Faultline: Lexi
an exclusive book club edition

By Mia Michele

Infinity House Publishing

Philadelphia

This novel is protected under the copyright laws of the United States and other countries throughout the world. Any unauthorized exhibition, distribution, or copying of this book or any part thereof may result in civil liability and criminal prosecution. The story, all names, characters, and incidents portrayed in this writing are fictitious. No identification with actual persons, places, or things is intended or should be inferred.

ISBN: 9798356479939

First Printing
2022

©2021, 2022 Mia Michele, Infinity House Publishing
All Rights Reserved

Originally published in its entirety and available as Faultline
(ISBN: 9798686356030)

The lyrics from *Annuzza Bedda* were written by Carlo Muratori for his album, Afrodite, ©1987, Carlo Muratori. A full detail of the song can be found here: http://www.carlomuratori.it/album-afrodite-carlo-muratori.php
All Rights Reserved

For my readers... By request!

Special Thanks

To my husband, Peter; my children; my BETA and ARC readers & reviewers; and my editors: all my thanks for everything that you do.

A special thank you to Carlo Muratori for permission to use the lyrics to his song, *Annuzza Bedda*.

Prologue

The screaming in her head was getting louder and louder. She could barely understand what was being said and tried in vain to subconsciously back away from the cliff that she had willingly found herself on. As she was pacing across the living room that suddenly felt too small, she stopped to look at the last photograph taken with her father before his death.

Only days from her college graduation, Lexi had leaned against his chair while he hugged her. Minutes before the image had been cut from life, she had told him about the promise of her dream job once her internship was complete, and happiness radiated from the eyes that stared back at her from the picture. In an instant, he was gone and her entire world spiraled into a nightmare.

Ten years were all but yesterday for Alessandra Masters. After earning both an advanced degree in Library Science and an honors degree in Italian, Lexi had been sitting at her college graduation, wondering which seats her parents had found since she hadn't managed to catch up with them before the ceremony. The bright lights as she had walked across the stage made seeing them in the crowd impossible, and, once all was said and done, she had mingled with her fellow NYU students and wondered where the hell everyone was.

When she saw her father's partner rushing toward her as the overcast sky opened into a spring shower, numbness inched up her spine. The man she had grown up calling *Uncle Sam* looked as though he'd been through hell. Twenty-two-year-old Alessandra hadn't known what real hell was at the time, but she quickly found out.

The front door opened, snapping her back to the present, and Sam was standing there. "You had better be joking."

"No joke. I told you: I got the job. I've already given my notice."

"No!" He threw down his holster and badge on the table by the door, just as her father had often done. "No, Lex. It's too soon. You aren't ready. You've been at the Smithsonian, what, a year-and-a-half? That's not enough time. It's not enough distance from the FBI."

"The job in New York was open. It might not have been there in another year or five." Her eyes pleaded with him to understand. "I had to at least interview for it."

"No, you didn't." He stalked into the kitchen and opened the fridge, grabbing a beer from the door. In a habit that had always annoyed her mother, he used the side of the counter to cause the top to spin off the bottle and across the floor.

"Mom would have yelled at you," Lexi said with a small smile. "That always drove her nuts."

He glanced at the bottle and chuckled before looking back to her, and his eyes were full of sadness. "She wouldn't want this for you, Lex. Neither would your dad. You've got to let this go. Please. Before you do something that gets you killed."

"Did Masseretti do it?" She took a few steps forward and, when Sam drank his beer instead of answering, asked, "Did he kill my dad?"

Sam sighed and dropped his head back. "Yes."

"Shoot him like a fucking dog in the middle of a dark alley? Leave his body in a gutter?"

"Lex, please."

Although there had been nothing in the FBI files that insinuated the Masseretti organization had ever killed anyone in law enforcement, Sam had been sure of their involvement, and her father's body had been found at *Café Lombarto*, one of the family's cover businesses. "No, Sam. Giovanni Masseretti has had ten years, and no one has even tried. I'm tired of waiting for someone else to figure out how to hang him. If no one has the guts to face him, then I will. I've got nothing to lose, Sam. I've lost everything anyway."

The numbness of that spring afternoon a decade earlier had only grown worse with time. Lexi had thrown away the internship in the Rare Books Department of the Smithsonian's library and the job she would have had translating and restoring rare Italian manuscripts. It had been her dream; the bullet that killed her father had ended her life as well.

Sam was watching her when she blinked her way back into reality. "I didn't come here for permission. I came to look at apartments and to let you know that I start Monday. I know this rushes the timeline. I'm working with what I have. I'm sorry, Sam." She picked up her purse and the keys to her rental car. "But you told me this was the play. You can't back out just because you don't want me to run the risk. The Bureau isn't even trying anymore."

On the way to Newark, the tears made it hard to drive. It wasn't Sam's fault that he didn't want her in New York, trying to outplay one of the most street-smart men the Organized Crime Task Force had ever gone up against. Lexi wasn't an agent- not in any real sense. She had been a librarian at the Academy. It wasn't until she had risked contacting the Director of the OCTF that Sam had confessed to her the Bureau couldn't officially send agents after the Masseretti family. However, he confided, if Lexi was willing to break all the rules, then maybe they could work together and figure something out.

His idea had seemed crazy, but Lexi had no reason to refuse. She was a shell of a human being anyway. Her mother had been diagnosed with late-stage breast cancer and had died that fall. When winter came and the numb threatened to completely obliterate her chances of seeing a new year, Lexi had vowed to do whatever it took to finally have some closure- even if it meant embarking on a plan that seemed destined to fail from the start.

When they had met for Christmas in the same house where Lexi had grown up and where Sam, who had gotten engaged to his partner's widow a year before she died, lived, Lexi had ended up with two glasses of wine as a result of Sam's proposal. "You'll have to leave the FBI," he said. "The Bureau will not put anyone under. The risks are too high for too little payout. The Smithsonian is hiring for an Assistant Librarian in Rare Books. You've been volunteering there for years. Get yourself hired. Create a new life and then, when the time is right, we can bring you to New York. Getting you into the family as the friend of one of the wives is probably the safest thing; then it's just waiting to overhear something. But it takes time, Lex. It's not overnight."

Despite how ludicrous his plan had sounded, Lexi's application for the Smithsonian had been easily accepted. After giving her notice to the FBI, she had moved into an apartment close to the library in DC and had settled into creating a life that she could transition to New York. She spent her spare time researching Giovanni Masseretti, the son and presumed heir to the *Don* of the New York family, learning everything she could about him.

On paper, Giovanni looked like an extremely successful businessman who liked women and alcohol. He had multiple avenues and investments along with a penchant for sex clubs, travel, and, interestingly enough, a lot of charitable giving. Although he was suspected of running drugs, there was no evidence that he used them, and part of his well-known activities included funding drug rehab centers throughout the state. It made no sense, but Lexi supposed that even gangsters were slapped by their consciences every now and again.

After eighteen months, a similar job became available at New York City's Main Library in Midtown. She hadn't bothered to tell Sam before applying. Once she interviewed and realized that she had misread the advertisement in her haste to apply- it was for the Director of Rare Books, not just a librarian working on the materials- she thought it was insane to assume she had a chance at the job. Over a month had gone by before the Human Resources Director called her with an offer that Lexi immediately accepted. She gave her notice to the Smithsonian and made appointments for the next week to view apartments in Manhattan.

Today had left her feeling like she was failing before she started. The costs were exorbitant, and the idea of living in the middle of New York City, even though she was coming from Washington, DC, was daunting. Lexi had been the quintessential librarian: quiet, bookwormish, and easygoing. As she tried to figure out an *in* for her unsanctioned undercover assignment, she knew that it was going to be an entirely uphill battle with a high probability of failure. Lexi had told Sam the reason she was nearby when calling to see if he was up for a visit, and he had completely lost his mind. She had eventually hung up, but trying to talk to him at home hadn't been much better.

Lexi sighed as she parked at the car return before walking to the Amtrak stop at Newark Airport. The high-speed line would have her back to DC in two-and-a-half hours. As she checked in, she tried to forget what she knew was true: Lexi wasn't cut out to be a federal agent. She had barely passed her annual weapons evaluation, and her psychological exams showed her as a woman who had given up her dreams to follow in her father's footsteps. She was breathing, but that was the extent of her living.

She finished up her final days of work; burning through her vacation time meant her last day closed out at three o'clock. Lexi was desperate to work off her nervous energy and debated going to one of the loud nightclubs she declined visiting with her coworkers. She picked up a coffee as she walked to her apartment, and a notification pinged while she flipped through her phone. *New article on: Giovanni Masseretti.*

She clicked the link and up flashed a photograph, taken outside of a building that looked like a museum and, according to the article, had hosted a BDSM-themed ball. As usual, he had a leggy blonde trailing behind him and Lexi was annoyed. Sam need not worry that she would get anywhere close to Giovanni. She had little chance to garner his attention short of gaining a few inches, shedding a few pounds, and dying her hair platinum. Not that she was trying to- he was her target and she was looking to nail his ass to the wall, not nail him.

That being said, as she read through the article about what the press assumed had gone on inside the towering walls and high security-laced building, Lexi found herself scanning through sites of local fetish events. She was leaving DC; she didn't have to worry about running into anyone that she had to work with later. As a single woman, she could get into the clubs without invitation and, in some cases, without paying a cover charge.

She packed up the final boxes for the giveaway bin once she got home before looking at her completely closed out apartment. Lexi needed to get out and try one last chance at feeling something- anything- before her entire life became focused on trying to infiltrate a mob family. At the very least, if she ever had the chance to talk to Giovanni, she would have the ability to say something other than *why did you kill my father*.

Lexi had nothing in the wardrobe she was taking with her that screamed out either black tie or corset, which the only event happening that night specified was the dress code. She had a dress from a wedding where she had served as a bridesmaid. While it was formal, she hadn't remembered it implying that she was into a night of bondage, domination, or anything else the event promised. She chuckled at the thought as she tried to find the box she had tossed the dress in.

She didn't accept drinks from strangers and found it difficult to do anything other than pay for half on dates. Lexi wasn't interested in a relationship; sex, sometimes, but relationships were things that seemed pointless when she couldn't feel more than emptiness and the ache of being alone in the world. Her failed attempts over the last ten years were proof of that.

She pulled the teal dress from the bag where she had already slated it for donation. As much as she had hated it when she had to wear it for the wedding, it would serve her well tonight with its toe-to-hip slit and knotted, open-waist halter top. After getting dressed, she found the silver stilettos she had been forced to wear with it- also in the donation bin- and had to root around in the bathroom drawers for makeup she rarely wore and had yet to discard. Finally, she made arrangements for a car as she tried to fix her hair, settling for a messy bun that she hoped look more chic than lazy, and ran outside to the Uber when the woman arrived.

Giving the address of the dance club, she noticed the woman's raised eyebrows in the rearview mirror after typing the street number into the GPS. "You go there a lot?"

"First time for everything," Lexi said uncomfortably.

"I guess."

The car dropped her off ten minutes later where a line wrapped around a colonnade, and Lexi debated calling the driver back. A man wearing a mask as though it were a masquerade party and holding a clipboard stopped to look her up and down. "Single?"

"Excuse me?" Lexi looked around, but it seemed he was talking to her.

"Single woman? Not part of a couple?"

"No." She stumbled through the answer. "Just me. I mean, I'm alone." She nodded when he smirked at her. "Yes, single woman."

"First time?"

"Is it that obvious?"

"You'll make it. Come on." He directed her to follow him around the line. "Single, female subs never wait in line. You're an automatic entry."

"I'm not a *sub*." She looked at the different outfits of everyone in line while fidgeting nervously.

He glanced over at her and chuckled. "Right. Like you said: first time." He waved to the door bouncer and Lexi bypassed the rope. "Have a good time," he added before, Lexi suspected, he returned to searching out more single women.

The club was bright and people were dressed as though they were at an art gallery- if an art gallery was both sexy and kinky. Lexi had never seen suits made out of leather but that, along with leather-trimmed tuxedos, seemed to be a staple of male attire. The women wore corsets and thongs or were painted in evening wear that plunged to navels and revealed far more skin than any formal exhibition Lexi had attended. Traveling waiters in only aprons served a variety of cocktails and finger foods.

Walking between the rooms where different demonstrations were taking place, Lexi was intrigued. Although she couldn't say anyone or anything she saw made her feel the cold around her soul recede, it was the first time where she actually considered that she could find herself, somewhere, if only she would give life a chance. As soon as she had the thought, she dispelled it. If she couldn't trust a man to buy her a drink, she sure as hell couldn't trust someone on such a grander scale.

"Cocktail?" As if reading her mind, one of the suits stopped her. His eyes drank her in from her high-heeled shoes and revealed leg up to her face where he settled his gaze.

"No, thanks." She continued to walk as he paced her.

"You don't look familiar. I haven't seen you here before."

"Visiting the area," she lied.

"Where from?"

"New York." Although he was good-looking, Lexi wasn't interested in sex with a stranger on her last night in DC and, as she tried to soak in the amount of kink around her, found it hard to concentrate, especially when he reached out to touch her arm suggestively.

"Really? What's your home club?" He watched her as she watched other people. His stare made her uncomfortable, as though he was trying to open her mind and read it like a book.

His fingers slid up and down her bare arm, and Lexi said the first thing she thought of, namedropping the club that had appeared on her notification. "Underground Met."

His fingers stopped moving as he gave her a more appraising glance. "That's pretty hardcore stuff." He turned slightly and pointed to a decorated staircase. "What you want is upstairs. I can show you."

What the fuck was she getting herself into? Swallowing down her inhibitions, she nodded slowly and followed him through the crowds. When they risked getting separated, he offered her his hand, which she nervously took, and the people thinned out once they passed through another bouncer at the top of the stairs. "What's your name?"

"Lexi," she said. The lights had changed alongside the décor. Rich reds and blacks adorned the center gallery, and the blue-hued lights were lowered to resemble a breaking dawn. "Yours?"

"Master Brian, but you can call me *Sir*."

Lexi stopped. "I beg your pardon?"

He chuckled and led her farther down the hallway. "If Underground Met is your speed, you'll probably get more out of this room than anything downstairs. The demo just started. Give him an hour, and he'll be into what you like."

Master Brian pushed open a large door to reveal a room that resembled a lecture hall. A woman was chained to a wooden X on the stage. Her evening dress was open, and Lexi flinched on her behalf when the man behind her flicked a massive whip against her back. The sound of leather against skin echoed in the room. The sadist dropped the lash again, and the stranger resumed the dance of his fingers on her arm. "There are private rooms on the top floor. *Fully-equipped* rooms."

"I'm gonna pass," Lexi said, both mesmerized and terrified. "I've got my own *Sir* at home who might be a bit pissed if I do anything more than watch. Sorry."

He gave her a good-natured smile, dropping his fingers from her arm. "No worries. Have a good night." Without any pressure, he was gone. Lexi was surprised by his easy response to her rejection.

She lingered in the room. After the sadist changed from a whip to a cane, Lexi slipped back into the main hall and found herself near a bar where women were serving as tables. She had decided to investigate another beautifully carved door when her phone chimed, and she pulled it from her handbag.

At your apartment. Where are you?

Sam hadn't told her he was coming, but she quickly texted that she was en route and made her way to the exit. Lexi used the car service app to arrange a pick-up from the corner closest to the event. When she passed by the bouncer who had walked her in, he stopped her. "That was faster than I thought."

"I have to go. Work." She lifted her phone apologetically. "Another time."

"I hope so." He winked. "It would be a shame to never learn your name." Returning his smile, Lexi continued to walk until she passed through the main gate.

Sam looked annoyed when she arrived home, but his eyes exploded when she got out of the car. "What the hell happened to you?"

"A date that wasn't going anywhere," she lied. "I didn't expect you after earlier in the week."

He held up a bag. "Sushi peace offering."

"Miso?"

"Is there any other way to say you're sorry?" Sam put his free arm around her shoulder when she smiled at him. "I didn't mean to sound like an ass. I was just shocked. But," he added when they went inside her garden apartment, "I have news that I think you're going to like."

"I'm listening." She grabbed a beer that she kept for Sam's visits from the fridge and began to unpack the trays of sushi. She dumped the entire steaming bowl of miso soup into a large mug and drank it as though it were tea.

"The Director gave some budget. It's still off-book, but I got you a small- and I mean *small*- apartment fifteen minutes from the library. It's paid for from today until December. If you've got anything going on by then, we can reevaluate."

"Seriously?" Her eyes widened. "That's great! Rents are insane."

"I know, but I think I have a great *in* for you."

"Okay." She lifted a piece of the dragon roll with wooden chopsticks. "Which wife is my new best friend?"

"Friendships only work if you can manage to keep friends, Lex, and that requires that you not isolate yourself." Sam picked up her tablet and typed in a website. "This," he said, passing it over, "is one of Masseretti's clubs. It's not far from where you'll live, and it is one of the few places that he spends at least a day or two a week."

"*He*'s the mark?" Lexi looked up at Sam. "The endgame for sure, but I can't play Giovanni. He uncovered every agent the Bureau sent under for him. Fuck, he's probably part of the reason they don't want to send anyone else."

"You aren't playing *him*. Find one of his people. Hell, flirt with all of them and find one who is dumb enough to risk pissing his boss off by feeling you up at work. All you need to do is get close enough to get shots of whatever is in his office. Papers. Pictures. Whatever you see." Sam pointed to the link he wanted her to click on; when she did, it populated her screen with a girl who looked about twenty. "They are," he read the print, "*always interested in employing only the best in the service industry*."

"Sam, that's hookers. He's hiring escorts."

"*Cocktail waitresses*," Sam pointed out, "not hookers. Not officially anyway."

"You want me to get a job as a call girl. Really?" Lexi dropped the tablet. "How much are you drinking these days?"

"I *wanted* you to get a job at the Smithsonian. I *wanted* you to stay working with books, behind glass, safe. That," he added, "is also what your parents wanted. *You* chose this- not me. I never wanted you close to this."

He paused to eat a piece of sashimi. "Look, Lex, the only jobs for a woman in Masseretti's world are mother, sister, wife, girlfriend, employee, or whore. Your options are limited. Get in, get info, and get out. That's it. If you get in and it's too hot, then just leave. It's an off-book assignment. No one is going to know if you bail."

11

"If I bail, no one will know why they killed him," she said, looking down at her plate. She pulled up her resume, quickly deleting the FBI and expanding how many years she had worked for the Smithsonian to create a seamless job history before overwriting her address with the new number and street from the small sliver of paper that Sam gave her. Saving it, she clicked on the email link and composed a quick cover letter. "I'm just a woman relocating to New York in need of a second job to make my rent." She pressed send. "Done."

Sam took a drink of his beer and reached for her hand. "If you get in there and it feels wrong, just go. Promise me that you'll walk out and go back to that apartment. Promise me you'll work at the library and have a life and live a dream. Don't get involved in something that is far over your head. Men like Masseretti- they don't play. They live this. They will kill you in a heartbeat and dump you in an alley."

She burned her fear with the miso. "I can do this, Sam. I can find whatever it is that's there. I can sort it and catalog it, and, if we're lucky, I can find what you can use to hang him."

Her tablet beeped in conjunction with the email icon illuminating, and she clicked on the little envelope. "Freddy is impressed that I can speak Italian and would like for me to come in Sunday evening for an interview." She started typing a response in her second language as Sam watched over her shoulder.

"What are you saying?"

"That I can meet him at six o'clock." She dropped the tablet on the table. "Tomorrow, the second-hand shop is picking up all of my furniture and stuff, so I'll rent a car and drive up the few boxes of books and clothes I'm taking with me. I can get settled in by then."

Sam took a key ring from his pocket and put it on the table between them. "If you go through with this, then you and I can't see each other. You can only contact me when it's over. Come to Northvale. I will bring you in, and we can go from there. But, Lex, you can tell no one. *No one,*" he repeated.

"You can't call anyone from the FBI. You cannot risk talking to anyone from your past. Do you hear me? You have to look perfect for this to work."

"I can do it." Lexi looked back at the tablet as it dinged when a confirmation came through. "Game on," she said, taking another bite of sushi.

1

The nightclub looked like regret in the making. Lexi would have called it more speakeasy than disco, which made sense since the Masseretti family had used it during Prohibition to run illegal alcohol. She had researched the history of the building that morning in lieu of unpacking, and Giovanni's apple hadn't fallen far from his grandfather's tree. He now used the same spot to run escorts, drugs, and God only knew what else. Lexi approached the long line and walked up to the bouncer at the door. The giant looked her over as she stumbled through her declaration. "I have a job interview at six with Freddy."

The bald man with a larger-than-needed gun tucked beneath his tight jacket laughed in her face. "Go home, sweetheart. You don't belong here."

Was that it? She looked around at the bodies pressed together outside, waiting for their chance to drink and dance the last night of the weekend away. Even in the short dress that she had bought specifically for the interview and the white, leather knee boots that, contrary to her reservations, had to be some of the most comfortable things she'd ever owned, Lexi didn't fit in. She didn't even own enough makeup or hairspray to compete, and she definitely wasn't edgy enough.

Her soft voice and *please help me* eyes weren't going to do the job, and she gave herself an internal pep talk, as she often did when she felt like she was on the verge of failure. Lexi straightened her back and reflected annoyance in her voice as she repeated herself, this time louder and after taking a step into his personal space. "Six o'clock. Freddy. Job interview. Did I stutter?"

The man raised his eyebrows, amused, and looked at her again before grinning. He said something into his headset mic before he stepped back and opened the door to the entrance. Lexi exhaled into the flashing lights and the chaos of music and conversation. There were scantily dressed women on poles, men and women grinding together on floor panels that lit up, and tables overflowing with men who, if she had access to the database, Lexi was sure would be recognizable from mug shots.

The large bar was a hotbed of activity, and she squeezed through people to get there, clutching the envelope she held against her stomach. It didn't help with the nausea her nerves had gifted her, but she refused to back down. She wasn't going to fall apart until she took the Masseretti family with her. The bartender asked what she wanted, and she had to scream over the noise. "I've got an appointment with Freddy at six. I'm interviewing for a job."

She heard him before she saw him and knew that Giovanni Masseretti was talking to her when she looked to her side where the man had materialized into a vacated space. He had spent most of his time in Sicily, moving to New York City ten years before and continuing to travel worldwide for his business dealings, and his suave accent reflected his life. "I can save you some time, *bambina*. This isn't the place for you."

He was dressed in a black suit with a crisp white shirt that was open at the top to reveal dark hair on his chest and the edge of a tattoo that she couldn't make out. The suit alone had probably cost a month of Lexi's salary. His tousled hair was cut short, and he had a nearly invisible scar under his right eye. Another tattoo, this one the tail of a snake that trailed up his hidden arm, was visible on the hand that took the bartender's glass of proffered whiskey.

Combating the fire that his voice coursed through her body, she narrowed her eyes when she looked at him. He watched her with a smirk that told her he believed the world revolved around him, and the attitude she had forced at the door slipped out unabated. "It seems like the men around here all have hearing problems. I said I'm meeting Freddy at six. Unless you're Freddy and it's six o'clock, why don't you run along and play messenger?"

Giovanni bit his inner cheek to avoid laughing at her and casually slipped his free hand into his pocket as he balanced against the bar. "Oh, *bambina*, this is definitely *not* the place for you." His gaze darkened, and he leaned close enough to her that she could smell spice and charcoal. "Because that mouth of yours would be broken before you even had a chance to take the floor." He yelled to the bartender before he moved back from the bar and started to walk away from her, reaching out from his pocket to use his thumb to swipe across her lower lip. "*Ciao, bella.*"

"Interview's over," the bartender said, sliding a flute of prosecco to her. "On the house, courtesy of Mr. Masseretti. And then," he tipped his head toward the door, "you should go."

Fuck, she thought, leaving the glass and turning to find Giovanni's tall frame disappearing from the crowd through a wide door. She tried to force herself between the mass of dancers, but people were everywhere and she wasn't used to walking in the heeled boots that she had only bought that morning. When she finally reached the back hallway, there was no one there and she eyed the doors that lined the corridor before walking toward a marked exit at the end. Hearing noise from behind one of the rooms, her trembling hand reached for the knob and it turned easily.

The sight stilled her, and she couldn't hide the embarrassment that choked her anymore than she could look away from the heat in his eyes as Giovanni watched her. He leaned against a large desk while a woman in a dress that was so short Lexi could see her thong sliding up her ass knelt in front of him. Her head bobbed as he tangled his hand in her hair. "See something you'd enjoy, *bambina*?"

She had seen countless situations in her head, but this wasn't one of them. She wanted to wipe that look off his face and shove his *bambina* bullshit down his throat. At the same time, the fact that he was standing there so calm and collected while Lexi thought she might implode had her thinking that Sam had been right: she wasn't cut out for this. Failure, however, wasn't an option. It never had been. "I have a job interview," she said between clenched teeth.

"Unless this is the type of job you are looking for, then I'm not sure there's much here for you." He was talking to her as though he were sitting behind a desk pushing paperwork back and forth instead of pushing a woman's head against his crotch. "But, by all means, come over and show me what else that mouth is capable of."

She could feel her cheeks pink when he pulled the woman back and told her to go. He continued to lean against his desk, his piercing black eyes never breaking Lexi's gaze. She refused to look away, both because she was determined to call him on his bullshit and because she feared catching sight of his cock. "Something you would learn working for me is that I don't like to wait and don't take kindly to my orders not being followed."

That fucking attitude. He was absolutely terrifying in his quiet authority and that smartass, *I-rule-the-world* persona that made Lexi's heart race. This was it. Make or break. Her heels clanked across the wooden floor as she slowly walked forward, and she stopped when their bodies were almost touching in order to bridge the gap by leaning in. "Let me say it for you in a language you might understand. *Appuntamento. Sei in punto,*" she purred into his ear as she pushed the envelope containing her resume against his chest harshly. "*Smettila di prendermi per il culo.*"

Telling him to stop fucking with her may have been the straw that broke his sense of humor. When Lexi tried to pull away, the gangster wrapped his hand in her hair, which she had painstakingly pulled up into a loose bun that was far more work than he made it worth. "*Bambina,*" he growled, the envelope falling to the floor between them. "It's *me* that *you* shouldn't fuck with. I don't think you understand the way that I play, and I doubt you have any idea of the rules."

The sexual tension radiated off of him like a hot stove, but what was infinitely worse was that Lexi felt *something*- and it wasn't fear. This was not the way this scene played out. This was not the moment that her mind decided to wake up. Her hands were against his chest, and she thought she might fall in the shoes that she had specifically chosen to give her more height. Yanking her hair pulled her body against his in tandem. "Get your hands off of me," she whispered when he drew his mouth close to her exposed neck.

"Where is your toughness now?" The stubble from his light beard moved along her cheek, and she shivered. "I thought you were going to speak the language I understand."

As he continued to hold her in front of him, Lexi thought that kicking him in the balls might be the only language left. She hadn't noticed her hands curling in the open collar of his shirt, her remaining defense before she fell to her knees, and her fingers were tickled by the dark curls beneath. He murmured something in her ear that was close to the Italian she dreamed in, but she couldn't understand the words before a loud alarm sounded in the office and he cursed. He turned their bodies so that she was held up by the desk when he let her go before he shoved his dick into his pants and zipped up as he walked behind them to look at the monitors displaying the club, inside and out. He repeated the explicative before grabbing her hand. Without stopping his stride, Giovanni drug her from the office. "Let's go."

"Go? Where?" Lexi stumbled after him into the alley that the exit door opened to. A smoky gray Portofino with the top missing sat alone facing the street, and he threw her in the passenger side before walking around to the driver's door.

"Anywhere but here." Giovanni went to turn the car on when they both saw the line of police. "Fucking son-of-a-bitch."

Her brain on autopilot, Lexi looked at the tight interior. "Take your seat as far back as it will go."

Barely giving her mind, he exhaled a guttural breath. "I'm not running down a dozen cops who can't pin anything on me in a fucking alley." He raised his eyes in surprise when Lexi pulled her already short dress higher in order to straddle him in the narrow front seat. "I'm up for a lot, baby girl, but this isn't really the time or place."

"It's better to have a reason to be in the alley when they get here." Her pulse was pounding as she leaned her head forward, her mouth hovering over his. "Plausible deniability of anything possibly illegal going on inside. You're just a guy in his car in a public space. Misdemeanor at best." She swallowed down the fear and felt excitement in its place. What the hell was she doing?

One of his hands was already burying itself in her hip and the other gripped the back of her neck, bringing her the remaining distance needed for their mouths to meet. She could feel him pushing against the tightly tailored slacks as she sat in his lap. His lips were softer than she thought those of a killer should be, but that was all that was soft about him. He crushed her against him, forcing her mouth open with his tongue and probing spaces she was desperate to keep hidden.

Ten years. Ten years of empty. Of nothing. Of cold. Ten years of numb were wiped away in those seconds when Giovanni Masseretti became her air. He had been a name in Sam's stories, a face from a photograph, the villain of her adulthood, and now he was the one thing that had woken her from a sleep that she hadn't believed it possible to open her eyes from. His kisses demanded that she yield while her body told him that nothing about her would be easy, and he bruised her with his rough hands against her supple waist. They weren't only opposites; they were star-crossed. The only thing she needed more than him was to never lay eyes on him again.

Lexi curled her fingers into his shirt and one of the buttons opened lower, giving her access to his chest where that hand buried itself in the dark hair that spilled out. She used her other to balance herself where his upper thigh met his torso. She heard a policeman slap the glass of the closed window although he could have easily called out to them and the convertible would have carried his voice. "The fuck, Masseretti!"

"Almost," Giovanni said, pulling away from Lexi and giving the cop a once over. "If you hadn't interrupted, perhaps sooner rather than later."

"Get out of the car-"

"What the hell! What are you doing?" Even from fifty feet away, Lexi recognized the FBI shield that hung from the approaching man. She didn't know who he was, but he was definitely an agent and he was pissed. She almost responded when she realized he wasn't looking at her but rather at the police officer who looked almost as annoyed.

"Who the fuck are you?" The cop toggled between the car and the suited man with a gun and badge pointed at him.

The agent was young- even Lexi knew better than to yell undercover business in front of strangers- but he was also incensed, and that made for a loose tongue. "You're ruining a well-placed sting. And why? To bust some guy in an alley with his girlfriend!" He looked at the car with disgust, either because he recognized the *guy in the alley* or because the idea of what the police had interrupted pissed him off even more than his screwed up sting. "Get the fuck out of here before I call my boss and have your pension."

Lexi was surprised. Why would the police raid one of Masseretti's clubs? Even had they suspected prostitution or drugs, it would have been a combined effort with the FBI. If the feds were running a sting nearby- on the club or elsewhere- there would have been an organized effort to make sure that neither crossed paths. Something would have been rescheduled. Why were the police here in force at all?

She looked at the officer, and the cop gave her a glare. Her cheeks burned with shame. What was she doing, straddled and practically on-the-clothes-fucking a stranger in a car? Had her father been the one stumbling upon her, he would have been disgusted, too. She stole another glance at the cop again when he cursed under his breath and looked at the driver of the Ferrari with anger.

Giovanni waved with the hand from the back of her neck. "I think those are your exit orders," he glanced at the man's rank, "Sergeant," before he pulled Lexi back to him while the man turned and stalked with rage down the alleyway. "Where were we, *bambina*?"

"*We*," she said, breathing heavily against his lips, "were nowhere, and I think I just heard my own exit orders." She tried to extricate her body from his, but he held her against him. His erection pushed against her panties while his lower hand inched her dress higher up her leg. "I'm leaving. You can let me go now."

"I don't often make errors in judgment." He didn't bother with acknowledging her declaration. The hand on her neck curled into the hair he had caused to fall down, and Giovanni bit the bottom of her lip suggestively. "Maybe there is a job for you here after all."

"I don't think so," Lexi said, still struggling to back away and ultimately giving up as she sat in his lap. She gave a slight shove to his chest, and he replied with the smirk she had seen at the bar. "I've seen the way you treat your staff. You were right the first time. You've saved me a lot of effort and probably saved yourself from my foot to your *palle, Signore* Masseretti."

"Gio," he corrected, his hand still woven in her mahogany waves so that he could pull her into the space she had only recently vacated. He pressed his lips to hers as he talked, and her heart decided it could pump faster. His voice dropped, that accent curling around her cold like a flame and pushing at it. "And I would much rather have your tongue than your foot."

"Keep dreaming."

He laughed and damn her if it wasn't the sexiest thing Lexi had heard in months- years. It was almost sexier than the way he called her *baby girl* and moved his hands through all of her secrets. She looked into his eyes and they burned her, as though he could see right through her.

The police were slowly wandering down the sidewalk at the end of the alley. Based on the increase in noise, the club had already started to discharge its people onto the street. If she didn't leave now, Lexi might not be able to convince herself to stay away from him- and that was a huge problem. "I need to go," she whispered.

He was going to argue but stopped when the exit door swung open. One of the bouncers she had seen before at the bar leaned out, looking around wildly before yelling, "Gio!" and rattling off his anger.

Giovanni's hand was no longer rough against her hair. Instead, he caressed her like a child with a treasured doll. He just watched her, ignoring the bouncer, and she felt naked in front of him. Lexi had no choice but to pull away before the night caused her entire plan to fall apart. This time, although his other hand was still on her waist, he didn't stop her from lowering into the passenger seat.

He sighed when he finally let her go in order to get out of the car, and Lexi straightened her skirt while Giovanni walked around to open her door. "It's only now six o'clock," he said, using his body to block her from walking away when she stood. "Don't you have an appointment to keep?"

"Give my regards to Freddy." Lexi tried to slip around him, but Giovanni gripped her wrist.

His voice was low. "I'm not used to not having what I want."

"That must be very frustrating for you- to be faced with something you want and can't have." She wasn't sure where the comment came from but, when he gave her a seductive chuckle and tipped his head back to see something in her that she didn't recognize, she lifted her arm so that his eyes found the wrist he held. "Goodbye, *Mister* Masseretti."

"It seems not only the men are hard of hearing here: Giovanni." His fingers relaxed, and she pulled her wrist from his grasp with a grin at his reply.

"Goodbye, Giovanni." She wasn't sure that he would let her leave, but she easily walked around him, only stopping midway down the alley when he spoke.

"You didn't tell me your name."

Instead of answering, she blew him a kiss over her shoulder and kept walking. She rounded the corner into traffic, and the woman she had been seconds before evaporated.

Her entire body was shaking. What the hell was she doing? This was crazy and she was insane for thinking she had the balls necessary to go one-on-one with a Mafioso. Whatever confidence she had managed became an overwhelming sense of embarrassment at what she'd done. She stumbled down the New York City block until she came to a side-street that offered her a reprieve from the crowds of people. Pressing her back into the wall of the building behind her, she thought she might puke.

Her father had always been an agent. As a child, Lexi had known that he was a leading member of the Organized Crime Task Force, but he had kept his work quiet. Her parents didn't discuss it around her, and she had never known what he actually did for the OCTF until after his death.

Having fallen in love with books at a young age, Lexi had never planned to follow in his footsteps. Her entire world changed after his murder. Nothing made sense, and, although she was close to her mother, the self-proclaimed *daddy's girl* couldn't find stable footing in a world without his belief in her and his support of her endeavors. Not even a full day after his funeral, she had applied for the FBI Academy.

No one- not her mother, not Sam, not even Lexi herself- had thought she would make it until graduation. The coursework was easy, but she was told outright at her psychological exam that she didn't have the emotional stability of a field agent. Combined with her average shooting record, she had skated through by the skin of her teeth and, she always presumed, sympathy for her fallen father.

Instead of an office, she had been assigned to the Quantico library where she had excelled. She had created cooperatives with local libraries, building community partnerships between the schools in the towns nearby and the FBI. After five years of working as one of the Associate Librarians, she had been promoted to the Assistant Director position; when the Director retired, she was named as Acting Director. She would have interviewed and achieved the promotion, too, had Sam not come to her with the plan for her to leave the Bureau and begin the unauthorized undercover.

Every attempt to bring down the Masseretti family from the inside had failed. Giancarlo Masseretti, the head of the family, had always managed to uncover even the smallest deception and, when he had backed away in favor of having his oldest son take on more of the family's leadership, Giovanni was just as astute. Of the three agents the OCTF had tried to insert over the ten years that Giovanni had been the de-facto head, all three had been uncovered within a month.

"Maybe that's the problem," Lexi had argued with Sam regularly. "You keep sending in people trying to be someone they aren't." Convinced that it wasn't a murder charge or even proving a drug trade that would be his undoing, she had tried, unsuccessfully, to convince Sam to build a case against the Masseretti organization from all of the little things that were ignored. It hadn't been a murder charge that destroyed Capone but tax evasion. Who better than a librarian to build a solid case against a family the FBI had never been able to touch?

Sam had not been swayed and had demanded she drop the notion. "You're too close to this to think straight," he had told her, emphasizing that she wasn't a seasoned undercover and had never been in the field. On top of that, she was the antithesis of the women who had the sliver of a chance at finding the type of information Lexi swore existed in plain sight. They were young college students who didn't mind the attention of men much older than they were for the ability to pay off debt or be sequestered mistresses in penthouses. "Even if I thought this play would work," Sam had said dismissively, "you're too old and too fucking smart."

Lexi had laughed at his assessment over her coffee as she sat on the porch of her childhood home during the last visit where they had been able to actually talk to one another instead of argue. "Then I'll outsmart him."

"Giovanni Masseretti doesn't get outsmarted. He's a narcissistic mentalist- and a damn good one. He uses women like he uses everything else in his life and doesn't care about anything or anyone. He's cold and ruthless, and his reputation..." Sam's voice had trailed off. "Don't do this. Don't even think about this. Your father wouldn't want this for you. Even if- and it's a big if- you ever got close enough, you have no idea what you'll be forced to give and what Masseretti will take. It's not worth it."

But Lexi hadn't listened. She hadn't listened when Sam told her to find peace at the Smithsonian in a job she had longed for. She hadn't listened and stayed away from New York. She hadn't listened to the last plea from her dying mother that she let go and learn to live again. And now, due to her inability to listen to the people who loved her, Lexi was seconds away from throwing up on a Manhattan sidewalk because of the visceral response she'd had to a murderous thug. She was barely able to take in air and thought the panic in her chest might give way to her collapsing against the hidden storefront.

"Just breathe, *bambina*." Giovanni's voice covered her like a warm blanket. His arms wrapped around her and brought her away from the wall, pulling her trembling body against his warmth. "I've got you." The hand with the snake that promised her the apple tasted sweet and was worth the fall touched her chin and raised her face to look at him. "You're going to be fine."

She couldn't help her honest reply. "It was a mistake to come here."

"It was completely a mistake," he agreed, the menacing glint back in his eyes. "You should have stayed as far off my radar as possible." Her heart that had never stopped running joined the race again when he pushed the hair he had messed up from her eyes. "Let me take you home, Alessandra."

"How do you know my name?"

"Six o'clock. Freddy. Did you stutter?" The smirk that made him look both handsome and dangerous painted his face. "Come on." He gently pulled her toward the car that sat close by. "I'm safer than a subway in that outfit."

"Somehow I doubt that," she muttered, debating the door he held open.

"Get in the car, Alessandra."

The lilt of the command made it sound like he was enticing her to refuse. After thinking better of it, Lexi sat down. She secured the seatbelt and called to mind the address of the bookstore that her apartment was situated over. "Five thirty-five-"

He cut her off. "Madison Avenue. More," he sought out a word, "*posh* than I would expect on a public librarian's salary."

He had read the resume she had dropped in his office, Lexi realized. "It's a shoebox on top of a bookstore." She echoed, "*Posh* enough that I was looking for a night job, but I'll manage, *Mister* Masseretti."

"Gio," he corrected for the third time. "*Sorda*, I'm sure you will." He navigated the traffic by tapping his fingers against the steering wheel, and Lexi wondered if it drove him insane to drive so slowly in a car that could hit sixty-miles-per-hour in under three seconds. "Forgive me, *bambina*, but you don't work as *le baldracche*."

She looked out the window, tearing herself away from the gaze that worked its way from her boots up her dress as he drove. "*Baldracche*. You're an asshole." When he scoffed at her response, she turned back to him with narrowed eyes. "Does your staff know you think of them as *whores*? It's amazing you manage to keep anyone employed with that attitude. Although after what I walked in on, I guess it's not just attitude."

"My *staff*," he said, emphasizing the word, "know that they are expected to keep my clients entertained."

"Yeah, not *just* your *clients*." She put the final word in air quotes.

He chuckled. "No. Not *just*. Entertained is one thing, but I don't fuck the women who work for me."

"How very PC of you."

At her smartass reply, Giovanni rested his hand on her leg, and the contact forced Lexi to look back at him. "You came to me for work. What you saw? That's the interview you were so anxious to get." He winked at her, and she took his hand in hers in order to put it back on his own leg while he continued to look amused.

It wasn't far from the club on East 58th to Madison and took Giovanni less time to drive than it took him to park. He maneuvered into a slot between two cars on 54th and got out of the Ferrari, walking around and opening her door before Lexi had fully untangled herself from the seatbelt. Fearful excitement pulsed beneath her calm demeanor when he pressed her against the Portofino. Her breathy voice mimicked her flush. "Thanks for the ride."

The devilish smile was back before his mouth lingered near her ear. "I should thank *you* for the ride." As he backed away, his lips and stubble rippled against her cheek, and Giovanni settled a hand against her waist. "Yet a thank you might imply that we are done."

"That's because we *are* done. *Buona sera.*"

"I think we're just getting started." He took to the habit he had picked up of playing with her hair. "But I could leave you pretty well *done* before night's end. Come home with me."

"That's going to be a *grazie ma no*. Goodnight, Giovanni." Lexi tried to move around him, but the hand on her waist slid to her wrist and pulled her back.

"I'll buy you dinner." He nodded away from her apartment. "There's a place down the block. It's perfect for you to grab a bite, and you don't know it."

"How do you know what I know and don't know?"

"You've haven't lived here long enough to know the hidden delicacies." When he winked at her again, Lexi could feel her resolve melting.

Where was the line between *hard to get* and *not worth the effort*? While Lexi wasn't sure about that, she was more than sure that she was not the person for this job. She was standing across from the man whom she had believed for a decade killed her father and had barely been able to decline the offer to go home with him.

She didn't feel disgust or anger; she felt want. She knew he was guilty- he had to be- but even that belief wasn't enough. She wanted to keep the feelings that he inspired because they choked out the emptiness. Being awake was a crystal clear look at how lonely and broken her life actually had been.

Fuck him and fuck her. Contrary to every course of right action, Lexi nodded. "But only because I'm hungry- not because I want to spend more time than necessary with you."

"That's only because you don't know how I spend my time." His fingers curled effortlessly around hers as he pointed her down the block and began to walk.

"After what I saw tonight, I have an idea." She pushed the hair from her eyes when her bangs blinded her. "In case you missed it the first time, I think you're an asshole."

"You aren't the first woman to tell me so. It's doubtful you'll be the last."

"I'm not interested in a place that cops raid- or the man who runs it."

"Fucking *runs it- owns* it, baby girl." He kissed her knuckles when she looked over at him and rolled her eyes before he maneuvered her against him and draped his arm around her shoulder. "And I think you're more than interested."

"A bit arrogant, aren't you?"

"The language of my people."

"*Figo*," she taunted.

The air left her when he pushed her back against a brick-and-glass restaurant front. When she fought against him, he only deepened his penetrating gaze while he moved one hand beneath her short skirt and rested it on her inner thigh. Realizing that he was using her struggle as an invitation to continue the game of chicken that she had instigated with her insult, Lexi stopped moving. She had no option but to give him that round, otherwise she would end up with his fingers inside of her on a Midtown sidewalk. "You purposely provoke me. At some point, I'm not going to stop, and you'll see the wolf you've unleashed." Before removing his hand, he slapped her through her panties.

They were in front of a pizzeria that could have been any of a hundred pizza shops on any of a hundred New York City street corners, and he pulled the door open while physically requiring that she step inside. Lexi tried to release her anxiety and desire into her inhale of tomato sauce and fire. "Gio!" The man behind the counter, who looked near in age to the thirty-eight-year-old man on her arm, rushed to the front. "Long time!"

After cursory greetings, Giovanni led her to a small table at the rear of the room where he had a clear view of the eatery, storeroom, and street. His back was to the wall, and he watched her with a look that made her uncomfortable. She shifted in the chair and glanced around the room before still finding his gaze cemented on her. "You're staring at me. It's disconcerting."

"You aren't Italian," he said matter-of-factly after the shop owner placed an overflowing antipasto plate between them.

"È molto astuto da parte tua," she interrupted.

Giovanni bit his lip before he continued his assessment of her. "Yet you speak Italian fluently. Even your accent, while *Napolitano*, shows skill."

"We have schools in the United States, and I'm a quick learner." She was about to smart off about his accent when he picked up one of the plump olives from the center and curled his lips into that same, danger-ridden smirk from before.

"Are you, *bambina*?" He pressed the olive to her mouth and it slipped between her lips, her tongue grazing his fingertips. "There's so much more I could teach you."

She finished chewing the olive before she sipped the wine that was placed in front of her. The red was far harsher than the sweet white wine she preferred. "The degree in my apartment says that my language skills are impressive enough."

"Nothing compares to a native tongue." When she looked away, he leaned forward and touched her cheek. "Your blush gives you away. I wrote the rules to this game, and I always get what I want."

"Who says I want to play?" When Lexi raised her eyes, he still watched her intently. Her entire life was a series of knots and damage, and that fucking look was starting to undo all the ones that her current lies required she keep tightly wrapped.

"You stood in my office and offered me the deck of cards." He lifted his own wine glass before whispering the equivalent of *game on* in the end of an Italian proverb. " *Allora, pedala.*"

"*L'apparenza inganna.*" Her nerves were balanced by her annoyance at the realization that Giovanni knew he was breaking down her resolve, and she surprised herself with her brazen reply. Lexi sat up taller, forcing the hand on her cheek to fall. "Your reputation precedes you, and I'm not your type."

"You look enough my type to make it interesting, *bambina.*" He drummed his fingers on the table in front of her, licking his teeth to stop from laughing. "And I like a challenge."

Insulted, she crossed her arms. "Unlike your *baldracche*, I'm not as easily impressed by Ferraris and accents. It takes something more than what's under the hood to make me interested in taking a ride, and I doubt you've got enough of what I'm looking for to make you more than an interesting night. You might want to stick to the game you know before you risk checkmate in the one you don't."

The moment she uttered the words, Lexi knew that she had not only provoked him but had issued a challenge he would be thrilled to accept.

After the experience on the street outside, she also knew that one of those alone would be impossible for Giovanni to ignore.

He breathed an amused half-laugh and stood, buttoning his jacket over what she was nearly certain was a holster and gun. He pulled her to her feet in a smooth move and nodded to the pizza maker as the pair slipped into the back, out of sight from the workers and other patrons. They had barely moved into the storeroom when Giovanni pushed her against a wall, causing her to yelp in surprise. One hand rested on her throat and the other was pressed against her torso, negotiating the space between her breasts and stomach.

"You don't want to play this game with me, *bambina*. The reputation you think you know? It is window dressing for what I'm capable of. In this case, my looks are *not* deceiving." When she refused to lower her eyes and forced through the trepidation from his growled assertion, the hand on her throat tightened slightly. The way that he had his arm across her chest had effectively immobilized her arms, and he leaned into her at an angle, keeping her legs apart with his knee.

The one thing that Lexi was sure of was that Giovanni wasn't going to kill her. As he pressed against her, she felt his erection; he wanted her and, damn it, she wanted to give in. "When I take you, you'll regret this challenge. Still," he echoed his possession with a harsh kiss, "with that mouth, you'll no doubt beg me for more after."

Her heart hammered against her ribs and her body felt hot. This was all wrong. This wasn't the reaction she was supposed to have. Lexi struggled in response to the struggle against herself, and he just balanced against her with more force. His mouth hovered above hers after another stolen kiss, and she tasted whiskey and smoke. His lips touched hers as he spoke. "I'm going to delight in making you mine."

She had been outplayed and Giovanni knew it. She was scared and her voice trembled. "Let me go," Lexi whispered.

The weight relaxed, his body a blanket instead of a burden. When she blinked, she saw the raw desire from before replaced with something akin to concern. "Breathe, *bambina*." He reached out and gently touched her, but she jerked back, which did little to stop him from continuing to caress her cheek. The voice that had soothed her on the street corner returned. "Don't be afraid. I take care of what's mine."

But she was afraid, and she sure as hell didn't want to be identified as anything resembling Giovanni Masseretti's property. Her body began to shake and she pushed beyond him, amazed that he didn't try to stop her. She ran through the restaurant and out the door, hearing the bells scream for her to get the fuck away from him as they jangled noisily.

It was only a third of a mile to her apartment. Although Lexi wasn't used to the chunky heels, she managed to make it to the side door of the antique bookstore before realizing she didn't have her handbag. Had she left it in the restaurant? The car? She used a coded keypad alongside the door to enter the apartment. Once locked safely inside, she ran up the stairs into the studio and collapsed at the foot of the bed. She would find a way to get her purse back later.

She wasn't a field agent. She wasn't conditioned for this kind of work. Could she live with herself if she got out of this? Lexi had pushed Sam so hard, but she had given no thought to how much her zero experience would impact her. In her head all she had needed to do was flirt strategically and then overhear information, steal data, and possibly- if she was lucky- maneuver herself into Giovanni's office long enough to look through and snap photos of whatever he kept onsite.

But Lexi had severely underestimated the gangster. Sam's contention that Giovanni Masseretti was viewed by everyone who knew him as danger incarnate had fallen on deaf ears. She was indeed *sorda*, just as Giovanni had called her tonight. It was clear to her now that the only thing he liked more than being on top of the world was being on top of a woman. For her worse, Lexi had directed his eyes to her as his next plaything.

From all of the accounts she had read, he was the ultimate alpha male; power was his aphrodisiac and mixing an edge of the violence from his real world into his fantasies fueled his sex. Lexi could still feel his hand against her throat and the pressure of his dick against her leg if she closed her eyes, and she hugged herself to dispel the thought. Better to feel the bite of the cold than to get burned by the warmth he was offering. What the hell had gone wrong to screw up her plan? *Everything*, she thought, starting with her leaving behind her job in DC to move to New York.

After ripping herself out of the dress and boots, she took a hot shower and pulled her hair into a ponytail. Her stomach rumbled, and she dressed in jeans and a loose fitting sweater that were much more fall appropriate than the dress had been. Although she didn't have her wallet, she took a twenty from a stash of money that she always kept hidden in her work bag for those moments when coffee was as much a necessity as air.

Looking down the block, Lexi noticed that the Ferrari was gone, and she heaved a sigh of relief. She walked in the opposite direction of the pizzeria to the café a block over that she had already confirmed made a light-roast coffee heavy with sugar and milk like she adored. She grabbed a half-sandwich from the cold case and one of the sweet lattes, eating a few bites at the bar that faced the street before she threw the majority in the trash. She was hungry, but the combination of nerves and unfulfilled sexual need made it difficult to stomach either the food or her thoughts. She said goodbye to the barista, who raised a silent hand in reply, before she eased back into the night.

Manhattan seemed brighter than it had been during the day, and it dawned on Lexi that, for living only an hour away for much of her life, she hadn't spent a lot of time in The City. She had grown up in northern New Jersey and her father had commuted in, trying to save his family from being tainted by his work. She had taken countless trips to Times Square and the Garden for events, but her youth had been full of books and quiet parks near her suburban home. She often wondered if her parents had settled so far north because there was no easy train ride into Manhattan, as though that would keep their family isolated from whatever horrors her father dealt with day after day.

When Lexi had been accepted into NYU, rather than be excited that she would be only a short trip away for midday lunches, her father had expressed concern. *The City isn't like New Jersey. Nothing looks like it is.* And isn't that what she had said to Giovanni tonight? *L'apparenza inganna.* Looks were often deceiving, and Lexi was just another of a million actors running through the play that was the lifeblood of New York City.

She walked slowly back to her apartment, constantly looking over her shoulder and unable to shake the sensation of being watched. She didn't see Giovanni and no one seemed out of place; the Ferrari was still gone when she arrived back at her door. She again bypassed the lock with her code and walked upstairs, realizing she would have no choice but to go back to *Disco Ballarò* tomorrow in order to locate her missing keys and wallet.

Coming to a stop on the top step, she looked into the small room that made up her entire life, and the cold of the numb was overshadowed by the chill of terror. Sitting on the small kitchen counter was her handbag atop a note scrawled across a subway map. *Allora, pedala.*

2

Lexi didn't sleep that night. There was no place to hide in the apartment, but that didn't stop her from looking everywhere and from sitting with her face to the stairs while she clutched a kitchen knife. Rationally, she knew that Giovanni had used the key from her purse to gain access to her apartment, but she didn't care. Away from him, the chemistry that they had ignited cooled, and she was left with a pit in her stomach.

Lexi stood to stretch the ache from her muscles when the darkness of night faded. She limped into a hot shower and let the water pound against her skin, grateful that the tiny apartment had harder-than-expected water pressure. Afterward, she stared at her reflection in the mirror and tried to see anything other than a woman with thirty-two unfulfilled and broken years.

Her gunmetal blue eyes were striking against the contrast of her pale skin and hair that looked as though brunette strands were kissed by light. She was everything that a mob girl wasn't, yet she had a clear opening that had never been expected. Did she play the role of the typical arm candy that Masseretti normally had trailing behind him? The miniskirts and overdone makeup? The expensive dye jobs and tight bodies?

She watched the eyes of the woman in the mirror transform. *No*, Lexi thought. She would be everything he couldn't have. She would be smart-mouthed where they were docile, provocative where they were permissive, teasing where they were dripping with easy sex.

If Giovanni wanted a challenge, then Lexi would give it to him. She had worried the night before that she would never get another chance. Seeing her purse on the counter, she knew for a fact that he would find a way for their paths to cross again. When he did, she would be ready.

She dressed in a stylish pencil skirt that fell just below her knees and a fitted top. Her heels were lower and made the fifteen-minute walk to the Main Branch of the New York Public Library easy. She took the elevator to the primary circulation desk on the third floor and waited in the lobby until an older librarian approached with a smile. "Alessandra Masters; I'm Dr. Rory Fisher." She reintroduced herself although Lexi remembered her from months before. "Welcome to the Schwarzman."

"Thank you." Lexi accepted the woman's outstretched hand and followed her through the spacious room. "Working here is a dream come true."

"Your CV speaks for itself. The Smithsonian? That's an amazing collection. We didn't really get a chance to discuss this at your interview, but what brings you to New York?"

"I just needed a change of pace," Lexi lied as they entered the smaller reading room. "The opening in Rare Books was fate telling me to make the jump."

"We are glad to have you. Your predecessor had been here for years. His stroke a few months ago left us wondering how long the vacancy would last. It's lucky for us that someone with your credentials was interested in the move."

They went over the initial paperwork, and Lexi was outfitted with keys and her badge. Dr. Fisher spent several hours showing her around the huge building before they returned to the third floor, where the older woman gave Lexi a large folder. "You're coming on board just before our annual library fundraiser. The Gala is our primary source of private funding and is mandatory. Friday, black tie. We close at four and the Gala begins at seven. You'll be expected to showcase your collection and engage donors." She smiled as she waved her hand around the room. "We are trying to break the stereotype of stuffy shelves managed by passive librarians."

Once Dr. Fisher slipped out of the collection room that housed books dating to the fifteenth century, it didn't take long for Lexi to submerge herself in the pile of active repairs and restorations. She met her archival page, and the two of them discussed a piece recently acquired from auction that had been damaged in a fire. These were the skills that Lexi had spent countless hours honing; it was what she loved. By the time her phone rang at the end of the day, she had fallen into her work with ease. "Alessandra Masters: Rare Books."

"*Ciao, bella.*" His voice was smooth, and Lexi looked around the empty office as though he was somehow there with her. She wanted to say something- anything- but words refused to form. In her silence, she heard his amusement. "It's not good for you to skip lunch, *bambina.*"

"Stop calling me that." She continued to look out onto the floor that housed the majority of the adult section, but the only person watching her was the Circulation Librarian. He lifted his hand in a wave when their eyes met. She didn't see Giovanni, but Lexi couldn't shake the sense that he was nearby. She walked through her collection quickly as his voice continued to drip with delight at her annoyance.

"Would you prefer English, baby girl?"

"I'd prefer Lexi- and that's if you had a reason to speak to me at all." She stood at the window that overlooked Bryant Park. He was watching her even if she didn't see him. The thrill of being chased was both unsettling and arousing.

"Alessandra." The way that Giovanni said her name made *bambina* almost preferable. It sounded dark and sexy. In those four syllables, she could hear all the things he had promised her the night before when he held her against the back wall of the pizzeria. "No, *bambina*, I think I'll call you what I'd like, when I'd like."

"Why are you calling me anything at all? I thought we established that I don't belong anywhere near you. Oh," she added, "and that you're an asshole."

His accent continued to untangle her. Whatever it managed to leave behind, his words continued. "Yet: here we are."

"I'm working. How did you get this number?"

"You gave it to me, remember? Perhaps I'm calling for a reference."

"You can take my name off your list. I'm not interested in working for you."

"That's good since, as I told you last night, I don't fuck the women who work for me."

"I'm sure your HR department appreciates that," Lexi answered dryly. His laughter surprised her. The sound was melodious and very much not something she thought should live anywhere near Giovanni Masseretti. She dropped her voice in the hope that no one would overhear. "But you're not fucking me either, so losing this number might still be your best option."

"You don't like me very much, do you, *bambina*?"

"Why would you think that?" Lexi panned her eyes across the park, looking for anything out of the ordinary. "What about you might lead me to *not* like you? The way you propositioned me in your office while you had another woman on the floor getting you off? The way that you slammed me against a storefront and manhandled me in the back of a pizzeria? The breaking into my apartment? The fact that on several occasions- including seconds ago- I referred to you as an *asshole*? What was it, Giovanni, that gave my feelings for you away?"

The phone clicked in her ear. "You need to eat. You barely touched your sandwich last night, and I doubt you've eaten at all today, save the cups of coffee that line your wastebasket."

Lexi could see his reflection in the glass, and she turned around. Did she look as nervous as she felt? She had promised herself the ability to stand up to him and to be everything he couldn't have, but could she? Could she avoid the attraction that pulled her to him like a moth to the flame? "What are you doing here, Giovanni?"

"I like to read."

"Really? Your reading level is probably housed on the first floor, although we don't keep porn in our juvenile collection. You might want to try the bookstore a few blocks over."

He pinched his lower lip between his thumb and forefinger in a poor attempt to hide his mirth. "It's time to go home. Your day ends," he looked at his watch, "now."

"It may surprise you, but I managed to get myself to work this morning. I can make it home without your escort." She returned to her desk and flashed him false concern. "Shocker, I know."

His ever-present amusement greeted her. "This mouth of yours is a treat. I look forward to all the different ways I'll transform it into obedience."

With far more bravado than she actually possessed, Lexi closed her laptop and picked up the messenger bag she had brought with her. "Not a chance, Gio." As an afterthought, she paused when she walked by him. "Or in the language you understand: not a chance, *Sir*."

He had her by the arm with a grasp that she thought might actually bruise. "Here you are, playing this game for which you don't know the rules again, Alessandra. You are pushing my buttons and daring me to respond."

Lexi met his eyes and forced herself to look at him without flinching, transforming her flirtation into overdone sweetness. "As you pointed out, Mr. Masseretti: Rare Books is closed. Do you need me to show you the elevator or should I ask Security to take you?"

His sexual aggression softened into a smile as he lowered his hand. "By all means, Alessandra: lead the way."

Lexi sauntered to the lift at the end of the empty collection while he echoed her steps. "Lost already?"

"I just like the way your ass moves in that skirt." When she stopped and looked over her shoulder to glare at him while she waited for the elevator to arrive, Giovanni had the audacity to wink at her. Lexi grit her teeth together to avoid saying anything else that he could twist.

He stood closer than was necessary in the empty elevator, and his fingers touched her spine through the lacy shirt. She debated telling him to stop but knew that he would only be emboldened to continue if for no other reason than to piss her off. His lips grazed her ear once they were walking toward the exit. "Where should we go for dinner?"

"Maybe *we* should work on your English since you missed the part upstairs where I said that *I* am going home. *We* aren't going anywhere."

"No." They stepped outside, and he fell in line with her steps down the stairs to the sidewalk. "It's time for dinner and, as much as I can fuck you in your bed or mine, you don't have any proper food in your kitchen. I'm not up for whatever takeout is between here and Madison."

Horrified, Lexi stopped and looked at him. The wind ceased to blow. The sun was no longer warm. The sounds of the hundreds of people around them died out completely. She had barely stomached the knowledge he was in her space, but the confirmation that he went through her things turned her blood to ice. "You went through my apartment?"

"There wasn't much to go through. A few cabinets-" Giovanni stopped himself when she quickly moved away from him, walking with a newfound quickness down the sidewalk. "My car is this way," he called out, pointing in the other direction.

"I'm not going anywhere with you."

It didn't take him more than a few of his long strides to catch up with her, grabbing her elbow and turning her around. "I told you, baby girl: I take care of my own. Don't be afraid of me."

"Don't be afraid of you? You fucking broke into my apartment and went through my things!" Her chest rose and fell with angry breaths. "Don't be afraid? What fucking game do you think you're running? Go back to Underground Met, and find someone else to play it with!"

Giovanni's dark eyes deepened, and he bit his bottom lip before he challenged, "Come with me. I'll teach you."

"Get away from me, Giovanni- I mean it. Get away from me, or I'll scream."

"You're in the middle of Bryant Park. Give that a try. See what happens." His grip tightened on her arm as she continued to struggle. "Stop the *Underground Met* nonsense that we both know in the present is bullshit. Dinner and home." He shrugged easily. "You have my word."

"I tried dinner with you last night. It didn't work out so well. Let go of me!" She tried to wiggle her arm away, and he applied more pressure, sending shockwaves through her. "You're hurting me, Gio."

"Then stop fighting." He didn't loosen his hand from her arm, and Lexi shivered beneath his stare. He emphasized each word slowly. "Stop fighting."

"Then let go." Although she was still scared of what he had done, Giovanni didn't terrify her. She was more annoyed by his calm control and his ability to coerce her into his play.

"I make the rules, *bambina*, and, besides," he leaned against her and deeply inhaled, "you may not want to like me, but you can't fight the fire that sparks between us." He pulled back and used his free hand to touch her face. "Stop this needless fighting. I'm going to win regardless."

Zero to two, Lexi thought. She decided to lose the round with her eye on the war. "I didn't sleep well last night. Since that was one hundred percent your fault, I will let you buy me dinner because I'm too tired to figure out an alternative, but then I'm going home. *Alone*."

Giovanni paused as though he wanted to say something but thought better of it. "The car is this way," he repeated, giving a gentle tug of her arm before he allowed his fingers to envelop hers as they walked through the park.

"How long were you here?"

"Not long," he answered, leading her to where the Portofino, although parked illegally, held no ticket. "I didn't need to be in order to know what you were doing all day."

Had he tapped into the CCTV of the building? She was disturbed at the thought. "A note for the future: that shit makes you sound like a stalker. You might want to tone it down."

"It doesn't make me *sound* like anything," he retorted. "I *am* stalking you. That's what one does to a target."

"I'm not your prey, Giovanni." Lexi stopped at the car when he held the door open, gesturing for her to get inside.

"*Bella mia.*" He ran his finger across the fullness of her lips before trailing it down her throat. Whatever appetite she may have had dissipated. *Zero to three*, she thought before he continued with his smooth voice. "Everyone is prey to the predator." When she made no attempt to move, looking behind him while she considered the option of walking her ass home and locking the door, he shook his head as though he had open access to her thoughts. "I don't think so. Get in."

That was the last thing she wanted to do, but Lexi got in the car anyway. "Where are you taking me?"

"Downtown," he answered, closing the door and walking around to the other side. The top of the Ferrari was closed and the proximity to Giovanni made it hard for Lexi to breathe. "I have a table at the best place in town."

Traffic was normal for a New York evening. The car's stereo crooned out a musician she didn't recognize, and Lexi wondered if this was all part of a grand seduction scheme. She couldn't deny her attraction and was determined to use that to her advantage, but, when Giovanni downshifted in the thickening traffic, her nerves electrified at signage for the Brooklyn Bridge. "I thought you said we were going Downtown."

"We are." He pulled to a stop in front of a valet at an expensive Park Place complex, and a suited bellman opened Lexi's door. Having already walked to her side of the car, Giovanni replaced the bellman and led her into the richly decorated foyer of the Woolworth Tower.

"*Buona sera*, Mr. Masseretti, ma'am," the concierge greeted.

"*Buona sera*, Philip." He briskly walked toward the elevator. Lexi slowed her stride in an attempt to stop, but Giovanni continued to pull her forward to the golden doors.

"This isn't a restaurant, Gio." She stumbled into the lift as it opened and an attendant keyed in the code for the penthouse. Her heart pounded in her chest while they ascended to the fiftieth floor.

When the elevator opened and they exited, he asked, "Do you doubt my intentions, *bambina*?" He slowly walked her toward one of the several floor-to-ceiling windows she saw. "It's not only the best place to eat, but it has great views of The City."

Giovanni wasn't exaggerating. It was a beautiful view of lower Manhattan. The sun dipped lower in the sky, casting reflections on the water that surrounded the island and creating the illusion that the Pinnacle rested above the rest of the world. He moved with ease through the vast foyer that held a variety of white couches in a near circle, and Lexi shook her head with a light laugh. "Of course you live *here*."

"I do when I'm in The City." He had already tossed his jacket on one of the seats before taking his tie off in order to open up the first few buttons of his shirt. "I have properties all over the world. I travel a lot."

"Owning a nightclub doesn't seem like an international feat."

"I have a feeling you know far more than you say, *bambina*." He walked over to her and took her bag, adding it to the pile on the leather sofa.

"Librarians often do," she answered, taking a step back against the window.

"Then I won't insult you with lies." Giovanni gently touched her chin before taking her hand and leading her to the staircase. "Unless you wish to see my bedroom before dinner, you should come with me upstairs."

"I'm surprised anyone has seen your bedroom," she taunted. "This place is more of a showplace than a brothel."

"Be careful." He gave her a rough but playful pull up the steps to the fifty-first floor, where they exited into an imposing kitchen of white marble.

"Instead of my bedroom, you'll end up elsewhere." When she said nothing, he gave her another of his signature smirks. "But you are right. I use other rooms for that."

"Sounds lonely." Lexi ran her fingers along the grey veins that wove through the white marble. She knew that she was exacerbating an already dangerous situation. Nothing in his jacket suggested that Giovanni did anything other than detest rapists. One of the murders that he was suspected of was a lower level enforcer accused of assaulting a college student. They had only found pieces of the man's body, and the chunk that he had done damage with had ended up mailed to the girl's house. Regardless, provoking someone with an inclination for violent, rough sex- even if consensual- wasn't the smartest move. Lexi looked up at him and stopped caressing the counter when she saw desire staring back.

"Are you offering to alleviate my loneliness?" Giovanni walked around behind her and dropped his fingers on top of hers. They pressed her hand against the cold stone. His breath was hot on her ear and his voice was low. "Many have tried, but all have failed."

Trying to return the dinner to even ground, Lexi said lightly, "I hope that isn't your mantra for cooking. You promised me the best food in The City."

He laughed and, once again, the sound caught her off guard. "You lighten me," he whispered into her hair before he walked to a refrigerator that was twice the size of a normal one. "I'm not sure that I like it."

"I think you do. Why the hell else are you incapable of taking the hint that I'm not interested?"

"Is that the hint you are dropping, *bambina*?"

"Why do you call me that?" She leaned against the pass-through into the dining room, and he looked over his shoulder at her as she specified, "*Bambina*. Why call me *baby girl*? You don't know me, certainly not well enough for that."

"Hmmm," he said noncommittally. Lexi doubted that he didn't have an answer; Giovanni was just playing with her. He removed a bottle of wine from an under-the-counter refrigeration unit and poured two oversized glasses of white. "I don't make it a habit to explain myself, Alessandra. I take what I want and expect the pieces to fall into place."

"I'm a person, Gio; not a piece on your personal chessboard." She took the glass he offered. "And I don't like you. Remember?"

He scoffed at her response. "You like me far more than you want to admit." He took a slow drink from his glass, watching her over the rim. "You can desire what you fear."

"You think I'm afraid of you?"

That arrogant smirk detailed his face again as he put his wine down and pressed her against the kitchen counter by placing his hands atop hers. "Did you know that your breathing increases to nearly double its normal pace whenever I am this close to you?" He leaned in, his scruff sending chills through her when it brushed against her neck. "That your pulse quickens and your body flushes when I touch you?"

She tried to move away, breaking through the arm that he had blocked her with. He moved with such a speed that she let out a small scream when he pushed her against the wall that joined the kitchen to the stairs. "That your eyes widen and your pupils dilate when I take your body in my hands? You want me and *that* terrifies you more than the fear of who you think I am ever could."

Zero to four. Without a word, he stepped back from her and returned to the stove, taking a large pan from an overhead rack. His voice lost the trace from moments before as he gave her a history lesson between heating water in the pan and mixing together what looked like pureed tomatoes with garlic, oil, and herbs in a bowl on the counter. "Ten years ago, this space came on the market. I had no interest in staying in New York, but who could say no to such a large ownership in a city that belongs to the entire world?"

"Living in the Pinnacle seems a little like overcompensating." The statement, which she knew would hit the mark, caused Giovanni to look up darkly from the stove, and Lexi momentarily feared his retribution.

"You tell me that later," he said in a voice that implied he didn't find her amusing. When the water in the pan started to boil, he forked in long strands of fresh pasta.

The wine made her feel braver, and she drank a hearty gulp. It had a taste that made it difficult to decipher the grape. She liked it, but she wasn't sure what it actually was. "What kind of wine is this?"

"Catarratto," he answered, stirring the noodles around. He transferred the pasta into the large bowl of tomato and added in some of the water from the pan before swirling in a handful of cheese. "It has a poor reputation, but as you told me before: *l'apparenza inganna*. This particular one is my favorite." Giovanni tipped his head toward her empty glass. "Careful, *bambina*; it is far stronger than the water you Americans call wine." He placed a dish in front of her and offered her a fork from a drawer. "Especially since you haven't had a full meal in at least a day."

"Careful, Gio," she mimicked. "It almost sounds like you are worried about me." She sat down on a bar stool and twirled the fork into the pasta. She knew that he was watching her, and Lexi provocatively took the first bite of the simple dish which was full of flavor. She was both annoyed and impressed. "This is really delicious," she said before taking another bite. "I didn't think you could actually cook." When she looked up at him, Giovanni used his thumb to touch the side of her lip, and Lexi counted up another loss in her head.

"My mother would be offended to hear you say that." He took a bite from his own plate.

The wine made the evening feel less like an assignment and more like the date that it was. Lexi didn't normally drink more than a glass and she felt the impact, but that didn't make her refuse his refill. "Do you have a large family?"

"I'm the oldest of six," he said while pouring more wine for himself. "My brothers and one sister. Rowdy bunch."

"And a mother who taught you to cook."

He chuckled. "Yes. Much to my father's annoyance, I think. But," he raised his goblet, "I can impress you with my *carrettiera*, so... Perhaps she was right. And you?"

He asked the question naturally, but Lexi couldn't imagine that Giovanni hadn't already looked her up. "You already know, don't you? You went through my kitchen cabinets. You don't strike me as the type who wouldn't have looked up everything you could find on me."

He didn't answer, just watching her with the arrogant stare that both iced her veins and caused them to incinerate in the next second. Was it possible he hadn't looked? That didn't make sense. Unsure but to make conversation, she said at last, "I'm an only child."

His next question made her doubt that he had pulled her background, and it stilled her. "Do you see your parents often?"

"Um, no. I, um..." She sighed and looked down at the food, licking her lips and trying to figure out what to say. "My parents are both... They-they died. My dad, ten years ago; my mom, two years ago next month."

"Alessandra, I'm sorry." He placed his fork down and touched her hand affectionately.

She thought her heart might go from beating a thousand-beats-a-minute to just stopping cold. This was it. This was the moment where, in his kitchen no less, she was going to call Giovanni out for what he had done. Instead, when he asked her what happened to them and his voice was gentle, what slipped out was, "My father was killed. They never figured out who or why." He cursed under his breath as the fingers around her hand tightened. "My mom: cancer." Lexi took a drink of wine in the hopes that it might put her out of her misery. "I'm sorry, Gio, but I really don't want to talk about this."

"Okay." When he tipped her head back to look at him, it was the compassion for her suffering that made Lexi want to fall apart. "You love books," Giovanni said, trying to change the weight of the mood. "Old and broken ones. New York had issue enough with their old, broken books to lure you from DC, likely because we have better coffee and better-looking men." He held his hands up in mock defense. "I took that from your resume. What did I miss?"

"Introverted librarian who loves old, broken books." She smiled at his attempt. "Just me, my books, and my coffee- the habit of which you totally got from stalking."

"Don't forget the better-looking men." He leaned forward to kiss her cheek before resuming his spot next to her while taking another bite of his dinner.

In seconds, he had moved her from tears to smiling. "I'll give you this: I cannot, to save my life, make anything other than a sandwich or a cup of soup from a can." Lexi laughed when he made a gagging sound before thoughts of her parents slipped out again. "My mother didn't teach me to cook, and my dad couldn't even fry an egg without setting off the smoke detector."

"I suppose that's something I can rectify."

"Take out rectifies it just fine." When she reached for her wine glass to drink away the memories again, Giovanni's hand touched hers and their fingers laced together.

"Enough, I think," he said softly. "Too much wine doesn't sit well on top of too much grief."

He was right. Her head was swimming. She stood up and felt uneasy on her feet. Before she could take a step, warmth flooded her waistline and Giovanni's hands were strong around her. "You aren't alone. I won't let you go," he whispered. "You are safe."

"I haven't been safe since last night," Lexi replied before her eyelids drifted closed without her consent.

3

The FBI had gone out for really nice sheets. Lexi pondered whether or not they would let her keep them as she became aware of the softness that covered her naked body. She would sleep naked more often if she had sheets like these in DC. They were heaven. Her hands brushed against the muscular torso of her bedmate when she turned onto her side, and she wondered if she could keep him as well. Lexi's eyes burst open at the thought, and she was blinded by the pale light of the rising morning. She thought she might choke on the breath that she held.

Giovanni's eyes were closed and he slept with the arm closest to her over his head. Peeking out was part of an extensive tree tattoo that wrapped around his bicep. Her fingers trailed down his side, over a scar that was jagged and she assumed was from a knife. She stopped herself at his defined abdomen, suspecting that he wasn't wearing anything beneath the sheet that covered the rest of him. Lexi didn't know if he was as asleep as he looked, and she was no longer interested in provoking him to find out.

She sat up and held the sheet around her chest while she looked around, but her clothes were nowhere to be seen. Although she didn't feel like she had done anything other than sleep, Lexi had very little memory after having dinner at the kitchen bar. How much wine did she drink? How had she gotten undressed? What the fuck did she do? The answers weren't in the skyline, but she kept her eyes trained on the sun decorating the buildings of downtown with shimmer as though the secrets were somehow contained in the reflecting light.

She jumped at the feel of his touch on her bare back. His voice dripped with sex, although Lexi wondered for a moment if that was just his accent and, by nature, a default of his personality. *"Buongiorno, bambina."*

She didn't bother to look at him. "I'm naked."

"Hmmm," Giovanni agreed, letting his fingers fall closer to her bottom as they continued to trail up and down her spine. "Beautifully so."

It was a struggle to keep her voice even. The more he touched her, the more he sent electricity through her, and it was erasing not only the numb inside that branched out like veins through her soul, but also her common sense and ability to think rationally. "Where are my clothes?"

"Laundered." His fingers became his entire hand, radiating heat across the middle of her back.

"I need to go to work." Lexi looked at her fitness band; the clock gave her ample time to get back to her apartment. She had to get the fuck out of here. The walk of shame would be far easier at dawn than if she showed up to work in the same clothes she left in.

"It's too early for that talk," he disagreed. "Come back to bed."

She coughed out the words. "No. Definitely not."

Her back was against the mattress with only the thin sheet separating them. "You misunderstand, *bambina*," Giovanni said under his breath before he lightly kissed her. "I wasn't asking."

As she breathed, her body touched him, sending signals of want and desire through her that were met and increased by the way he looked at her. Lexi wanted to turn away, but she was captivated by him even though she knew that the longer she stayed, the more trouble she was asking for.

"Do you know how easily we could solve all this tension between us?" Giovanni dropped his mouth to her neck and she shuddered. She clutched the sheet between them while he slowly moved his lips to her collarbone. One hand slipped beneath the sheet, and those fingers curled into her hip. "The last thing you would be worried about is work."

She could barely pant out a single syllable. The hangover mixed with the sensations that pulsed through her at every kiss and move of his fingers. "I," she tried helplessly. His mouth crushed hers while her betraying fingers tangled in his hair. Giovanni's kisses were rough, but his hands were rougher. The sheet was in danger of being shredded as he moved his body against hers, barely avoiding a connection that would destroy whatever assignment Lexi thought she was trying to craft.

She arched her back and gave a small cry when his teeth buried into the sensitive skin of her neck. She pushed back at him, but he easily pressed her hands down against the mattress while her body urged him to keep going. She finally managed to say his name. It was a plea, and Lexi wasn't sure if she was begging him to stop or to undo her completely. His breathing was ragged when he dropped his forehead to hers, his fingers biting into her wrists while he held her beneath him.

"Fuck." He lifted his body up and stalked into the bathroom at the far side of the room. She heard the shower turn on, and Lexi stared at the ceiling from the bed while she tried to figure out what to do.

What had just happened? What had happened the night before? She was convinced that they hadn't had sex. Giovanni had told her as much. Still, the fact that he hadn't tried to take advantage of her in her inebriated state surprised her. After all of the innuendo and outright sexual foreplay, how- and why- had he undressed her and put her to bed, sleeping next to her?

Lexi took the robe from the chaise in the corner before she walked through the bedroom that was as large as two of her apartments. It sat behind the stairs that she had taken to the second floor the night before and exited into the foyer. She went the opposite way and opened the other door that she saw.

It wasn't shock that settled on her. She had read enough about Giovanni to presume what he was into, but being inside his private space made Lexi feel as though she had become a voyeur to a fantasy that she had no business looking at. Her fingers slid over the deep purple duvet before they touched the cold metal of the four-poster bed. Splayed across the comforter was a carved paddle with strands of braided leather curled from one side. The leather was soft beneath her hand, but she could only speculate as to what damage it could do if slapped against skin like she had seen the week before. She didn't risk touching the cuffs that were already attached to each of the lower posts and wasn't surprised to see handcuffs peeking out from the headboard.

Had he thought to bring her in here last night? Was this what the wine had saved her from? What it had kept her from? Lexi was distraught by her thoughts. More disquieting was how she debated sliding her hands into the rings and risking where the morning might take her.

"See something you like?"

Any smartass quips she had weren't coming to mind. Provocation was not in her favor; this was *his* space with *his* rules. Although she had considered the idea just seconds before, even Lexi wasn't still drunk enough to entice him here. "You are surprisingly quiet, *bambina*." He was behind her, and she flinched when he touched her back, as though his fingers were the whip and she his slave. He slid her hair from her neck before he kissed her gently on the space he had scorched by his passion before. His tenderness was oddly out of place in this room. "No suggestion? You choose to not tease me here?"

Giovanni curled his hand around her waist to the loose knot that she had tied in the robe. With little effort, he pressed his hand against her bare stomach. "Where is that smart mouth I love so much?" She couldn't even swallow let alone talk. Her entire body was frozen to the floor while his hand moved lower on her belly, dangerously close to her final undoing. She leaned her head back against him, unable to stand on her own, and heard satisfaction in his arrogance. "It isn't so easy to toy with one who could break you, is it?"

He rolled his hand along the body she longed to hide from him, and Lexi wanted to give in. She needed to give in. Even if everything fell apart and she had nothing left, the memory of being alive for the last twenty-four hours would be enough. She would figure out how to live with herself; Lexi didn't know how, but she would.

She searched for the words that would let him know that she wanted him, but she didn't know what to say. After a few seconds of silence, he turned her to face him and she shuddered at his icy stare. Terror and shock widened her eyes.

His voice was a growl, and she knew exactly why he was referred to on the street as *The Wolf*. "Don't fuck with me, Alessandra. I promise that you will regret every moment." When she tried to lower her gaze, taken aback by his change in tone, he tipped her face up harshly. "Consider this your last warning. The next time you're here, I'll take what I want, and the fear in your eyes will do little to stop me from possessing you completely."

Giovanni wasn't interested in her. He just wanted to break her the same way he seemed to break any other woman who got close enough to him—and Lexi had been the fucking idiot who thought the simple fact that he was good enough at what he did to wake her up was worth the cost of throwing her entire life away. She hated that it hurt. Worse than the hurt, she hated that tears sprang to her eyes.

The second his hand dropped from her face, Lexi ran from the room. She tore into the bedroom and saw an outfit that she recognized from her closet laying across the chaise where the robe had been before. She no longer cared that Giovanni had been in her apartment again. She ignored the underwear and pulled on the pants and sweater, vowing to be out of the bedroom before he returned. Her shoes from the previous night were beneath the seating, and she slipped into them easily.

Inside the great room, she snatched her purse from the leather couch and incessantly pounded her fingers against the elevator call button, knowing that once would have been more than enough. Lexi didn't see Giovanni and no longer had the ability to worry about where he was. She just wanted out and she wiped away the tears, forcing herself not to dissolve into a mess in the foyer. Fuck him for showing up at the library yesterday. Fuck her for going to that goddamned club in the first place. When the elevator opened, the attendant made no comment about her disheveled hair, and Lexi wondered how many times he had seen similar. Probably too many to remember. "Main level, ma'am?"

She couldn't risk speaking and nodded, pressing her body into the corner. She didn't breathe until the elevator was hurling her back to earth. When the golden doors opened, she kept her head down and almost ran from the building. She was disoriented when the exit spilled her out onto Park Place. Her Midtown apartment was only about four miles away; in the haze left from the night before, Lexi had no idea where Sixth Avenue was and wasn't about to ask for help. Within ten minutes, she had found the City Hall subway and disappeared down the concrete steps.

The Six had her to 51st Street in half-an-hour, and she clutched her arms around her chest as though it was December instead of September. Her hands were still trembling when she arrived at her apartment, and it took her multiple attempts to get inside. Lexi bolted the door and had barely made it to the bathroom before she puked up the wine from the night before.

She cupped her knees against her chest in the tiny shower. Sam had been right. Lexi wasn't cut out for undercover work. Whether because Giovanni Masseretti had seen through her ruse the same as he had with every other undercover meant to entrap him or he was merely as dangerous of a playboy as she suspected regardless of anything else, Lexi had been outmatched and played.

She kept her head against her forearms and sobbed. She had failed. She had failed Sam, she had failed the Bureau, and she had failed her father. His death, left unprosecuted for close to a decade, would be just another unsolved mob hit.

Her tears were laced with the memories of the last few years, when she had watched her mother move from a heartbroken widow into a woman rediscovering her life only to have her days cut short. At some point, Shannon Masters had looked in the mirror and made the choice to live again, something her daughter had yet to learn. As she comfortably rested, sedated by morphine during her final hours, Shannon had held Lexi's hand and tearfully told her, "The best thing you can do for yourself is to forget and move on. Learn to live again."

"Living again isn't something I'm capable of," Lexi had replied. If her father's death had started the cold inside of her, then losing her mother at only thirty-years-old had cemented the numb to her soul.

"You're wrong," Shannon had choked out. "The feelings will come back when you don't plan for them." She had been holding onto Sam's hand as he sat on the other side of the bed. "With someone you never expected. Don't hide from it, Alessandra. Embrace it. Live again no matter the cost."

It was one of the last things she had said before she fell asleep. Shannon hadn't woken up again, and the conversation was the final memory Lexi had of her mother. She had refused to listen, but maybe Shannon had been right. The knowledge that Lexi had been awakened by her father's killer broke her further, and she tried to drown beneath the shower. The numbness was easier to live with.

She dressed in a pair of gray slacks and a cream turtleneck sweater, opting for low cut brown boots. Keeping her hair down, Lexi covered the brokenness in her eyes with dark sunglasses and spent the next fifteen minutes convincing herself to call Sam. He had told her to come to New Jersey when she was finished, but she wasn't sure that she wanted to give up her new life. She simply didn't want to deal with Giovanni anymore. After this morning, she hoped that he would leave her alone.

Greeting her new coworkers on her way to her third-floor desk, Lexi felt the pieces of her life falling into place. She opened her laptop and launched the start-up software, the image of the library flashing on the screen. This life was everything she had always wanted. It was what she had spent years studying to do; even as an FBI agent, working with rare books was how she had spent her free time. She had been volunteering at the Smithsonian for as long as she had been in the DC area. *This* was her dream. What did she risk by staying in New York?

Quitting now would guarantee that she never returned to the Bureau. Sam had told her that she could reapply until she aged out, but why would she? She hadn't lasted forty-eight hours undercover. There was no way she would be anything other than permanently assigned to the warehouse of law enforcement materials at the Academy. Was that really what Lexi wanted to do with her life? While she may have been good at her job in Quantico, she hadn't loved it. It had just been something to keep the days moving forward with her eyes trained on finding answers.

The almost twenty months she had been employed by the Smithsonian, by contrast, had been a dream. Making the move to New York, although she had done it as the first step of getting close to Giovanni and discovering the truth, could still be part of that dream. She had snagged a department directorship. She was the head librarian of a rare books collection. This was what she had always wanted and, ten years post-graduation, she had made that goal a reality. Maybe Lexi was looking at this wrong. Maybe she should see this as a gift and try to pull her life together.

Giovanni hadn't hinted that he knew who she really was. The entire thing had been a cat-and-mouse game to get her in bed with him. She didn't know why he had stopped last night when he had the upper hand; maybe it was the one shred of dignity he had left after a life of violence and murder. By morning, he had seen it as failure.

Why else would he have treated her so harshly? The desire to make her leave had raged behind his eyes. He had been successful in that quest, and knowing that she had lowered her defenses enough for him to do so hurt. Lexi hated him for that pain. She hated him for being the one her mother had promised her would be waiting to wake her up. Shannon should have warned her instead.

If she stayed in The City and Giovanni never looked in her direction again, Lexi would still have escaped from the life that hadn't been real. She had her dream job in a place that offered her the chance to create a new life. Maybe it would even offer her the chance to wake her soul up to someone else. Her mother had found two great loves. Why couldn't she?

Lexi stopped, the thought she might vomit too strong. Giovanni wasn't a great love. He was merely hot enough and sexy enough that he had burned her brain awake. Now she had to burn him from her memory, perhaps with someone else, perhaps not. She wasn't that far yet.

She tried to refocus, but her thoughts were on Giovanni and the morning that had unfolded, catching her completely off guard. Lexi turned to the pile of restorations and copy requests that sat on the edge of her desk, and pushed the memory of Giovanni from her head as she started to work. After visiting with a small class from a local MLIS program and giving a tour of the collection, she decided to break for lunch and walked down the stairs to the first floor for a bagel and coffee.

"Hey. It's Lexi, right?" The male librarian smiled at her while he paid for his lunch and waited at the edge of the counter.

"Yeah. Hi." She couldn't remember his name and hoped he would fill in the gap.

"Luke. Head of Circulation," he said, looking around them and, after she had paid, using his bag to point outside. "Do you want to have lunch together? There are a lot of areas in the park. It's nice to just get out of the building sometimes."

She didn't really want to say *yes*; unable to figure out a way to say *no*, Lexi agreed and followed him into the early afternoon. They sat down at a small table beneath a large tree that afforded them shade. "You're from DC?" Luke asked.

"New Jersey." She unwrapped the bagel and broke it into pieces while panning her gaze around the nameless, faceless people. Was Giovanni watching her? "I moved to DC after school."

"What's the Smithsonian like?"

"It was great." Lexi looked back on her time there with a measure of satisfaction. The collection was amazing, and she had learned skills that, had it been another place and another time, she would have considered valuable and worth the painstaking effort.

"Do you miss it?"

Luke was trying to make conversation, and Lexi picked up on the fact that he might be on the verge of asking her to have more than lunch to talk about it. She wasn't up for that at all and needed a gentle way to let him know. She hated the lie almost as much as she hated that it was Giovanni she thought about as she told it. "I do, but I missed my boyfriend more." Lexi shrugged and looked back at her bagel. "Long-distance thing. It was one or the other, and the open job here made the choice easier."

Luke gave her a guarded smile as he ate chips from the open bag in front of him. "I get that. Makes sense."

She managed to get through the painful lunch by discussing Luke's path from university to the New York Public Library before she made an excuse to return to her work. After the day before, Lexi was surprised when her day passed without incident. There were no phone calls, no mysterious visitors, and no gangsters dragging her to a waiting Ferrari at the end of her shift. She worked later than she needed to, waiting on the phone call that would tell her Giovanni had been stalking her again, but that call never came.

It was closing in on six o'clock when she locked up and said goodbye to the security guard as she walked out into the cool breeze of a Manhattan fall. The sun set the sky on fire. Walking passed Rockefeller Center, she grabbed takeout from a burger joint. Lexi got home just before darkness settled and sat at the built-in desk by one of the few windows to watch the people walking through Midtown. Her apartment was quiet and empty.

Although she kept the knife from the kitchen by her bed, she eventually fell asleep in cotton sheets that weren't nearly as luxurious as the ones she had woken in. Light streamed through the apartment's tiny windows in the morning. Lexi half-expected to reach out and find a body next to her, but she was alone and lumbered to the shower. It was as though Giovanni Masseretti had never existed. She promised herself that she could live with that as hot water slapped her in the face before she dressed. Lexi still hadn't bothered to grocery shop, and she left the apartment for the café that was in the opposite direction of work to grab a yogurt and the first of Wednesday's supply of coffee.

Sitting at the counter, she balanced the spoon in her mouth in order to click on the notification. *New article on: Giovanni Masseretti.* The photograph showed him looking just as sexy as he had been at the bar on Sunday but this time with a dark haired woman leaning against him. They laughed as they sat behind an exterior table. The photograph had been taken the night before at an Uptown restaurant. She tossed the half-eaten yogurt in the trash without bothering to read the article.

The woman was beautiful, and Lexi hated her guts. She shoved her phone in her bag and slipped between the people in line as she took her coffee and walked down the busy sidewalk. It wasn't the mystery woman she hated; it was Giovanni for replacing her so easily- and with a fucking brunette. Lexi could live with another blonde draped over his arm; *that* she expected. His changing preference to a woman who looked more like her was a slap in the face.

When she got to work, she vowed to wipe all care from her thoughts. The building was already preparing for Friday, and she passed by gigantic bouquets on every counter. When she got into her own office, she fingered a heavy gardenia bloom that filled the vase on the edge of her desk. The vase was larger than the others she had seen walking through the library, and she wondered why hers wasn't just roses but held a variety of flowers, like ranunculus and orchids. Maybe the different departments had different themes for the dinner, she considered as she tried to figure her life out.

Giovanni the man had been a distraction and Giovanni the killer was a fail. Sam had told her that it was okay to quit and live out her life. He knew her father better than anyone; if her parents had wanted nothing but for Lexi to move on, then it was time to start. Having a life well-lived would have to be enough to deal with the fact that she would never know the truth. It made her sick, but what the hell other choices were there?

She managed through a working lunch as she learned about what typically happened during the fundraising dinners. After leaving work on time, she made it to one of the dress shops in Rockefeller Center twenty minutes before close. The woman who greeted her was not amused. "I'm sorry," Lexi apologized. "I need a dress that can be ready by Friday. I don't care what it looks like- you can pick from what you have. It just has to be formal enough for a fundraiser."

When the woman looked her over and measured her, only to disappear and pull out a dress with a price tag that made Lexi internally scream, the librarian plastered a smile on her face and dutifully tried the dress on. Other than being too long, which the in-house seamstress promised was an alteration that she could have done right away, the dress hung and cupped in all the right places. She could pair it with the stilettos she had kept from DC and slid her credit card across the table as the clerk rang up the purchase. She would deal with hating herself when the bill came in.

She managed to leave the shop only ten minutes after they closed and hoped the commission would cover the annoyance that the employees may have felt. There were street vendors exacerbating her hunger as Lexi walked aimlessly toward home, eventually finding herself outside of the pizzeria that Giovanni had brought her to. "You're an idiot," she said to herself, pulling back the door and stepping inside. The same man from several nights before was making pizzas behind the counter, and she knew that he recognized her when he looked behind her before making eye contact again. She smiled her best smile and greeted him in Italian. *"Buona sera."*

"Buona sera." He looked over her shoulder again. He was a native New Yorker and switched to English. "What can I get you?"

"Just a slice. Plain."

"To go?"

Did he want her to go? She looked out the window where his gaze kept going, but none of the people drew her attention. Lexi returned her eyes to the counter before she saw an empty booth and pointed. "No, I'll eat in."

He lifted his hand to acknowledge he would bring the pizza to the table she had searched out before he used a large, wooden plank to put the slice from the case into the fire. As she slipped her workbag next to her, the man came from around the counter and placed a glass of wine in front of her. "I'm good, thanks," she said, trying to refuse, but he only smiled and waved her off while he returned to waiting customers.

"Deaf Italians must be my thing," she muttered under her breath, scrolling through her phone. As much as it annoyed her, she typed Giovanni's name into the search box. The change in color showed her that she had already read every immediate response to her query, and she clicked on the images tab instead. Popping up first was the picture with the brunette from the night before; she swiped it away. There were all sorts of images: Giovanni at restaurants, clubs, with women, alone, at a ribbon cutting for a drug rehabilitation center in upstate New York. She lingered over one of him half-naked on a beach and zoomed in on the tattoo she had seen on his chest. Lexi chuckled as her pizza was dropped off. It was a fucking wolf on *Il Lupo*. Of course it was.

The pizza made her wish she had ordered a second slice. It was everything a piece of pizza should have been, and Lexi knew she would deal with the risk of seeing Giovanni just to make this a haunt. Why had she run out on dinner two nights before? The food might have been worth dealing with him.

She put her phone in her bag to avoid looking at it, opting to eat her dinner in peace. Looking at pictures of Giovanni would only make things worse. If she didn't think about wanting him in bed, then she would think about wanting him in prison- and those things were not in the immediate future. When Lexi finished her dinner, she bussed the dishes to a sideboard and waited at the register.

"Have a good night," the pizza maker said, ringing up the person who stood behind her as he passed across a large box to the man.

"I haven't-"

"*Buona sera.*" He smiled at her. "Tell Gio that Marco says *hey.*"

Lexi sighed. "Yeah. I will," she lied, lifting her hand. "Thanks."

"Good night," he echoed again, turning back to his customers.

It was dark outside, and Lexi held her bag closer to her arm as she walked the few minutes home. She changed her mind; she would avoid that restaurant. There had to be pizzerias just as good that didn't think she was a mobster's girlfriend.

By the time she showed up to work on Thursday she had, once again, given herself the pep talk to avoid thinking about Giovanni and, after she had filled her empty desk drawer with the things she would need for the Gala the next day, decided she was going to take her advice. Fuck him. There were millions of men in New York City. She could find another one to make her heart race- and that one wouldn't be a drug-running, hooker-pimping, murdering Mafioso.

Her workday ended, and Lexi found herself playing with the roses while waiting for the phone to ring, someone to tell her that her ass looked nice in the skirt she was wearing, or a Portofino waiting to take her anywhere but home. She wasn't getting off that easy. Based on the frustration she felt, she wasn't getting off at all.

Walking to work on Friday with a dress bag thrown over her shoulder from the pick-up that morning, Lexi gave herself yet another *you can forget about him* internal chat and almost felt like a normal person. She hung the dress on a hanger in the staff bathroom where several other bags had been left and kept her mind on work through the shortened day.

The library was buzzing with excitement. The annual fundraiser was the highlight of the year, and most departments were stressed as they tried to serve the public and maintain a clean and organized collection. Rare Books was the envy of the building. The majority of their requests were distance and little was required to keep the floor looking pristine. The building eventually closed, and the staff worked to ready themselves in offices and bathrooms while caterers, event planners, and musicians overtook the landmark building on Fifth and 42nd.

Looking at her reflection in the mirror, Lexi pulled a few ringlets of freshly curled hair to frame her face and accentuate the long silver earrings she had paired with her emerald green dress. The backless gown with a plunging neckline displayed her curves without looking trashy. There was a hint of a bite mark on her neck, but she doubted anyone would notice after she used a necklace of overlapping discs that matched her earrings to cover the lingering bruise.

A voice came over the PA system to warn that the doors of the Gala would soon be opening while Lexi locked her personal items in her bottom drawer and took a position near the front of her collection. There was a string quartet playing soft music in one corner and a full bar had appeared in another. As the building welcomed rich philanthropists from all over The City, uniformed servers rotated through with a variety of cocktails and hors d'oeuvres. This would continue until the guests were led into the large reading room that shared the third floor with Rare Books. Nearly the size of a football field, Lexi could see that the space had been transformed into a site fit for a royal wedding.

Putting on her best smile, Lexi began to talk with the people who wandered in. She answered questions about the library's mission and its origins in 1911, along with specifics about the antique books housed in her room. A businessman who seemed more interested in her neckline than the book he inquired about stood a little too close, and an elderly couple with a love of German binding tradition were her save from continuing the discussion with him. Lexi had just explained a restoration technique to the group when her entire body electrified.

"Do you find our materials compare well to those of the Smithsonian? They are, I believe, considered one of the world's premier collections." He may have presented it in a way that made him sound unsure, but Lexi had no doubt that Giovanni knew what he said was true and didn't need her to teach him.

She looked over her shoulder, her eyes focusing on him as though he was the only person left in the room. His tuxedo was a deep gray, nearly black, and tailored to fit his body. He had shaved down his stubble and his dark eyes picked up the light from the chandeliers. He held two flutes of the champagne that had been making their way through the floor.

Lexi bit back a laugh when she saw his charming look transform into a glare at the man closest to her. After the couple she had been chatting with excused themselves and the man made himself discrete, she raised an eyebrow. "Jealousy looks less fitting on you than that tux. I would have figured you for Armani," she added, "but I don't think they do that shade of black."

"Piana," he answered. "And I'm not jealous; I'm territorial. Those are *not* the same."

"Do tell." Lexi rolled her eyes as she crossed her arms over her chest and watched him with amusement.

"*He's* jealous." Giovanni tipped one of the glasses toward the man who watched them from across the room. "He wants something that isn't his. I'm protecting what's mine," he said, taking a step closer to her and leaning down to kiss her cheek. "There is a world of difference." When she scoffed but didn't reply, he held one of the glasses out. "I almost hesitate to offer. I don't think your office is nearly as enticing as my bedroom."

He was intruding on her life, and Lexi hated herself for still wanting him. Why had he suddenly decided to come back? Had he been on the guest list from the start? *No,* she thought as she saw him settling into the role of unraveling her. Giovanni had come back for her, but Lexi couldn't risk him again. She had wanted him all week, yet, in the moment he returned, Lexi knew that she wouldn't survive when Giovanni decided she wasn't worth the effort once more. She took the glass and pretended to show him the collection as he walked alongside her toward the back windows. "I've decided to take your advice."

"Have you now, *bambina*? And what advice have I given that you have finally decided is worth taking?"

"I'm not going to fuck with you." She couldn't make sense of what she saw in his eyes at her comment and had to look away. "I'm finished playing the game. I fold." Lexi turned back to the people entering the room, smiling at him professionally before leaving to greet them. "*A'risentirci*, Mr. Masseretti."

She kept herself occupied and away from Giovanni, who talked easily with her coworkers and fellow donors. She bit back annoyance at the way many of the women threw themselves at him. Their eyes met, and Lexi saw amusement at her frustration when he tipped his glass in her direction. In reply, Lexi tried to forget the gangster even existed and focused on socializing. When dinner was finally called, she sat down in her prescribed seat only to sigh when he appeared next to her. "How did I know that you would find yourself assigned to this table?"

"Where else would I sit?" Giovanni leaned over and kissed her sweetly which saw several raised eyebrows among the other staff although the donors had the decorum to ignore the gesture. She saw Luke watching them from a table over, and her cheeks reddened before she looked down at her hands. Dr. Fisher delivered a welcome speech while the servers plated the first course and filled wine glasses, and Lexi kept her focus on her boss. When she touched the stem in front of her, Giovanni whispered in her ear, "Be careful, baby girl, or I'll have to take you home again." The threat was enough to make her reach for water instead.

Her table was awash with discussion of current events and how they related to library services, but Lexi was barely able to articulate organized thoughts. At some point during the meal, Giovanni had rested his hand on her thigh to sear its imprint through the fabric of her dress and into her soul. When dinner was over and the staff were asked to return to their stations while donors wrote checks and picked up thank you gifts from the various collections, she was relieved to see that she had earlier letters in the alphabet; Masseretti was assigned to the Children's Department on the lowest level.

Although she could have changed out of her gown and peep-toe heels, Lexi was too wired to spend the time doing so. She didn't want to deal with getting a taxi in order to carry everything home and decided a walk through the chilly night air might clear her head. No one in New York City would think twice to see a woman strolling Midtown in an evening gown. She noted to the librarian who would be covering Circulation the next day that she would come in over the weekend to pick up her things. With a final goodbye, Lexi walked out the main entrance and down the steps toward the sidewalk where a light rumble of thunder made her wonder if the stilettos were a good idea.

"Would you like my driver to take you home?"

He was leaning against the platform that held one of the entry lions. As much as Lexi was loathe admitting it, Giovanni looked like a model in the well-cut tuxedo, and she was painfully attracted to what she knew for a fact she should stay the fuck away from. The numb that would come when he threw her away would be far worse than the one he had forced to recede. She needed to keep walking, but her body refused to cooperate and she raised an eyebrow at his offer. "Am I no longer important enough for you to take me home yourself?"

Smirking, Giovanni didn't miss a beat. "*Perdonato, bambina,* but of all the goodbyes you could have chosen, you were clear that you no longer favor my company."

"I don't recall favoring your company to start with."

The way he slowly walked over to her made it appear that he owned the sidewalk. "Raphael is the man I trust most. I would value you more than I value my own life to send him on the simple errand of driving you home. However, if you would prefer the risk of my humble escort…" He let the offer linger as he offered her his hand.

"Everything about you is a fucking risk." Lexi pulled her bottom lip into her mouth in a nervous habit. "The word- in English and Italian- is *no*, but you just don't understand *no*, do you? You might want to try your lines on one of the cheap, underage girls who would give nothing more than to be your kept arm candy. I'm old enough to know better." She pushed through his outstretched arm before stopping at the loud clap of thunder. Lexi looked up at the sky as it sent down a cold rain. Was Mercury in retrograde? Was the entire damned universe set against her?

Giovanni took her hand and ran with her to an armored BMW X5 that waited by the curb. Although she hadn't made note of it several nights before, the slate metallic was a unique color. They climbed into the open door and she pushed the wet hair from her face, remembering, "This car trailed us Monday night. It was parked behind the Ferrari when you picked me up from work."

"I don't often drive myself." He spoke to the driver before he leaned back in the seat. "I enjoy it, but," he shrugged, "it's not the safest choice."

"Yeah," she snorted. "Nightclub owners are a high-ticket item."

He ignored her response. "I have a proposition for you, *bambina*."

"The answer is already no." She turned her body away from him and hugged the car door, feigning interest in Midtown.

"You have no idea what I'm to propose."

"If you are the one proposing it," Lexi countered, "then it doesn't matter what it is." The car maneuvered through the late-evening traffic until it entered the FDR and the East River appeared out her window. "This isn't the way to my apartment."

"There are better sheets at mine."

She looked over at him. "Has no one ever said *no* to you and meant it?"

"People tend to know better." Although the words were a warning, his face softened. "Why did you do it?"

"Why did I do what?"

"At the club. Why did you follow me? Why did you choose to navigate the police?" Something about the way Giovanni watched her led her to think that these questions plagued him.

She recalled their meeting at the bar. Lexi still couldn't understand why she hadn't walked out. From that first encounter, she had known that the only way to survive Giovanni was to avoid him. But that damned numbness… The numb had been silenced by his voice, and she needed it to go away. She gazed out the window and replied with a truthful lie. "I didn't like being rejected for no reason."

"I had my reasons."

"Not blonde enough? Too old? Length between the floor and my knees too damned high?"

He cursed under his breath. "You reminded me of my sister." When Lexi looked back at the comment she hadn't expected, Giovanni trailed his fingers along her cheek. The tenderness in his touch mirrored his voice. It was far more dangerous than his anger when she provoked him. "I rejected you for your own good. You deserved better than what my club would offer you." They sat in silence for a few seconds, just watching one another. "We are both going to regret this," he said before he pulled her closer and kissed her, treating her like glass that he could easily crush beneath his grip.

"You say that like we don't both regret it already."

4

The door to the X5 opened when the car stopped underneath the covered entrance of the Woolworth Tower. Giovanni stepped out gracefully before lowering his hand; after gathering up the skirt of her dress, Lexi slid out of the back seat. He took off his jacket and draped it around her shoulders even though they were only outside for seconds. With his hand on the small of her back, he guided her into the elevator and they were silent until the lift stopped at the fiftieth floor. She followed him into his apartment. "I don't think I agreed to come back here. Didn't you offer to take me home?"

"I did." He untied the bow tie, letting it hang around his neck.

"Gio, I'm in shoes that make it difficult to walk and it's raining. I want to curl up in warm pajamas, watch bad television, and remind myself that I'm staying the fuck away from you over a pint of ice cream."

He was biting the inside of his lip, and she knew that he debated openly laughing at her. He took her hand and brought her into his bedroom. "I didn't pack your pajamas," he said, opening a large drawer. He offered her a La Perla shirt before putting the matching bottoms on the edge of the bed. "But I don't mind sharing."

"What do you mean?" She stood there, holding the silk button-up while he kept his eyes on her and unfastened his cuffs. When he didn't answer, she said with more annoyance, "Gio, what does *I didn't pack your pajamas* mean?"

The cufflinks and tie on his dresser, he began to unbutton the white shirt. "Do I need to speak Italian for you, *bambina*? When I went to your apartment to get some of your things for the weekend, since I assumed you would not be amused to find yourself here and without whatever lotions and such you prefer, I neglected to pick up anything for you to sleep in."

Lexi threw the shirt at him, which he caught squarely in the chest before laughing. "This is why you don't have a girlfriend, Gio."

"*Bambina*, I have many girlfriends-"

"No." She shoved her finger in his chest after he threw the top onto his bed, pushing into him with the anger that flowed out in waves. "You have one-night stands and women who use you as much as you use them, but you have zero understanding of what a normal relationship actually looks like. Maybe it's because you aren't capable or because no one ever bothered to explain to you that you don't get to rule people like you do an empire. I am not a thing. I am not someone you can just play around with until the fancy passes you. I'm not your *baby girl* that will sit home while you fuck your staff to prove who's the boss. It's not about what's down here." Her voice was louder than she intended when she harshly grabbed his crotch before tapping her fingers against his chest. "If there's nothing of merit here!"

She stalked out of the room, going back to the main elevator and touching the call button. When it didn't light up, she pushed it over and over again while cursing, "Come the fuck on."

"I'm not used to women running from me."

"Well, that's a shocker. You clearly know the wrong women because no one should stand for a man who breaks into their house and throws them around alleys like they are a rag doll." He was so close to her that she felt the heat from his body before he slipped his jacket from her shoulders. His hand touched her bare skin, and he leaned forward to kiss her upper back. "I want to go home, Gio." Was she crying? Why was her face wet? Why did her voice sound so choked up? "Just let me go. Please."

When he turned her around, his fingers fell over her tears like they were braille and he sighed. "I am not the man for you," he admitted, using his thumbs to wipe her tears away. "These will only be the first of many, and I will hate myself for each and every one, even as I push you to them."

"Then let me go," she whispered. If he called the elevator, then Lexi promised herself that she would get the hell out of New York City. This belief coexisted with the part of her that didn't want to leave 2 Park Place at all and wondered what, for better and worse, staying would cost her.

"I think we are too far beyond that." He leaned forward and her mouth was his in an instant. "I will do better," he murmured before cupping her face in his hands, "to be the man you deserve and not the man I am."

"Why do you think that's enough?" When he pulled back to look at her, Lexi thought she saw a chink in his tough exterior. "I told you earlier tonight. I can't play this game. You don't want *me*; you want a challenge. But that won't be enough, Gio. You'll want to win, and I will let you break me for the sake of not making that easy." She dropped her head as a new tear slid down her face.

"I don't want to break you."

"That's exactly what you want to do!" She looked up at him. "You can't suddenly change your mind now because you realize I truly want to go!" Lexi slammed her hand against the elevator, but the call button still didn't light up.

"I'm not used to being told no," Giovanni said, his hand returning to her back. "And every time you challenge me, it just makes me want you more. I always get what I want, and I don't care who pays the price for that."

"Why would you think that I would want that? That any woman would? Jesus! What the fuck is wrong with you?" Lexi could hear the tears that weighed her words down.

Giovanni exhaled in frustration and didn't answer. "Come to bed," he said almost apologetically. "Your dress is wet. Your skin is cold. I don't want you to get a chill."

Lexi took a shaky breath. He wasn't going to call the elevator and, truth be told, she wasn't going to force him to. She walked beyond him into the bedroom and, after picking up the shirt, locked herself in the bathroom. One of her travel bags, filled with a variety of the lotions and washes she had barely unpacked onto her sink, was on the built-in vanity. She took off the shoes and wiggled out of the dress. After she slipped into Giovanni's shirt, which hung just below her bottom, she washed her face with one of the washes from the satchel. Looking up at the clean-faced woman in the mirror, she saw fear and vacancy. *You wanted this*, she reminded herself. *You got yourself into this, and now you've got to make it out.*

Lexi had no idea who Giovanni really was. None of this made any sense. The man on the street? The violence and sexual tension? That Giovanni she understood. He scared her and made her feel like she had lost before she had even tried to play the game, but she could rationalize him. That man fit in with everything she had read.

But this Giovanni? The one who touched her gently and spoke to her as though he actually cared? She could not rectify this man with what she knew. To her detriment, she wanted both versions. What did that say about her? And how much worse of a person was she if she factored in every story and rumor Sam had told her? She covered her face and leaned against the counter.

Giovanni had only pursued her because she had dared to tell him she wasn't interested. Once she slept with him (because that, Lexi thought, was inevitable), would she be relegated to the pile of women he had left in his wake? Would her life fizzle because this entire tango was driven by his pursuit of her? Or had he decided that she was something worth working for, even if he didn't understand why either? If he was legitimately interested in her and then discovered her betrayal- Lexi cut off the thought. She refused to think about that at all and zippered everything back into the bag. How much longer could she hide in the bathroom?

It was quiet outside the room. What had he planned? He mentioned her staying for the weekend. Had he thought this through? Had he assumed that she would go along with whatever plan he had?

He had to have known better than that. Giovanni knew that she would fight back. That had to be part of the allure. If he thought that he had broken her, would the spell be broken, too? Lexi was torn with her next move, but Giovanni was more adept at playing on this chessboard; she would be at checkmate far sooner than she realized if she stumbled.

She opened the door and looked into the empty bedroom. She walked through the large room and, as she entered the foyer, heard noises from the floor above. Lexi quietly ascended the stairs to the kitchen that she had seen on her earlier visit. Giovanni was at the pass-through, wearing the matching pajama bottoms and holding a small container while he took a spoon from a drawer. "I have gelato." He flashed an apologetic half-smile. "No ice cream."

His demeanor had changed. Lexi didn't know how much he was strumming her strings but decided to play along. "Same thing."

"Not even close." He flipped the top onto the counter and put the spoon into the chocolate before offering it to her. When she opened her mouth, the cold spoon slid between her lips and the silky dessert exploded her taste buds. "While I can provide you with gelato and pajamas, I'm afraid that convincing you to stay away from me…" He didn't finish the sentence, instead refilling the spoon and returning it to her mouth. "Apparently, I don't need to attempt much to convince you of that."

After the second bite, Lexi picked up the top and put it back on the pint. She was close enough that her body brushed up against his bare chest, and they stood motionless until he tossed the spoon in the sink and returned the gelato to the freezer. Giovanni used his fingers to stroke her lips before he dipped down and kissed her lightly. "Come to bed with me." One of his hands rested on her lower back and the other curled beneath her hair at her neck. "Let me hold you until you fall asleep. We'll discuss the rest in the morning."

"I don't trust you," Lexi said, looking into his eyes.

Giovanni lightly nodded before kissing her again. He slid his hand from her back to her fingers, leading her downstairs to his bedroom. After turning down the sheets wordlessly, he gently pulled her into bed with him.

"You're trembling." He settled her against his chest after bringing the sheets and thick comforter up to their waists. "Are you cold?"

"No." Her reply was muffled by him, and he adjusted himself in order to look down at her with concern.

"*Bambina*," he sighed, his voice low and raspy, "when you watch me with those wide eyes, I want to possess you until your terror is replaced by desire. And yet, I fear that you will always be afraid of me, which is probably the right choice as much as I wish it otherwise."

Lexi didn't want to give in, but he was her secret addiction. Giovanni stroked her face and, when his lips softened against hers, she slipped her tongue into his mouth and encouraged his deepening kiss. *You're a liar*, her mind chastised. She had told Giovanni *no* repeatedly only to have her body tell him *yes*. He rolled her beneath him, and Lexi's hands curled into his back and neck while her legs wrapped around his thighs. She could feel his hardness pressing through his pants as though desperate to break out and into her.

"You should go now, Alessandra," he said between breaths, "or I won't let you leave. You should know that. You'll be mine. Forever." It was a final warning as Giovanni devoured her mouth and ripped open the three-hundred-dollar nightshirt, its buttons flying through the room. He dropped his mouth to her neck while his hands brutalized her breasts with their rough massage. "You aren't going anywhere."

Lexi cried out when he bit into her neck, drinking her in as though she were wine. Her fingers knotted in his hair while she tousled beneath him in response. His hands on her wrists easily subdued her, and she could barely say his name before his mouth was over first one nipple then the other while his fingers found solace by digging into the tender spot between her waist and hip. She gasped when his tongue flowed over her belly like a waterfall before disappearing in the space vacated by the panties he destroyed in an easy rip of fabric.

Her back arched with wave after wave of a pleasure that he addicted her with by hit after hit. When he came back to her mouth, Lexi tasted herself on him and her eyes were captured by the darkness that overwhelmed him when he pushed beyond defenses he had already disarmed. He filled her and she shuddered, breaking their gaze and clutching his shoulders to combat the pain of his size ripping through her narrow body. "Fuck," Giovanni said between gritted teeth. He threw her to the bed, balancing on his knees. His hand was wrapped around her throat, and she gripped his wrist with both hands while he slammed into her body. "You are so fucking tight around me."

Lexi's eyes rolled back as he thrust deeper, her breath catching and releasing as a moan. The fingers around her neck hovered between safety and danger, and the compression enhanced the fury of desire that flooded her with every move. When Giovanni roughly threw her onto her knees, she choked on the change and grabbed the hand that wrapped in her hair in order to yank her head back. He used the move to pull her in front of him and, without warning, rejoined their bodies together.

He pulled her hair before his open hand slapped her ass harshly, and her voice came out in staccato bursts that mimicked his pounding of her as she felt her orgasm begin to start. "That's right, baby girl," Giovanni whispered, his hand tangling more in her hair while the other wrapped around her waist to touch the swollen flower that he had caused to burst open from its blossom. "This is mine. *You* are mine."

Her voice was a cry of his name and he growled, "Mine," fucking her with an intensity that she'd never before been exposed to. He fingered her roughly while she clenched around him. Her body begged him to slow down, to let her go, to relax her back into the sheets that were wet with sweat and sex, but The Wolf had been unleashed and Giovanni used his body like a weapon. A second orgasm hit her like a punch to the stomach when his cock began to throb and explode as he cursed and emptied inside of her.

He collapsed his forehead against her head as she hovered above the bed. When their bodies fell back to earth and hit the mattress, Giovanni pulled her against him and she felt his heart thundering. She tasted salt and sex on him when she kissed the wolf tattoo that was almost hidden by neatly manicured chest hair. He held her tightly, his arms warm around her, and she closed her eyes. Between the lullaby of his slowing heart and whatever he hummed while his chin rested against the top of her head, Lexi found the numb receding into the darkness, and she drifted to sleep.

5

Lexi knew she was being watched, and she squinted to combat the morning light. She blinked the image of a well-dressed man in a chair next to the bed into view. Giovanni drank from a demitasse, and his gaze made her shiver. He was every bit the Mafioso that his file had made him out to be, from the soles of his shiny loafers to the crisp collar of his starched shirt. "You're beautiful when you sleep."

She used the silver sheets as a cover and sat up, leaning against the pillows and headboard. "You're a stalker." He didn't answer, but a smirk appeared as he took another sip of espresso. "And it's rude to not bring enough coffee to share."

"Based on the shit I saw on your desk, you wouldn't be able to handle real coffee." He offered her the cup. "Prove me wrong."

She couldn't stomach black coffee and watched him return to his drink, satisfied that he had called her bluff. She felt sick when the night before settled against her like a weight. "What happens now?"

The darkness returned to his stare. When he spoke, Lexi wasn't sure if Giovanni didn't want to understand or if the expression was lost in translation. "What do you mean?"

"Challenge accomplished, right?" Lexi curled her legs beneath herself as she sat forward. "You win."

She didn't see him put the cup down. He materialized over her and held her flat to the bed, his hands cutting into her shoulders. Anger dripped off his heavily accented words. "So you're a whore now? Just my game?" There was rage in his eyes. "*Quando finisce la partita il re ed il pedone finiscono nella stessa scatol!* Fuck, Alessandra!" He pushed into her arms as he used the momentum to stand up, running a hand through his hair.

He was menacingly mad. Lexi had insulted him and he paced the room, throwing looks that could kill in her direction until his cell phone vibrated on the bedside table. "*Cosa?*" he answered harshly before storming out of the room.

Her body was sore from the rough sex and Lexi needed a shower. The hot water scorched away the pain, and she balanced her hands against the wall while the panels of wet heat hit her from multiple directions. *When you finish the game, the king and pawn end up in the same box*, Giovanni had said. In her case, it might be a pine box or perhaps the mud at the base of the East River.

She wasn't sure how long she stayed beneath the scalding spray, but eventually Lexi turned it off and took an overly soft towel from the heated rack that hung alongside the shower. After roughly drying her hair with it, she wrapped the dark brown cotton around her body and secured it with a knot at her chest. Looking in the mirror, she leaned forward to caress her lower throat. Where he had pushed against her the night before, a bruise in the shape of his hand was forming.

She exited the bathroom and found a dark gray, three-quarter length sleeved dress angled across the bed. Lexi looked around, but Giovanni wasn't there and the floor was silent. She dressed in the matching underwear that had been folded neatly on the duvet before slipping the soft cotton over her head and adjusting the fabric as it fell slightly above her knees. The collar was high enough that it covered her neck, and she didn't have to see the reminder of his hands on her. She pulled on the socks and brown knee boots that were next to the bed. She wasn't altogether amused by Giovanni's adult version of dress-up but, looking in the full-length mirror, had to admit that she looked the part of a thirty-something New Yorker enjoying a fall day.

The rain from before had left a sheen on the city below, and Lexi watched the skyline for a few moments to try and gain the courage needed to face Giovanni in the light of day. She had spent as much time away from him as she could manage, having used the dryer that hung on his bathroom wall to blow her hair out into chunky waves to kill several more minutes. She looked in the mirror a final time before exhaling a deep breath and venturing into the hallway.

Voices led her upstairs to the apartment's third floor. Neither in English nor Italian, she recognized the musical Sicilian dialect between the men gathered in the great room that abruptly ceased when she exited onto the floor. Giovanni made no secret of appraising her looks. She thought she saw approval at her appearance, but being on display in front of strangers left her uncomfortable. Lexi shifted her weight between the balls of her feet as she pointed to the steps and turned to leave. "I'm sorry. I can go."

"Stop." The command instantly halted any movement she had considered. He stood and rattled off an order to one of the men before he took her hand and led her to the couch, sitting her down next to him. The man he had spoken to, who had to be close to seven feet tall with the build of a football linebacker, brought from the bar against the wall a delicate cup of coffee he had lightened with milk. He had to crouch into an almost bow to present it to her, and she managed to choke out, "Thank you," when her trembling fingers took the saucer and handle.

As though she hadn't entered into some sort of prearranged meeting, Giovanni continued. He rested a hand on her knee and slowly curled and relaxed his fingers while managing to avoid inching her dress higher. After a few minutes, the five men stood together and the four bodyguards left via an elevator that mirrored the stairs on the opposing side of the floor. Lexi stayed on the couch as Giovanni took another espresso from the bar where her coffee had come from. "You look nice," he complimented. His voice offered the hope that their final moments in the bedroom had been erased from his memory.

"Thank you," she murmured. "You have good taste." Placing her cup on the coffee table, she stood up and took a few steps toward him. "I... What..." Lexi sighed and tried again. "Are you upset with me?"

"Should I be?" That dark look was back in his eyes when he put his demitasse on the marble countertop. He had most certainly *not* forgotten their previous discussion.

"Gio, I-" Her voice skidded to a halt when Giovanni took two long strides toward her and stopped just before hitting her.

"If you ever call yourself out like a whore again, I will make it so that you won't be able to move for a week without remembering why," he growled, his fingers sitting on her lips in a warning. "Don't try me."

Fear flooded her in heat when he turned on his heels and was quickly replaced by anger. Had he just threatened her because she had thrown his own *I like a challenge* bullshit back at him? After making it clear to her that she had been a pursuit from the start? "What, Giovanni? Are you the only one allowed to make me feel that way?"

His eyes betrayed shock, amusement, and arrogance all at once when he faced her. "What did you just say to me?"

"I asked if the only one who gets to treat me like a whore is you. Did I stutter?" She took a step forward before adding, mockingly, "Do I need to say it in Italian?"

"You are treading on thin ice," he warned.

"You toss me like trash before you subject me to the whorehouse of your office. You decide that I'm suddenly worth your time so you break into my house to prove to me how tough you are before you buy yourself into my work. You bring me home only to dress me up like I'm some sort of doll to parade before your friends. And I'm the one on thin ice?" The heels of her boots smashed into the floor before she gave him a light push in order to get around him. "Fuck you, Giovanni."

"Fuck me?" He had her by the throat against the wall closest to them before she could get even a few steps away. "Fuck me? Is that what you just said?"

"You don't scare me," Lexi said, keeping her eyes on him as he applied more pressure to her neck.

"That's a fucking shame. I have two speeds: hard and harder. I don't do gentle, and I don't do disobedience. You're going to learn that sooner rather than later." She heard the snap of his belt as he used his free hand to undo the buckle and knew he was going to follow through on his earlier threat.

"What are you doing?" Lexi used both hands to claw into him, but he didn't even flinch. His leg was squarely between hers; even though the skirt was free flowing, she couldn't shift her weight enough to free herself. "Gio, stop."

"I thought you weren't afraid of me." He let go of her throat only to push her chest against the counter and curl his fingers into her hair.

"Gio, stop. I'm not kidding."

"What did I tell you about *stop* before," he snarled into her ear. When she didn't answer, he yanked on her hair and she yelped. "What did I tell you?"

"That if I provoked you, I would see The Wolf. Gio, please." She wrapped her fingers around his. Lexi was scared of what he might do to her, and her voice trembled. "Please don't hurt me."

She could hear his angry breathing and didn't know if her pleas were enough to stop him. Between the wetness between her own legs and the sensations of confusion, fear, and desire that overwhelmed her, she couldn't begin to imagine what Giovanni was feeling. He pulled her upright, wrapping his hand around her neck and resting the curled belt against her stomach. His erection burned into her ass. "I don't make it a habit to bark and not bite, *bambina*." She gasped when he tightened his hand before he lightly snapped the leather against her stomach, causing her to jerk against him. "I doubt we'll make it through tonight before my belt explains what my words have failed to."

When he stepped away from her, Lexi steadied herself on the barstool. Had she not known the type of proclivities he had from reading about him, the playroom next to his bedroom that she had wandered into after the first night she'd spent with him would have given her an idea. Face-to-face with the streak of his sexual violence, she was left wondering who the hell she was if it turned her on to even imagine what his threats were capable of achieving.

Her hands were shaking, and Lexi tried to breathe through her panic and emotions. Her closed eyes snapped open when a voice told her that she wasn't alone. "*Signora?*" It was the massive man who had brought her coffee. Where the hell was Giovanni? "It's time to go."

She didn't have the courage to ask where they were going. Lexi followed his outstretched hand to the stairs, walking down in front of him two flights until they reached the first level of the penthouse. The main elevator was already waiting and they stepped into it, where the bellman announced their descent before he coded for the ground floor of the building. When they arrived, she followed the bodyguard through the bright foyer and outside to where another armored car, this one a 550i sedan in front of the X5 from the night before, waited with Giovanni already in the back seat. The valet opened the door and the gangster looked up at her before he sighed, annoyed by her lack of movement. "Get in the car, Alessandra."

"Where are we going?" His look said, *don't make me tell you a second time*, and she thought better of refusing the order. Once she was seated next to him, Lexi asked her question again.

"Long Island." He texted something on his phone and didn't look up.

The Masseretti patriarch owned a chunk of beach off the coast of Long Island, and Giovanni went there for lunch every Sunday according to Sam. Lexi couldn't imagine why he was bringing her there at all, let alone a day before he normally would go to visit his parents for their weekly gathering. "What's on Long Island?"

"You ask a lot of questions, *bambina*." The mobile vibrated again, and he responded before he put it away and looked at her with a tight smile.

"You divert a lot of questions, *Il Lupo*."

Giovanni laughed the rich melody that enveloped her. *"Il Lupo,"* he repeated. "That's rich, baby girl."

She watched the view merge from the Brooklyn Bridge into the interstate as the car sped toward the coast. "Were you really going to hit me?"

"Yes." Giovanni looked at her as though cataloging the emotions that passed through her face at his confession.

"Why didn't you?" He didn't answer her right away which, oddly, scared Lexi more than the idea that he would have actually whipped her with a belt.

He looked away, his eyes scanning the scenery. "Because you were legitimately afraid of me."

The drive took nearly two-and-a-half hours, but Lexi didn't try to talk to him again. The voices in her head had been stunned into silence for the first time in years, and she watched the traffic ebb and flow until the car stopped at an East Hampton marina. While the bodyguard from before opened Lexi's door, Giovanni got out on his own and met her. He took her hand and led them to a Lazzara that sat anchored at one of the docks. A public gentleman, he offered her the first step onto the luxury mini-yacht before he gave the order to shove off to the island. "It's only a few minutes," he said, looping the hair that the wind blew in her face behind her ear.

They had barely hit the bay that would spill out into the Long Island Sound if they went far enough when they were approaching a smaller version of the recently departed harbor. The engine settled as the boat maneuvered into a slip. When they docked, Giovanni exited first before giving her a slight tug when she didn't immediately start walking. "Come on, *bambina*. My family doesn't bite."

"Why are you bringing me to meet your family?"

They followed behind two bodyguards and in front of two others, one of whom held a brightly wrapped package. "Perhaps because it's my niece's birthday and I thought it would be an easy way to bring a woman home.

Perhaps because I wanted to show you that you aren't simply a conquest." He shrugged. "No doubt, *capatosta*, you will find a less honorable intention."

"*Capatosta*? Really? You think *I'm* hardheaded?" She stopped moving, and he looked back at her.

"If you don't walk, I'll throw you over my shoulder and carry you inside."

"What would your family think of that?" she challenged.

"They know me, *bambina*. They'd just debate whether or not you were Calabrese instead of whatever mutting it was that crafted you."

"Mutt?" Based on the curve of his lips into a smirk, Giovanni was trying to piss her off and knew that he had delivered a direct strike. Lexi clenched her jaws together. "Did you just call me a fucking *mutt*?"

"That is the American way, yes?" He smiled broadly at her, as though he hadn't just levied a slur. "This melting pot of culture and backgrounds? Maybe I need you to explain it to me in a language I'll understand."

Don't do it, Lexi, she commanded silently. *Don't give him what he wants.* She started to walk forward, her arms crossed over her chest so that he couldn't take her hand, and she heard him chuckle as he kept a few paces behind her. "I'm going to put you in dresses every day," he said, adding insult to injury. "They mold to your ass in a way that I enjoy watching while you walk."

Before she could tell him exactly what she thought of his dress fantasy, they approached the walkway for the island's main beach house. He put his hand on her waist, causing Lexi to slow as the door opened and a woman in her late-fifties appeared on the porch. She looked between the pair with a smile that lit up her face and raised her arms, exclaiming, "Giovanni!"

Dressed in an uneven tunic of varying shades of red over white capris that hugged her petite frame, Maria Masseretti was stylish and matronly. Her salt and pepper hair was bobbed at her shoulders and she was tiny, even in the stacked sandals she wore. She balanced on her toes in order to wrap her arms around Giovanni; although he leaned down, he towered over the older woman to kiss her. "And you," she said, her voice flowing with a delicate accent that reminded Lexi of Giovanni in his considerate moments, "must be Alessandra. Welcome to our home."

"Thank you." Lexi smiled and accepted her outstretched hand that quickly transitioned into a hug. It had been so long since she had felt a mother's affection, and a balm overshadowed the younger woman's orphaned heart. She pulled away before she choked up, saying, "It's a pleasure to meet you."

Sandwiching herself between them, Maria took each in arm and walked into a spacious foyer that connected to multiple rooms. An older man was coming from the kitchen to their left and stopped at the start of the long hallway in front of them. He held a demitasse in each hand and placed the coffees on a side table to embrace his son with a warm greeting. Giovanni's response was muffled against his father's broad shoulder, and the man pulled away to look at Lexi after offering his son one of the cups.

Giancarlo Masseretti's chocolate-hued eyes gave her an idea of where her lover's intense stare came from. Although Maria looked prepared for either a walk on the beach or a visit to Long Island to shop, her husband was dressed much like his son. His jacketless suit was gray, and his vest was crisp against his bright white shirt. He was almost as tall as Giovanni and, although he was heavier and his beard was mostly gray, Lexi knew that, his son notwithstanding, Giancarlo was the most dangerous person on the island. "Alessandra," he said, pursing his lips so that the *r* of her name rolled at the end. "My son brings home a girl- and an American girl at that."

Giovanni chuckled, resting his free hand on Lexi's waist and pulling her closer. "Be nice, Pop."

"I am nice." He watched Lexi with a look that begged for a response. Giovanni's trademark amusement danced in his father's dark eyes. "Perhaps I am simply trying to understand what she sees in you."

Lexi shrugged. *"La lussuria è cieca."*

Giovanni choked on his coffee before he glanced at her with raised eyebrows. His father smiled at her reply while his mother outright laughed. Maria took her arm and directed Lexi into a designer kitchen. "You speak Italian."

"I can get by." Lexi grinned, watching Giovanni follow his father down the hallway until they disappeared.

Maria's face was bright as she poured two cups of coffee. She radiated happiness, and Lexi was reminded of parties with her own mother. Shannon had loved to entertain. Their house had always overflowed with friends, especially during the holidays. Memories she hadn't considered in years began to pop into her head, and Lexi tried to focus on Maria's voice to stay in the present. "How did you meet Giovanni?"

"I'm a librarian." She took the pottery mug that was offered. "Gio is a donor to one of our special collections." She had seen his name alongside a hefty gift to Rare Books after the fundraiser, making the answer technically the truth. It had a far better ring to it than *I interviewed to be a call girl at one of his clubs.*

"My son: a patron of public arts." Maria seemed to know there was more to the story, but she simply smiled. Lexi couldn't help but wonder what the twinkle in her green eyes meant. "Have you known him long?"

Long enough, Lexi thought. "Not really."

"Sometimes it doesn't take long," Maria said with a knowing wink.

Lexi looked away as her cheeks started to burn and turned her attention to the oversized windows that surrounded the kitchen, giving way to a panoramic view of the beach outside. She tried to redirect the conversation. "Your home is beautiful."

"*Grazie.* After so many years in The City, it is good to live away from the noise." As if on cue, the front door opened and there was a sea of sound as several children appeared.

"*Nonna! Nonna!*" There were three of them yelling as one. Lexi watched Maria's face curl into the joy of being a grandmother as she kissed each. A beautiful woman with long dark hair that rested over her shoulders and eyes the color of cognac entered behind them alongside a man that was tall but stocky.

Lexi nearly gagged on her coffee. It was the woman from the news article- the woman that Giovanni had been photographed having dinner with earlier in the week. Moments later, there was an increase in the noise as several men, women, and more children entered the house. The first woman, who was very pregnant, looked at Lexi questioningly while Maria continued to hug and greet everyone.

After placing her purse on the counter, she walked toward Lexi with a smile that was so reminiscent of Giovanni's smile that Lexi was surprised she hadn't realized who the woman was when she had initially seen the photograph. The brunette introduced herself, and Lexi felt ashamed of her earlier anger. "Theresa," she said, her voice almost void of the accent that was still firmly wrapped around the brother who hadn't lived stateside long enough to shake his European roots. "I'm Gio's sister."

Before she could answer, Lexi felt a hand on her waist. "This is my girl, Alessandra," Giovanni said, his declaration causing Theresa and one of the men who had wandered next to her to look between the two in silence.

"Girlfriend?" The man with wavy chestnut hair exclaimed with shock before he whistled. His hazel eyes were wide with surprise. "No shit!"

"Lorenzo!" Maria admonished, waving her hand around to signify the children that were everywhere. "Language!"

"Sorry, Mama." He stepped forward as his younger sister had and introduced himself along with the blonde next to him who waved before running after a toddler. "I'm Gio's brother, Lorenzo. My wife, Cecilia."

"Lexi," she said before Giovanni tightened his grip.

"Alessandra," he corrected. Lorenzo just laughed and gently smacked his brother's cheek.

The house was lively with his siblings, their spouses, and children. The kitchen overflowed with the lunch that would celebrate her granddaughter, Anna, and Lexi assumed Maria had been cooking all morning. The little girl loved being the center of attention, but it was her *Zigi*, a pet combination of the Italian word for uncle, *zio*, and Gio's name, that captivated the beautiful three-year-old. Much to Lexi's shock, Giovanni stopped to play with the child whenever she approached him, holding her arms up and begging, "*Zigi!*" When their eyes met during one of those encounters, it was impossible to see the man who had threatened her with a belt only hours before. He was carefree and jovial. It was unsettling and endearing all at once.

"My mother says you are a librarian." Lexi turned to see one of Giovanni's brothers in front of her. The light gray of his eyes popped against his olive skin and his smile was bright. "Carlito."

"I am, yes." She apologized. "I'm still learning who everyone is. I'm sorry."

"I'm fourth. Old enough to know better, but young enough to still get away with something. Vince and I are the quintessential middle children," he joked.

"I haven't met him yet," she said, her eyes searching as Carlito pointed to a tall, slender man with a ponytail in the corner with Lorenzo and a woman with nearly black hair that was braided down her back.

"That's Vincenzo and his wife, Cara." Approaching the group were a petite redhead who was dwarfed by a muscular, husky man with sandy hair and eyes that were so blue Lexi noticed them from across the room. Carlito added, "That's Matteo and his wife, Sara. He's the runt of us, but," he laughed, "you'd never know it to look at him."

He pointed to the several little boys who ran around with the ones who had come with Theresa. "Theresa and Frank's boys: Ruggerio and Niccolo. Those three are mine: Carlo, Luca, and Orlando. The other four are Lorenzo's: Michael, Tony, Frankie, and Tommy." He pointed to a brunette with glasses who laughed with Theresa and Cecilia. "That's my wife, Deb."

"Your kids are beautiful," she complimented.

"They are a handful," he chuckled. "Especially with Deb working on her doctorate, but," he wiggled his hands, "that's what a hands-on dad is for."

"You're a stay-at-home father?" Lexi asked with surprise.

"I work from home," he clarified. "The boys are in school, and I work for Giovanni's holding company from a home office. If I have to go into Midtown, I schedule it for when they are busy."

She debated asking what he did for his brother but decided against it. "What's she studying?"

"Archeology." Carlito looked back at his wife. "I actually met her at a fundraiser for Hunter College. She was one of the students giving a keynote, and I ended up writing a far larger check than Gio appreciated."

Lexi laughed with him. "I guess love doesn't have a price tag."

"Gio disagreed, especially when Deb wouldn't even talk to me." He drank from his wine glass. "She was dating someone else. It took me a while to sway her to my side of the fence."

"Do I want to ask?"

"Saved." He grinned with a wink as Maria approached, and Carlito embraced the tiny woman. "How are you, Mama?"

"I'm good, I'm good." She was still looking at Lexi with those knowing eyes, and the younger woman wasn't sure what to make of it. Was she simply happy that her son had finally brought a woman home? Had he talked to his parents about her? Maria had known she was coming, so he must have. What had Giovanni said? "Are you having a nice time?" Maria asked.

"I am. Thank you. Are you sure that I can't help you with something?" Lexi looked back toward the kitchen. "You've worked so hard on everything. It seems awful that you have to clean up the mess, too."

Maria waved her off. "Nonsense. It's what mothers do."

After a few minutes of conversation surrounding the food, Lorenzo offered a walk along the beach to his siblings and their spouses. "Go," Maria encouraged. "I will clean up."

When Giovanni took her hand, Lexi didn't have much choice, although it seemed strange to be with them as the completion of his pair. "This tends to be a tradition whenever we are together," he explained. "Everyone walks, tells any recent news we'd rather not share among the parents and kids, stuff like that. Usually ends with Matteo kicking someone's ass with a football."

"Wait? There's something you *aren't* good at?"

He pulled her closer and exhaled a light laugh. "I didn't say that."

"Who's going first?" Lorenzo's wife, Cecilia, asked as they walked.

"Gio," Theresa answered.

"The fuck you say! I don't have any news." He gave his sister a pointed look when she looked over her shoulder at him.

"The expression is *what the fuck*," Theresa said with sarcasm, "and the woman with you says otherwise."

Giovanni pulled Lexi closer to him. "You can see her," he retorted. "I'm not sure what else you want from me. An invitation to look?"

Theresa turned again on the verge of saying something but, seeing Lexi's blushing face, seemed to think better of it. "Who's next?" she said.

Vincenzo, the brother that Carlito pointed out, turned and began to walk backward. "We've got news." His wife punched him in the arm. "Ouch."

There was a round of cheers before either could say anything, and Giovanni leaned against Lexi's ear. "Vince and Cara have been trying to have a baby for the last year."

They stopped at a fire pit surrounded with chairs. As she went to sit down, Giovanni pulled her into his lap instead. "There are enough chairs," she argued.

"My lap is far more comfortable."

"I feel what's in your lap," she smarted, adjusting her ass against his bulge before he pulled her face closer to him for a kiss. "And I don't think *comfort* is your priority."

"If you encourage me, *bambina*, I'll take you to a secluded spot on this beach to get more *comfortable*." He kissed her again.

Cecilia sat in the sand and leaned against Lorenzo's legs. "Since Alessandra is new, let's tell how we met."

Lexi chuckled when Giovanni groaned into her neck. "We can leave for that secluded spot now," he whispered.

"I was going to a beach concert and got lost," Cecilia said, leaning her head back and smiling when Lorenzo dipped down to kiss her. "Needless to say, the directions I got included ones to Manhattan." People laughed, and, when Theresa implored them to get a room, Lorenzo kicked sand toward her.

"I can tell the story of how Gio and I met your true love," he said to his sister, earning him a dirty glare.

"I'll help," Giovanni offered.

Theresa cut them off. "I met Francesco at a culinary exhibition." She stuck her tongue out at Lorenzo and turned to look at Lexi. "I had just gotten to Florence for a study abroad and ran into him on one of the first weekends I was there. It was love at first sight." When he took her hand from the seat next to her, she looked over and smiled at him. "I'm lucky he loved me enough to endure the men of this family." She gave Giovanni a raised eye. "Your turn, *Zigi*."

Giovanni pulled Lexi tighter against him. "Should I tell them the truth?" he asked, kissing her hair.

"Gio is a donor to my library," Lexi quickly interjected.

"That sounds like a truthful lie." Carlito laughed, ending up on the receiving end of a playful smack from his wife. "Like something you would tell parents so they wouldn't know the actual truth."

"The truth," Giovanni said, shifting her so that he could see his siblings, "is that Alessandra saved me from a traffic stop and, in return, I took her home. The rest is *private* history."

"Saved you from a traffic stop?" Theresa was intrigued now. "In that Portofino? This I have to hear."

"There's nothing to hear." Giovanni shrugged. "No story to tell."

"No story you're willing to tell, you mean." She grinned. "I'll work it out of one of you. Just wait." Theresa looked around, as though they were missing someone. "Where's Raphael?"

"Pop wanted to talk to him."

"I didn't see Felicity either." Vincenzo's wife, Cara, spoke. Her accent was light and different from the ones around her. "Did she not come with the baby?"

Theresa answered, "Gianni is teething and was a mess. I talked to her this morning. She called to tell me she was staying home with him."

Lexi tried to keep up with the different conversations. It was clear that, although they were family, the couples gathered legitimately enjoyed being together. As Giovanni nuzzled her hair and kissed the nape of her neck periodically, Lexi couldn't help but find herself believing things were real. The afternoon progressed while the siblings joked about the different things going on in their lives and debated current events before they took the walk back to the house. As Giovanni had mentioned, Matteo picked up a football, and Lorenzo opted to stay outside with him while everyone returned to the waning party.

"My brother hasn't ventured into the girlfriend waters in..." Theresa brought a glass of wine to Lexi after everyone was settled. "Forever, I think. I've seen him with women, as has most of New York, but he's never bothered to give them names or brought one home. This is a rare show of something more than the asshole I normally get the pleasure of seeing. And," she added, "after watching you with him today, you might be able to show him a shred of normalcy."

Theresa grinned at her over her glass of carbonated water while Lexi shook her head. "I don't know about that. *Non puoi insegnare niente a un uomo. Puoi solo aiutarlo a scoprire ciò che ha dentro di sé.*"

"Even Galileo would struggle to get Giovanni to see something he didn't want to see." Theresa's eyes fell behind Lexi, who jumped when the man in question draped his arm around her.

"Talking about me?" he asked.

"You know we are." Theresa drank her water. "Her Italian is better than mine."

"Her cooking, too." He winked, and his sister punched him in the arm.

"I don't cook," Lexi said apologetically.

"Neither do I," Theresa answered. "Not well anyway. It's why I married a chef."

Before the conversation could continue, Giovanni kissed the top of Lexi's head. "We need to go, *bambina*. It's time to say goodbye."

"You aren't staying?" Maria asked when she hugged her son. "You are welcome," she added, her eyes darting between both Giovanni and Lexi to make sure they understood her invitation.

"No, Mama. I have to work." He gave her an extra squeeze. "Next week. I promise."

"With Alessandra," his mother added, giving Lexi a hug goodbye and whispering, "A strong woman will be good for him."

Lexi wasn't sure that she was anywhere close to a strong enough woman to reign in Giovanni. "Thank you again," she said graciously. "Everything was delicious."

"Come back and I'll teach you." Maria beamed. "I'll teach you his favorites."

Giovanni smirked. Before he could betray her lack of culinary skill, Lexi thanked the matriarch again. "I'll look forward to that."

The breeze blew in from the water while they walked back to the boat and the day eased closer to sunset. "Did you have a good time?" he asked, rubbing his fingers over her knuckles.

"Everyone was really nice- except you of course." She bit her bottom lip with the tease and winked at him when he glanced at her coolly.

"I don't do *nice*."

"I don't know about that. Anna seemed to love you just fine, *Zigi*."

Giovanni drew Lexi closer to him as he waved to the two of his brothers who had lingered behind on the beach when everyone else had gone inside. "That goes without saying. Anna has me wrapped around her little finger."

"It was adorable." Being beneath his arm was making it difficult to concentrate. "I'm not sure your father liked me too much."

Giovanni chuckled. "He doesn't like anyone." He stopped walking and gave her a raised eyebrow. "*La lussuria è cieca?*" When she blushed at his reminder of her words, he grew serious. "Is your lust all that's blind?"

"With you, I feel like Homer." She looked away from him and her heart sank. "Why did you bring me here, Gio? It's going to be that much harder to walk after I've seen you act like a normal person. And after this morning? I can't stay. I can't do this."

He licked his lips before pouting in contemplation. "I think you can handle all that I can give you. You won't always like it," he said darkly, "but you'll handle it."

"I don't *want* to handle it, Giovanni." How much of her refusal was fear of him and how much was fear of herself? Even Lexi wasn't sure. "And now I'll have to explain to your poor mama that her choir boy isn't going to have someone to make his favorite spaghetti!" She pulled her hand and kept walking when he started to laugh at her response.

"*Choir boy*? Fuck." Giovanni doubled over and, after she shot him a glare, stood up to sing *La Cura* at the top of his lungs.

"What the hell are you doing?" The Italian rolled off his tongue as Lexi turned around, pressing her hands to her mouth. To their credit, the bodyguards were ignoring the entire performance, save the one man that she often saw Giovanni with. He watched the rendition with a smile and, when she met his eyes, didn't even pretend to look away.

Her face reddened when Giovanni approached her, taking her hand and singing loudly while the other arm swirled in the air like an opera singer. Lexi knew the sound had traveled back to the open windows of the house when his family began to pour out onto the porch. His voice was beautiful, and it only served to deepen her attraction. "Gio, stop!"

His brothers had ended their football game and Lorenzo said incredulously, "Is Gio fucking singing?"

Matteo, the youngest of the brothers, laughed. "That's what it sounds like!"

This commentary only fueled her embarrassment, and Lexi tried to drag Giovanni toward the boat. When he belted out the last notes and his family applauded, their laughs and yells echoing along the beach, he had the good nature to turn and bow as he let her pull him down the dock. He was still laughing once they had succeeded in boarding.

"You just can't lose, can you? You've got to have the last word! And you can even fucking sing, which infuriates me more!" The boat shifted into the open water, and Lexi dropped her head. "Damn it. Can't you be bad at *something*? At this point, I'll take anything."

He kissed the top of her head as her hair blew wildly in the wind. "I'm bad at us it seems."

"There is no *us*, Giovanni."

He stood to the side and looked at her. "After last night- after today- you still believe that?"

When Lexi's eyes met his, she was convinced that Giovanni really could see into her soul. "You were right that first night in your apartment. You said that I knew more than I let on." She gazed over the water. "I know who you are, Gio. I knew who you were before I went into the club looking for a job and I-I," she stammered, "I thought I could handle it. I thought I'd keep my head above water and I'd be fine. But the whole thing- I couldn't. I can't."

"That's work. That's not me."

"It *is* you." She looked at him and could feel tears starting to form. "Just because you don't pull the trigger doesn't mean that you aren't the one killing." Lexi stopped, horrified. Those were words she was never meant to utter.

He bit his lips and exhaled, looking beyond her. She watched him in the twilight before she covered her face with her hands. He leaned forward and kissed her forehead, holding her until the boat docked. Giovanni helped Lexi onto the pier, saying nothing when he joined her in the sedan.

The traffic was light as the two cars wove back through the Hamptons toward The City. Giovanni didn't try to deny any of what she had called him on, and Lexi didn't know what she could possibly say to undo the damage. *You fucked up*, she thought to herself.

The mixture of sun and wine from the day started to catch up with her; when she blinked, they were pulling in front of the Woolworth Tower. Giovanni's arm was around her and she rested against his heart. His other hand gently touched her hair. When she leaned up, he forced a smile and grabbed her hand as she moved closer to the door. "Come upstairs with me: not because of who you think I am, but because of who you've seen. Come with me not because I won't let you go, but because you don't want to leave."

"Gio-"

"Come upstairs with me knowing that, for however long you are able to stay, I will take care of you. I will push you and force your tears. I can't change who I am." He paused, watching her intently. "Come with me even though you know I will never let you beat me."

Lexi was stuck in her seat. She had no idea what to say or how to even breathe. He hadn't defended himself against anything she had said. He hadn't apologized for the way that he roughly handled her, and she knew he'd barely even started. "You're free to go and I won't blame you when you finally walk out the door," Giovanni said quietly. He pushed her hair from her face again. "Just not tonight."

This Giovanni was vulnerable and open. His eyes were empty of the rage and the darkness. They told her that things weren't what they seemed, that looks could truly be deceiving. They promised her the sliver of a chance, and, although she knew that all great romance stories ended in tragedy, she couldn't make herself give him a different answer. "Not tonight."

6

He kissed the top of the hand he held then blinked back the Giovanni from before. He tapped on the window and the rear door was opened by the waiting valet. When Lexi got out of the car, a late summer wind had replaced the coolness of the day. Giovanni's phone vibrated in the pocket that was next to her, and he removed it as they got in the elevator.

His voice changed to annoyed. Although she didn't know what he said, she assumed the conversation wasn't one he wanted to have. When they arrived in the apartment, Giovanni took her upstairs into the kitchen and opened up a leather folder that held countless menus. "Order whatever you want. I have to work for a while." He kissed her again before disappearing in a room that shared the floor, shutting the door behind him.

Was this what she was signing up for by agreeing to his impassioned plea that she stay? Lexi dropped her head into her hands. What the hell was she doing? Was she even trying to be the FBI's proxy? Lexi may not have known who she was anymore, but she knew enough to realize that whatever undercover operation she had initially embarked on wasn't real.

She didn't look at Giovanni as a mark; she looked at him as a lover. Perhaps most terrifying to her own understanding was that she didn't see him as the killer she knew that he was. There was no way he couldn't be based on the things she had read in his jacket. But killing her father? Fuck, this was all wrong. It was all sorts of wrong.

"You can do this," she whispered, tossing her head up. She just had to trust herself. Her mother had always taught her to see what was in front of her- not what she wanted to see, not even what she hoped to see. Could she attempt that with Giovanni? Could she risk that? Could fate be so cruel as to finally let her feel a desire to live again with someone who was the entire reason that she had died in the first place? Even fate couldn't be that coldhearted.

She flipped through the binder and settled on a menu of Chinese. Lunch seemed like forever ago even though she wasn't that hungry. She heard voices upstairs. Were there hidden bedrooms on the upper floors for his bodyguards? How much food did she need to order?

Giovanni had offered her little in the way of instruction, and Lexi had no idea what the expectation was. She cursed when she realized that she didn't have her cell phone and lifted the receiver to the landline that hung on the kitchen wall. "*Buona sera*, Mr. Masseretti. How may I help you this evening?"

Why the hell had the phone automatically connected her to the concierge? "I was hoping to order dinner for delivery."

"Yes, ma'am. What can I have brought for you?"

She rattled off the restaurant's name and a variety of dishes, assuming that Giovanni had to at least like Chinese to have the menu in the binder. "Do you want me to come downstairs to pay?" Immediately after asking, she remembered that she didn't have her purse. It was still at the library, locked in her desk along with her phone.

"No, ma'am. Mr. Masseretti keeps a card on file for his orders. I will take care of this right away, and Jacob will bring it up." The call disconnected shortly after he wished her well.

She leaned against the kitchen counter. How long was Giovanni going to work? Should she tell him that she had ordered dinner as requested? Would he be annoyed if Lexi checked out the apartment? He had decided she was staying for the weekend. It was his own fault if she found something he wanted hidden. Maybe she'd borrow another nightshirt, although she couldn't imagine Giovanni would be thrilled to have her sitting at dinner with his bodyguards in nothing but a top that barely covered her ass.

She went downstairs into his bedroom and wandered into one of three walk-in closets. It was as large as the main section of her apartment and served as a personal gym. There were weights and a hanging punching bag alongside other equipment, and she wondered how often he used the room in order to keep the well-sculpted body she had enjoyed.

The next closet connected to both the bedroom and the bathroom, and was nothing but designer suits and more shoes than she had ever owned in her entire life. "Fucking fashion plate," she muttered, walking through the bathroom and into the mirrored closet on the other side.

This one held rows of shirts and pants, as well as a section of women's clothes and shoes. Fingering the different choices, she saw that they were her size and uncomfortably knew that it wasn't coincidence. The dress she was wearing hadn't just materialized out of thin air. Giovanni had specifically bought it because, like the overkill of dresses hanging in front of her, it was his preference.

She pulled out the first of the built-in drawers and touched the neatly folded lingerie. The second drawer looked like negligees she had never imagined herself wearing. She lifted one of the delicate pieces. Lexi wasn't sure how something with so much lace could be comfortable to sleep in, but she held onto the black babydoll and opened the next drawer. The silk tanks and shorts at least resembled something worth being called pajamas, and she lifted out the shorts from the black pairing.

After dropping the nightwear on the bench that sat in the middle of the closet, Lexi slipped out of the boots and socks, putting them under the bench, before she stripped and tossed the clothes in the closet's hamper. She had painted her toenails a deep gray before the Gala; without the fancy silver shoes to reflect the color, they looked like the sky when it stormed.

After stepping into the thong that had been wrapped with the nightie, she put on the shorts that barely covered both ass cheeks. It took her two attempts to figure out where her arms slid into the strappy negligee. When she looked in the mirror Lexi knew that Giovanni would be more than pissed if she walked out of the closet wearing a top so sheer that her breasts were on full display. Not that she would ever do that, but she sure as hell wasn't temping either his jealousy or his territorial tendencies.

She took one of his white shirts, buttoning it up just enough to reveal a hint of cleavage and lace, and rolled the way-too-long sleeves up to her elbows. The shirt hung lower than the shorts, and Lexi wondered what he would think of her mismatched clothes and bare feet when he returned from whatever *work* it was that he was doing.

She had already seen the first floor and returned to investigate the second floor of the apartment. Off the kitchen, she found a pantry that was stocked and organized along with a laundry room. A hallway held three doors, and two of the rooms were stunning guest suites that were fit for a luxury hotel. Lexi avoided the last room where Giovanni had disappeared; from there, muffled voices that she couldn't translate filtered into the dining room centerpiece of the floor. It held a rectangular glass table with twelve upholstered chairs. Giovanni had been in his element with his family, and she could practically see the room filled with the large bunch she had spent the day with.

Having grown up with just her parents, who had also been only children, and without grandparents by the time she was ten, Lexi had never experienced a gathering like today. Just as Giovanni had pushed the numbness away, being surrounded by the laughter and the easiness of his family had covered up the loneliness she had felt since before her parents had died. She wanted to believe that Giovanni was more than what she feared. She wanted him to be what was in front of her and not what she had read or been told. Giving him a chance meant more than just the sex and the lack of numb. It meant having the opportunity for a life she had only seen from the outside.

It also meant that Sam would hate her.

Lexi leaned against the window and looked at the traffic from fifty-one floors away. Sam would never forgive her if she forgot who she was supposed to be for who she wanted to be. She had felt so aimless for a decade and everything about the last week had been so fast. How was this where she felt safest? How was this where she felt most real? Most *her*? Was she really willing to trade Sam and her entire life- everything she had believed and still had to believe- for Giovanni? For a man who might one day wake up and, just as he had decided he had to have her on Sunday, could decide to tell her to go as he had on Tuesday?

    Lexi walked up the stairs to the third floor where she had been that morning. The great room was currently being used by three of the four bodyguards she had seen. They worked on tablet computers and talked back and forth, acknowledging her with nods when she entered.

    The linebacker with a shaved head who had brought her coffee that morning offered help. He looked like he was in his early-thirties, and she guessed he was from Brooklyn based on his accent. Lexi almost asked his name. Would he tell her? Was that information she was allowed to have? She politely declined his request and, rather than explore that floor, continued up the staircase to the next level, a mezzanine that overlooked the great room below and ended the private elevator access.

    The floors were getting smaller as the Pinnacle rose into the air, but even this room was easily the size of her apartment. Art covered the walls. Some of it bore nameplates of artists she recognized, but other names were unfamiliar and had recent dates. Was Giovanni a lover of art or was this just something to occupy empty space?

    She found a piece she particularly liked hidden in one of the room's corners. The picture of a large house with a stone wall was painted in oil against canvas, and the bright reds and golds of flowers were waves of dried paint. In the distance of the house, she could make out trees dotted with greens and blacks and, on the other side, yellows and bright oranges. The painting was warmer than most on the walls, and it inspired a sense of contentment when she looked at it.

    Her fingers hovered over the name plate and the date from eight years before. *G.D. Masseretti. Addivintari.* She didn't know what the title word meant; the spelling was wrong for any Italian words she knew. The word closest, a reflexive verb that meant *to come to*, didn't really make sense with the painting. And Giovanni an artist? Maybe she would ask him about it.

She took the stairs up to a library. Oversized, stadium-style seats led Lexi to believe that this was some sort of theater room as well, although she didn't see a screen and wondered if it was discretely hidden in the paneled ceiling, but it was the walls of books that caused her to fall in love instantly. If she lived here, this would be *her* room and she would never leave.

Wherever there weren't windows, the walls were lined in full-length bookcases, and the rectangular staircase was replaced with a circular one. Her fingers dithered over the spines. *I like to read*, he had told her. These weren't the children's books (or the porn) she had chided him with. In multiple languages, there were books on art, history, military strategy, psychology, and an array of fiction ranging from classics to modern pieces that she wouldn't have expected. Seeing what was in front of her was getting more difficult by the minute.

She kept ascending, and the stairs deposited her into a completely windowed tower with no furniture at all. The floor, instead of the wooden planks of the previous levels, was thick, black rubber. There was a small refrigerator in one corner and a table with, not that she was surprised, a single-shot coffeemaker and disposable cups. Giovanni might avoid drugs, but he had an addiction to caffeine that even she couldn't rival. If he didn't own stock in a few coffee bean farms, maybe she would suggest that be his next investment.

The steps shrank into a metal staircase that curved to the roof. She pushed the door open, and the view from the terrace nearly sixty floors from the sidewalk gave her pause.

New York City at night was an amazing sight. The higher the view, the better she had always thought, but this was the most phenomenal view Lexi had ever seen. Each terrace was different. On one, off which she could see the northern view of The City, Giovanni had a marble table with matching benches. On the western view, he had placed a variety of metal sofas and chairs with a corner bar.

Still, it was the east view that captivated her soul. There was nothing but the terrace. It was nearly open to the entire cityscape. Lexi saw the bridges awash in light while traffic traveled back and forth to create a twinkling of white in either direction. She could have stayed forever in this one spot and rested on the edge, letting the wind rip through her hair. Even the coolness of the evening wasn't enough for her to go inside, although she buttoned the shirt higher and unrolled the sleeves down to her wrists.

"This might be my favorite place in the entire apartment." When she turned around, Giovanni was standing outside the door to the lower level.

"It's not technically *in* the apartment." Although she was teasing him, the view could easily become her favorite place as well. "It's beautiful."

"Yes, you are."

She chuckled without acknowledging the compliment. "No doubt you use this view to charm all the ladies."

"Not this one; this one is mine." She returned to the views from the railing while Giovanni walked forward to stand next to her. He had taken off his jacket and his sleeves were pushed high. She could see the scar of a bullet that had gone through his forearm sitting on the border of a cross tattoo. He noticed where her eyes had fallen, saying, "One of many."

"The bullet or the tattoo?"

He looked down and made a fist, causing the muscles in his arm to flex before releasing the stress and looking back at her. "Both."

"I haven't seen that many," she said, remembering the wolf, the part of the tree, and the snake, but not really calling to mind much else. "How many are there?"

He shrugged. "I don't keep up with the scars. Enough? Too many? Thirteen tattoos."

She ran her fingers over the scarred skin at the base of the ink. "What happened?" Lexi looked up at him questioningly and could see a fight between the man in the car who had asked her to stay and the one who had thrown her against the bar stool to punish her only that morning. How much would he tell her?

"Don't ask." He ran his free hand through her hair then used it to pull her closer, kissing her lightly before directing her back to the door that would lead them inside. "Come on: dinner is downstairs."

"That's faster than I thought."

"Philip knows that I don't like to wait," Giovanni smarted.

The food had been unpacked from a large box and the white, fold-up containers were displayed in a line. "You ordered enough for an army," he chuckled. "We'll be eating Chinese food for a week."

We. How long did he expect her to stay? "You have a house of people, Gio, and I had no idea what you like."

"What I like doesn't come in a box." Giovanni swiped his finger across her blushing cheek before taking a few steps away. He took a bottle of rosé from the wine fridge and used a corkscrew to open it. "My men don't stay here. They live on the floors below."

"They live *here*? In this building?"

"Yes." He looked up at her. "Forty-ninth floor for Raphael, and the other three you've met are in the three apartments on the forty-eighth. Why?"

The Woolworth Tower was one of the most expensive properties in New York. The estimation for the penthouse alone was over seventy million dollars. One of Sam's complaints had been that they couldn't find paperwork on how Giovanni had been able to buy it. There was little to suggest the apartment was even listed before he had just appeared with the address.

He was watching her intently, and she tried to come up with something to say since it was clear she was thinking. "You must pay far better than I presumed. Maybe I'll submit my resume to be your personal librarian."

He poured two glasses and pushed one toward her with a guarded laugh. "Somehow I don't think I could afford what you would cost me." He brushed his knuckles across her jaw. "You're wearing my shirt."

"I liked it better than that *kinkwear* you put in the closet."

"*Kinkwear* isn't a word."

She lifted the shirt seductively. "Then what would you call this?" she asked, flashing him the lower part of the negligee before laughing when he grabbed her by the shirt's placket.

He began unbuttoning it from the collar. "I'm not sure I'll look at my shirts the same way," he joked before his hand stilled at her neck. He pushed the shirt to the side. "The fuck."

Lowering her eyes to where he looked, she saw that the light bruising from before had deepened in color. "It's fine. It doesn't hurt," she said when he cursed again and stepped back. Lexi held the shirt closed while he paced away from her. "Come on- I'm not the first girl to end up with bruises from you."

The look he gave her was unbridled and full of anger. The way he growled her name and bit his own teeth to avoid unleashing his rage terrified her. "It doesn't hurt," she repeated. What the hell was wrong with him? After the amount of manhandling he had subjected her to, how could he imagine there would be no physical reminders of their encounters? Had he forgotten the room that was only a floor away and what he did there? Lexi chuckled and tried to lighten the situation. "Did you think your belt would have marked me less this morning?"

"Fuck, Alessandra!" Giovanni was on her in a second, having pressed her against the fridge. "You just can't help yourself! That fucking mouth!" His hand was in the same position that had caused the bruising, and he cursed before dropping it and backing up to the counter. No longer facing her, he finished his glass of wine.

"What is your problem?"

"My problem?" He looked back at her and dropped the glass so hard that she didn't know how it hadn't managed to break. "My problem is that you tempt the beast, *bambina*. You play the first moves but are terrified once your pawns are taken off the board, and I stop the game." He took a few steps closer to her. "You know who I am. There's nothing here that you don't see," he said between gritted teeth. "You know that all I want to do right now is beat that fucking smart mouth off of you and then fuck you until it revives so that I can have excuse to do it again." Seeing her body tense, he threw his hands up. "And you know that seeing you, both scared of what you know I'm capable of alongside that goddamned look that says you want to see just how far I could take you over the edge by doing it, fucking unnerves me."

"Do you want me to go?" she whispered.

"Of course, I want you to fucking go!" Giovanni slammed his hands on the marble, and Lexi jumped.

Lexi backed up to the stairs. Confusion and doubt combined with the wine to leave her stumbling against the rail. He had practically begged her to stay only now to tell her that he wanted her to leave. He accused her of playing the game, but she had no idea what board they were using or any of the rules.

She sprinted down the steps to the lower level and realized that she didn't have shoes on. Not wanting to stay any longer than necessary, Lexi went into the closet and took the first pair of sneakers she saw. When she walked out, Giovanni was leaning against the elevator. There was no sign of the anger she had seen upstairs. "Going somewhere, baby girl?"

"You want me to leave. I'm leaving." Lexi didn't walk closer to him, tossing her head toward the elevator and forcing her body to hold the tears back. "Call the elevator."

"No."

"You don't get to say that to me." She shook her head. "You don't get to tell me to go and refuse to let me leave."

The arrogance she had witnessed from the very start was back. "My game. My rules."

"*You* told me to leave! And what was it you said to me in your office? That if I stayed with you long enough then I would know you don't wait and people always do what you say!" She made herself take a step forward. "Point taken; I've learned. Call the fucking elevator and get out of my way."

"That mouth." He rubbed his jaw with the hand that showed off the tail of the asp. "Go upstairs and eat dinner. I'll be back tonight." Without touching her, Giovanni walked to the private elevator on the other side of the room, and Lexi practically ran to the main lift, pressing the button and seeing no light appear. She was trapped.

Lexi didn't want to eat. She drank part of the wine before she dumped the glass and put the untouched food in the refrigerator. The last place that she wanted to go was the bedroom, but she had no phone and wasn't about to go into his office to ask for access to one. She had taken off her watch for the Gala and had no concept of time. Minutes or hours could have passed with her sitting on one of the bedroom window seats, curled up and watching the lights outside. Lexi eventually gave up on waiting for him and crawled into bed.

No matter how she adjusted the blanket, she alternated between feeling hot and cold. Giovanni's supima shirt felt like burlap and she took it off, folding it over the back of the bedside chair. Her constant moving made the shorts uncomfortable, and she stripped down to the panties and negligee. When sleep continued its refusal, Lexi returned to the view, this time sitting on the chaise. She curled up beneath a soft blanket that was draped over it, closing her eyes at last.

"Come on, *bambina*." She could hear his voice even in her sleep, and the sweetness was painful after their last fight. His strong arms lifted her from the chaise as though she weighed nothing as he whispered, "The bed is far more comfortable."

"It's too big," she said sleepily, trying to focus her tired eyes.

He smiled and touched her face lovingly. In the light of the bedside lamp, she noticed the scuffing on his knuckles, and her body woke up immediately. How long had she slept? What had gone on while she was out? She took his hand and rolled her fingers over the cracked skin. "What happened?"

"Don't ask," he said, just as he had when she had asked about his scar on the terrace. She could see the memory of them in the kitchen behind his eyes. "It doesn't hurt."

Lexi felt sick. She knew exactly what had transpired. "Who did you hit because you wouldn't hit me?" When Giovanni didn't answer, she also knew that she was right. "Who? Did you go to one of the clubs you own for some *interviewing*, too? Make sure to cover all of your bases?"

The growl replaced the gentleness. "Don't, Alessandra."

Lexi pulled away from him and stumbled off the other side of the bed. "Why the fuck not, Giovanni? Afraid you won't be able to stop?" Why did the idea of another woman make her so angry? So hurt?

She had forgotten- that was why. Giovanni had made her forget that this was just an assignment and that there was no reason for her to give a damn. He had convinced her to see him, and Lexi had decided to ignore everything she knew. Being here, in this position- again- was her fault. Caring about him and letting him hurt her was her penance for her stupid heart. Let him fuck and beat the hell out of every woman this side of New Jersey! She didn't care!

But Lexi did care. She cared a lot more than she wanted to admit to herself and a lot more than she wanted Giovanni to know. The truth wasn't that he had unlocked her heart. It couldn't be that. It was jealousy. Why else would the hurt of his betrayal sting so much? She was envious of the blondes and the escorts and whoever else it could have been- that had to be it. It wasn't lust or, fuck her if she even thought it, some screwed up version of love.

She stalked around the bed to where he stood, his fists clenched at his sides. "You fucking bastard." Without a single thought for what would come next, she slapped him as hard as she could. "Go fuck yourself, Gio. I'm done."

Had she done it because she knew he wouldn't be able to stop? Had she purposely poked the bear in order to get the response she knew would come? He was far taller and stronger than she was, and Giovanni was most certainly a better fighter. He had her flat on her back against the bed, one hand tearing into her hair while the other pressed into the bruises around her neck and throat. One knee was harshly planted between her legs; although she used all of her strength to struggle against him, there was nothing she could do to loosen his holds. The look on his face was a combination of desire and rage. "Too fucking far."

"So do it. Whatever it is you want to do to me, do it." Lexi swallowed, feeling the pressure on her throat and knowing that he could crush her in a second if he wanted to. She finally managed to choke out, "*Allora, pedala.*"

He used her hair to turn her around, shoving her roughly against the bed. "You have no idea what you've done," he whispered dangerously as she heard the buckle of his belt open. His detached anger was terrifying, and Lexi wondered for a moment if she had misplayed the hand. Her fear took over and she tried to move, pulling her hands behind her head to grab at him. "Fight back, baby girl," he chided, and his words were cold.

This wasn't the Giovanni she had seen on the street or even in the great room this morning. This was a step beyond. This was the killer who could, if he chose, hurt her. This was the voice that had ordered bodies floating in rivers and buried in ditches.

Lexi didn't know the difference between the man who had beaten the undercovers sent to try and destroy him and the man who tied up and whipped women to satisfy his own kinks and urges. Were they one and the same? If so, how could he possibly know where the line was with her? Lexi felt anxiety start to overwhelm her and clawed at his hands when he yanked her to stand. "Stop!"

"That word," he snapped brusquely, "means *nothing* to me."

Pulling her off the bed had given her a slight advantage, and she used his change in weight to drop her leg behind his, displaying a move she had been taught in the Academy to disengage from an attacker. They both fell to the floor, and the belt skidded from his hand. Getting onto her knees, she tried to stand in order to run, but Giovanni was ready for her and grabbed her ankle, causing her to stumble. "I guess the Smithsonian teaches more than how to repair old books," he said with arrogance.

Lexi kicked out at him and freed herself, making it to the door. She managed to grab the handle, but Giovanni slammed it shut as she opened it. When he pressed his body against her back, she could feel how much the encounter had already aroused him. In that moment, although she had no idea what he would do to her, Lexi's true fear dissipated and she was no longer trapped in her own head.

Giovanni was a double-edged sword who could do far more damage than she could sustain. Knowing that he was operating on sex and not rage allowed her brain to click into play. She wasn't terrified; she was finally awake. Giovanni thought he could be strong enough for the both of them, but was he strong enough to know the limits Lexi herself didn't understand? Was he enough to calm the beast inside of her?

She shoved her body against him to create space, but he only laughed as he tossed her back on the bed. When she pushed up in an attempt to get to the other side, he used his knee on her lower back to push her down and curled his hand into her hair, forcing her head against the mattress. Lexi felt the expensive leather trace the curve of her skin and closed her eyes. Her tears saturated the sheets below as she prepared herself for the blow. "Do it," she whispered.

She heard him shudder when she truly consented to his game. Giovanni pulled her hair tighter and his knee weighted her while he balanced on the leg he kept off the bed. She could feel the belt still in his hand when he ripped the thong to shreds, the sides cutting into her hips as they tore at the seams. Seconds later, the soft leather bit into her ass as it lashed against her bare skin, and she gulped in air.

Lexi didn't know what she had expected, but it wasn't that. The impact initially was soft to the touch before a millisecond later every nerve ending was on fire. Her brain lit up across the board. She was unable to scream, having barely been able to breathe before the second hit, harder than the first, lay its marks across her backside.

"Enough?" Giovanni's voice was harsh and barely registered. Lexi was struggling to cope and clenched her eyes tightly as her fingers threatened to tear holes in the sheets. A third drop of the belt slapped her. Whether it was because her ass was already raw or because his wolf was finally being stilled, this one felt even harder, and she managed to choke out a sob between her rapid inhales and exhales.

Lexi didn't know how to say that she was done. There weren't words in her vocabulary to tell him that she couldn't take anymore. The monsters in her head were quieted, and her body couldn't withstand another blow without shattering the silence into the lack of trust she feared was waiting on the other side.

When she heard the belt hit the floor and felt the knee come off her back while the hand in her hair loosened, Lexi knew that Giovanni understood without her saying anything. She panted with relief and pulled herself to her knees with the intent of crawling to the other side of the bed. Before Lexi could move away, his hand returned to her, grasping her shoulder and positioning her body in front of him. Giovanni was inside of her seconds later, roughly claiming the body that he already owned. He tore the thin babydoll from her and left it hanging at her wrists, using the same hand to grab one breast and pinch the nipple so hard that she cried out.

She was dripping wet for him, and he was thick from the need to possess her. She couldn't help but respond to his deep thrusts by moving her body back against him. Flooding her were sensations of pain and pleasure, fear and desire. There was no rational thought process; had there been, her brain would have probably told her to run.

Lexi had known from the start that Giovanni's game was one she had no business playing. Yet, here she was, encouraging him to fuck her like this, giving him the last remaining permission needed to completely break her. Her eyes were sticky from crying, and, when he moved the hand on her shoulder to her throat in order to pull her head back to kiss her harshly, he tasted the salt on her skin. "Even your tears are beautiful."

She couldn't speak, rushed by all of the things she had never been meant to feel. Freedom breathed in as heaviness because Lexi didn't know how to process what she was experiencing or who Giovanni had unleashed. When he pulled himself from her and threw her down on her back, she closed her eyes. "Look at me," he demanded. "Look at me or I'll do this all night."

Lexi couldn't take him all night. She needed to fall. He had wound her tightly, snapped her cord, and sent her outside of the gravitational pull of her own orbit. She needed to tumble back to earth so that she could remember who she was.

She opened her eyes and came face-to-face with The Wolf she had only seen glimpses of before. His eyes were drugged by the sex and the fight. The harder he pounded into her to satisfy himself, the more he commanded her body to release. She needed to hold onto that, to maintain some sense of personal ownership and control, and Lexi longed to deny him this want. To fight back, she closed her eyes tightly again.

"Open your fucking eyes." He growled each word as though it was its own sentence while squeezing his hand around her throat. It wasn't enough that Giovanni knew he owned her; he wanted to see that she understood his possession in her own eyes. She played the only card left and kept them closed, feeling his fingers grow even tighter as his speed increased. His voice boomed the order again while the lack of oxygen needed to process the command made her feel lightheaded. *"Ho detto apri quei fottuti occhi!"*

Her orgasm completely obliterated her and she arched beneath him, accepting his own while her eyes involuntarily opened and she dropped her head back, seeing downtown out the window while at the same time seeing nothing at all. Giovanni collapsed on top of her, his shirt sticking to her skin. She didn't know how long they laid there before eventually he pushed up, his hands on either side of her, and she knew even beneath closed eyes that he was watching her.

His fingers were gentle against her face as he moved the matted hair from her forehead. "*Bella*," he murmured, trailing his hands down to where the bruises on her throat had deepened to purple. He leaned forward and kissed the marks. "I'll run you a bath."

When she heard the water turn on in the tub that took up a windowed corner of the bathroom, Lexi opened her eyes and tried to sit up. Everything hurt. Her arms hurt where she had fought against him; her legs hurt from being roughly pushed apart; her ass was throbbing and raw against the sheets that should have felt like laying on a cloud. She stood up and her knees buckled, causing her to grab the bed for support as she tried to walk toward the bathroom.

She thought she was falling, but she never reached the floor. Giovanni held her in his lap, sitting them both in the bedside chair where she had seen him watching her that morning. Was it only that morning? Twelve hours? Eighteen? What fucking time was it? What had happened to her? Every feeling that had been turned off while she was lifted above earth came on like blinding light behind her eyes. It was fire in her veins- agony, pain, that godforsaken numb- no, worse: fear of the numb.

Lexi didn't know who she was or why she had been freed by this, by him. The world was quickly approaching as gravity forced itself upon her, and she lost it. When her mind exploded, so did her body, and her tears were the result of massive sobs. She clutched his shirt with her hands while he held her and rocked her as though she were the baby girl he had promised her she was. "Shhh, *bambina*," he whispered, kissing her hair. "My beautiful, sweet girl." Another kiss to her head. "You are everything I want, everything I need."

His words weren't making any sense, and that just made her cry harder as she buried herself into his chest. "I won't let you go," Giovanni promised. "You're safe."

But he wanted her to go. He had told her to go. He had beaten someone else to settle his rage enough to even look at her. And what had Lexi done? She had provoked him to the point that she had felt everything he wanted to hurl at her.

What the fuck was wrong with her? Why had she done it? Worse, why had she been relieved at the first blow against her? Why, in the middle of the pain, had she felt the stings of peace and letting go? Why, as she was captive beneath his rough hands, had she felt a measure of freedom? There was nothing okay about any of this, and maybe she was just as fucked up as he was.

Giovanni carried her into the bathroom and held her in his lap as he turned off the water. She could see the steam rising and the smell of lavender drifted up, giving her an understanding of why oil rested on the sheet of heat that filled the porcelain oval. With hands that were suddenly silk against the ivory that he had resculpted, Giovanni lowered her into the tub. She grimaced when the water hit the cuts on her ass, and he rested her head back on a towel rolled up to support her neck.

He stood up to undress, and Lexi finally saw the involved tattoo she had only managed to catch the edges of before. The tree was intricately woven from words with the roots creating a beautiful script of his last name, but Giovanni moved toward the shower before she focused on the details. Lexi couldn't imagine where thirteen were hidden, although she saw another curving pattern that trailed down his spine.

He quickly washed away the remnants of their night before he turned the water off. Hidden on the side of his right bicep, she could see words inked into his muscular arm. "What does it say?" she asked when he emerged from the glass encasement. Her voice was raspy; her throat felt scratchy and it hurt to talk.

"What does what say?" He wrapped a towel around his waist, knotting it against his tight stomach. As he did so, Lexi noticed another scar, this one jagged and camouflaged in the line of his abdomen.

"The back of your right arm. It says *ig* something."

"*Igitur qui desiderat pacem, praeparet bellum.*" He ran a hand through his dripping hair to get it from his face and water dotted the floor at his feet. "If you want peace, prepare for war."

Lexi didn't want to think about the war that was being waged inside her own soul. It felt good to feel weightless in the water and to ignore everything else. Giovanni leaned over the edge of the tub in order to steal a gentle kiss. "I'll get you tea for your throat," he offered before walking toward the door. "And some ibuprofen for everything else."

Lexi started to laugh, but the action hurt and she sank deeper into the hot water. She still didn't understand why she had done what she had done. She felt both liberated and flushed with what felt a lot like embarrassment. What would she say if the time ever came for her to debrief? Hopefully she would have better lies by then. The thought made her feel sick, and she was more afraid of herself than she was of Giovanni.

7

Lexi eased out of the deep tub. After drying off as quickly as her aching body would let her, she put on the robe from the wall hanger and ventured into the quiet penthouse. Ascending to the second floor, she assumed the others in the apartment were already gone. Giovanni was replacing a tin in one of the cabinets while he removed a steaming kettle from the stove top. She could finally make out the tattoo that covered his spine; it was a line of thorns that stretched from his neck to his waist. He turned when she approached and said gently, "I would have brought the tea to you."

"I can walk." It hurt like hell, but Lexi refused to give him whatever satisfaction knowing that might offer. She waited for a comment of *I'll do it harder next time*, but Giovanni said nothing. He submerged the mesh bag of tea leaves into a large cup beneath a stream of boiling water, and his demeanor in the silence made her nervous. "Are your men still upstairs?"

"No, it's just us." He looked up as he brought the cup to where she stood before he reached into another cabinet and pulled out a bottle of ibuprofen, putting three of them in front of her. "If you want something stronger…"

"No." Lexi swallowed the green pills dry before she picked up the tea. She walked into the breakfast room to look out the window, and its night views showcased the lit up city around them.

"Drugs not your thing," Giovanni said, more as a statement than a question.

"Definitely not my thing." She sipped the black tea. "Shouldn't be anyone's thing."

"The world disagrees with you." He came behind her and settled his hands on her shoulders before his fingers massaged the knots that he had assisted in the formation of.

"That's because the world chooses to ignore the damage. It's because *people*," she said, not adding *like you*, "convince them that they aren't selling their souls to the devil with each hit." She shrugged her shoulders and he stopped, moving his hands in front of him as he crossed his arms. "This isn't something you want to talk to me about, Gio."

"Why's that?" His voice was still calm, holding no signs of the man before.

"Because if the internet is right and part of how you afford the tea I'm drinking and the bed I've slept with you in is paid for with the blood of addicts, then there is about a zero percent chance of this ever going anywhere." She took a step away from him and turned.

She wasn't sure what she thought might happen. Would he flip his switch again? Would she end up against another wall? He did neither, walking closer to her in order to run a thumb over her lips. "You simply cannot help that mouth."

He kissed her and, when he pulled back, Lexi noticed the damage again. She exchanged the mug that she put on the table for his hand. "What happened?"

"Nothing that has left me worse for wear."

She sighed his name before dropping his hand and returning to her cup. "I don't ask questions that I don't want the answers to. And this?" Lexi looked back at him, nausea settling over her. "*This* had to do with me. I want to know."

"Bare-knuckled boxing." Giovanni looked down at his flexing fingers. "With one of my men."

"Did you win?"

He laughed. "I sure as fuck didn't lose."

"Did he piss you off? Were you angry at him?"

"I was angry at *you*." The admission goosebumped her skin. Looking into his eyes made her uncomfortable, and she dropped her gaze. "Don't worry; Manny comes from an MMA background. There is nothing I gave him that he couldn't handle, and he got enough shots in to make it an even ass kicking."

Angst rose in her throat, and she drank more of the scalding tea to force it down. "Why?" she choked out. "Why would you do that?"

"Because it was the safest option. Suffice it to say, I didn't expect your response an hour ago." He offered her his hand, but Lexi stood rigid with the cup, still unable to look at him. "And I neglected to *interview* anyone, here or anywhere else."

This entire thing was a giant mess. Giovanni had beat the hell out of one of his bodyguards because the desire to unleash his anger on her- anger, she had to admit, she had pushed him to and encouraged- was unmet. She didn't consider anything he had done to her abusive. Lexi had enjoyed the rough sex from the night before and, although she was nervous about what she felt after their most recent encounter, there was nothing they had done that was without her consent. But could a man who was this intense, who was so aggressive and physical, be safe? Would his sexual sadism evolve into brutality? Would his dominance become cruelty one day? Would Lexi even be able to tell the difference? "This isn't going to work," she whispered.

He stepped closer to her and kissed the top of her head before taking the cup and putting it on the table. "After tonight, I think it might work far better than you suspect." His voice was soft, sweet. "Come to bed, baby girl. We'll talk in the morning."

Lexi didn't think she would be able to sleep, but she drifted off far easier than seemed possible. Her body melted against his as though created to be his missing piece. To the caress of his fingertips along her spine and the sound of his heartbeat, she fell into a dreamless sleep that didn't end until she opened her eyes to daylight. By the time she had wrapped herself in a robe and walked upstairs, Giovanni was at the bar, reading on a tablet that he tossed to the side when she entered. "Coffee?"

"Thank you." She took the cup that he streamed milk into before offering it to her.

Fully dressed, he emanated sex. She doubted anything he wore would do much to change that. Still, Lexi wondered what necessitated the suits he wore each day. Looking at the way his jacket hung, she wondered if it was simply to hide the automatic that she was nearly sure he had holstered around his shoulder. To his credit, Giovanni had done a decent job of keeping it hidden while she was with him, and she hadn't seen it at all when they went to the Hamptons. He smiled at her before he spoke. "What would you like for breakfast?"

"I don't eat breakfast."

He ignored her. "We can order in from the French bakery two blocks away or, if you would like to go out, walk down once you're dressed."

She was curious as to whether or not he would find her amusing when she said, "Did I stutter, Gio? *No, non faccio colazione.*"

He picked up the phone on the wall while she drank her coffee. "*Buongiorno*, Caleb. The order I gave you this morning? Yes, thank you." Replacing the phone, he returned to his espresso. "I don't think I've ever force-fed someone croissants, but there is a first time for everything."

He walked around to the bar that created the pass-through into the dining room and picked up a red, square box with the name of the jeweler scripted in gold. Giovanni placed the box between them and tapped it with his fingers twice. When Lexi made no move to touch it, he said, "Open it."

"What is it?" There was no way she was opening a Cartier box. She probably couldn't afford the box itself, let alone whatever thing was in it- and the financial cost of whatever that was wasn't even where her worry lived. Whatever he was offering was too costly for her to consider, and she shook her head when her eyes met his.

"If you open it, you'll find out."

"Gio-"

"Did I stutter?" Giovanni chuckled. *"Primo passo: aprire la scatola."*

Placing her cup on the countertop, her fingers found the split in the box. It was just a box. A very expensive box. A box that she had no business opening- but still a box. She lifted the lid and inhaled sharply as she murmured his name. The white gold cuff had been channeled with more diamonds than she could count, each grouping separated by onyx circles with triskelions, and Lexi thought she might not be able to breathe again. "I can't-"

"Thank you," he interrupted, whispering against her hair and, when she made no move to pick the bracelet up, doing it for her. "I think the words you are looking for are *thank you*. They aren't *I can't*."

After putting it around her wrist, he removed what looked like a metal toothpick from his pocket. Once the bracelet was secured, he slid the sliver of platinum into the clasp before harshly pulling down on the stick. He tossed the broken remnant in the red box and leaned against the counter.

"What did you do?" The two-carat band was heavy against her wrist, and she turned it to get a better look. "Why would you break the clasp?"

"It's not a clasp." He returned to his coffee. "It's a lock."

"How do I take it off if it's locked?"

"You don't." When the wall phone rang, he acknowledged that the elevator would soon be bringing breakfast before returning to the spot in front of her, as though waiting for Lexi to argue.

"How do you expect me to shower?"

"With water." Arrogance saturated his words. "I can teach you if you've forgotten how."

She bit her lip in frustration before raising her arm. "How do you expect me to walk down the fucking street?"

"It's on your wrist, *bambina*. It won't impact your ability to place one foot in front of the other."

"Why would you spend thousands of dollars on a woman that doesn't even like you?" she exclaimed.

Giovanni laughed and walked downstairs. She heard him thank the elevator attendant and then his steps as he returned. He placed a large bag on the counter and began to take out fruit and pastry, ignoring her annoyance. "You know that I can't accept this," she said softly.

Lexi watched the light create multicolored reflections against the diamonds and her stomach hurt. What was she doing? There was no way to rationalize any of this. The entire relationship, from start to now, was something out of one of the poorly-written chick-lits that the library circulated en masse. She couldn't do this. She couldn't live with what she knew wearing this bracelet would require. It wasn't her. It couldn't be her.

No, Lexi thought. It was because she was afraid that it very much *was* her, and she wasn't sure how to cope with that. She forced herself to ask, "Is this because of last night?"

"I'm not paying you for sex."

"Not the sex," she said, trying to ignore the feeling that was heavier than the cuff.

He grinned as he continued to unpack things from the bag. "I'm not paying you for that either."

"Do you feel ashamed? Is that what this is about? You got up early and called in favors down on Fifth Avenue because you felt ashamed of beating the fuck out of me last night?"

"I didn't come close to beating the fuck out of you," he said with a wink. "We'll save that for next week."

Lexi snapped his name in frustration. She was unable to instigate him and his easygoing attitude was pissing her off. "Is this some sort of guilt thing?"

"Baby girl, I don't feel guilty about last night. Not even a little. I bought it last week." After plating a croissant and berries, Giovanni took an unpacked container of butter and spooned a dollop on the plate before he pushed the offering toward her. "Had you not been so involved with your work, you would have had it Friday."

"Friday? That doesn't make any sense. I left here on Tuesday morning. You had no idea if you would ever see me again!"

"I brought it with me to the Gala as an apology. You were simply too annoyed with me, and I enjoyed the chase."

The man had brought a bracelet worth thousands of dollars to a woman he hadn't spoken to in days- a woman that he hadn't known existed even a few days before that. "You did everything possible to make me leave Tuesday. Why?" Lexi looked at him and wondered if he could see the hurt from that memory. "Why would you do that only to want me back?"

Just as they had when he'd explained his rejection of her at *Disco Ballarò*, Giovanni's words stunned her into silence. "I wanted you to have more than I felt, at the time, I could offer you." After a few moments, he added, "I reconsidered. Now eat." He nodded toward the plate. "I wasn't joking about the force-feeding."

Lexi knew there was little he wouldn't follow through with, and she tore a small piece of the croissant to placate him. When he saw her eating, he began to eat his own breakfast, glancing at his phone and typing replies to messages that came in. "I'll be leaving today," he said nonchalantly. "Work."

"Interviews?" Lexi asked, earning a dark chuckle.

"Watch yourself. Last night was only a sampling of what I'm capable of."

Her ass woke at the mention of the night before and she shifted uncomfortably, but that wasn't enough to reign in her attitude. "Don't pretend you don't have women for every day of the week, Gio. I can read *Page Six* as well as everyone else."

He tossed the cup of coffee back in a single swallow. "First," he said, pulling the cup down, "the women I date and the women I employ are two different things. Second, let me ask you a question, *bambina*. Would you consider a man with another woman slander?"

"I think most women would say yes." She took a berry from the plate and turned it around in her fingers.

"Why do you think that is?"

"Because betrayal hurts," she answered. The implication that every interaction with Giovanni was based on betrayal wasn't lost on her, and Lexi felt convicted. She looked down at the plate to avoid his gaze.

"I would wager feeling betrayed by someone you trust to take care of you probably does more than *hurt*." Placing his fingers on her chin, he lifted her face so that she could look into his eyes. "Do you trust me, Alessandra?"

"I don't know," she whispered. If the day came when she trusted him, then Lexi would have no choice but to confess every secret. God help her, she already believed him. Trust was right there, beckoning her to give in. She was no better than dead the second Giovanni was able to prove to her that he was worth that.

"Do you know the difference between *ferire* and *danneggiare*?" Giovanni walked back to the built-in espresso machine and started another cup.

"*Ferire* means hurt, like a cut or some sort of injury. *Danneggiare* is actual damage: real suffering and harm."

He nodded as he turned around. "You should know something about me. When I say something, I follow through. I'm not an easy man to deal with. I know what I want in life. If I can't get it, then I take it." His intense stare both calmed and chilled her with its brutal honesty. Giovanni took the cup that the machine finished and drank from it.

"Last night with you was a taste of what is to come. I *will* hurt you- your mind, your soul, your body." He put the cup on the counter and walked over to her, gently forcing her eyes to return to his from the floor where she had dropped them at his most recent confession. "But I will *never* harm you. I will cross your lines and destroy your boundaries, but I will never force your true limits. You will choose to trust me to know what it is that you can endure rather than fear what your mind says you cannot take. You belong to me not only because I want you, but because you want me to own you. The price that I pay for your gift is a refusal to harm you- no matter what. You can let go of whatever doubt lingers, whatever fear it is that drives you. You can trust that you are safe from the world and from yourself."

"From you?" Her throat felt tight with the challenge. "Who will keep me safe from you?"

"You have nothing to fear from me." Giovanni took a deep inhale of her hair before kissing the top of her head. "Nothing at all."

Lexi wasn't sure what to say. She could handle the anger and the violence because she could understand their origins. But this? His honesty was too much, and she wanted to flee. She wanted to run as far from him as possible and never think of him again. Had she not been sure before that she was outmatched, Lexi knew it for a fact now.

"Now you," Giovanni whispered as he stepped back and looked into her face. "You must give me a word that tells me I stand on the line between *ferire* and *danneggiare*. When you believe you risk harm, you must give me the word that ends the game. Know, *bambina*, that once you utter the word, the game is over. The king and the pawn return to the box."

Lexi nodded and lowered her eyes again. He was giving her a way out, a way that would end whatever relationship they had, be it a week, a month, or longer. He wasn't offering her a safe word that would still his belt or stop him from unraveling her; Giovanni was giving her the key to unlock his hold on her. Even this early in the game she wasn't sure that such a word truly existed anymore.

Satisfied that she would come up with her answer, he kissed her again before walking toward the room that housed his office. He stopped at the sound of her whisper. *"Oltre."* Lexi turned to watch him through the pass-through. "I choose *oltre*."

He gave her a sad smile. "So be it, and may I never hear that word cross your lips."

Giovanni disappeared behind the door as Lexi released a deeply held breath. Her body nearly collapsed against the counter, and she was grateful that he was gone so that she didn't have to force anymore food into an already upset stomach.

She returned to the bedroom downstairs. Despite the tailored suit she had seen Giovanni in, all that she wanted was a pair of her favorite ripped jeans and a comfortable pull over- neither of which she found in the closet. She chose a maroon sweater dress before putting on the knee boots from the day before and pulling her hair back into a loose braid. Once dressed, she forced the courage needed to confront Giovanni in his office.

She lightly knocked and heard his voice beckon her inside. Lexi peeked her head in the door that she barely cracked, and he stood from behind the desk. She didn't enter the room, which looked like it had been ripped from an architectural magazine. "Are you alright? Do you need something?"

"I-I'd like to go back to my apartment. I need to go by work and…" Lexi didn't know what to say and stammered, "I-I need to go and think somewhere else."

"Be back by tonight." Giovanni didn't seem bothered by her request and came around the desk to meet her at the door. He took her hand and began walking her down the stairs, while he used his free hand to lift his phone. "Raphael or Ricardo can-"

"No, Gio, I-I don't want you to send anyone with me. I'd rather walk."

"We're downtown. Midtown is quite the stroll." Giovanni used his thumbprint to unlock the elevator before he pressed the call button and said in refusal, "Raphael can take you."

"Gio, please." She squeezed his hand and implored, "I can't be a piece on your chessboard."

"The queen is the most treasured piece."

"And she moves in every direction- alone. I want to go. I *need* to go." Lexi bit her lip and looked up at him from beneath long eyelashes. "May I please go?"

Giovanni's silence gave her no insight into what he would decide. She had purposely asked if she could go rather than demand that he let her leave, hoping that her deference would tip the cards in her favor. "You'll always be free to go. You aren't a prisoner." The elevator door opened and a uniformed bellman appeared.

Lexi stepped inside while Giovanni watched her, the hand with the asp sitting over his lips. What was he thinking? Did he wonder if she would come back? Was that even a choice? He could easily find her if she failed to show up. "Alessandra: tonight," he said quietly as the doors began to shut. She wasn't sure if that was a threat or a reminder as he disappeared behind the closing panels.

When she stepped onto the street, the gusts of wind blew into her face and she wished she had sunglasses to keep the glare of the real world from blinding her. She felt a lifetime away from her apartment and wanted the long walk to clear her head. What the hell had she gotten herself into?

Thinking rationally, there was nothing about the last week that made any sort of sense. She was not the kind of woman that Giovanni Masseretti kept on his arm. She had seen the parade of blondes online. According to Sam, the Bureau hadn't bothered to approach them because the women were never around long enough. From everything Lexi had seen in her countless searches, long-term relationships were definitely not Giovanni's thing. If he was spending thousands of dollars on every woman he slept with, she mused, then the real secret was how he didn't go broke.

The bracelet on her wrist was heavy, and it left her feeling even heavier. She knew the significance: he had just cuffed her. Other than a basic understanding of the dynamics that included cuffs and collars, Lexi had glossed over that part of her research into the man who seemed to eschew commitment. She would have to either look it up once she got back to her apartment or ask Giovanni directly, and she really didn't want to deal with more of his honesty right now, not when she wasn't able to be honest with herself about how much she wanted to tell him the reason she had shown up at his bar in the first place.

She passed between the different groups of people on Broadway, their voices a symphony of languages and tones. Lexi wasn't walking with any sort of speed. Her mind was moving too fast, and she slowed her body down to address the range of emotions and feelings that were drenching her like a storm. She had left Park Place a little after ten in the morning but didn't reach her apartment until noon. Using the keypad to get inside, she walked up the stairs and collapsed on the floor in front of the bed.

As a teenager, Lexi had always felt things more intensely than everyone around her. She hated it because, whether she was afraid, angry, or overly happy, those feelings often escaped as tears. Her shoulders heaved against her knees as she clutched them to her chest. She didn't know what she felt or why. She was a librarian: her life was made up of cataloging materials and making them fit into neat boxes. She needed to catalog herself but had too many subject cards to manage even a basic attempt at organization.

When her heavy breaths finally calmed and she wiped her face on her sleeve, Lexi stood up and stripped from the dress, exchanging it for some ragged jeans with holes in the knees and a cable knit from her tiny closet. Since Giovanni had neglected to add such things to his dress-up pile, she opened one of her larger duffle bags and tossed in a few pairs of jeans, sweaters, and the dress she had discarded.

Her laptop was on the desk that was part of the windowsill and she sat down, typing in *BDSM cuff significance* before burying her head after reading through the first of several entries. What the ever-loving fuck had she just agreed to?

> *Similar to the significance of a wedding ring.*
> *Indicative of a submissive's status.*
> *Signal of ownership.*
> *Transfer of power.*

"Fuck." She poured through the different links. "No. No. No." Lexi closed the computer and looked at the thick- and locked- cuff around her wrist. How in the hell was she supposed to be okay with this? And why the fuck had he decided to behave in such a way with a complete stranger? Giovanni barely knew her! He didn't know even the most basic things about her!

She stood up to pace the small room. She had to keep her shit together. Lexi simply needed to look at this the same way she looked at everything else. She just had to organize and detail things out so that they made sense. The problem was that her feelings were in the way.

It was easy to catalog books with distinct subjects. It had been nearly as easy to look at people emotionlessly and slide them into boxes. The last week had done nothing but decimate Lexi's ability to do that with Giovanni. All of the feelings she had thought were dead and buried had rushed her, and the world seemed to change pace.

Not the world, Lexi thought. She was the one who changed when she was with him. She felt free and open, even though that usually meant responding to whatever bullshit was coming out of Giovanni's mouth at the time. When she caught sight of herself in the bathroom mirror, she was fingering the bracelet around her wrist and her face held a soft smile at the lone thought of him.

"Fuck, Lexi," she said aloud, hitting the sink and looking at her reflection. "He killed Dad!" She tried to force the girl to listen. "Pretty bracelets, great sex. None of it matters. He's a fucking killer! If he ever realizes who you are, you are just as dead. Wake the fuck up!"

But Lexi knew that she was already awake. That was part of the problem.

The eyes in the mirror asked her to consider the fact that there was no evidence that Giovanni even knew who her father was, let alone that the Masseretti family had ever killed an agent or cop. Still, Sam had been so sure and had spent years trying to piece together how they had failed. There had to be something that Lexi was missing.

John Masters had never loved being in the field and had preferred information gathering and organization. After Lexi's birth, he had traded going undercover for a promotion to supervisor and work as an analyst. In addition to mapping out the possible avenues of agent embedding, he had worked tirelessly to make sure background identities withheld scrutiny and that agents were emotionally prepared for the hell that undercover work would require.

Masters sat at a desk in Manhattan. Why would Giovanni kill a paper-pusher when he didn't even kill moles? The three agents that, over the last ten years, had been tasked with trying to unravel the Masseretti syndicate had all been found out within weeks. While they had been returned to the Bureau with the shit beat out of them, they had all gone home to their families. Lexi's father had been shot in an alley. It didn't make sense.

Lexi tore herself away from the mirror. Thoughts like these wouldn't serve her in any meaningful way. She had left DC with the singular need to destroy Giovanni even if it killed her. What was she supposed to do now?

Lexi started to pace again. She had fallen for his charm. She had fallen for everything about Giovanni- and she had fallen hard. She dropped her head against the wall that she stopped in front of. Fuck the whole world. Lexi was no longer sure that Giovanni had done what she had set out to reveal. She didn't know why, but it just didn't feel *right* anymore.

How could she even begin to prove that? Could she risk telling him the truth and just ask? Giovanni had said she had nothing to fear from him, but that was because he had no idea who the real Alessandra Masters was. The cuff picked up the stray beam of sunlight that poured into the apartment and laughed at her with its shine. His need to claim her just made things all the worse.

After shoving some cash into her pocket and putting the boots back on, she tossed the bag over her shoulder and left the apartment to walk the fifteen minutes to the library. Although Rare Books was closed on Sundays, the building opened for a few afternoon hours, and Lexi sequestered herself in the collection with a sandwich and extra large coffee from the downstairs café.

She worked on restoring a page from the book she had recently started from her pile of repairs. It was tedious and required her full attention. When, three hours later, Luke curved his head into the reading room to tell her that the library was closing in ten minutes, Lexi felt an enormous sense of gratitude that she had been able to focus on something other than Giovanni and the mess she had gotten herself into. Standing up and feeling sore throughout her lower body, however, brought her mind back to the night before, and she wondered if her ass held rectangular bruises or if her brain just remembered each whip.

She added the personal items she had brought to work for the Gala into the duffle bag and, after shoving her phone with its zero missed calls into her back pocket, sprinted to the elevator that Luke had held for her. "So," he said as they walked through security and into the afternoon, "the boyfriend? You didn't mention it was Giovanni Masseretti."

"Do you know him?" Lexi did not want this conversation and offered up a prayer to whoever might be listening. Based on Luke's continuation, that saint must have had a full inbox of petitions.

"Everyone in New York knows who he is." He stopped walking at the top of the stairs to the sidewalk and reached out, taking her arm but unable to complete his thought. "He's, Lexi, um..."

"He's something," she finished. Lexi shifted her weight and slid her bag forward to create a wall of personal space between them. "Was he rude? Did he say something at the Gala? I'm sorry if Gio was rough around the edges. He doesn't always play well with others- especially men."

"No, he wasn't rude." Luke shoved his thumbs in his pockets. "Not at all. He was really polite. I just..." He sighed and his gaze was a mix of disturbed and worried. "You know who Giovanni Masseretti is, right, Lexi? I mean, DC isn't New York so maybe you don't. But you said you two were dating distance..." His voice trailed off again with a conversation that, although he had started it, clearly made Luke uncomfortable.

Was he trying to bring up the fact that Giovanni had constantly been photographed with other women? That it was no secret what her *boyfriend* did in his spare time? The suspicions of what he did for a living? "Don't believe everything you read," she said, trying to offer him a polite smile. Defending Giovanni was something that would take far more time and patience than she had. "Articles don't always paint the clearest picture."

"Photographs do." Luke looked around nervously. "Look, I know you don't know me, but you seem like a really nice person who wouldn't want to be mixed up with a guy like him. I'm worried for you."

Lexi looked at her watch. "Maybe we can talk about it when I'm in tomorrow. I really need to go." Luke seemed to realize that she wasn't going to continue the conversation, and he stayed behind as she walked away. Lexi had barely managed to get to the main sidewalk when she stopped. "Not sure I'd come back?" she asked with annoyance.

"It's supposed to rain again." Giovanni took the bag from her, the movement causing her braid to smack her in the face as he did so. He passed it to the linebacker who took it to the X5 that sat at the curb. "Who's your new friend?"

"Careful, Gio: that sounds like jealousy over territorialism." She didn't like the look on his face. It made her concerned for Luke. "He's just a coworker."

"A lot of conversation for a coworker who spent the last few hours with you."

"It's your fault. This conversation was about you." Giovanni looked back at her with a raised eyebrow, and Lexi playfully pushed her finger into his chest. "I'm not defending you, FYI, so keep your bullshit out of the papers. I don't want to be painted with the brush that you seem more than happy to let the press color you with."

Giovanni gave another look behind her before he leaned forward and kissed her. "That's fair."

"It's more than fair," Lexi scoffed, causing him to laugh as he kissed her again, this time biting her bottom lip in a move that made her lean into him and wish they were alone on the sidewalk. "You're being mean," she whispered. "If he's still watching us, you are doing this for spite."

"Just asserting dominance."

"Your bracelet choice and my sore ass prove that you've done enough of that already." Lexi stood taller and looked up at him. "Now why are you really here, other than to be a stalker?"

"I wanted to tell you in person that I'm leaving." He took her hand in his. "I have to go out of the country for some business. Come with me."

She opened her eyes wide with shock. "I-I-I can't, Gio. I'm due to work tomorrow. I've got four restorations that the previous librarian left on-going. I can't just *not* show up."

Lexi steeled herself for an argument, but he gave her an authentic smile and ran their joined fingers across her lips. "Of course. Your work is," he sought a word, "admirable. I would never ask you to leave it. Sadly, my work while less," he smirked, "*admirable*, is needed."

"How long will you be gone?" she asked as he led her from the park.

"A week. My flight will be back Saturday." When they settled into the car, he asked, "Are you sure I can't convince you to come with me?"

"I wish I could, but-" She was interrupted by a vibration against her butt, and she navigated the back seat to pull the phone from her pocket. "Hello?"

"Alessandra? Dr. Fisher."

"Dr. Fisher," she greeted, wondering why the Library Director was calling her on a Sunday. "How are you?"

"I'm well. The reason I'm calling, Alessandra, is, um, it is a very strange request. I'm sorry to put you in a position like this." The woman sighed apologetically. "I know this is an insane question, but do you have a passport?"

"A passport? Yes, I have one." She began to suspect the reason why Giovanni hadn't pushed his *come with me*. He had already set the response he wanted into motion.

"I received a call this morning from Ursino, asking if we could lend them our Rare Books Director for a week while their librarian is away."

"Ursino? In Catania?" Lexi was confounded, and the look on Giovanni's face only made her more so. "I'm sure there are people far more qualified."

"They asked for you by name and, in addition to a very generous donation to offset our loss for the week, offered to fully cover your travel expenses and accommodations along with a daily stipend."

"I bet *they* did," Lexi muttered through gritted teeth.

"I know you have a few ongoing projects. I can get coverage for your collection and have your page stabilize anything you were working on." Lexi thought she might hyperventilate. It wasn't Dr. Fisher's fault that she was sleeping with Giovanni. The older woman, still contrite, tried to sound enthused. "Your flight leaves later today. The director said that he will contact you and make arrangements directly."

"I'm sure he will." When Dr. Fisher said goodbye, Lexi echoed her and threw the phone into a pocket next to the door. She was so irritated that she couldn't stand to look at Giovanni's smug grin, and she stared out the window.

"Trouble at work?" he asked innocently. She spun her head around to eye him angrily and watched his smirk deepen. "Did you forget what I told you?"

"You've told me so much over the last few days, Gio, that I have no fucking clue what you mean."

He rubbed his stubble and chuckled into his hand. "I always get what I want, baby girl."

"Fuck you, Gio."

At this, he broadly laughed. "I'll take that as an invitation."

"Do you enjoy this game of buying people like stocks? Of using people who have no idea who the puppetmaster is?"

"It's the way of the world."

"It's disgusting," Lexi countered. "It's wrong. I don't like being pulled around like a fucking doll. You aren't moving me; you're strangling me."

He seemed to consider this for a moment. Leaning back in his seat, he sighed and waved his hand, as though that could eradicate her frustration. "It's done now."

She exhaled angrily and returned to the window. Had Lexi expected an apology or for Giovanni to change his mind? His consideration for her position might be the best she could hope for. She ignored him until the car entered the Queens Midtown Tunnel. "Where are we going?"

"JFK," he answered as he sent a text.

"JFK! I don't have my passport!"

"It's taken care of." Addressing an incoming call, he no longer focused on her.

Lexi's fingers curled into her thighs. Giovanni had broken into her house again, and she felt her rage rising. She tried to use the drive to Terminal One to settle her emotions, but, as the car pulled into the Alitalia section and one of the bodyguards opened the door, all that Lexi wanted to do was refuse to exit and force Giovanni to take her home. He couldn't make her get on a plane.

The way he said her name as he stood, hand extended, led her to believe he could do exactly that. When she made no move, he added in a low voice, "I will drag you from this fucking car and carry you onto the plane. Don't tempt my hand, *bambina*. I thought you learned that last night." She didn't need another reminder; her body was still sore. She furiously took his hand, which he used to yank her from the back seat. "You're learning."

If this was part of what she needed to know, then Lexi feared she would have a steep learning curve.

8

Giovanni offered her a chance to see the world in a way that would have been impossible before him. From the private lounge at JFK to the luscious seats in First Class that allowed her to fall asleep for half of the trip, these weren't her routine flight experiences. As she woke to his fingers sliding down her face and that smile that made her heart race, Lexi wanted to escape and enjoy it all. Seconds later she remembered she was pissed off at him for getting her out of the country. She turned her head away, annoyed.

It was impossible to fly nonstop to Sicily, and they landed in Rome after eight hours in the air. It felt too early and her body revolted against being woken from the comfortable recliner, but it was already midmorning. If she didn't force herself to wake, then sleeping at night would be difficult. When they arrived at a private jet already prepared for departure, Lexi settled in for the hour-long flight and graciously accepted the sparkling water offered by a flight attendant that she was nearly certain Giovanni had slept with based on the way the woman fawned over him while he practically ignored her. Although Lexi had planned to continue the silent treatment because she was still pissed, she couldn't help herself. "Do you interview your flight attendants, too?" she asked when the woman walked by them after the pilot signaled their takeoff. He looked over at her with a look that implied an answer wasn't necessary to her insinuation before returning to his mobile.

Giovanni had been right: Lexi couldn't control her mouth around him. While she had never been the type of child to smart off to her parents or teachers and she was an adult who rarely even showed her frustration to anyone that wasn't close to her, she couldn't seem to avoid pushing his buttons. She was quiet and reasonable before her parents died. Had she happened to intersect with Giovanni in that life, would he have woken her up in a different way? Would she still find herself incapable of not encouraging the responses he seemed all too willing to give her? She whispered sarcastically, "Didn't take much to silence The Wolf."

The fingers of the hand next to her curled around Lexi's wrist while he continued to work on his phone with the other. Giovanni didn't even bother to look over at her, instead bringing her arm to his lips. Lexi squirmed in her seat when she felt his scruff tease the delicate skin on her wrist before she covered her mouth with her other hand and turned to the window.

His bite was both sensual and sadistic. The pain danced with the desire that flowed through her entire body. She clamped her jaws to avoid alerting the plane to what he was doing, and her free hand fled from her mouth to grip her handle as she nearly leapt from the seat. His teeth released and his tongue lingered over the indentation, ending in a kiss before he put her hand down to answer his phone.

This is what you get for instigating him at every turn. The voice in her head was getting louder. When Giovanni got up and walked into the part of the cabin where the two men who had accompanied them were seated, she was grateful to have the space to breathe. Lexi looked down at the red imprint of his mouth on her wrist and fingered the marks on the skin he had managed to break. When she looked to where Giovanni leaned against an aisle seat and talked with his men, he winked at her deviously.

The plane was soon descending toward the sea that was all around them. When it touched down on the runway that weaved between mountain and water, Lexi braced herself as gravity forced her back and the sound of the slowing plane raged through the air. The flirtatious flight attendant welcomed them to Palermo while she offered more refreshment and seductively leaned over Giovanni, who was again seated, but Lexi heard nothing except her heart pounding in her ears.

The first thing that hit her when she followed Giovanni off the plane was the heat. She took in a deep breath of the heavy air. Her sweater was out of place, and she feared being overheated by the time they reached the convoy of armored cars that waited for them at the base of the jet's stairway. "Are you expecting company? Heavy packer?"

"No." Giovanni led her to the third in the line of five, while the two men who had accompanied them each went into one of the cars that bordered the vehicle. He opened the door for her and waited for her to get inside. "We don't have luggage."

"Do you expect me to work naked?" Lexi suddenly felt like there was something very important that she didn't know when Giovanni covered his mouth to hide his laughter and watched her with amusement. "What?"

"Nothing." The car moved forward down a single lane road. Lexi knew that voice. It dripped with gameplay. "I know your Italian is very good. How is your geography?"

They were surrounded by water which made sense because Sicily was an island. There was water everywhere, and the major cities were all bordered by the sea. As the Falcone Borsellino Airport was fading behind them, she tried to rationalize what she was seeing. "We flew into Palermo. Why not Catania? Ursino is in Catania. Why did we fly into an airport on the other side of the island?" When his grin grew, Lexi knew that she was on the right track. She wanted to ask *where are we going* but took the more concrete option. "We aren't going to Catania, are we?"

"I can take you to Catania if you would like to visit. Great city. Beautiful architecture. And we will have some time while I'm here."

She tried to settle her nerves. "There's no week of restoration at Ursino, is there?"

"I'm sure their staff is busy restoring every day-"

Lexi didn't want to hear proof of another lie and she interrupted him, frustrated. "Where the hell are we going?"

Pretending her leg was a map, Giovanni placed his fingers at her knee. "Palermo," he pointed out before trailing his fingers up her thigh, "south to Menfi."

"Where the fuck is that?" He chuckled at her indignation when Lexi pushed his hand from her leg. "You think this is funny, but I don't. I want to know where I am."

"Trust me." He leaned back in the seat as though that were the easiest thing in the world and would solve all of Lexi's problems.

"Then stop lying to me!" She turned back to the window as they sped down what had to be a highway. "I have no idea where we are going in a convoy of cars that would make the President's security look like a group of toddlers. I don't like this. I don't want this." Lexi looked back at him, but Giovanni was silent. "You let everyone who knows me believe I'm going to be in Catania. If something happens to you or me, then I have no idea how to get out or where I'm even running from. Gio, please." She took his hand when he looked away from her and out the window. "Even if I could tell you that I trust you, you don't trust it here or we wouldn't be sitting in an armored car." His unbuttoned jacket had opened in such a way when he turned that she saw the holster. He grabbed her wrist harshly at the touch of her fingers to the gun's grip. "And you wouldn't be carrying a gun."

"Baby girl, I always carry a gun." He shifted back in his seat and released her wrist to interlock their fingers. "You just haven't seen it." She tried but failed to pull her hand from his. "Sicily is not New York." When Lexi shook her head as if to disregard his clear warning, he turned her hand slightly, causing pain to radiate through her wrist. "I'm not joking, Alessandra. I forbid you to go anywhere alone."

"You *forbid* me?" She laughed angrily. "I'm not a child, Giovanni."

"Do not force my hand, *baby girl*." The look in his eyes iced her. He was deadly serious but added, "Nothing will happen to you. You don't need to worry." When Lexi didn't answer, his voice was softer. "Menfi was settled in antiquity. It's been owned by the Arabs, Spaniards, Italians... It's a beautiful mix of culture and people. The architecture is astounding for such a place. We are not far from the sea. You can even see Tunisia on a clear day."

"It sounds beautiful." She didn't bother to look at him.

"You are afraid." Giovanni squeezed her hand. "That's good. It will keep you aware of your surroundings and of whom to trust."

"Who can I trust, Gio? You? Would *you* trust you?" Lexi raged in his silence. "You always get what you want, and you don't care how high the cost or who pays the price. At some point, people will ask if you are worth it. You'd better hope you are the vintage you think you are."

The drive was comfortable. They entered Menfi, and Lexi was annoyed by her response when they traveled down the dusty road toward the fortified estate. She was like a small child, transported to a fairy tale. "*Addivintari*," she whispered, the gallery painting making sense.

She leaned forward in her seat, trying to take in the picturesque view of the olive fields, the grape vines that were delicately looped over themselves, and the citrus valley that seemed endless. The sky was unlike any other blue she had ever seen, and the car came to a stop in front of a tree-and-flower-lined fence made of stone that could have dated centuries. A bodyguard she didn't recognize opened the door.

Lexi shielded her eyes from the sun and looked out over the fields below. The rolling hills of fruit and flowers trailed into the sea, and she almost believed they were at the edge of the world. It was extraordinary, but she was hot and her skin felt plastered to her sweater. Giovanni took her by the hand and pulled her toward the gate that was already open. "There is much more to see than this."

"Another ten thousand square feet?"

She could hear the humor in his voice. "Stop. It's somewhere in the neighborhood of six times that." When her eyes widened once they entered the courtyard, where flowers embellished the antique stonework, he added, "I bought it as a family home. When we are all here, it's barely big enough to avoid killing Theresa."

"Your sister was lovely," Lexi fired back, taking in the details of the architecture and beauty as they walked into the air conditioned foyer. In a room to the side, a middle-aged woman in a uniform wiped down a massive dining room table. "If you don't think so, that's only going to make me like her more."

"You are trying, aren't you? Do you think I have no recourse?" Giovanni grinned broadly at her. "Keep teasing with that mouth and you'll find out that, New York or here, I'm still the one in control."

Lexi was completely teasing him and her wrist still smarted from his bite, although that did little to dissuade her. Was she hoping he would prove his words? It was disturbing to consider. "I thought you were working. I wouldn't want to distract you from your important- if not admirable- work."

When she parroted him from the library's steps, he chuckled and squeezed her hand before bringing her to a wide staircase. "Most of the living space is on the first floor," he said as though her tour guide. "There are upper wings that do not connect to one another. They enter via stairs in the house and have a second exit into one of the courtyards."

Lexi accompanied him to where the stairs ended. In some ways, the suite was ripped from a thousand years before with the swooping arches and stone, yet it belonged on the cover of a modern living book. They were in a sitting room whose windows showcased both sides of the house, if she could think of the *baglio* as that. On one side, an olive grove was surrounded by bright pops of wildflowers. On the other, grapes traversed the hills like women dancing.

Giovanni tossed his jacket onto a couch, and she swallowed down the lump in her throat. He was no longer trying to hide the holster that carried a 9mm SIG Sauer P226. He slipped his hands into his pockets and lazily walked through the room, silently commanding she follow.

The main room led into a bedroom that reminded her of his Manhattan apartment but with a décor that was in line with the age and style of the building. Even though the air conditioning kept the house cool, the windows were thrown open and she could smell the sea while long curtains swirled when the wind blew. The bed itself was a four-poster canopy that was open all around with drawers making up the base; it was covered in a green and gold duvet over sheets that reminded her of the dress she'd worn to the Gala. Lexi ran her hand over the comforter, and the diamonds around her wrist picked up the sun as it shone through the wall of windows. There were two leather chairs, one in either opposing corner and each in front of open doors that she could see were closets. A glass door showcased the outside on the exterior wall.

The bedroom ended in a bathroom that, if possible, managed to put the Pinnacle's master en suite to shame. The marble walls looked more like a spa than a house. One housed jets that could have easily spanned twelve feet across and was boxed in glass; four overhead shower heads hung from the ceiling. Not to be outdone, the corner soaker could have fit at least half-a-dozen bathers and resembled a small swimming pool more than a tub. The vanity held only two sinks while taking up an entire wall. "You must burn through money."

"I can't take it with me." He shrugged. "I should enjoy life while I have it."

Lexi nodded toward the gun. "If you have to carry one of those to ensure that, you may want to rethink some life choices."

Giovanni turned on the balls of his feet and returned to the bedroom. "You think you know me?"

"I think I know how to read."

"Most of what you've read isn't true." He sat down in one of the chairs and rested a foot over his knee. "It makes for a good story, but it is fiction crafted by people with nothing but time."

She felt emboldened. "Are you telling me that those scars are fiction? That you've never fired that gun?"

Giovanni's gaze could freeze the sun or cause the icecaps to melt. There wasn't anger or annoyance as he watched her, and that made Lexi even more uncomfortable. She waited for him to say *don't ask* and was surprised when he inquired, "*Facciamo un gioco, bambina?*"

"Maybe you are out of practice, Gio, but talking to another person isn't usually considered a game." She leaned against the bed while he smirked at her. "But, if you'll explain the rules, I'll consider it."

He held up a finger. "You can ask one question in exchange for turning yourself over to me, for whatever I wish to do to you, for one minute."

"You want me to pay for asking you questions? With sex?"

"Now," he said with understanding, "I will not charge you for those two questions since I am a kind and generous man." Her eyebrows shot up and he chuckled. "In the future, those would be worth two minutes of your precious time. Do you have more questions?"

Lexi knew he was absolutely serious and worded her sentence carefully. "I think you should explain to me clearly the rules of this game. I assume that you will answer my questions honestly in exchange for your *quid pro quo*."

"I will. I'll tell you nothing but the truth." She was sure that Giovanni saw her breath tie a corset of knots in her chest. "How much are you willing to pay to find out what it is you wish to know?"

"This payment system is based on sex and not on you hurting me."

"I won't say no to pain, but nothing you ask will inspire me to anger or to punishment."

His confessions would never leave the room. Even if Lexi showed up at the FBI the moment they returned to New York, she wouldn't be able to debrief her exchange of sex for information. She would risk whatever he could put her through to find out the truth, and Giovanni knew her answer before she said at last, "I'll play."

"I thought you might." Giovanni opened his hands over his knees, inviting her to begin. "Ask what you want to know."

Each question would cost her sixty seconds and Lexi wanted to make them count. "Have you ever killed someone?"

He didn't flinch and his eyes didn't leave hers. "Yes."

"Just yes? No details?"

"If you want specifics, you will need to ask specific questions." He held up three fingers. "You are already up to three minutes."

"What? I asked you one question!"

"Four." Giovanni held up one finger for each question he repeated back to her. "Have you killed someone? Just yes? No details? What?"

"You can't be fucking serious," she seethed. "I asked you one *real* question, Gio. You're cheating."

"No, I was clear in the rules. One minute for each and every question. You can stop the game whenever you wish. I, most likely, won't choose to play it again, but you have complete control of how far we go."

Lexi was grinding her teeth. Giovanni had set her up and she had walked straight into the trap. She had to plan her real questions to avoid tripping up again. "Why do you do this? Why live a life that is nothing but drugs and crime?"

"My life is far more than that," he countered, looking at her with interest and recrossing his legs. "I'm not sure what you're reading, Alessandra, but easily ninety-five percent of my business is completely legal."

"It's the other five percent and that SIG against your chest that has me worried." *Shit*, she thought; she had overstepped by being able to identify the gun. "At least, it looks like the one the Seals had on display at the Smithsonian."

He reached into the holster and lifted the gun, placing it on the table next to his chair. "It bothers you. You would rather I, what? Be afraid?"

"Oh, Giovanni, I think you *are* afraid." Lexi watched her own fingers roll up and down the comforter for a few seconds. "I think you build walls because you are afraid that it's all just a front. That *you are just a front*."

He laughed at the suggestion. "What I think is that you don't believe me when I say that nothing will inspire punishment. Very clever, *bambina*. Just remember: I'll own you for however many minutes you end up with."

Lexi's fingers stopped moving as she looked back at him. "Why do you run drugs? You don't use them."

"You sound sure of that."

"There's nothing I've seen that would imply you actually use anything other than caffeine. Your espresso habit is probably an addiction in its own right."

"Coffee and sex," he agreed. "I don't use drugs."

"Why do you sell them? You easily have spent millions on addiction recovery programs. Why do that only to create the patients you are trying to save?"

Giovanni sighed and stood up, walking to the door that led to the patio. He looked outside. "Do you remember meeting my family? My brother, Matteo?"

She could see the younger man in her mind. "Yes. He liked football."

"He does, yes. When he was in college, he indulged in a variety of vices. Often he was drunk and smoking, but once he went too far."

"What happened to him?"

"He nearly died. Losing him would have killed my mother. He was her son." Giovanni faced her. "I realized all of them are someone's son. What I import is clean, and, for those who cannot stop themselves, there are options available to help them."

Lexi leaned against the bed, stunned. Had he really just admitted to selling drugs while in the same breath expressing remorse and a desire to help those that he corrupted by the sheer nature of what he did? She tried to find another question, but her head was spinning. "And the women?"

"Women are…" Giovanni grinned and the empathy was gone. He was back in the game. "I'm not sure what you want to know. Do I like women? You wasted a question if you didn't know that was a yes."

She had to stay on her toes if she wanted to get away with more answers than time owed. "Are your nightclubs fronts for prostitution?"

"First, prostitution *should* be legal. There is nothing wrong with a woman making money for something she would give for free if only she desired the man in question."

The weight of the bracelet against her arm felt heavier. "That does not answer my question."

"I won't deny that arrangements are made and business is conducted. My *staff*," he smirked, "are well-paid for their work and, on top of that, are granted generous donations by their benefactors. I know of several who have graduated with extended degrees and no debt. Is what I offer them any worse of prostitution than life forcing them to sell their souls to pay for a simple education?"

"Gio," she muttered. "That's not the same thing and you know it."

"*Tutto fa brood.*" He shrugged again and leaned back against the wall. When she exhaled angrily at his expression, he looked at his watch. "I hate to cut this short, but I have a meeting soon. Any more questions?"

"How many people have you killed?" The question slipped out before she could stop herself.

"I don't remember. Enough."

His answer froze her to the floor. "Any cops? FBI? Anyone like that?"

"Since I think you don't understand grammar very well, I will only count that as one question instead of three."

"You can count it for all three as long as you answer." She needed his response and would pay anything he required for the simple *yes* or *no*. She took a step forward, trying to stand on her own even as she braced against her fear. "Count it for five. I don't care."

"No," he said, biting the inside of his cheek before he answered further. "I don't kill cops. It's not their faults they chose a side that puts them in opposition to me. They believe they are fighting for a common good, for law and order. They simply don't have the power they need."

She was both stilled and angered. "They don't have the power because men like you take it away from them."

"*Men like me?*" Giovanni stood taller. "Tell me, Alessandra, about these *men like me*." When she didn't reply, he filled the silence. "*Men like me* rose up from the people when foreigners came in and decimated those they considered weaker and less than. *Men like me* protected the villagers from the thugs in power who raped, stole, and beat them into submission."

"I don't need a fucking history lesson." Lexi crossed her arms. "What happened to the people of Sicily was awful."

"*Men like me*," he continued, "traveled to New York to find that the American dream only applied to people who had a little less brown in their skin and an accent that made English far more accessible. *Men like me* created safety and order for immigrants who just wanted a better life and a future for their families."

"Stop acting like you're Robin Hood!" Lexi exclaimed. "*You're* the outlaw, Giovanni- not the fucking hero robbing from the rich to give to the poor!"

"The outlaw," he said, nodding his head with annoyance. "The outlaw according to whom? To the same people who did nothing but force those with hope and goals into tiny compartments of life where they could barely breathe? *Men like me* took the wealth they had brought with them and offered loans to the people who looked up to them as their protectors. *Men like me* helped them start the stores and the businesses that, under the ruling Americans, they would have been left to sweep the floors of."

"*Loans?* Do you understand what the term *loan shark* means? They weren't offering them help; they were putting them into a debt they could never get out of!"

"Don't put the men who decided to play American and use everyone they came into contact with to build their power in the same category with the *men like me* who actually gave a damn about their people and wanted to see them successful." Giovanni was watching her with a look that said he believed himself analogous to the feudal lords who didn't just rule over people but made sure they were legitimately cared for. He scoffed, "*Men like me.* You have no fucking idea who *men like me* are or what we do. You hear a last name and think we are all the same. How does that make you any different from those who founded your country and stole it from the people who, to their dismay, already lived there?"

Lexi felt the hairs on the back of her neck stand up. "Are you trying to call me out on American history?" She took a step closer to him. "You stand here and give me this speech about helping the poor and oppressed, and you want to look at me as some sort of oppressor? I'm a fucking woman, Giovanni. I didn't even get the right to vote until a hundred years ago, and I still don't have equal protection under the law! Fuck you if you think different. And," she said, pointing her finger angrily, "I don't hear a last name and think you are all the same. I could care less where your people came from or what color they were or anything else. I care about right and wrong. I care about the things that you do and try to convince yourself are worth it. You are who you are? Let me tell you who you've shown me you are. You build empires by destroying the people beneath you, and you don't care who you step on as long as you never touch the ground. That's who you are, and your last name probably wouldn't change that by much if it was fucking *Smith*."

Lexi wasn't sure what he was thinking as he watched her from across the room with eyes that never failed to get under her skin. He slowly walked over to her and stopped to kiss the top of her head before whispering, "I've crawled on the ground." There wasn't anger in his declaration rather the suggestion that she understood him as he understood her. "Beneath the whip of your tongue, I feel I crawl even more in the dirt at times."

Giovanni stepped away from her, and Lexi turned around when he lifted the SIG from the table. He checked the safety before returning it to the holster as she asked, "Did you really tell me the truth?"

"I have no reason to lie to you." His gaze made her feel as though he had looked inside of her soul and knew every hidden detail. He pointed to one of the closets. "I had some things brought in for you. I would prefer you stay on the property until I'm finished. I will have lunch laid out for you. Let Raphael know what you wish for dinner if you have preferences, and the cook will prepare it." He glanced at his watch again. "I have to go. Oh," he turned back after he took a few steps, "because I'm sure you want to know: the answer is fifteen."

9

The swimming pool was perfection; swimming while two strangers sat on the deck and talked about her was not. When Giovanni left, Lexi debated taking a shower and changing clothes, but catching sight of the swimming pool when she walked by the door to the outside made her rethink her options. If he wouldn't be back until dinner, then she would be on her own for hours.

"Fuck you, Gio," she muttered when she walked into the closet he had directed her to. Either he brought a lot of size-eight women to his secret hideaway or he had ordered an entire clothing boutique delivered. There were rows of dresses, ranging from simple day pieces to long gowns. She didn't see any of her preferred jeans and t-shirts, and she recalled his threat to dress her as he liked. In one of the dressers, she found matching sets of underwear that looked more fuckery than functional. Lifting up one of the lace brassieres, she threw her head back and exhaled her frustration. A few drawers down, she found some athletic wear, which actually made her happy. The hills would be an achy run but would give her something to do.

Alongside the workout gear, she saw several bathing suits- although that was a misnomer. There was nothing suit-like about the choices he had made. There were at least five sets of briefs that would barely cover her ass combined with tops that more than showcased her breasts. The underwear would cover more!

Tossing her sweaty jeans and sweater into a corner chute that ushered her clothes somewhere else- probably a furnace if Giovanni had his way- Lexi pulled on a brightly colored, saffron bikini and slipped her arms through a sheer cover. The center of the closet had enough shoes to rival what she had seen in his New York apartment, and she wondered if he had bought her a pair of every shoe in Sicily as she selected a pair of decorative flip flops from a lower square.

She walked down the balcony steps to the outside where an infinity pool sparkled in the afternoon sun. There was no one around and, after leaving the shoes and cover up on a lounge chair, she jumped in, swimming to one end before looping back and swimming to where she had started. Standing up, she pushed her wet hair back and blinked. Where she had been alone before, two men now stood.

They walked from the main house toward a covered table, and she recognized them from New York. One was the massive linebacker who had made her coffee; the other was not nearly as tall and had a slighter build. He was older than the huge bodyguard and looked about the same age as Giovanni. Based on the way he carried himself and his near constant presence alongside his boss, Lexi assumed he was in charge. He gave her a slight bow of his head in greeting. "*Signora.*"

"*Ciao,*" she murmured, not sure of what to say.

"*Don* Giovanni ordered you lunch. Would you prefer it brought outside?"

Even if he wasn't around, Giovanni couldn't relinquish control for even a moment. She didn't feel like pushing her luck. "I can eat it inside after my swim, but thank you."

"Of course, *Signora*."

"You can call me Lexi," she said, offering a smile. If these were her bodyguards while she was here, she could at least make their jobs slightly easier.

"*Don* Giovanni would disagree, *Signora*."

This really annoyed her, but she couldn't do a damn thing about it. He wouldn't even accept his family calling her anything other than Alessandra; why had she considered the idea that he would allow someone from his crew to use something as familiar as *Lexi*? "And should I call you *Signore*?"

"Raphael, *Signora*." The man, whose eyes were more slate gray than blue, smiled a wide grin, as though he found her amusing.

Her mind immediately went to the night of the Gala, when Giovanni had offered to have his driver take her home. He had told her that Raphael was his most trusted bodyguard. "Why aren't you with Giovanni? He told me that you're the person he trusts most."

He continued to watch her with interest before he shrugged. "Today, *Don* Giovanni has trusted me to watch you for the afternoon."

Lexi leaned on the side of the pool. "But why? He told me to stay here. If he's out, then why would he keep you here and put himself at risk?"

Raphael didn't answer, instead turning to his companion and beginning a discussion in a low voice. Did Giovanni not trust her to stay on the estate? It was a valid concern; she didn't really listen to him about anything else. Lexi swam another few laps in the pool to ponder the idea. Why would he leave without the person he trusted most to have his back? Had he not left? Giovanni didn't tell her, specifically, that he was leaving; he had just said that he was busy.

The pool was in a courtyard that didn't face where the cars had dropped them off, so she couldn't see if there were other vehicles. Lexi balanced her chest against the patio and kicked her feet slowly while she panned her eyes around the back of the house. A shadow passed in one of the lower rooms. A sheer curtain blocked a detailed view of the man on the other side, but she recognized Giovanni by the shape of his body. After a few more laps, she pulled herself from the water and accepted the towel Raphael offered her.

The bodyguard whose name she didn't know went into the house while Lexi dried off and tied the cover up like a robe. "Lunch will be served in the *salina*," Raphael said, trailing a few paces behind her and to the side. "Please let me know your preferences for dinner, and I will issue them to the kitchen."

"I don't have any preferences." Lexi dried her hair with the towel. "Whatever they had planned is fine." She followed his lead when he took a few long strides to get in front of her to open the door. Soon they were in a room that, while it opened into the main house on three sides, faced the outside with a wall of doors that were open to the fields. A table large enough for four was decorated with a single place setting. "Are you not eating?"

"No, *Signora*." He pointed to a room off to the side before he pulled out her chair. "I will be in here if you need me; Ricardo will remain outside and will take care to not block your view."

She wanted to ask if Giovanni was still at the house as she suspected, but Raphael walked into the other room and she was alone. A short, plump man in a white chef's coat and hat appeared from the room across from her and gave a small bow as he placed a plate of antipasto and a larger-than-needed glass of wine in front of her. "*Buon appetito, Signora*."

"*Grazie*." She was starving; there was zero reason to insult the poor cook because she was annoyed with Giovanni.

What kind of man fabricated a fake job in order to create a reason for his lover to accompany him on a trip? A man with an ego the size of its own galaxy and enough money to buy the world, she mused, and one who was incapable of taking *no* for an answer. The more she pushed him, the more he would push back if only to win.

She wondered if the olives and wine came from the property. With so many options at his disposal, why were drugs and murder Giovanni's choices? Of course, Lexi had to admit, he had this many options because of the life he led. Still, couldn't he at least consider better? Wasn't there better to consider? And what would her life look like the longer she spent with him?

Lexi nearly choked on a piece of spicy salami at the question as it innocently passed through her mind. Had she actually forgotten who she was? In only a week, Giovanni had her unable to see clearly. *Keep your head in the game*, she commanded.

The problem was that Lexi didn't know what game she was playing. She had never desired to be a federal agent. She had chosen Italian for a degree and then had decided to pursue her love of books and research by completing her Library Science degree at the same time. She had spent nearly every waking moment taking classes or doing homework, and had managed to complete both the degrees in five years, pulling full summer loads and working on campus doing various jobs in whatever minimal time she had left. She had pushed everything into school, and, by graduation, had already lined up an internship to begin learning the techniques for restoring antique Italian manuscripts. At twenty-two, she had been full of dreams and promise.

Her father's death had depressurized her, and Lexi had plagued Sam with questions he couldn't answer. Why had her father been killed? Why was no one looking for the answers? Who had destroyed their family? After Sam had confessed his suspicions that her father had finally uncovered the mole the OCTF had been looking for, her world further crashed. His belief that the Masseretti family was responsible for the actual killing became the tiny bit of focus she needed to keep breathing.

Sam had begged her to reconsider the Academy, as had her mother who couldn't cope with the idea of losing her only child in addition to her husband, but Lexi hadn't listened. When her acceptance from Quantico had arrived, rather than elation, she had felt nothing. She had reported for her four months of training and focused on graduation. Her classmates had discussed their goals of working for the Bureau while Lexi mourned the life she had planned alongside the loss of her father. Instead of hating the endless drills and pressure, she tried to let it fuel her desire for revenge.

But revenge didn't make her into a better agent. When she graduated and was given permanent dispatch to the FBI Library, she tried to make the most of her love of research by learning everything she could about the mob families that still ran New York, chief among them the Masseretti's. She would take the train back monthly to visit her mother and would pump Sam for information. As the years went by, she began to consider what it would take to bring Giovanni to his knees. After the last agent that the Organized Crime Task Force had tried to insert failed, the idea of trying to imbed a woman in lieu of a wiseguy began to take shape.

After deciding that, statistically, the best option for avoiding detection would be a relationship with a low-level mobster, Lexi had pitched the idea to Sam, who outright rejected her plan. He refused to back her and admonished her for even considering a transfer. Lexi had never planned to talk to the OCTF Director, but, when he had been at the Academy for an awards ceremony, she had ended up confronting him about her father's death and the Bureau's lack of action. She had barely made it home from the evening when Sam had called her in a rage. Was she crazy? What was she thinking? Hadn't he told her that he would take care of it?

Shortly after, Lexi had celebrated her twenty-eighth birthday with her mother and Sam, who took the occasion to tell her that they were dating and were interested in pursuing something more. She had no hard feelings; they had been friends and had both loved her father. She wished them well and gave her blessing before returning to the Academy and her job. Before she had left, her mother had repeated Sam's message that Lexi move on and forget about trying to hold the Masseretti family responsible for something that there was no concrete evidence for pursuing.

When Sam had suddenly changed speeds, Lexi had assumed it was a combination of her constant harassment alongside her mother's death. She had never planned to end her FBI career. She had never thought she would find herself surrounded by rare books and living her dream. She sure as hell had never seen herself finding some sort of, dare she even think it, *happiness* with Giovanni Masseretti.

Giovanni was everything she was not and the image of everything she didn't want. She had dated off and on in college; during her twenties, Lexi had cycled through a few different agents and even a local assistant district attorney. Her longest relationship had been another librarian- and that was only six weeks. Thinking back, she had judged Giovanni for going through women like they were an endless supply for his use. She had been little different in her speed dating of men that she had possessed no connection with.

Lexi had been the problem; she simply wasn't open to whatever they were offering. The men had all been nice and accommodating, yet she was bored. There was no flicker of fire or spark of something that caused her heart to beat faster. The sex had been decent, but it paled in comparison to the heat that Giovanni brought to the table. The memory of him pushing her against the pizzeria was still exhilarating. The more recent memories of his bedroom and his belt made her flush.

She cut her thoughts off as she saw the cook returning. He looked down at her half-eaten plate of food. "Is not good?" he asked in broken English.

"It's very good! *Questa è più che buona. È spettacolare!*" Lexi offered him a kind smile. "I'm just tired from traveling, that's all. It's really wonderful."

"I bring you something else?" He was clutching his hands as though her not eating greatly disturbed him.

"No, I'll wait until dinner." She smiled at him with her newly decided request. "Giovanni mentioned letting you know what I would like."

He nodded. "I cook for you what you like." This seemed to lighten his mood until she spoke.

"Can you teach me how to make *carrettiera*?" When the chef looked at her quizzically, she repeated the request in Italian and he shook his head.

"No, *Signora, I* cook for *you*. You don't need to work."

"I want you to *teach* me." Self-depreciatingly, she laughed. "I can't cook. I don't know how. I want to learn to make *carrettiera*."

"But *Don* Giovanni-"

"I want to make it *for Don* Giovanni." She stood up when he took her plate and noticed Raphael in the doorway. "Raphael, am I allowed into the kitchen?"

The look on his face betrayed that he found her request odd. He looked at the plate of antipasto. "Are you hungry?"

"No, I want to learn how to cook, but I think that the chef is concerned that I'll be doing something Giovanni wouldn't like. Did he say I couldn't go to the kitchen?"

"No, but-"

She looked back to the chef, who was still shaking his head. "See? *Don* Giovanni doesn't care. It's fine. When should I meet you?"

After killing time in a first-floor library, Lexi took a walk around a trail near the house. It pissed her off to have an escort everywhere she went, but the scenic views were beautiful. She could see all the way to the coast; wherever she looked, the landscape was lush and overflowing with colors. To combat the heat of the afternoon, she took another swim before she showered and dressed. The bright red of the wrap dress brought out the natural streaks of auburn in her hair and the blue trim incited her eyes to shine.

She thought the chef looked nervous when Raphael brought her to the kitchen. "Are you sure, *Signora*? I can cook for you. What if you are burned?"

It would probably be less painful than some of what Giovanni had already subjected her to. "I'll be fine. Don't worry." She clapped her hands together. "How do we start?"

Based on the few ingredients that were on the counter, pasta shouldn't have been difficult. It looked like some flours, a few eggs, salt, and water. How hard could it be? After crafting two balls of dough that the chef deemed impossible, she started her third attempt. At this rate, they wouldn't be eating dinner anytime soon. However, with a nod of his head and a "*Buono*," the final ball was considered acceptable.

After he taught her how to create a tomato puree, she minced large cloves of garlic, which she added into the tomatoes before streaming in olive oil. Finally, while the chef looked on in terror, she chiffonaded fresh herbs and stirred the thin strips of green into the bowl. The pasta that she cut into thin, flat noodles cooked in the boiled water in what seemed like seconds, and she tossed them in with the tomatoes before dropping a hearty handful of cheese that she had grated herself into the mixture alongside drizzling a thin stream of the boiling pasta water.

She heard Raphael cough from the doorway. He didn't say anything, but Lexi assumed that Giovanni was finished with whatever he was doing and that she was being given the option to go to him before he found her. "*Grazie*," she said to the chef graciously. "I will try to remember everything."

"No," he said emphatically. It was clear that he was as nervous of her dinner attempt as she was. "I cook for you tomorrow."

Giovanni was walking through the courtyard as she stepped outside. He had his hands in his pockets as though he had been strolling the property and his gun was missing. She wondered who he had spent the afternoon with but didn't want to ruin the evening by asking. As he approached, he smirked and looked at her dress. He fingered the bib of the apron she had forgotten to take off and, after she untied it, slipped it over her head to give it to Raphael's waiting hand. "Don't you look like a *casalinga*."

He kissed her after wiping a smudge of flour from her cheek, then pulled out her chair from a table on the candlelit promenade. After sitting down next to her, Giovanni poured from an iced bottle of rosato. "I hear you're attempting to poison me tonight."

"Your poor chef seems worried about that possibility." She took a drink of the cool wine and leaned back in her seat as the older man approached the table with two plates that looked not only edible but beautiful. "If you hate it, don't tell him. He was miserable when I asked to cook, and I think he would have given anything for me to leave his kitchen alone."

Giovanni watched her over the hand he balanced his lips on. "It's not the role of a gentleman to eat first."

Lexi made a production of turning around and looking throughout the courtyard. "I think you're safe; I don't see any gentlemen around." He chuckled then took a bite from his plate while keeping his eyes on hers. In that moment, while she waited nervously for his response, Lexi thought she might serve him a run-on sentence of the truth instead of the pasta dish. She had suspected before, but now she knew. She was in love with Giovanni.

She had read psychology briefs her last week in DC as she tried her best to prepare for what life undercover might encompass. Falling in love was usually an immediate and unstable response driven by lust and desire. Lexi had blown off the report, promising herself that she could keep whatever lust rolled her way at bay because she would be sitting in front of a killer. That alone would be enough. Knowing Giovanni was responsible for her father's death would be a constant knife in her heart, making it impossible for her to develop any feelings, stable or otherwise.

She had expected her need for revenge to cause a flashing devil to appear over Giovanni. Instead, she had felt the heat as he eradicated the numb. She may have felt fear because of what she knew he was capable of, but it wasn't hatred for what Sam had assured her Giovanni was guilty of. Now, not only was she wrong about her suspicions of his past, but Lexi was also wrong about how she would respond to him. Heartbreakingly wrong.

Watching him eat the first meal that she had ever attempted to make for anyone, Lexi knew that she had no choice but to somehow find the words to tell him the truth. The lies of omission were the vestiges of the emptiness and they pushed at her resolve, promising her that Giovanni would never be able to forgive or accept her. As she felt the edges of the cold trying to wrap around her, Lexi knew that she had to risk his hatred rather than undermine her love. She blinked to try and laugh off the heaviness when he reached across the table to stroke her face after saying her name softly. "Sorry. I was waiting for you to drop dead."

Giovanni took another bite and shook his head. "You're a shitty liar."

He had no idea, and that made his comment hurt far more than it otherwise would have. Every moment with him was a betrayal. When

Giovanni found out, what would he do? Lexi tried to smile as she redirected his attention to the meal. "How is it?"

"It's quite good. You made it?"

"From the third attempt at pasta to the sauce: all without burning myself." She waved her fingers before reaching for her wine. "I even managed to avoid cutting these off!"

Before she could lift the glass, Giovanni had her hand and kissed her fingers. "That's a good thing, seeing as I like what these feel like." When she blushed, he returned to his meal. "Eat, Alessandra; I know you haven't eaten well."

"What is your obsession with food?"

"*Il cibo è vita.*"

"That sounds like the mantra for an eating disorder." She took a bite of the *carrettiera* and, while her sauce was thinner than Giovanni's had been, the taste was fresh and she was impressed with her attempt.

"You speak fluently, but did you not visit to understand the people and the culture?"

"I spent my time studying and trying to eek out two degrees while working." She moved her fork back and forth. "I fell in love with languages when I was in high school: first Spanish, then Italian. For better and for worse, Italian stole my heart." Lexi thought about the two-week trip to Italy she had planned after graduation and tried to shake off the memory. "But, to answer your question, my Italian experiences are limited to the ethnic churches I like to visit for spaghetti suppers and pizzerias where I'm manhandled in back rooms by inappropriate men." Whenever Giovanni watched her, she wondered what he was thinking and, at the moment, he was looking at her like he knew every secret and every truth. "You're watching me again."

"I like watching you. Eat," he commanded, dropping his eyes to her barely touched plate.

She cocked her head. "Pay for it."

"What?" he asked with a laugh.

"You like games; play a game with me. For everything you tell me about yourself, I'll take a bite." She looked at her plate. "It'll probably be far less painful for you than those fifteen minutes I owe."

Mischievousness and amusement shone in his eyes. "Alright."

"And it has to be something you haven't already told me. None of this *I'm the oldest* stuff. I know that already." She poised the fork full of pasta and, after a few seconds of silence, asked, "How much do you really want me to eat something?"

He tapped his fingers on the bowl of his wine glass before saying at last, "When I was a kid, I thought I'd grow up to be a policeman."

"You're lying." She couldn't even move the fork.

"Eat." He took a drink of wine. "Or the game's over and I'll add five minutes to your running tally for breaking your word." After she ate the forkful of pasta, he continued, "No, it's true. My mother even has a picture of me in a policeman's uniform. I think I was six? Seven? I don't remember."

"What changed your mind?" She twirled more pasta onto her fork. Giovanni a cop? That was an impossible thought.

"I was a kid." He ate from his own plate. "*Comandare é meglio che fottere.*"

"You realized that power was better than sex as a kid? Damn, Gio, no wonder you're so good at this." When he grinned, she ate her required bite and poised another.

"I was meant to do this," he said, after a moment. "This is who I am."

"None of us are *meant* to be something. We choose it. We become it. We embrace it or we hate it, but it's our choice nonetheless."

"And you, *bambina*? Are you what you have chosen to be?" That intense stare was back.

She didn't know if he'd earned it, but she took a bite regardless to create space. "I never saw myself like this, no."

Giovanni leaned on his wrist while he watched her prepare another fork of pasta before he rolled up his right sleeve and extended his arm on the table. On his lower forearm, she saw the scar. "It's from a bullet," he said, causing the muscle to flex. "It's from the first time I was shot; I was seventeen."

"Oh my God," she whispered. "Seventeen? What happened?"

He sighed and bit his bottom lip. "In the heart of Palermo, there is a night club that I frequented as a teenager. I was drinking with friends and I, perhaps unintentionally, perhaps not, insulted the girlfriend of a visiting *Don*. He didn't appreciate it."

"He shot you?"

"No," Gio said as he shook his head. "He offered me a job."

"What?" The fork stopped midway to her mouth and Lexi gave up, dropping it and trading the silverware for her wine glass.

"As we stumbled into the night, several of his bodyguards approached while the Boss watched from his car. When they drew, so did we. The first round went through my arm, but," he shrugged, "I have two."

Lexi paused to consider this. She had struggled to be a decent shot with her right hand; holding a gun in her left hand felt awkward and she couldn't imagine firing it with accuracy. "You switched hands." When he nodded once, she swallowed before asking, "And you killed him?"

"No, I deserved it." He chuckled. "I was running my mouth."

Lexi's eyes widened. "You don't shoot people for insulting your girlfriend!"

"Would you like to know what my father said when I showed up, shot and bleeding?" Giovanni refilled his wine glass. *"Imagine a world where men knew that to dare insult a woman would result in a bullet to the arm.* Do you think we would have women raped when they were merely walking from their dorm to a library if men knew that even looking let alone daring to speak could get them shot?"

Lexi did her best not to flinch, but the comment slapped her in the face. Was he admitting to killing the hitman who had raped the college sophomore several years before? "What did you say?"

"You spent several years on a campus. Did you feel safe traveling the grounds at night?" He took a drink of his wine. "I don't think Theresa was out of anyone's sight for the four years that she was away. Of course," he laughed, obviously thinking of his sister with fondness, "after growing up the baby of five brothers, she is probably more capable than most of protecting herself."

"And she managed to find a husband that you didn't have to shoot in the arm," Lexi said with a smirk over her wine glass. When Giovanni merely smiled, Lexi realized that there was more to the story. "What *did* you do to him?"

"I didn't shoot him." He opened his hands innocently.

"If you expect me to finish this last bite, then you owe me more than that." Lexi pushed the food around her plate.

"I was right when I said you reminded me of Theresa." He nodded at her as if to say, *eat*.

"How so?"

"You both get away with murder."

"I don't know that my ass agrees with that statement." At this, his grin deepened into a smile, and she had to look away. "And those fifteen minutes you're lording over me say that I'm not going to get away with anything. I will more than pay for it."

Giovanni chuckled again. "Theresa studied architecture with a minor in fashion. Her last semester, she convinced our father to let her study in Florence. Now," he shifted in his chair, "you must understand, *bambina*: nothing is hidden."

Lexi remembered her two-bodyguard detail. "She had people with her."

"Every second of every day. It became a game." He moved his fingers as though playing chess and smiled a devious smile at Lexi. "The more she tried to hide, the more we simply hid the surveillance so that she believed she had won. Eventually, she thought that we had given up. She would maneuver these elaborate meetings with girlfriends and then try to sneak away. She once pretended to be sick and in the college infirmary, only to escape down an emergency exit. My father even called to yell at her for eluding security, all while we knew exactly where she was."

"She's your sister, Gio, not your target." Lexi crossed her arms and scowled. She felt angry for Theresa. "She should smack the hell out of you."

"When she found out, she did but she," he played with his glass before returning the look of overplayed innocence, "hits like a girl."

Fuck, he was sexy. Lexi wanted to show him exactly how hard she could knock that smile off his lips- right after she threw herself in his lap and devoured them. She fought the urge. "No wonder she thinks you're an asshole."

He scoffed. "Less now than then, I'm sure."

"So what did you do?"

"Her deception was obviously about a man. No one cared about her coffees and shopping trips. Why so much deception? A man. A Florentine." The way he said it implied disgust. "Of all of the men in Italy, she couldn't be bothered to find one who came from the island or even one of the great cities. No, Theresa had to fall in love with a fucking Florentine."

Lexi decided to fuel the fire. "Florence is a beautiful city with a rich history." She took a grape from a bowl of fruit that appeared on the table when the chef discretely removed their empty plates. After rolling it along her bottom lip, she placed it in her mouth, similar to Giovanni's feeding of her an olive at the pizzeria. He was still watching her intently when she slowly licked her fingertips. "Florentine men are probably an exemplary example of the sexy Italian that us girls are so easy to fall for." She pursed her lips as though the idea were a delicious one and added, suggestively, "*Amato molto bello.*"

Giovanni bit his lip before he responded. "I know what you're doing."

"I'm just giving Theresa's husband the benefit of the doubt." Lexi returned the raised eyebrows and open-handed innocence. "You were saying?"

He growled and shifted in his seat. "Lorenzo and I decided to go to Florence ourselves. Theresa hadn't expected that and, when we showed up at Francesco's flat- where she had spent the night- she was mortified. She gave some song about how it was true love, but we didn't listen. We left with a half-naked Francesco and with her crying after us."

Lexi's annoyance was back. "She was a grown woman, Gio. It's not like you weren't sleeping around."

"The difference is that he was sleeping with *my* sister."

"I bet the girls you fucked were also someone's sister. At the least, they were someone's daughter." Lexi took another drink of her wine while he didn't bother to refute her. "Your double standard is appalling." He didn't continue and she picked up another berry from the bowl. "This counts as a bite and I'm still waiting to hear how you didn't shoot him."

He shook his head slowly. "What are we up to? Sixteen? Seventeen?"

"I'll deduct time if you can't manage to keep up your end of the bargain," she smarted back.

"Lorenzo and I took him to a friend's place."

"You have friends? That's a shocker."

He chuckled after a drink. "Seventeen. We weren't going to hurt him, merely convince him to fuck someone else's sister. Unfortunately, we didn't know then that he has a severe allergy to alcohol."

Lexi stopped eating the fruit she was toying with. What had they done? Waterboarded him with wine? "What do you mean?"

As he remembered the event, Giovanni didn't even have the grace to look penitent. "We were practically drowning him with bottles of whatever we had handy. Francesco, not once, said anything except how much he loved Theresa, how he was going to ask Pop to marry her, and then, all of a sudden, his throat started to swell. We nearly killed him- completely by accident. We got him to the hospital, but," he laughed, "Theresa was so pissed she didn't speak to us for weeks."

"You really are a piece of work."

The chef returned with full hands. He presented a snifter of something alcoholic to Giovanni after he placed the plate with a *biscotti di mandorla* accenting a wide-bowled cappuccino mug in front of her. Even in the candlelight, she could see the elegant artwork in the foam.

When she looked up, Giovanni was leaning against his palm again, still watching her. Once the chef left, she decided to fuck with him some more. Lexi lifted the cup and dipped her tongue into the foam. After drawing it into her mouth, she licked her lips before murmuring, *"Ottimo."* The look of heat was written all over his face, and she relaxed in her chair.

"Eighteen." Giovanni smirked. "You aren't getting away with this."

She drew her shoulders up and lowered them to push her chest forward before suggestively twirling her finger in the hot milk foam and sucking it off. Lexi felt the thought before it registered in her head; she could play this game. He wanted her to play, but, more importantly, *she* wanted to play it alongside him. "I thought food is the pleasure of life. Isn't that the quote? Or do I need a native tongue to explain it to me in a language I'll understand?"

Giovanni stood up and grabbed her by the hand, dragging her toward the house. "I can't run in heeled sandals!" She screamed in surprise when he easily tossed her across his shoulder and stalked to the stairs leading to their bedroom. When he deposited her on the edge of the bed, she bounced and slid slightly backward.

His hands made easy work of her; one pulled her up by the dress's belt, simultaneously opening up the wrap, while the other decimated her hair as it directed her to his mouth. His kiss was rough and his tongue devoured hers; he bit into her bottom lip. "*Quando mi fai questo, perdo la testa,*" Giovanni said between harsh breaths. "You tell me you don't know the rules, but I think you're fucking with me and, goddammit, I don't even care anymore."

Before she could answer, he had her on her back and was on top of her, the wrap dress open and revealing the set of silver lace that she had paired with it. "Fuck," he sighed, running his hands over the barely covering fabric. "You fucking sit across from me, dressed like this. *Sei proprio una provocatrice del cazzo.*"

"Coming from a lesser man, I'd consider that insulting." She lifted her freed hand and trailed her fingers down his arm. "I might even have to shoot him."

Before she could breathe again, he had her pressed between him and the wooden bed pole. Just as he unhooked her bra, she heard a knock and then the door began to open. She gasped and grabbed at the dress while Giovanni turned and covered her with his own body. "*Che cazzo vuoi?*" he growled angrily.

"*Mi scusi,* Don Giovanni. *Credo che siamo già tutti d'accordo.*" Raphael's face indicated that he understood Giovanni hadn't wanted to be interrupted. He switched to Sicilian after his apology, and Lexi tried to turn off the part of her brain that knew something bad was about to happen.

Every muscle in his body was taut when Giovanni turned back to her, brushing her face with his fingertips. His voice was low, a cross between sexual need and gentleness. "I have to go, *bambina*. My apologies. I will," he kissed her delicately, "find a way to make this up to you."

Lexi's breath was slowing down and, as Giovanni neared the exit where Raphael had once stood, she called out to him, "Five minutes." He looked back over his shoulder. "You owe me five minutes of whatever I want." She retied the dress but never broke eye contact. "It's the price for leaving."

Giovanni didn't answer, smiling lightly with a nod before walking into the front room of the suite and out the door. Lexi fell back against the bed and exhaled deeply. She was completely riled up and thought her entire body might explode from want. She heard car doors slam and she got up from the bed, walking toward the balcony and seeing lights as they tore down the road. Where was he going? What was so important that Raphael had come to get him?

She was nothing but a ball of energy that needed to decompress. Lexi returned to the library she had found before, but she couldn't settle on anything to read. She tried a few books, but nothing held her interest. She nearly asked Ricardo, whom she saw lingering from a distance wherever she went, if he wanted to play cards but figured he would say no. Aimlessly wandering around the massive estate, she found a room that met her needs. When she saw her bodyguard watching her from the door, she decided to save him the trouble of following her back to her room. "I'm going to change clothes. I'll be back."

He nodded only to trail behind her. She nearly told him that she knew enough of the floor plan to get back but decided against it. At this point, she could see the bodyguards. Remembering the cautionary tale of Theresa believing she had managed to shake them gave her enough concern that Lexi didn't want to attempt anything similar. In that game, Giovanni would always win.

Ricardo waited outside the main door while she went into the suite alone. After pulling out a pair of compression shorts and a sports bra from the drawer, she dressed while keeping her feet bare. She didn't need footwear to practice the kickboxing that she had started learning before moving to New York.

Ricardo gave a quick look of surprise before looking away and following her back to the first-floor gym. She found tape and wrapped her knuckles and toes before she powdered her hands and began to work out her sexual frustrations on the bag. The bracelet added a weight to her right hand that she wasn't used to. It seemed odd to box in such an expensive piece of jewelry, but Lexi didn't have much of a choice; she continued to punch and kick the bag.

Her body was covered in sweat by the time she heard Giovanni talking to someone as he walked into the house. When he appeared in the doorway and watched her with a grin, she ignored him until he addressed her. He looked just as he had when he had left, except for the holstered SIG that had returned to his chest. "Not a room I thought to find you in."

"I didn't think Ricardo would be interested in boxing me, and I wanted to hit something. I'm sure you understand how that is."

He bit the inside of his cheek and said seductively, *"Culo, quella bocca."*

"I offered," she said, throwing her fist into the bag again. "You declined."

"That's not the way it happened." He approached her and put his hands on her waist. "Work."

"You owe me five minutes." Lexi put distance between them by pushing her fingers into his chest as he chuckled and stepped back.

"And how will you use those five minutes?"

She hit the bag again before standing and making her challenge. "Box with me."

"I don't think so."

"Not up for the game?" Lexi shifted her weight. "Afraid you'll lose?"

He scoffed. "I've seen your moves. You wouldn't stand a chance."

"Afraid you don't really know how a girl hits?" She continued to provoke him, knowing full well that they had an audience of at least half-a-dozen bodyguards hidden only a few feet away. As Ricardo had waited, two men she hadn't recognized joined him. Giovanni's arrival had returned

Raphael, and he was followed soon after by two more men. "Afraid to find out?"

When he removed the holster and placed it on a table behind him, she saw his pleasure at the challenge. "You're already up to eighteen," he said, walking slowly toward her.

Lexi knew she would get no real chance to strike first so she planned for a defensive counter. He wasn't going to throw a punch, she presumed. He would try to incapacitate her and then use that to inflict enough pain that she would confess defeat. While she expected as much, she knew that it was the split second between being grabbed and then his choice of where to inflict pain that would be the sweet spot. He stalked toward her in his designer suit and leather shoes, but Lexi had the upper hand. She had no clothes he could pull on, and her bare feet gave her a stability that she hadn't had before.

"I'm surprised you aren't running away, baby girl. Isn't this the point where you usually search out the elevator?" he teased.

"I'm just wondering what it was tonight that has tired you out so much that you can't manage a walk to the other side of the room faster than my grandmother." When he leapt for her and easily captured her, Lexi lowered her center of gravity and threw him over her shoulder, hearing him hit the wooden floor with a thud. Rising from her knees, she smirked when he looked over his head at her from the ground. "You fight like her, too."

"Nineteen." Giovanni stood up and took a step closer to her. His voice gave away his enjoyment of her game.

"I think I may have to start deducting time if you can't move faster than my Nana." Giovanni wouldn't be easy to throw off again. She calculated exactly how far she needed to get outside into the courtyard. Lexi couldn't let him grab hold of her, and she watched his body language for the tiny change that would tell her he was coming for her. She nearly missed the cue. He caught her arm as she turned around him, her sweat aiding her slip through his fingers. Even though she got away, he had slowed her down enough that he was right on her heels.

He grabbed her and pulled her against him just as she reached the swimming pool. "When I get you inside," he growled, "I'm going to enjoy the time I have completely owning you."

"You should go ahead and make it twenty," she whispered before throwing her body backward. Together, they splashed into the pool. As she came up for air, she saw the bodyguards standing on the patio, and she couldn't help laughing before Giovanni pushed her head beneath the water. She bobbed back to the surface still laughing. "I hope," she sputtered, "you have a personal dry cleaner here or those pants are ruined."

Giovanni held her tightly in the water, waving his hand to the guards. "I like it when you laugh like this." He pushed the hair from her face before he kissed her delicately. "But if this is your attempt at beating me, I think you've failed."

"I don't know about that." Lexi grinned. "Now I'm not the only one who's wet."

10

After a few minutes, Raphael brought large towels and Giovanni pushed his body out of the pool, cursing. "You have more clothes and shoes than most women do." Lexi laughed as she pulled herself onto the patio. "I think you'll find replacements just fine."

He wrapped her in a towel. "I might just take yours and force you to stay naked."

"That's not a threat you'll follow through with." Lexi leaned against him to whisper, "Cross dressing didn't show up as one of your kinks in any of my Google searches." She pulled back and bit her lip. "Prove me wrong, Gio."

He dropped his head back, exuding a sexy chuckle. "You know the game," he said before kissing her again. "That makes it all the harder to say goodnight."

"Goodnight?"

"I need to take care of some things." He ordered one of the men to bring new clothes to his office. "I would come back to the bedroom, but I don't know that I could get away without fucking you until you fell asleep."

"Your loss," she answered before knotting the towel around her chest.

"It is. Indeed." Giovanni kissed her a final time, letting his lips rest against hers. "I will make this night up to you tomorrow."

She watched him walk inside, surrounded by his entourage of armed guards. Ricardo waited by the door, and Lexi gave him a small wave before bypassing the main level and walking up the stone staircase that led to her balcony. Once inside, she took a steaming shower and dressed in one of Giovanni's shirts instead of choosing a silk negligee from the variety of choices that lined a drawer of her dresser. As much as she wanted to wait for him to return, the boxing had done the trick. She had worked through the sexual tension, and her body was ready to follow her brain into sleep.

It was dark when Lexi opened her eyes and saw him sitting in the bedside chair closest to her. Where had he gone? What had he done? He was still wearing his vest, shirt, and slacks, but his tie was missing and the top button of his shirt was open. The light from the full moon illuminated the magazine floorplate of the SIG in its holster. The heat from his hand caused the ice in the glass he held to shift as it melted, breaking the sound of his near-silent breathing.

Giovanni stared at her in the darkness. She sat up, her hair falling around her shoulders; unsure of herself, Lexi stood and took a few steps forward. Giovanni didn't move, continuing to watch her as she shyly approached. Coming to a stop in front of him, she knelt down.

It was hard to read his gaze, and she had no idea what she could offer him. After all of the sexual tension from earlier, sex seemed the easy answer. Reading the little information she could see said that Giovanni needed more from her. Even though Lexi wasn't sure what that meant, she curled up between his legs and laid her head against his thigh. Her arms lightly cradled his leg and waist.

She felt his hand against her head; his fingers gently caressed her hair and, in that moment, in spite of everything wrong about them, the world felt right. A sense of contentment fell over Lexi as she closed her eyes. At some point, she began to doze back to sleep and was startled when Giovanni stood up to remove his holster and gun. He lowered himself to scoop her into his arms and, wordlessly, tucked her back into bed. She watched him undress and walk into the shower. Her fitness band told her tired eyes that it was still an hour or so before sunrise, and she eventually fell back to sleep to the sound of the water.

When she woke again, the sun was already shining through the windows and she was alone. Draped across the chair where she had seen Giovanni a few hours before was a summery white dress covered in lemons that looked ripe for squeezing. Leather sandals in a matching yellow and with squared heels waited beneath the chair. On the table where he had placed the SIG before he carried her to bed, a vase full of freshly cut flowers nearly overflowed. She lightly touched a bloom on her way to the shower.

Once she slipped into underwear and blew her hair into long waves, Lexi dressed as she assumed Giovanni had intended. After securing the sandals, she exited into the empty sitting room and pulled the door to the hallway open. "*Buongiorno*, Ricardo," she said pleasantly to the man who stood ready.

"*Buongiorno, Signora. Don* Giovanni asks that you join him for breakfast."

She was pretty sure that Giovanni had done nothing of the sort and had ordered her brought to him like she was a cup of his beloved espresso, but Lexi appreciated Ricardo's attempt. She walked in front of him down the stairs, following his hand when he guided her through the house to the courtyard and a covered side porch where Giovanni sat with coffee in one hand and his phone in the other.

When he saw her, Giovanni waved her forward, and Ricardo slowed so that she could continue alone. He hung up the phone when she approached. Her hair flowed over his hand as he softly wrapped it around her neck to pull her close for a kiss. "*Buongiorno, bambina.* You look beautiful."

She took him in. He wasn't wearing the suit jacket he had tossed in a chair next to him and had paired his charcoal vest, tie, and slacks with a dark shirt. The SIG she abhorred had returned to his chest. "*Grazie. Buongiorno.*"

"I ordered breakfast for you." He opened up his hand to offer her the seat next to him on the outdoor couch, and the sunlight lit up his watch when he waved at someone she didn't see. "Something you'll like, I think."

"That has me slightly nervous coming from you." She saw the chef approaching. He sat down a demitasse refill for Giovanni along with a shapely glass that looked almost like shaved ice accompanied by a slice of thick, buttered bread. "*Granita?*"

"*Granita di mandorla.*" Giovanni nodded. "The almonds come from just down the road, and Fernando makes a loaf of *brioscia* daily."

"*Grazie,*" she said to the cook as he left. She turned back to Giovanni. "You aren't having anything?"

"I've been up since before the sun." He smiled, but the look didn't reach his eyes.

Lexi remembered the night before with a pang of worry. "Are you alright?"

Giovanni reached out and touched her hair, much as he had when she had knelt in front of him, and she unconsciously closed her eyes, curving into his hand. "I'm touched to know you care."

"I do care." Lexi opened her eyes and pulled away. "Do you doubt that?"

He touched her mouth with his thumb. "Sometimes what we see in front of us is difficult to believe."

He didn't answer her question, and Lexi wished she had sunglasses to keep the hurt from that simple refusal off her face. She used the spoon from the small plate to break into the *granita*, but she only played with the cascading shards. When Giovanni touched her shoulder, she looked up at him. His voice held secrets she couldn't begin to uncover. "It was a long night, but it's taken care of and I'm fine."

She turned back to the shaved ice, rewarding his answer with a small bite. The dish was sweet with a distinct almond sting that transported the taste to savory as the ice melted and she swallowed. "It's very good," she said, glancing at him. "I've never had an almond version before, only fruity and sugary."

"Very American."

"It's what the mutts like," she replied, taking another bite. "We can't all be perfect and Italian."

At her reply, Giovanni grinned and this one lit up his eyes. "What is your background, Alessandra? Despite your Italian name and hardheadedness, you are not from Calabria."

"My mother's family is Scottish. She was an amateur ballerina who had hoped to dance before she became a teacher. She loved Alessandra Ferri and, when she got pregnant, decided to name me in her honor." She thought of her mother with fondness and missed her more than she had before. Her mother would have known what to do. Lexi wished that she could talk to her one last time. "Mom wanted me to dance, but I was awful. I didn't have the temperament- or so *Madame* Villet told me on several occasions. By the time I was twelve, my mother gave up and told me I could stop lessons."

"You miss her."

"Very much," she choked out. Lexi stabbed at the ice with her spoon. "I kept her cell phone active after she died. At first, I just- I couldn't get rid of it. I couldn't imagine someone else having the number. I don't know. That sounds stupid."

"It doesn't," he reassured her, his fingers delicately stroking her back.

"When I miss her a lot, I call it just to hear her voice. During the important parts of my life that she's missing, like getting the job in New York, I've even left her messages." She wiped a tear before it fell. "That sounds so insane when I say it aloud."

His voice was full of compassion, and Giovanni transformed his fingers into an arm around her. He pulled Lexi against his shoulder so that his lips could graze her temple. "It's not insane, Alessandra. It's love. Love makes us do things that defy all reasonable explanation."

Lexi forced an exhale so that she could pull herself together and she sat up, trying to go back to the conversation with hopes to clear her head. "Masters is Welsh."

"So it seems I was mistaken," Giovanni said, easily moving the discussion forward. He offered her a smirk that she couldn't help but grin in response to. "You aren't too much of a mutt after all."

"Several generations in, I'm sure there is enough mixed in to make me more of a mutt than you are." She lifted the bread which shared the texture of a French brioche and was sweetened by the creamy butter. "And you, of course, are as full-blooded Italian as they come, am I right?"

"Not *Italian*." He scoffed the word as though the mere thought was offensive.

"Sorry. *Sicilian*," she corrected with a laugh. "I know there's still a lot of contention, even a hundred and fifty years later."

"Even if you were right, Italy is not *one* people, but many. Sicily, even more so. You don't need to look farther than my family to see that."

Lexi thought back to his father, who Giovanni was a younger replica of, and his tiny mother with the twinkling, green eyes. He had brothers who were blonde down to his black hair; their eyes, too, had been a range of colors as had their skin tones. While all of them shared the smile that Lexi recognized from his mother, Theresa was as light as Lexi was and Giovanni looked as though he had been made of bronze. They were very much the same and yet incredibly different.

"Today," Giovanni continued, "many still speak their regional dialects as their native tongue. Everyone learns Italian in school and, unless you are a *nonno* who refuses to adapt, all the people can communicate in a common language, but it is much like the northern countries of Europe. On top of those differences, Sicily is its own unique culture; to call it merely *Italian* would be to call the Welsh or Scottish *English* because England owns the right to the land."

"Is this one of the many reasons you don't like Florentine men? They have no hope of being Sicilian?"

The melody of his laughter filled the air. "My nephews and niece are now mutts because of Theresa's affinity." He ran his fingers up and down her arm. "We are all mutts on some level, I suppose. My father was born and raised in Palermo, but my mother came from Catanzaro."

Lexi smiled at the memory of his threat to carry her across the deck to his parents' home and the comment that they would have questioned whether or not she was from Calabria, where the people were known to be stubborn and hotheaded. "Your mother is Calabrese."

"Oh yes," Giovanni said, drinking his coffee. "And Theresa is much like her. All of you women are nothing but headaches."

"Perhaps if you Sicilians would learn to listen, you wouldn't have to worry." He smiled at her when he replaced his empty cup on the tray that covered the coffee table. "How did your parents meet? Palermo and Calabria aren't exactly close."

"My mother visited Catania for a school trip. My father was in the area, saw her, and," he slapped his heart with his open palm, "was hit by the arrow of love."

"That is so romantic." She took another bite of her *granita*. "What a sweet story."

"It's very sweet, *bambina*. He kidnapped her from the hotel where she was staying and brought her home."

Stilled midswallow, Lexi finally let the melting ice slide down her throat. "You're joking, right?"

"She was quite unimpressed by his declaration that she was to be his wife and mother his children. According to my father, he sent word to her parents that they could either attend a wedding or a funeral."

"He was going to kill her?"

"No." Giovanni laughed, standing up and lifting his jacket from the seat next to him. "It was a threat aimed at my grandfather: *give your daughter in marriage or I'll take her*. It was a different time."

"I see where you get your *I take what I want* attitude." She let him pull her to her feet and they began to walk in the direction he led. "So what happened?"

"My grandfather gave his blessing once he knew with whom he was dealing. My mother, however, wasn't convinced and wasn't permitted to speak at the wedding. The priest pronounced them married without her consent, and she opted to bite my father when he tried to kiss her."

"I like your mother even more."

"I bet you do." They stopped in front of a Mercedes S550 that was sandwiched between two BMW X5s, and she asked where they were going when he opened the door. "Into town. We have an event to attend: a marriage celebration for the Mayor's daughter."

"On a weekday? That's a bit odd."

"Life here is different. Every day is a new day; weddings, babies, deaths… They are all reasons to come together. They specifically waited until I would be back to have their reception."

"Why?" she asked as they settled in and the car moved forward. "Are they friends of yours?"

He paused as if trying to figure out an explanation. "This is *my* town," he said at last. "My choice of home, if ever there was one and, similar to the Cardinal who always visits the town church dedicated to him whenever he is in Rome because they are his people, these people are mine. They know that, and they expect that I treat them that way." He touched her bracelet as it sat against her crossed knees. "It is part of what being their *Don* means to them. It is part of what being me entails."

His answer made Lexi's thoughts return to the previous evening. "What happened last night?" When Giovanni looked out the window instead of answering, she reached for his hand. "I'm not here to judge you, Gio. Whatever you did, whatever happened…" Lexi felt conflicted, but her concern for him overshadowed her own fears of whatever he may have done. "I just want to know that you're alright."

"Don't ask me to tell you things that will make you run from me." The car turned from the drive and twisted through the coast until it approached the Agrigentian town. They parked in an area outside of the roped off downtown where people danced, and the crowd was loud with singing and celebration.

Police stood at the entrances to the square and, although they were in uniform, they held drinks or socialized. Giovanni's men spread out around the largely open perimeter, and Lexi unconsciously held his hand tighter. He reassured her. "We're safe here. There's no need to worry."

"Tell me that when you don't carry a gun everywhere you go."

The hand around her waist drifted down to her ass. "I don't take it *everywhere* I go." She twisted around and lightly smacked him. "Twenty-one," Giovanni countered with a chuckle.

"Nineteen," Lexi returned. She accepted the arm he offered her and followed him into the reception.

The songlike Sicilian language floated around like a cloud. Lexi could pick out words that were similar enough to Italian or Spanish with their Latin derivatives, but she was lost by the resulting combination of the languages with Greek and Arabic. It was impossible to know in any real sense what was being said.

When Giovanni introduced her, he spoke in Italian and she greeted them in such; when the townspeople spoke to her, they used the common language of the country. Several of the teenage girls who giggled whenever Giovanni walked nearby asked if she would speak to them in English, since they were learning the language in school and wanted more practice. When he excused himself after reminding her that she was safe and to enjoy the morning, Lexi found herself wishing she had bothered to add another language to her field of study as the world around her exploded in conversation.

"You his wife, yes?" One of the girls looked at her with an open smile when Lexi choked on her drink. "*Don* Giovanni? He find you in New York?"

Who the hell was she supposed to tell them she was? The girls giggled again as she blushed and Lexi said with a light laugh, "I guess I should hope I don't run into his girlfriend."

The trio, clearly understanding, laughed harder and the one who had spoken before shook her head. "*Don* Giovanni has no girlfriend. Many wish it so, but," she shook her head again, "he no say yes."

Lexi looked behind her. Giovanni was sitting at a table in an outdoor café with the man he had introduced as the Mayor. They were looking at a file of papers, and she smiled when her eyes found his before turning back to the girls. "Does he visit here often?"

The girl closest to her seemed to be searching out the words in English. "Every months. Three. Sometimes for a while, he stay." She began to answer in Sicilian before stopping. "Sorry. I forget you no speak Sicilian."

"I would love to learn," Lexi said authentically. "I do speak Italian if you'd rather."

"No, no!" she exclaimed. "We watch movies. We want to speak English like girls on TV."

Lexi drank from her glass and the girl who'd yet to speak asked, "You come to live here? With *Don* Giovanni?"

"Live here? I don't think so. I'm a librarian in New York."

"Librarian?"

"*Una bibliotecaria*," she explained. The girls nodded with understanding. "I repair old, broken books."

"We have library here!" The girl who presumed Lexi was Giovanni's wife pointed down the street. "You be there when you live here!"

Lexi wasn't sure how to explain that she doubted they would ever see her again, so she just listened to them talk about the town while they pointed out things nearby. The band began to play dance music, and the girls left her to flirt with a group of teenage boys.

Under the guise of exploring the area, she walked closer to the outdoor café where Giovanni now sat with a fiftyish-year-old man she hadn't been introduced to. From the facial expressions, it almost seemed like Giovanni was giving some sort of medical advice. She saw him touch his heart and trail his fingers down as though he were trying to explain blood flow. When he repeated the word *cori* several times, she assumed she was right based on his movements and the proximity to the word *cuore*. She was close enough to pick up some words, but, for the most part, the noise made trying to understand what was being said impossible.

The bride approached and Lexi offered her a sincere smile. "*Congratulazioni! Migliori augur.*"

"*Grazie, Donna.*"

"No, no." Lexi laughed and played with the stem of her prosecco and blood orange cocktail. "It's not, I mean, I'm not. We're just, um, no."

The bride chuckled as she looked behind them to where Giovanni sat. Lexi followed her gaze and saw that he was watching the pair while he listened to a different man in front of him. "You don't wish to marry *Don* Giovanni?"

"I don't know that *Don* Giovanni would wish to marry me." She would be lucky if he didn't shoot her for insulting him.

"People often do not see what is in front of them." The woman, beautiful in her white dress, looked down at the sparkling rings on her finger. "It took me years to see that which was always there."

"Did you know each other a long time?"

The woman searched for her groom, pointing him out as he danced with several men while the group laughed. "As children. But he was, how do you say, not what I wanted to spend my life with." She looked back to Lexi. "He was not always good."

"Isn't that usually the truth," Lexi agreed.

"But sometimes good is not what we think is good, you know?" She drank from her glass before saying, "Sometimes a good man has to do things that make him not good to be good."

What was the woman trying to tell her? How much might Lexi learn if she tried to understand? "I think that sometimes we convince ourselves the things we do are worth the cost, but that's rarely true." She picked up a few other words from Giovanni's conversation; once again, it seemed like he was giving some sort of advice.

The women could speak and watch each other but, with a minor shift of their bodies, could watch Giovanni as well. If this bothered him, he didn't show it, probably, Lexi assumed, because she couldn't understand a damn thing that he was saying. When the chair in front of him vacated, he said something to Raphael, who nodded, and then he turned back to a waiter who approached with coffee. As he left, Giovanni stood while an older man, wringing his hands and with tears already streaming down his face, approached.

The man tried to fall to his knees, but Giovanni caught him and patted his back before pulling him into an embrace as the man heaved. Gently, he guided the gentleman into the chair and then sat down across from him. Giovanni leaned forward and touched the man's knee while he continued to softly weep. "What's going on?" Lexi asked the bride.

"That is *Signore* Pascarelli. His daughter." She shook her head. "It is very sad."

"Did she die?"

"No, no. I..." The bride looked around uncomfortably. It was clear to Lexi that she wasn't sure if she was supposed to share the knowledge she had, and the younger woman finished off her flute nervously. "I am not sure what to say."

"Would you rather switch to Italian?"

"No, no. It isn't that." She stumbled over her words. "You know, um, *Don* Giovanni- he is the patron of this town. He makes sure things are good."

He had told her as much in the car. Giovanni had referred to the people as his own and, looking down at her wrist, Lexi could only presume the meaning behind his words. "Right. He told me something similar."

"When things happen to anyone, they happen to *Don* Giovanni- do you understand? If you steal from store, you would be stealing from him. Yes?"

"Okay, yes." Lexi nodded.

The bride exhaled shakily and lifted her hand to a traveling waiter. She took a new glass and waited for Lexi to drink the remainder of hers. "Have another," she encouraged. Unsure of what the woman was preparing to tell her, Lexi complied. The bride changed her posture to turn her back to Giovanni, dropping her voice even softer. "All know that there are rules that *Don* Giovanni will not tolerate breaking."

Lexi felt her stomach start to churn. What the hell was Giovanni responsible for and why was the old man crying? "Did he do something to *Signore* Pascarelli's daughter?"

She whipped her head up. "No, no, *Donna*, you misunderstand. *Signore*'s daughter was, um... She lived in Siracusa, with her husband and family. She was very happy. But her husband, he, um, he was involved with some people." The woman was getting more uncomfortable as she continued to confess, and she deeply exhaled every few sentences. "These men, they are not like *Don* Giovanni. They have no honor, no dignity among women and children."

The rising nausea continued, and Lexi was grateful the bride had suggested another drink. She drank half of the mimosa and glanced back at Giovanni, who was clearly trying to decline something. Their eyes met as she saw him extend his hand toward her. The older man nodded before they continued the discussion. "What happened?"

"These men, they broke into her house. They beat and raped her." She shook her head and shivered. "It was awful. She is still in hospital." She paused again to drink. "Everyone knew, but the police, they could do nothing."

It's not their faults... They simply don't have the power they need. Lexi could practically hear their discussion from before. "But Giovanni could do something." She looked down at her shaking hands. When the bride was quiet, Lexi looked back to her. "What did he do?"

"I don't know," she said honestly. "But, based on *Signore* Pascarelli, I will guess that his daughter no longer has to worry." When Giovanni approached the pair, the woman deeply bowed her head. "*Don* Giovanni: you honor us by coming to my wedding celebration today."

"The honor is mine, *Signora* Miccucci." Giovanni reached out and gave the woman a light hug before he kissed each of her cheeks. "I do, however, expect a dance with the bride before we leave today."

Lexi watched as the woman's face lit up and she bowed her head again. "It was lovely to meet you, *Donna*," she said as she excused herself and went to greet other guests.

"White dress fantasies, *Donna*?" Giovanni remarked as the woman walked away.

"Definitely not." Lexi finished off her drink. "Just further proof that your people are hard of hearing."

He stabbed at his heart in distress. "Your words cut me deeply, *bambina*. You think I'm not husband material?"

"Apparently, you are an amateur cardiologist." She felt satisfaction when a look of uncomfortable surprise passed over his face. Rather than admit that she didn't really understand what she had overheard, Lexi sought out the gentleman she had seen Giovanni talking to earlier and pointed. "He should probably see a real doctor to make sure he is well."

Giovanni rubbed his jaw like he had been punched and looked around. "What else?"

He seemed legitimately concerned. Did she actually have the upper hand for once in their time together? Lexi knew that she should admit she had no idea, but she wanted to make him squirm. "I do hope *Signore* Pascarelli and his family are able to heal from the trauma inflicted upon them." Giovanni's eyes were nearly black and, when a shadow settled on them, it chilled her even further. Still, Lexi continued to push. "I was too busy in my own conversation to understand exactly what it was that you did but, clearly, he is appreciative, *Don* Giovanni."

She had barely uttered his name when Giovanni grabbed her arm harshly and walked her away from the crowd. Lexi struggled, and he applied more pressure. "You're hurting me, Gio."

"Then stop fucking with me." Giovanni turned her so that he could still watch the crowd while being far enough away to avoid being overheard. "You don't speak Sicilian," he said between gritted teeth.

"You're awfully sure of yourself."

"You like this game far more than you realize is safe for you." His voice lowered as he leaned closer to her while still watching the area around them. "Part of what gives me the power I have is the ability to read what is right in front of my face in order to eliminate any real threat. The second you believe you can lie to me and get away with it will be the day you feel much more than the belt that, obviously, did not do its job well enough."

Giovanni pulled back and looked at her with eyes that Lexi knew indeed saw what was in front of him. She choked on the nervousness that even her brazen attitude couldn't temper, and smug satisfaction crept back into his gaze. "You don't speak Sicilian," he confirmed, "but you read very, *very* well. I will make sure to direct what books you have access to in the future."

Lexi pushed up from the wall that was behind her when she found her fear stronger than her courage. She tried to slip around him, but Giovanni's body stopped her. "This front you put on, Alessandra, is ill-fitting. Stick to the clothes I select for you; I promise that they fit you much better." Satisfied that he had made his point, he stepped to the side and let her go.

After returning to the group of revelers, Lexi took a sparkling water from a waiter. Several of the different townspeople made conversation with her, and she tried to shake off her feelings. "*Donna?*"

She turned and recognized the man from before. Not bothering to correct him, she asked kindly, "*Signore* Pascarelli: *come sta?*"

"Would you like to dance, *Donna*?" He offered her his hand. "It would be my honor."

Lexi didn't have the heart to refuse him. She put her water on a nearby table before placing her palm in his. The song was slower and much older than the pop music that the band had played earlier. They joined many elderly couples who were dancing in the square; at least, Lexi mused, Giovanni wouldn't consider *Signore* Pascarelli a threat he would need to shoot.

The old man didn't want to speak with her; he simply wanted her company. Since Lexi didn't know what to say that might ease his suffering, she danced in silence. When the song ended and the Mayor offered her the next dance, she politely accepted to have an excuse to avoid Giovanni. She eased in four more dances with four more men who spoke to her about her visit and lauded their *Don* to her; one sang the words of the song in her ear, his aged voice causing her to smile. When their dance ended, she thanked him before she turned to go. "Did you save a dance for me?"

The traces of his earlier angst were gone and the amusement was back to light his eyes. She wanted to smart off, but the words felt rough in her throat. "That almost sounded like a request, *Don* Giovanni."

He exhaled softly with a grin before holding out his hand. "Dance with me." After a small pause, she gave in and he cradled her against his chest with his hand pressing into the small of her back while gliding her in a tight circle. His voice vibrated against her ear. "You're annoyed with me."

"Apparently, you don't like my clothes or my reading selections," she said dismissively. "So what is it that you find so damn appealing about me that you've whisked me halfway around the world to make the point that you want to do nothing but change me?" Lexi hadn't expected the explosion of hurt that accompanied her softly spoken words.

Neither, it seemed, had Giovanni. He leaned back to look into her eyes, but she turned her head to the side to avoid him seeing her pain. "It seems you are more than annoyed."

"Not annoyed, Gio: out of my league. You've made that crystal clear." Her body was rigid, and she longed for the dance to end. The closer she was to him, the more she lost who she was.

Giovanni touched her cheek; when she risked a look at him, she found concern in his gaze. "This game," he sighed, "may undo us both."

Lexi no longer wanted to play. She knew that the game would end with her being destroyed. When they returned to New York, the safest thing for her to do was to return to her real life and to accept that Giovanni wasn't in her cards. They were too different, too incompatible. Their passion was fire, and they were incapable of avoiding burning the other. She opened her mouth to tell him that she was finished, but he placed his fingers on her lips. "Shhh. Don't say it." He brought the hand he held to his heart, and she unconsciously rested her head on his chest while they gently swayed together until the song ended.

After a delicious lunch, the reception began to disband and shops opened. The barriers that had blocked off the square were removed and traffic resumed. The Mercedes approached, slowing alongside where Lexi stood with Giovanni while he spoke with the Mayor, and he excused himself to open the door for her. After a few moments, he slid into the seat next to her and they were back on the road toward the estate. "The afternoon will be another perfect opportunity for a swim or walk through the vineyards and groves. I've made reservations for dinner."

"Perhaps you'd like to select what I wear," she said, still looking out the window. "That way, you assure it fits in the manner you prefer." Even though she refused to look at him, Lexi knew that he was grinning and it pissed her off.

"You stepped into the Colosseum, *bambina*. You shouldn't have been surprised that the lions bite." She was silent and continued to watch the road. "You shouldn't ask-"

"For the answers that would make me run. Thank you." Angrily, she turned in her seat. "I heard you the first time and the second time and every other time you've said it. Let me explain this to you in small words that maybe, just once, you'll understand. The more you treat me like I'm going to run, the more you create a self-fulfilling prophecy. The more you leave me without information, the more I'm going to fill in the blanks with what other people tell me, what the gossip columnists write, what I infer and overhear, and what gets posted online. You tell me that most of it isn't true, yet it's all I've got." The car pulled to a stop in front of the house. "At the end of the day, I have to believe someone."

11

When Raphael opened the door, Lexi didn't wait for Giovanni to answer and she stepped out of the car. Instead of going into the house, she walked toward one of the trails she had explored the day before. Part of her hoped that Giovanni wouldn't follow her, and she hiked without looking behind her even though she knew he would never let her be alone. She eventually sat down on a precipice that allowed her to see the coast in the distance. She took her shoes off and pulled her legs close to her chest, resting her head on her knees as she gazed out toward the sea.

Giovanni allowed time for her anger to lessen before he sat down next to her, offering her a tall glass of iced tea. "What did you overhear?" he asked, joining her in watching the coastline.

"What does it matter? It's not like I actually understood any of it. But you knew that already. Not to worry: your secrets are safe. The *baby girl* is just as ignorant now of whatever the fuck it is you've done as she was this morning."

"It's not about keeping you ignorant."

"Bullshit. It's about control. It's always about control with you. Control your people. Control your men. Control me. Control the whole goddamned world."

Giovanni sighed. "The world is not nearly as black and white as you want to pretend it is. You think that wrongs can be corrected and made right, but the truth is much colder than that, Alessandra. Wrongs cannot be fixed. Mistakes cannot be undone. Prices must be paid, and restitution to the injured must be required."

"And you get to be judge and jury of your piece of the world," she said dismissively.

"What is it that should be done? What part of the system that you believe in is without bias and actually works as designed?"

Lexi finally looked at him. "You act like the system is damaged all the while you are the one breaking it!"

For the first time, she could see true frustration as he stood up. He ran a hand through his short hair. "What can I say that will settle this until the next time?"

Lexi scoffed as she raised herself alongside him. "At least you recognize that, with you, there will *always* be a next time!"

"What the fuck do you want from me?"

"The truth! I want to know what the hell happened yesterday. I want to know what created the way I found you this morning. I want to know why a grown man fell apart in front of you today. What did you do?"

Lexi thought he would just shut her out and leave. She expected his silence to end in his absence, but Giovanni exhaled harshly and his voice was even when he spoke. "Two weeks ago, the man you saw today, Giorgio Pascarelli, visited me during one of my stops here. His daughter had been viciously attacked. His grandchildren were terrified to go back home." Lexi could feel his disgust as Giovanni paced a few steps away only to turn back. "Giorgio was distraught. When his son-in-law wouldn't give him any sort of information, he came to me, as his *Don*, to fix the problem and restore his daughter's and his grandchildren's safety.

"I went to visit his son-in-law and persuaded him to talk to me." Her pulse started to increase and she forced herself to stay silent. Lexi could imagine what type of persuasion Giovanni had come up with, and she began to nervously move her fingers back and forth to focus on something else. "It seemed that he enjoyed gambling and had lost more money than he was able to pay back. He owed a considerable amount, and, to encourage a payment plan, his lender had ordered a message be sent."

"They attacked his wife."

Giovanni pointed his finger at her accusation. "For what it's worth, they were wrong." He walked back to the precipice and kicked a rock, creating a small cascade of dirt that fell over the edge. "The lender knew what his tellers were collecting and that the interest rate was far too high for the loan. He didn't realize that, although they may be customers of his particular bank, her original account belongs to my firm."

It was intriguing to see how easily Giovanni was able to tell the story with words that could never prove anything against him. Lexi was actually impressed and wondered if he would dip into the unchartered territory of unadulterated truth. "So like any good banker, you opted to settle his debt."

"No." Giovanni's eyes were cold. "Had he attempted to make restitution and they attacked his wife, I would have fought on his behalf. Instead, he was left to settle his debt alone."

The implication took away the heat of the Sicilian afternoon. "Where are *Signore* Pascarelli's daughter and grandchildren now?"

"Yesterday, a private nursing staff brought her to Giorgio's home, a few miles from here. Her children had been moved into his home weeks ago while she was recovering from her injuries."

"Was that why you left? To go see her and make sure she was settled?"

"No." Giovanni watched her face and she knew that he was waiting for the response that would signal what he presumed: telling her the truth would cause her to flee. "Shortly after we arrived, I met with my fellow banker to discuss interest rates and loans. We came to an agreement that would leave Giorgio's daughter and her children debt-free, and then I personally held her husband responsible for his overdraft. I left in the evening in order to permanently fire the tellers, and, while you slept, I delivered proof of the account closure to Giorgio on my fellow banker's behalf."

Was it possible to feel blood draining? Lexi wasn't sure, but it felt like gravity was pulling down on her entire body and she found it hard to stand.

She had no doubt that Giovanni had just confessed multiple murders to her. The small stones from the path buried into her bare feet, and she was thankful for the pain. It kept her from succumbing to shock.

He walked back to her and ran his fingers across the bracelet. After lifting her hand, he placed a kiss on her knuckles. "*This* is who I am. If I have stopped you from seeing all the facets because I doubted your ability to understand, then, as you said, you will have no choice but to one day decide who to believe and it will, I fear, not be me." Giovanni placed her hand over his heart and she could feel it thudding beneath his shirt and vest. "You were right when you said that we choose to embrace or flee from who we are. I choose to embrace my life for what it is. I won't apologize. I can't."

It was hard to find any words. Lexi nodded slowly before Giovanni began to walk her back toward the house. "I won't always be able to tell you things. Knowing is dangerous. If my accounts ever need to be settled, then your lack of knowledge frees you from liability."

"Do you have many *accounts* that will need settling?"

"I don't believe I have any; but those who have had loans called in may feel differently." He stopped walking and squeezed her hand. "Regardless of what I choose to tell you: ask. I *want* you to know, but I have to weigh what I want and what you need with what will keep you safe. You, Alessandra, must know when to no longer ask." He removed his vibrating phone from his pocket and glanced at the number before letting her go. "Take a swim or relax by the pool for the afternoon. I have to take this."

In seconds, he was gone. Lexi walked back to the bedroom, where she put on red fabric that was barely fit to be called a bikini. She alternated between swimming and stretching out on a recliner by the pool. Realizing she didn't have sunscreen on, she eventually settled beneath a large canopy, where the combination of stress, heat, and exercise lulled her into a nap.

"Excuse me, *Signora*." It seemed like she had barely closed her eyes when she heard Ricardo's deep vibrato and his voice reminded her of New York. For a few moments, she forgot she was in Sicily. Lexi blinked reality back into existence as she sat up on the deck chair. "It's getting late, and *Don Giovanni* thought you might want a shower before dinner."

She thanked him and accepted the bottle of water he offered her before she walked back to the terrace that entered the bedroom. The room was empty, and Lexi was surprised to find that there was no preselected outfit waiting for her. Upon exiting the shower, she looked around; there was still no dress chosen. She had no idea where they were going or what would be acceptable. What the hell was she supposed to wear?

Lexi had been annoyed at Giovanni's habit of selecting clothing for her, but, as she fingered the variety of dresses in the closet, she could see his consideration. Over the last few outings, she hadn't worried if what she was wearing was not enough or too much. It had seemed controlling at the time, but now Lexi saw it as part of his need to protect and take care of her. By taking that simple choice from the table and deciding for her, she was free of the stress and the worry surrounding events she couldn't adequately prepare herself for. She would never admit this to him, but Lexi wondered if Giovanni already knew and this was yet another part of her learning curve.

After finally deciding on a nude gown with navy embroidery that accentuated her cleavage with its deep V and gave the impression of sleeves with faux bell overhangs that covered up the fact the dress was actually sleeveless, she picked out a pair of three-inch, navy mules that peeked out from beneath the floor-length dress. Once she slipped into the gown and managed to navigate the zipper, she realized that, when she walked, her left leg would be revealed from toe to upper thigh, thanks to a slit in the dress. She opted to keep her neck bare and selected a pair of long earrings that she chose to believe were cut glass instead of consider that she would easily have a paycheck draped from each ear. She had always been on the bleachers when it came to wearing the fashion she had flipped through in various magazines. Seeing herself in designers whose names she had only read about was both exciting and intimidating.

After blowing her hair dry, she debated trying to style it before Lexi pulled her long waves into a messy bun that she easily pinned into place. Several wisps framed her face and a few tendrils fell along her neck from the chic stack. She swiped on a layer of moisturizer and, after covering her lips in a sheer lip balm, looked in the mirror.

She wasn't sure who the woman staring back was. Lexi Masters, former agent of the FBI, seemed like a faded ghost. Whatever leftovers of the numb, dead-inside woman that remained were being burned away by Giovanni's disarming honesty and the kisses he seemed unable to withhold. *Alessandra.* When he called her by name, she felt like a different person than the Lexi who had left DC with a half-assed plan and hell-bent on revenge.

Whatever she had set out to prove, Lexi had failed. Giovanni had told her that he hadn't killed her father. Although she had nothing but his word, that was as much evidence as she had from Sam to the contrary. They had nothing concrete to tie him to the murder. Was she willing to allow Giovanni's denial to weigh equal to Sam's argument? If they balanced and she was left to choose, had Giovanni given her the ability to be blind to her own emotions in order to see the truth or had he clouded her vision in order to delude her into submission?

She wasn't blind, Lexi thought. For the first time in ten years, she was seeing clearly. The weight of the pain was being lifted and she could finally move. Giovanni had freed her from the chains her father's death had locked around her soul. With him, she could breathe again. Watching herself in the mirror as wave after wave of understanding played behind her eyes, Lexi had to look away from her reflection. Everything would fall apart when she confessed. Lexi couldn't imagine another way. How would he ever forgive her?

She longed to just settle herself at his feet again as she had the night before. In that place, with his hand resting on her head and delicately stroking her hair, she had relaxed away all the stress and tension of every argument and every fear. That had to mean something, right? Even though they seemed to fight incessantly and battle at every turn, the fact that they each felt so strongly in those small moments had to matter. Didn't it?

The longer she thought about it, the more she created nerves that threatened to overwhelm her. Lexi forced herself from the room and slowly pulled back the door to the alcove that descended to the main floor. Ricardo stood guard, as she was now accustomed. "*Buono sera, Signora,*" he greeted.

After she replied, he walked down the steps with Lexi several paces behind him. She lifted the dress slightly to avoid tripping and hoped she looked presentable enough. What type of restaurant were they going to? Was she underdressed? Overdressed? They drew closer to the main floor, and she heard Giovanni with several other voices in discussion. Despite the desire to run back up the steps once Ricardo disappeared into the room in front of her, she had no choice but to keep walking.

When she stepped inside the large den, everything stopped. There were six men, including Raphael and now Ricardo, standing throughout. Giovanni, who had been sitting on a leather couch in the center of the room, immediately stood, buttoning his tailored jacket over his vest. He looked her up and down while he took a few steps forward, and she found it difficult to breathe. He touched her fingertips to spin her slowly around while his other hand rested over his mouth. His pointer finger slowly moved back and forth along his full top lip and, when he noticed every other man in the room looking at her, he gifted them a glare they all understood. The couple was suddenly alone, and Lexi heard doors opening and closing to the vehicles outside.

Finally, Giovanni spoke. "*Bellissima* is not a strong enough word. You leave me speechless." Heat flooded her cheeks with embarrassment at the compliment. "I should make sure I have extra bullets," he added. His eyes were full of mirth, and she couldn't help but laugh at the suggestion he would have to defend her honor.

The drive to the coastal resort took about twenty minutes, and Lexi watched the sun set the sky on fire as it lowered itself toward the sea. When they arrived at the country estate that had been transformed into a luxury spa, twilight had just fallen and the courtyards were alight with candles and hanging lights. As they exited the car, the sounds of a strings ensemble carried on the wind. Giovanni placed his hand on her bare back and led her to a podium where the maître d'hôtel looked over reservations. When he raised his eyes and saw them approaching, he immediately came out from behind the stand. "*Don* Giovanni!" he exclaimed. "*Bona sira! Bon vinuti!*"

"*Buono sera, Stefano.*" Giovanni answered in Italian and, immediately, Stefano made the correction when he greeted Lexi.

"*Buono sera e benvenuta, Signora.*"

Lexi answered politely before he led them to a beautifully prepared space that overlooked the vineyards. The table was set apart from the one for six nearest them, where their security detail was seated. "Do you always go out with this many bodyguards?" Lexi asked as they settled. "It seems a little much for grabbing a slice of pizza."

Giovanni sampled the wine he was offered before he waved the sommelier to pour their glasses. "It depends on the time and place, I suppose. Better safe than sorry."

"Spoken from experience?"

"It's been a long time since I've been caught off guard." He touched her hand and let his fingers trail to the bracelet. "I see you've figured out how to shower and walk without losing your cuff."

"I've even managed to box and defend myself against the local *cattivo ragazzo.*"

At this, Giovanni outright laughed. "Do you remember what happened when you called me a choir boy?"

"You serenaded me on the pier," she remembered fondly as her cheeks pinked at the memory.

"Imagine what I'm capable of if you believe me a *bad boy.*"

She reached out when he called her bluff and began to stand, pulling him back to his chair. "Twenty-one."

"Twenty-two," he countered with a wink. "I think I earned at least twenty-one with that pool stunt last night."

Lexi rolled her eyes. "You are what mothers everywhere warn their daughters about. Stop acting like you don't know that."

"Did your mother warn you about me?"

"Constantly." Although the word slipped out as a joke, Lexi couldn't avoid remembering the many conversations she'd had with her mother that featured Giovanni. What in the hell would Shannon Masters say to any of this? Lexi's fingers unconsciously played with her napkin. "She wouldn't have judged you based on anything someone else told her," she said, wondering why she bothered to say anything at all. "My mom was big on judging a book by what she read, not by how others reviewed it or by the cover."

He fingered the stem of his wine glass. "Smart woman."

"She was." Lexi nodded. "Great dancer. Great teacher. Great mom."

"And your father?" he asked, looking at her with interest. "Would he have judged my book by its cover and the public reviews?"

Lexi chuckled. "He would have hated you on sight. *Hated*," she repeated emphatically. "I'm not sure there is much of anything you could have done to change that."

"If my daughter brought me home, I would hate me, too," Giovanni agreed, letting his finger follow the curve of his wine glass. "Perfection inspires jealousy."

Lexi laughed again. "That attitude. The tattoos would have pissed him off first, but your attitude would have been the nail in your coffin. Dad wouldn't have even cracked open the book." As she considered the idea of introducing Giovanni to her parents, she neglected the realization that John Masters would have seen a profile and criminal rather than the man who had become his daughter's choice. "You would have been lucky to get off the porch before-" Her voice choked to a halt.

"Before?" Giovanni asked good-naturedly. Concern edged out humor when he noticed that she had paled. "Alessandra?"

"Before he shot you," she whispered, barely able to cough the words. He blew out a deep breath and reached for her hand. "It was a terrible joke," she said, looking down. She had actually forgotten. In a completely pointless moment of meaningless, joking conversation, Lexi had been given the briefest reprieve from ten years of nearly nonstop thoughts.

As if fate was offering them a chance to start anew, a man in a crisp, black chef's coat approached their table and greeted them warmly. "*Buono sera, Don* Giovanni, *Signora*," he said with a slight bow. "Tonight, we have *arancini* to start." He placed a plate of fried balls in red sauce between them. "In addition to a fresh salad, I have sourced the most local ingredients for our famous *pasta alla norma*."

"*Grazie*," Giovanni said, nodding his approval. "*Buono*."

Lexi used her fork to cut into the deep fried risotto ball and tried to lighten the ache that begged to linger. "It must really suck when you are in New York and the world doesn't revolve around you."

"Baby girl," Giovanni smarted, "the world *always* revolves around me."

"How is there enough room for it to revolve when your ego has it ripping at the seams?" she sassed in reply.

He pressed his lips against her ear and whispered, "Twenty-two."

"I don't think I deserve that." She shook her head. "I'm not giving minutes away. You have to earn them."

"My game. My rules."

"I'll remember that." Lexi put her fork down.

It took him a minute to remember their previous evening, and he grinned at her. "If this is the hill you wish to die on tonight, I can promise you a half-hour you won't soon forget."

"Half-an-hour? You just jumped quite a notch there, *Don* Giovanni." He looked over at her with raised eyebrows. "You struggled to understand my six o'clock appointment. Perhaps numbers just aren't your thing."

"You," he said seductively as he took her hand, "are my thing, *bambina*."

The question was an unconscious slip, and Lexi didn't want to know the answer in as much as she had to know. "How many *bambine* have there been?"

"The fuck you say!" Giovanni sighed and dropped his head back. "Alessandra, fuck."

She lowered her eyes and said softly, "I've found the hill I wish to die on; although, I think I'd like to be drunk when I die on it." She reached for her wine and swallowed half the glass. When she looked back at him, he was watching her and slowly shaking his head. "Okay, I'm ready. Drop the bomb. Hit me."

He chuckled despite himself. "Alessandra, you don't want to have this conversation."

"Did you want me to start first?" She lifted her wine glass as though it were counting for her and playfully began. "The first-"

"Stop. I think I'd rather not hear what I've already had the *pleasure*," he said sarcastically, "of reading."

Her glass stilled in midair, and she slowly lowered it back to the table. Lexi had known that he would have researched her after their initial meeting. What the hell had he found out? Had whatever background check he'd run included former lovers? Shit, it must have.

How had he uncovered that but not realized she was a former FBI agent? Had Sam been able to cover up her background? Giovanni couldn't possibly have known the truth and risked taking her to visit his family or conducting business around her. Lexi tried to wipe the shock and angst from her face, putting herself back at the mercy of the play. "You're a fucking stalker," she muttered. "Will there ever be a game that I win?"

"Most certainly. When I'm dead."

"You're someone who probably shouldn't tempt fate with comments like that." Deep down, she knew she would risk losing every battle if she didn't have to contemplate losing him. The thought terrified her, and Lexi tried to gloss over it by forcing an attitude. "I know what you are trying to do. You think if you can piss me off because you're a stalker, I'll forget what I asked in the first place. It won't work." She drained her entire glass of wine and sat it down before fidgeting with the bracelet. "How many? Do you recycle this through woman after woman?"

This time when their eyes met, she knew that her words had stoked the fire. Instead of being warmed, she risked getting burned. He had placed an elbow on the table to support the chin he rested on his knuckles. His pointer finger pressed against his top lip, and he watched her with an intensity that made her uncomfortable. She squirmed in her chair. "Number issues again? Too many to remember?" she asked, trying to divert her feelings.

Using the hand that he had been leaning on to hold up a single finger, Giovanni sat back in his chair. She hadn't thought she could get more nervous, and she laughed to cover up the sick feeling. "You're lying."

"No, there have been plenty of *ragazzine*, but they were *ragazzetta* not *bambina*. That, Alessandra, is all you."

"Why?" The wine wasn't strong enough, Lexi decided. She wished that the waiter would refill her glass because Giovanni wouldn't be doing her any favors.

"*Why*, what? I thought your Google searches had uncovered my kinks." He took a drink from his own glass then folded his hands in his lap. "Women who are *willing* to be used and owned are everywhere." She looked away from him and clenched her jaws together, returning her gaze to him when he drew his fingers up and down her arm. "And then you step into a club you never should have been in the first place and," he used his hand to express an explosion, "a fucking bomb goes off."

"You called me *bambina* when you met me. Why?"

"*Boh.*"

"You don't know? You locked me in a bracelet that costs as much as a year at NYU and you don't know?" She thought back to the countless photographs of women she had seen. "Did all of them stumble in looking for a job only to end up stumbling into your bedroom?"

At her derision, he grinned. "You almost sound jealous, *bambina.*" When she didn't answer, he adjusted his body language and glanced around the courtyard before settling his gaze back on her. "There are places one goes to find women of a similar opinion. We were looking for each other; they didn't *stumble* anywhere."

"Except out the door when you were bored." She was grateful when the waiter refilled her glass far higher than she knew Giovanni would have, and she drank more courage from it. "I don't think any of the gossip pages had you at more than a month."

He shrugged and didn't deny it. "My relationships were arrangements not romance, and the women in question weren't interested in renewing the contract after the introductory period." Giovanni returned to touching her arm, letting his fingers move to caress the top of her hand, and Lexi felt glued to the table.

"If you treated them the way you treated me last week, I can understand why."

The chef approached with another waiter and placed in front of them a green salad with red onion and what Lexi could smell was a citrus vinaigrette alongside brightly colored pasta. "*Buon Appetito, Don* Giovanni, *Signora,*" he said with a bow before leaving them alone.

Lexi had decimated her appetite by the discussion she had chosen and feared the train hadn't even fully derailed when Giovanni said offhandedly, "Last week barely scratched the surface of what those women were capable of withstanding."

She was having an allergic reaction to his truth and could actually feel the air around her heating up by twenty degrees while her throat constricted. It hadn't been his confession of killing several men; it was the knowledge that he wanted to completely own her and that she would let him. She would let him pick her clothes and lie to get her out of the country. She would let him choke her against walls, destroy her attitude with his belt, and fuck her until she forgot that she had ever belonged to herself in the first place. Not only would she, but she would come back for more the next day. "Now I want to run," she whispered.

"Only now? That's far longer than some." Giovanni seemed completely unfazed by her reaction and took a bite of his pasta. "You should eat, *bambina*. They are known for this dish." When she didn't move, he lifted her fork and offered it to her. "A bite for a question- wasn't that your game? And I've already offered you so much more in exchange for nothing other than a second glass of wine."

Swallowing even a bite of the pasta was difficult. "Why do you do it?"

"Why do I do what?" When Lexi wouldn't look at him, Giovanni tipped up her chin with his fingertips. "This was the hill you wanted to die on, Alessandra. Either open your arms for the next shot or wave the white flag. Either way: this was your game, not mine."

"Why do you mix sex with violence?"

"I don't. *Aggression*, yes, but violence implies a need or desire to do real harm. I don't hurt women for the desire to hurt them. That doesn't get me off. Stress relief. Anger management. Punishment. Entertainment. Enjoyment." He nodded before he sobered. "But I'm not a sadist who brutalizes without reason except his own pleasure."

"I guess that's comforting." She couldn't look at him. What the hell was she doing? Why was she still sitting here? Wasn't the safest thing- for her body and her heart- to tell him that she wanted to leave? But that was not an option. Lexi had been right before; she was just as fucked up as he was.

Giovanni took a drink and swirled the wine in the glass before he put it back on the table. "As to *why*? I suppose who I am plays out in every aspect of my life, most certainly in how I fuck."

"Was that all it was? A good fuck?" She finally stole a quick glance at him. Where did she fit into his answer? Was she simply something to pass his time, just like the rest had been? When he spoke, Lexi focused back on her meal and pushed the pasta around with her fork.

"Should it have been anything more? It's my entire life, Alessandra: women, business, buying a pair of shoes. What is mine is mine, and, when people are mine, I want them to know that I take care of what's mine and discipline when needed. I even fight with my men on a fairly regular basis, just to keep them on their toes and to remind them whose they are."

"I see a recurring theme." She looked back at him from her plate. "Did you love any of them?"

There was zero hesitation in his answer. "No. My attraction to them wasn't driven from that hope. I didn't go looking for anything other than sex and they knew better than to assume otherwise." He sighed and Lexi could see that he didn't like where the conversation had turned. "My *raggazzine* all knew what they were getting into. I didn't hide how hard I play or what I expected, and, when the introductory phase of our game ended, they knew their limitations and chose to conclude our arrangement. None of them left hurt or feeling abused; if anything, they knew far more concretely the type of man to avoid."

"And is that how I'll leave? Knowing who to avoid in the future?" *All men*, Lexi decided. Giovanni had destroyed the memory of every man before him, and she couldn't imagine another man coming close to unleashing the feelings he had manipulated. When he tired of her, she was finished. She wouldn't recover.

"You won't be leaving. I won't let you leave, but the truth is that you don't want to go. Not really. Are you scared of the unknown? Yes." Giovanni called a waiter over and, in Sicilian, ordered something brought.

"This is all new for you. What you feel for me. What you know I feel for you. The aggression, the pain, the fact that you enjoy what I do to you even as you hate yourself for it." Lexi looked up at him with eyes that told him he was surely crazy. "You don't want to admit it, but being out of control in a position that could leave you broken causes your heart to race- perhaps even more so than knowing that you don't want me to stop."

"I don't trust you to know when to stop." The waiter appeared with a large bottle of sparkling water and poured a glass for her before adding a second in front of Giovanni and placing the bottle in an ice bucket.

"That, *bambina*, is a mistake. Do you really think that I would continue without your consent? When you have been truly afraid, have I not stopped?"

Lexi thought back to their encounters. Even when he had wanted to continue, he had stopped each time until she had finally verbalized her agreement. She replaced her wine with the water and didn't answer. Finally, she met his gaze and asked, "Will it always be like this?"

"With you and that mouth, probably." He ran a finger along her bottom lip with a smile. "But punishment is only one aspect. Every tool and response can be used for much more pleasurable experiences. I promise."

She thought about the belt cutting into her ass and shook her head. "I doubt your belt will ever bring anything other than pain."

"It can, but it wasn't meant to pleasure; it was meant to punish. If you had enjoyed it, then I would have failed and I don't fail, *bambina*. Ever." He rolled the pad of his finger over her jawline. "Still, even as you didn't enjoy it, I could feel your body responding. With your lack of experience, I can only imagine that you felt confused and unsure, but you can't deny that relief flooded you with each hit."

Lexi could feel herself blushing beneath his assessment. How could he possibly know what she was feeling? Was this how he had discovered the undercovers sent against him? Was Giovanni simply so good of a mentalist that he could read those in front of him like Lexi read books? "I've been doing this a very long time," he said, proving her thought. "The only way to walk the line between *ferire* and *danneggiare* is to know how to see the difference."

"One day, you're going to skip ahead and miss what's written between the lines. One day," she whispered, "you're going to do far more damage than you can fix." Was it fear? Was it the fact that she knew where her feelings had led her and she couldn't bear to accept them? Was it that she was a liar who was desperate to tell him the truth?

"What is it, Alessandra, that scares you so much?" Giovanni's voice was full of understanding. "I don't think it is who I am- I think you believed you knew enough of that to be, if caught off guard, not utterly shocked. Is it who you are?"

"I don't know who I am anymore." Her voice was so low that she was unsure as to whether or not he even heard her.

"*Allora tu appartieni a me. Essere mia.*" Giovanni lifted her hand into his and kissed her knuckles gently, before running his fingers across the bracelet. "Not because I've chained you in a cage or because you fear that life has clipped your wings. Know that you are always free to fly away and, instead, choose to belong to me because that sets you free."

"I don't know that I can afford your freedom, Gio." She wiped away a tear and pushed slightly back from the table. When he stood alongside her, she folded her arms across her chest and kept her head down. "I need a minute."

After taking a few steps onto the patio, she stopped a waiter. "*Dov'è il bagno, per favore?*" He directed her down an interior hallway, and she stood inside the bathroom for several minutes, trying to breathe. She wished she could splash cold water onto her face or, even better, bury herself beneath a cold shower.

Lexi thought she may have preferred Giovanni's lies over his telling her the truth. She hadn't expected to fall in love and, as much as she couldn't handle the risk, knew when she looked at her reflection that she was too far along to stop. All that remained was the choice of whether or not she would be willing to sacrifice everything she would lose to gain him. Was he worth it? Was she?

When she found the courage to return to the table, Lexi tried to adjust her posture so that she didn't feel as weighed down by their discussion. The seriousness from before had already been replaced as Giovanni commented, "If you don't eat your dinner, I'm not sure I'll be able to accept dessert with a clear conscience."

"I wouldn't want to add guilt to your plate," she murmured as she lifted her fork.

"Life is too short for guilt." Giovanni beckoned the waiter and made a few comments before the man bowed and left. "*Mangia bene, ridi spesso, ama molto.* Are you ready to come off the hill now?"

"I'm still breathing, so most likely not." Lexi let her voice trail away before she bit her bottom lip and looked at him. She forced herself to focus and walk away from the game with something other than the loss of several more pieces from the board. On top of that desire, she was legitimately intrigued. "I am curious about one thing."

He folded his napkin and took a deep breath, before flicking his hand at her and resting his hands together as a throne for his chin. "Do ask, *bambina.*"

"What did they call you? Your *raggazzine.*" She took another bite from the plate to encourage his answer before she chuckled. "You don't strike me as the *Daddy* type."

"No. Not my thing." Something passed behind his eyes and, although he said, "I wouldn't use a word my own daughter might one day call me," Lexi couldn't help but suspect that there was something more to it.

"So," she coaxed. "What was it? I know it had to be something, *Il Lupo.*"

Giovanni tried to avoid smirking, using his thumb and forefinger to smooth the pout of his lips. "*Il Padrone.*"

"No shit? Seriously." When she knew that he was amused by her response, she lowered her voice and said with mock seriousness, "*Il Padrone*. Is that what you want me to call out in the throes of ecstasy as well? It doesn't exactly roll off the tongue."

"When you are gagged, not much does."

Game, set, match, Lexi thought. "Fuck, Gio. You just have to win, don't you?"

"Always, baby girl. Always. Besides, I like the way *Giovanni* rolls off your tongue just fine." The waiter approached with a plate of dessert and, balanced in his other hand, a wine with two thin flutes. After placing the plate between them, he deposited the glasses and Giovanni took the bottle from him. "*Grazie*," he said, indicating that he would pour.

Dismissed, the waiter backed away while Giovanni streamed a healthy amount of golden Ben Rye into the crystal glasses. Lexi watched him and finally gained the courage to ask, "They never used your name?"

"Sex, *bambina*. I wasn't looking for something else."

"That's cold."

"It's the game," he countered.

She leaned back in her chair, watching him as he settled the bottle alongside the water in the ice bucket. "Why didn't you ask me to call you that?"

"Asking isn't really my forte." He winked at her to further her annoyance.

"Neither is answering a direct question." She drummed her fingers on the table. "Why, Gio? Did you think you'd scare me away? Did you forget? Why?"

"Because I wanted it to be real. I wanted *us* to be real." He mirrored her position in the chair, as though they were stalemated in a match that only one of them could win. "You aren't my game, Alessandra; you're my girl. I didn't lie to you before. Whether you choose to stay or go, you'll always be mine. This is as real as I get."

Lexi was silent. The wine hadn't made her courageous enough to either confess or challenge. When he took the conversation in a different direction, she jumped at the chance to get out of her own thoughts. "Vincenzo, the chef here, comes from Pantelleria. His *baci* is some of the best on the island."

Giovanni picked up one of the floweresque pastries and tore it, allowing the pillow-like pastry cream to spill onto his fingers. He brought the delicacy to Lexi's mouth and, as she parted her lips, she tasted the sweet, powdered sugar glaze and soft crème that combined to create a sensuous dessert. His fingers lingered in her mouth and she tightened her grasp, sucking the cream from them and watching as his amusement morphed into sexual need. When he picked up another piece of the pastry, she said with invitation, "If this is your idea of force-feeding me, maybe I'll refuse to eat in the future."

"Careful." His voice exuded sex and Lexi wondered if he could hear her heart pounding. He placed a second bite in her mouth along with his fingers, pressing them slightly deeper, and she unconsciously took hold of his wrist. "I wouldn't want you to choke."

Sucking his fingers clean again, Lexi's eyes drifted to the plate and the broken profiterole. She dipped her finger inside and made a slow production of licking the cream, purring her approval of the taste. She forced her eyes to remain on his as they danced a very public, sexual tango. "I'm not sure that you can choke me on something that rolls so easily off the tongue, *Il Padrone*."

She finally calculated a scored point when Giovanni shifted in his seat uncomfortably before he stood up. "Perhaps I'll gag you just to keep that mouth at bay." Beckoning over Raphael, who was already standing, he said something Lexi didn't understand and then pulled her to her feet.

"Maybe that's only because you don't know what my mouth is truly capable of," she replied, looking at him innocently.

There was something incredibly sexy about the way he bit his bottom lip, as though torn between sexual frustration and humor at her push back.

He took her hand and began walking toward the entry of the restaurant, only to go in the opposite direction of the way they had arrived. They walked around the swimming pool, full of scantily-clad guests, and into a wing of the hotel. "Where are we going?" she asked.

"To find out what your mouth is truly capable of." He pulled her to a room where she saw Raphael use a card to open the door before walking back toward the restaurant. Giovanni pulled her inside and shoved his hand in her hair, dragging her into his mouth and crushing her against him. Her knees threatened to buckle and she held his wrists in order to stay standing as he devoured her lips like he was starving. "You fuck with me incessantly." He yanked her head back. "All because you want me to fuck you until you forget who you are."

What inspired Lexi to say, *"Faccia ricordare, Il Padrone,"* and to allow her legs to fold in front of him? Was she fucking crazy to call him *Master*? She had already instigated him at the table; he didn't need any *remind me* encouragement to take things further.

She unzipped his pants and found a bulge that couldn't be contained by the silk boxers he wore. Giovanni cursed and tangled his hands in her hair. "Fucking *Il Padrone*," he growled. "When I'm done with you tonight, you'll know exactly who owns you, baby girl."

The dress wasn't flexible enough for Lexi to do more than stay in a forced kneel in front of him. When her lips parted and he pushed his cock into her mouth, she thought his threat of choking her might be true. He wasn't gentle and didn't give her time to catch her breath, violating her with each need-filled thrust.

She balanced one hand on his muscular thigh and used the other to wrap around the base of his shaft. As she sucked him deeper and heard his guttural growl of want and satisfaction at the feel of her tongue and throat, Lexi pushed her own limits in order to steal the self-control that Giovanni refused to cede to her. This was a battle she was intent on winning, and she moved her lips around the tip in a circle while she simultaneously sucked vigorously. The hand at the base of his dick moved to fondle his balls, and she paired the movement with moving her tongue down the length of him only to inhale him back into her mouth.

"Fuck, Alessandra." He breathed her name harshly, giving her more than enough motivation. Giovanni roughly took out his need to regain control of his body by contracting his fingers in her hair, trying to force her head back. "What the fuck are you doing to me?"

She murmured a wordless response before she repeated the move from before, allowing her tongue to trail from base to tip before sucking him deeply down her throat. When he cursed again and tightened his fingers, she felt the warm, sticky trophy of his defeat explode in her mouth. Rather than pull away, she swallowed while her lips were still around him and continued her sucking. "Fuck, Alessandra, stop," he panted. She dug her nails into his thigh and gave another harsh suck before he pulled her to her feet by her throat.

Stumbling back from him, she grinned with satisfaction at her prize, slowly moving her fingers along her mouth. "I'm not sure the *crema pasticcera* from Pantelleria comes close to that from Palermo."

Giovanni threw her against the bed and ripped the dress by its hidden zipper to strip her out of it. He didn't even bother to take his own clothes off before decimating the lace panties that dared to cover what he wanted. She was wet, but he managed to rip into her by shoving his still-thick cock inside without pause. He held her hands behind her, pinning her to the bed, and she moaned as he fucked her roughly in order to reclaim the control she had mercilessly stolen from him.

Lexi felt the wave of an orgasm approaching. Giovanni slapped her ass with his palm, and she choked on his name as she buckled beneath him before he delivered another stinging blow. "You won't sit down tomorrow without thinking of me." She could barely utter his name, and he spanked her again. His fucking was unrestrained, and she clutched the duvet as he pulled her closer to a second explosion of fulfillment. "Where's your bravery now?

You talk about other women and question me with that fucking mouth," he growled, pushing himself even deeper into her as she cried out. "I want you to feel me in your throat just to shut you up."

"I already have," she gasped. When he continued to slam into her but she heard the unbuckling of his belt, Lexi tried to push up only to be knocked back to the bed. Whatever request she had died when Giovanni looped the belt around her throat like a leash. He pulled her back, making it impossible for her to plead with him to stop. She was forced to balance her knees on the bed to avoid being strangled and, when he pushed into her from this angle, she felt him deeper than before and could do nothing but exhale bursts that begged him to fuck her deeper, harder, longer.

She was on her hands and knees. When he tightened the belt, she raised herself toward him. When he brutalized her ass with his hand, her back arched and the belt constricted. She could barely breathe and, when he ripped through her soul, the orgasm that rocked her body shattered Lexi in a way she had never before experienced. The lack of freedom to breathe had heightened her climax, and she aimlessly fell against the bed. Giovanni dropped the belt and let her roll to her back. Her legs were spread open in front of him and, with hazy eyes, she watched him tear his clothes off before he climbed on top of her.

Her hands were already over her head, and he used his tie to loop them together in prayer before he strung the silk through the intricate metalwork of the headboard. In seconds, he held her waist and was inside of her again. Lexi threw her head back while sounds of pleasure escaped her lips. "Your body was made for me," Giovanni extolled, before thrusting into her deeply again. *"Potrei continuare a scoparti per sempre."*

Lexi could barely remember life without him. When he pulled her legs against his chest in order to fuck her even harder, she could see on his face that he wasn't going to stop until he was the only key that ever turned her lock again. His fingers wrapped around her throat while he completely obliterated her with his throbbing cock. His sweaty body collapsed on top of her and she was content to stay, tied to his bed, beneath him, for as long as he'd keep her.

After catching his breath, Giovanni balanced on his forearms and untied her wrists. She felt sensation rush back into them and curled against his body. "That mouth," he murmured, kissing the top of her head. "Why did I wait this long to claim that beautiful mouth?"

"Claim? I'm pretty sure I won that round." Lexi chuckled sleepily and, even though her eyes were closed, knew that he was smiling.

12

His fingers trailed from her temple down her cheek, and Lexi purred her approval as he continued from her neck to her chest. One nipple came to attention in response to Giovanni drawing circles around it. He lowered his head to gently suck the peak while he created a second one on the other side and repeated the action. "What are you doing?"

"We have to go," he answered. His fingers drew down her stomach and she arched her back toward him in reflex. "We have a flight to catch."

She looked out the window before his fingers slipping inside of her brought her attention back to the bed with a gulp of air. One hand was wrapped around his wrist and did little to change his course of action while her other clutched the sheet. "Stop watching me."

"I like watching you, especially like this."

With a simple change of movement, Giovanni had her entire body convulsing and she whispered his name desperately. Before she could beg him for the ability to breathe, he had buried his face between her legs. Using his hands to hold her wrists down at her side, he devoured her as though she were his breakfast spread.

The stubble on his face added an additional layer of sensation to the symphony his tongue was conducting. Her body was his orchestra, responding to each rise and fall within the measures he wrote with pulses and staccato bursts of breath while he brought Lexi to a crescendo. As his sexual opus increased from *molto vivace* to *sforzando* and she no longer could think about anything other than her own desire and pleasure, the scale erupted off the sheet music that he created, and she shuddered her final *fermata* by calling out his name and clutching his hands.

Giovanni slowed but didn't stop. Instead, he used his tongue as though she were the pastry from the night before. "*Dolcissima,*" he murmured before leaning back and licking his lips. When Lexi rolled over to bury her face in a pillow to cover her blushing and with embarrassment begged him to stop looking at her, he added, "*Come il miele.*"

His hand slapped against her ass playfully and Lexi grabbed the sheet. He yanked it onto the floor. "Time to get dressed. We've got to go."

"Go where?"

"Catania." Annoyance flared when she failed to move. "Get up."

"You're already up," Lexi teased. Her eyes cleared from her night of sleep and morning of his mouth all over her. She lazily relaxed on the bed. "Can't we just stay here all day? Catania can wait. I can see Ursino later."

"I wish Catania could wait." Giovanni moved so that he was next to her and, when he kissed her, Lexi tasted herself on his lips.

"You don't have to wait." She further answered him by wrapping her legs around his waist to press him against her so that she could bite his lower lip. She was still drunk on him yet needed another drink. When he pushed her back on the bed and forced himself inside of her, the ache of sex gave way to her body's acceptance of him.

"I don't have time to fuck you the way I want," Giovanni told her harshly, "so I'm just going to use you."

Even half-asleep, Lexi couldn't stop herself from provoking him. "*Fammi vedere cosa sai fare.*"

"That fucking mouth," he said menacingly. With a slap across her face that caused her breath to catch from desire instead of pain before he encircled her throat with his fingers, Lexi gasped and arched beneath the powerful thrusts that sent her body into waves of want. "When I get you back home, I'm going to teach you better manners."

Lexi couldn't get the words out in a continuous sentence as he fucked her to fulfill his own need and roughly manhandled her. "It seemed you liked my manners just fine last night," she managed. Her fingers curled into the wrist of the hand around her neck and she felt her stomach tighten in anticipation as Giovanni treated her body like it had been created explicitly for his desires. When he came inside of her, he tightened the fingers around her throat, sending her reeling into her own explosion, and dug his other hand into the tender skin of her hip.

He looked down at her before he lowered his lips to hers. "I could do this every day and never get tired of seeing you high on me."

"If you aren't careful," Lexi said when he moved off the bed, "you'll end up with an addict." And she would end up in rehab because she wouldn't be able to cope without him.

Giovanni lightly laughed while picking up his discarded slacks from the floor. "I can live with that."

Could she? Lexi scooted up against the headboard, feeling him all over her skin and inside of her body. He pulled on his pants while checking his phone. The sky was lighter than evening would suggest and the sun had yet to rise. "Why are we up so early? Is this one of your sadistic torture techniques?"

"I'll show you sadistic when I get you back home if you don't move that ass," he threatened. Giovanni picked up her dress from the floor and tossed it to the edge of the bed before taking the fragment that had been her lace panties.

"Did you just put my panties in your pocket?" When he didn't answer, Lexi crawled to the end of the bed and took the dress. "Freak."

"I've been called far worse."

"The fuck, Gio!" She looked over the mangled fabric. The zipper was halfway out of the dress and the seam had been ripped. It was barely held together as one piece. "Do you have any idea how much this dress costs?"

"I bought it," he shrugged, "so I can break it."

"You are unfuckingbelievable. I hope you go broke." Lexi wanted to be annoyed, but she couldn't stop laughing. "How the fuck do you expect me to walk out of here? Naked?"

"Naked works for me." He repeated her earlier comment from the bed with a sneer. "Show me what you can do."

"You say that, but I call your bluff. You don't want your men to see me naked. I'm surprised you can even cope with those pieces of floss that you dare call bikinis." She rose from the bed and slipped into her shoes. "I'll walk out of here like this."

"Are you challenging me?" Lifting an eyebrow, he stood from tying his shoes and a devious grin flashed on his face while he buttoned his shirt. He left his vest undone and pulled the holster over his arms before sliding the SIG into it. "Do you really think you'll win? This is Sicily, baby girl. My men see naked women whenever they go to a beach."

Time to move the queen, she thought as she sauntered over to him and leaned against his chest in order to whisper, "Naked *women*. Not *your* naked woman, *Il Padrone*." Lexi stepped back and, satisfied that she had backed him into a corner, smirked. She started to walk toward the door.

"You continue to misjudge me, *bambina*." He threw her over his shoulder and slapped her ass when she squirmed to get down. Giovanni didn't even bother to cover her up with his dinner jacket as he opened the door to the patio outside.

Lexi didn't realize how close they were to the road. His men were already spaced between the room and the driveway, with Raphael next to the door. Giovanni yelled out, *"Toglile gli occhi di dosso cazzo,"* and they all looked away as they walked toward the vehicles. By the time he dumped her into the back seat of the Mercedes, the men were already inside their respective cars. Giovanni tossed his jacket at her and settled into the seat next to her. "In case you'd rather walk when we get back."

"I can't believe you did that." She slipped her arms through the jacket and held it closed while she faced him.

"Unlike you, my men are obedient." He played with a strand of her hair that was in her face. "One day, you'll learn that I always win."

"One day, that attitude will cause you to lose," Lexi warned. Although she had meant it as a playful retort, the thought settled against the wine of the night before and she felt nauseous.

She thought she saw some sort of understanding pass across his face before he tucked the hair behind her ear. "The House always wins in the end." His voice was much softer than she expected, and his warning was more chilling because he sounded almost sad. "Betting against that will leave you with less than nothing."

She should have avoided the casino, Lexi thought when she looked out the window while he answered a call. She had never been a gambler and playing Giovanni Masseretti was not the game to start with. She didn't know the rules and wasn't even sure she could bluff enough to keep any chips on the table.

Lexi had to tell him the truth. He might kill her and mail her piece-by-piece back to New York. He might beat the hell out of her and drop her off at the field office when they returned in a few days. Lexi had no idea what he would do, but she couldn't imagine Giovanni would accept who she was and how she had lied to him with no repercussion.

What would she say? *I used to work for the FBI and I quit so that I could entrap you into admitting that you killed my father.* Could she possibly tell him that she no longer knew right from wrong? Lexi watched the rising sun change the sky as its rays reflected against the sea. Could she tell him that she'd fallen in love with him and didn't want to walk away? Would he believe her? After all of her omissions and lies, would Giovanni trust anything she said?

He hung up the phone and, when he touched her bare knee, she looked at him. The quiver of her voice betrayed her thoughts. "I'm not a gambler. I should have never come into the casino in the first place. I should have never tried to play a hand in a game I was destined from the start to fail." Her voice faltered as she choked up. *Just tell him,* her heart begged her brain. *Just say the words and let the chips fall where they may.* "I'm not who you think I am." It was all she could manage before she broke down.

"None of us are, Alessandra." He reached out and pulled her into his lap, holding her against his chest as tears spilled down her face. She clutched his shirt in her hands and felt the gun pressing against her side. Who they both were simply made her even more desperate, and she buried her head against him. "The House takes us all down in the end."

Giovanni held her until the car came to a stop in front of the estate. No one disturbed them, perhaps because they weren't willing to risk Giovanni's earlier command of *avert your fucking eyes,* and were content to have him decide when it was safe for them to do their jobs again.

He opened the door and eased her directly from his lap to the driveway outside. Lexi clutched the jacket around her and sank against him as he led her through the gate. "We need to leave in an hour," he said gently, not bothering to comment on their conversation in the car. "Wear comfortable shoes and," he waved his hand around her torso, "cover your shoulders with your dress."

She almost asked where they were going, but she simply nodded. "You aren't coming?" Lexi questioned when he stopped outside the door.

"I need to check on a few things." Giovanni followed the curve of her jaw with his thumb before kissing her. "Remember what I told you last night," he whispered against her mouth. "*Essere mia.* Don't place a bet. Get the fuck out of the casino and leave the chips for another player. Let me deal with covering the cost of the play. *Scegli di essere mia.*"

When she stepped inside the room, Lexi fell against the wall and wept as quietly as she could. Giovanni had no idea what he was saying. She poured herself into the shower and sank to the floor, the sounds of the water covering her tears. When they returned from Sicily, she would tell Giovanni everything. Although he would hate her, she couldn't continue to lie to him. She owed him this much, but the agony that this was the cost of her love was too much to withstand.

Lexi forced herself to breathe. They needed to leave for the airport. If she didn't pull herself together, she wouldn't last until they got back to New York. She had a few more days with him; Lexi had to create the memories that would help silence the numb that would no doubt come with Giovanni's loss.

She wrapped herself in a towel and stumbled into the closet, searching for something to mask how much pain her breaking heart was in. There were few casual dresses with actual sleeves. and she had just selected one that cuffed mid-forearm when she heard the shower turn back on.

The white dress was simple, combining the cotton material with delicate eyelets, and she paired it with matching platforms that laced midway up her calf to where the dress stopped. Lexi was surprised to find a white, floral headband amidst the collection of barrettes in the drawer where she had found hairpins earlier, and she left her hair down, resting the band at her crown. The woman in the mirror looked carefree and relaxed. Out of habit, she grabbed a sling bag but had nothing to put in it. She had no idea where Giovanni had put the duffel she had left work with.

The shower turned off as Lexi emerged from the closet into the bedroom, where she saw Giovanni drying off with a towel. When he saw her leaning in the doorway, he tossed the towel on the bed and began to dress. "Like what you see?"

"I was looking for where you've hidden my wallet and phone. The free show is just an added benefit." She sat down in the chair nearest her and slowly crossed her legs at the knee. "Thirteen, huh?"

His lips curled into a smile. "Still trying to figure out where they all are?"

"There's that really involved one on your arm and the thorns on your back." She pointed at one she hadn't seen because it was under his watchband. "There's something on your left wrist that I'm just now noticing."

Giovanni pulled on his boxers before he secured his watch. "It's a sprig of lavender."

"I'm not even going to ask what that signifies." Lexi kept recounting as she stood up and walked over to the bed. "The snake, the cross, the words, and the wolf make seven. What am I missing?"

"Perfect opportunity to investigate." He leaned forward to kiss her.

She rested her hand on his torso. The left side of his chest held the head of the snake at his collarbone and the wolf that was over his heart. Her fingers followed the asp as it curved around his left arm to where it ended on his hand. "There's something here." She pointed to something she had initially considered auxiliary to the serpent. "A map?"

"The island of Sicily." He made note of the two shaded sections. "Palermo and Agrigento."

That made eight. She held his hands and recognized a small symbol on his right ring finger by the way the three stokes of the wheel spiraled upon themselves. "I can't say I'm too surprised by this one. Nine."

She turned his hands over, but his right wrist was empty. She let one hand slowly drive over his abdomen back up his chest, and her fingers hovered over the numbers she found on the right side. The date would have put him around fifteen. "What's significant about March twentieth?"

"That's one for another day." He lifted her fingers and kissed them. "Move on. Ten."

Lexi was dying to know what the numbers meant, but she continued her search. She rested her hand on what she now saw was a far more involved tattoo on his arm. "Wow, Gio! I hadn't seen just how detailed this one is!"

The tree wasn't just any tree. While she had noticed that the roots created the name *Masseretti*, the tree itself was Giovanni's entire family. The trunk curved up into branches; on the left, the trunk was his father's full name while, on the right, his mother's. The branches bore the full names of Giovanni and his siblings, with Giovanni at the branch on the left side closest to his father and traveling up by age with his sister at the top. To the right, the branches carried the names, Lexi assumed, of their spouses, with

Giovanni's corresponding branch left empty. On some of the branches, there were leaves, each with a smaller name, representing one of his nephews or his niece. "This is spectacular."

"I'll have to add to it soon," he noted. "Theresa's new baby will be here in October, plus Vincenzo and Cara's baby next year." His hand touched her face and she looked up at him as he whispered, "And then there's you."

She felt her cheeks start to warm and looked away under the guise of moving behind him to investigate his back. Lexi drew her fingers along the thorns that trailed down his spine and stopped on his right side with a laugh. "How did I miss this?"

"No idea."

"No, not just the tattoo. How did I miss the imagery from the picture before?" She ran her fingers along the triskeles of the woman's three legs. The thin lines of the trinacria artwork etched the symbol of both Giovanni's heritage and, by coincidence, his lifestyle into his skin.

"Most would."

"The Gorgoneion is beautiful." The head of Medusa, rather than terrifying, was gorgeous, with wide eyes that looked almost three-dimensional. Instead of snakes, her hair was flowing pieces of wheat.

"An artist in New York did that one as well as the tree you like. She's quite talented."

"She is," Lexi agreed. On either side of the thorns, she saw the final two pieces. She had initially thought of them as extensions of the spinal artwork, but, looking at them directly, she could see that, although they were stylized as thorns, the names were the two Sicilian provinces he had alluded to earlier: Palermo, in grayscale, and Agrigento, in traditional black. She lifted the shirt he must have placed on the bed before his shower and offered it to him. "Thirteen." Walking in front of him, she opened her hands. "To zero."

"That doesn't surprise me."

"I'm afraid of needles. I can't imagine sitting down and letting someone draw on me with one. I barely survived getting my ears pierced at twelve."

"It doesn't hurt as much as you would think. The pain depends on the where as well as the amount of detail." He began to button his shirt after pulling on dark slacks. "It fades after the first few minutes."

"I'll pass." Lexi leaned against the bed. "Low pain tolerance."

"That's a lie." Giovanni looked up. "I might figure out how to use a tattoo gun just to prove a point."

"I don't know that I want to be your canvas after having seen how detailed your artwork can be." She laughed and took a few steps back. "Oh. My bag?"

"Ricardo unpacked it in the closet when we arrived." Giovanni switched to one hand in order to button his cuffs before he answered his vibrating phone. "*Salu.*"

Lexi returned to the closet, opening the few remaining drawers she had yet to explore in search of her cell and wallet, but they only held jewelry. She yelped nervously when she turned to see him watching her. "It isn't nice to sneak up on people."

He cocked his head to the side with a smile. "That skirt is far too long for how I would prefer to spend the morning."

"I guess that's the hazard when you allow the freedom to choose clothes." She turned back to the closet and finally saw the tiny edge of her bag beneath the bottom row. She pulled it out and unzipped it before looking up at him. "Where are the jeans and sweaters that I packed?"

"Not here."

Lexi glared at him as she removed her wallet and phone. "I'm not a doll for you to dress up, Giovanni. I'm a grown woman."

"A *disobedient* grown woman."

"That has little to do with my clothing choices." After she shoved the bag back in its place and stood, she turned her phone on, putting it alongside her wallet in the purse before she walked toward the door. "What? No smartass quips? Too early for you? Not enough caffeine?"

When she was close enough, Giovanni grabbed her arm. He pulled her close to him and whispered seductively into her ear, "That mouth begs me to make your ass difficult to sit on." Responding to her quick intake of breath, he used his free hand to slowly caress up her leg. "And yet that tongue deserves to be rewarded. You leave me in such a quandary."

Lexi didn't even realize her eyes were closed and she was trembling with desire. Damn him for knowing how every touch and every lilt of his voice manipulated her defenses into acquiescence. When Giovanni allowed his hand to go beneath the dress and she felt his hand between her legs, her head dropped against the doorframe behind her. "You are already wet for me," he purred in her ear before he chuckled again and lightly smacked her. "Time to go, *bambina*."

"*Sei un fottuto sciupafemmine dongiovanni*," Lexi said with frustration. Calling him a womanizer would surely get a rise out of him.

She thought he might bend her over the dresser and fuck her until she couldn't move, but he just laughed. "*Dongiovanni*," he echoed, recognizing the double entendre of using the insult that carried his name, a word to imply the stereotypical Italian lover. "Thirty-one."

Exasperated, Lexi walked out of the closet and stopped abruptly at the sight of the SIG on the night table. When she asked, her voice was devoid of the joking they had shared only seconds before, as though seeing the gun had dropped her back into reality. "Why do you carry this? Do you really think you'll need to use it?"

He approached from behind and put his fingers on top of hers as they rested next to the gun. "Better safe than sorry," he repeated from the day before. "It's a deterrent in as much as a weapon."

Why hadn't her father drawn his own gun? How had he been shot, point-blank and facing his attacker, having never even gone for his piece? "I hate guns."

"Everyone hates guns until they need one." Gracefully, he put the holster on before picking up his jacket from atop the bed. "I'm surprised you have such strong feelings. They are quite the American fascination."

"People who wouldn't shoot another person shouldn't have guns. They aren't protection; they are a liability." The words slipped out before she could check herself. Although they were true, it was something that Lexi rarely discussed because it put her at a severe disadvantage. When she had mentioned it to her weapons instructor, she had been chastised. What kind of FBI agent wouldn't be able to shoot when needed?

Still, Lexi knew herself enough to know that she would hesitate. Even as a child, she had hated her father's gun. As an adult, although she knew how to use the Glock she had been issued, it was because she was required to and had little to do with her belief that she could actually pull the trigger. "I could never kill someone else."

It was one of the few times Lexi thought she saw him truly surprised, but he quickly recovered. "I suppose it's good that you weren't interviewing for my security then." Giovanni draped his arm around her, pulling her against him before murmuring against her ear, *"Con me sarai sempre al sicuro."* He gave her a gentle squeeze and led her downstairs, to where Raphael was discussing a map with the men.

Giovanni looked at his watch before walking her outside of earshot. "Get something to eat," he ordered, pointing toward the kitchen. "We're leaving in ten minutes. I've already had Fernando prepare a few things for you to consider."

"I'm fine."

"Eat," he said, stopping her arguments by placing his finger over her lips. "Or I'll follow through with making it uncomfortable for you to sit."

Still annoyed by his pussy slap from upstairs, Lexi couldn't avoid the challenge. "Prove it," she muttered beneath his fingers.

The erotic darkness that passed over his face proved that Giovanni enjoyed the provocation as much as she did. His voice graveled the threat she longed for. "I'm going to enjoy watching you relive every slap when you try to move today."

"All I'm enjoying is listening to that voice of yours as you threaten me and seem unable to follow through. After all, we're leaving in ten minutes and I need to eat."

Her smartass response hit the mark Lexi thought it would, and he dragged her into the kitchen where the poor chef was pouring warmed milk and coffee into a travel mug. Before he could greet them, Giovanni growled, "*Andarsene.*" The older gentlemen didn't need to be told twice; he stopped twisting the top on the cup to scurry from the room. Pushing her hands against the island, Giovanni snarled, "You just cannot stop yourself, can you? You want this even though you have no idea what it is you are asking for."

He was right, Lexi realized. She had no idea why, from the start, Giovanni had inspired her desire to incite him at every turn. In her work, she was the perfect example of a demure librarian born fifty years too late. She wasn't a provocateur; if anything, she was known for being able to deescalate any situation. With Giovanni, the words and attitude slipped out. Lexi had initially thought that she was simply acting a role. As she trembled with anticipation, she now doubted that assessment.

"What? Nothing? Not enough caffeine?" He threw her words from the bedroom back at her while yanking her dress above her waist. She audibly swallowed, but her mouth was too dry to speak. "I'm not sure my hand wants to deal with this ass," he snapped.

Before she could move, the scream of wood hitting flesh echoed through the kitchen, followed by her stifled scream. The pain radiated across her backside seconds later in a delayed response that had her fingers gripping the steel island that Giovanni forced her body against even as she tried to back away. "Jesus!"

"*Don* Giovanni," he corrected. "I'm not quite Jesus yet." Before she could say anything else, he delivered a second, harsh blow. "*Dongiovanni-*

isn't that what you called me this morning? I think the full phrase you used was *you're a fucking womanizing dongiovanni*. Wasn't that it?"

She couldn't catch her breath. Unlike the belt that had cut into her skin and sent a coursing sting through her, the cutting board that Giovanni used as a paddle was a solid plank of balanced pain across her cheeks. It was a sensual torture that made her want to back away while she leaned forward. When the wood connected with her ass a third time, she gulped back the tears that came to her eyes. She was nearing how much she could handle, but the word to stop died before it even formed. "Fuck with me, baby girl," he growled. "Keep it up. I can do this all goddamned day and night."

"I know," Lexi panted.

He yanked her into him by her hair, his lips against her ear. "And you want me like this. You fucking do this on purpose."

"I can't beat the House if I don't learn how to beat the game."

Giovanni slammed the wood against the metal, and it reverberated beneath her fingers until he turned her around. Momentarily, she saw something other than the sport on his face. "You don't beat the House by knowing the game. You beat the House by forcing the game that is played to be yours." He clenched his jaws together and took a few steps away. "You fucking unravel me."

She unraveled him? Lexi leaned against the island barely able to move. "You aren't the one whose ass is numb," she mumbled.

He looked back, and his frustration ended in a sigh as arrogance crept back into his eyes. Giovanni picked up the coffee that still sat on the counter and screwed the top on tightly before giving it to her. "This will have to suffice until Catania. Maybe it will occupy your mouth until I have time to give you more etiquette lessons."

13

"What is that?" Lexi looked at Giovanni with shock.

"This whole *I'm a quick learner* doesn't seem to hold true," he said with a smirk as he pulled her toward the eight-passenger H145.

"That's a helicopter!" she exclaimed. "You own a helicopter?"

"I *chartered* a helicopter," he corrected. When she continued to force him to drag her forward, he added, "It's no different than taking a taxi."

Lexi had never been in a helicopter and wasn't thrilled about the prospect. "Can't we just drive? Or take a plane from Palermo?"

"It's a three-hour drive- at least- and to get there from Palermo means driving an hour north on top of the flight. It's less than an hour once we are in the air." He stopped and assessed her. "Are you afraid?"

"Afraid? Why would I be afraid? I mean, it's not like these things crash all the time and leave no survivors."

Giovanni laughed before he continued walking. "The H145 is safe. They are employed all over the world for civilian and government use; it's not going to crash." He looked at her and she thought he might change his mind when he said, "You are legitimately concerned."

"I don't like being in the air," she said after a moment. "I don't do roller coasters or parasailing or helicopters. Planes are a necessary evil that, if I could, I would do without."

"You don't like the sense of not having control and not trusting whoever does." He nodded with understanding and grazed her knuckles with his lips. He repeated, "The H145 is safe. I've used this company for the last few years; they haven't had a fatal crash in at least a decade. *You*," he specified, "are safe. I wouldn't take you up if I thought otherwise. Don't worry about trusting the pilot or the helicopter. Trust *me*."

She clutched the coffee that the cook had prepared although she had no desire to drink it and repeated to herself: *it's only sixty minutes*. The clamshell doors at the back of the helicopter were open, revealing two sets of four seats, each pair facing another pair, and Giovanni helped her step inside before following her. When she sat down in the leather seat, a wave of pain washed over her and she deeply inhaled.

"Is something wrong?"

When she saw the knowing smile on his face, Lexi refused to give him the satisfaction by confirming what he knew. "Just getting comfortable."

"Make sure to really sit deeply in the seat," he encouraged.

She almost told him to go fuck himself, but thought better of it. Lexi forced through the pain in her ass as she secured her seatbelt. Giovanni offered safety headphones; after putting them on, she looked out the window. Once the six-person security detail loaded in and the doors were locked, Lexi closed her eyes and prepared for take-off. "It's a beautiful view," Giovanni said, leaning against her shoulder and pointing out the window. He waited until her eyes followed to say, "You can see Africa from this vantage until we move over the island and head inland toward Catania."

Watching the world pass beneath them was fascinating. Nearly as soon as they had lifted off, it seemed like they were starting to descend. She could see a large airstrip coming into view, and the helicopter landed on a smaller heliport at the large Fontanarossa Airport a little over an hour after it had left Menfi. "See?" Giovanni told her, patting her leg affectionately. "It wasn't that bad."

He helped her off the helicopter, and Lexi looked around as a line of cars pulled up. Biting back the urge to comment on the amount of security, she entered the third car in line that he directed her to. "We're on the ground until tonight. We'll check into our hotel for breakfast, then head to the library."

"Hotel? I thought we were going back tonight."

"We are." He settled into the seat and unbuttoned his jacket.

"Then why are we going to check into a hotel?" She finally drank from her coffee and was pleased to see that the cup had kept the drink hot despite being an hour old. "We don't even have luggage."

Lexi could almost feel the scale she sat upon, as though Giovanni was weighing her and trying to decide if he really wanted to tell her the truth. Finally, he made a decision and, after replying to a message that vibrated his phone, began to explain. "Many bankers have multiple jobs: bankers, restaurateurs, real estate developers-"

"Amateur doctors," she interrupted.

He smirked. "It is a busy life."

"It sounds it. I can't imagine what you went to college for to wear all of these hats so effectively."

His smirk deepened. "It is commonplace that, when one banker visits the home of another, he will encourage the friendship and hospitality of his fellow banker by utilizing his hotels, clubs, restaurants, *et cetera*, regardless of how short his visit, and will pay a premium for the services."

Lexi listened to his explanation and drank the coffee to scald what he had just confessed. For years, the Bureau had been trying to figure out the methodology for how Giovanni and those like him cleaned their money enough to transition into legal businesses that, it appeared, were untouchable. She looked out the window at the sea when the traffic began to slow upon their approach into the more densely-packed city. Her mind tried to process the truth of both this confession and the one the day before. "Why would you tell me this?"

Giovanni shrugged. "You asked."

Was that all it would have taken? Devoid of humor, Lexi's first response was to laugh; if she did, she might puke. Just as he had so easily told her how he had murdered in order to restore safety to *Signore* Pascarelli's family, Giovanni now had shared his technique for money laundering.

She hated to admit that it was actually a foolproof technique. The money collected by hotels and restaurants was practically untraceable; what better way to legitimize than to open businesses that anyone could- and would- use, then cycle money through them, knowing that whatever money was spent would be returned tenfold. The premium served as interest for the privilege of laundering the money in the first place; everyone benefited and everyone made money, all while law enforcement tried to figure out where the money was coming from and how it was materializing in ways that were impossible to prosecute. Like any good businessman, Giovanni declared an insane amount of income and paid his taxes. He wasn't trying to hide it; he didn't need to. By the time the government took their cut, the money was clean.

  Traffic was crawling as the car turned from the coast and moved toward the heart of the city before the line of SUVs stopped in front of a multistoried, palatial hotel. After a few seconds, the doorman opened the back door and Lexi followed Giovanni into sounds of downtown Catania. It reminded her of a relaxed New York. The sidewalks were alive with people walking and talking, eating at cafes, and coming out of the shops that lined Via Etnea. When Giovanni took her hand, Lexi followed him into the brightly decorated lobby.

  The concierge greeted him by name before handing him a large envelope, and, as though he had been to the hotel a thousand times before, Giovanni strolled through the marble and glass entryway like he owned it. There was a waiting elevator that took them to the top floor. "Did you reserve the entire thing?" she asked when they stepped into the emptiness

  "People are probably eating," he said with a laugh. Giovanni used a keycard from the envelope to open a room door. "I'm not being *that* hospitable." Once inside the room, he offered her the key. "Raphael will have one, as will Ricardo, but this is on the off-chance that you get separated- which you won't." His tone implied that there would be hell to pay if she tried to shake her security. "Sicily is not-"

  "Sicily is not New York. I know." She took the key and slipped it into her handbag.

"Give me your phone." He held his hand out and waited for her to place the small rectangle in his palm. She wasn't sure what he was doing, but when he finished typing something, he returned to the main screen and gave it back. "If you get lost, if anything happens once we are apart, you call. Call me. Call Raphael. Call Ricardo."

"Call someone. I get it." Lexi looked down at the phone and noticed she had a missed call. While Giovanni talked to Raphael, she looked at the log and noticed the exchange for the library. She took the opportunity to explore the large triple suite while she waited for the international call to connect. The view was stunning as she watched Mount Etna smoking in the near distance. When she heard, "Rare Books," on the other end of the phone, she sat down on the stairs that led to the second floor of the suite. "Hey, Suzanne; it's Lexi. It's way the hell early in New York. What's up?"

"Lexi! Hey! Yeah, I got called in to do third shift to help out with the biannual weeding. I needed a break and am doing some repairs for a bit. How's Catania?" Her page sounded excited to hear from her. Even though her life felt like fiction, a sense of normalcy fell over her when she heard the friendly voice. "Enjoying Ursino?"

"It's amazing," she lied. She hoped her coworker wouldn't ask what project was so important that Lexi had been flown across the world, especially since she had yet to even visit the library. "I'm sorry I missed your call. Things have been hectic." Giovanni watched her from a bar where he already had placed a demitasse of espresso. "Is everything okay?"

"I'm working on the Mariccetti from 1788. It's in rougher condition than we thought. The page damage is extensive and the entire thing is just so dirty. The cover was the least of the issues."

"The cover can be reconditioned," Lexi noted, remembering the large book in question. "The page damage is unfortunate. The document tape can correct minors, but are we talking missing pages? We will have to order milled pieces to insert. When I checked before I left, we were out of clean pages that date that far back." She grunted with frustration. "If we have to insert, then that's going to completely change the makeup."

"I didn't see too many missing pages," Suzanne said. Lexi could hear the woman drinking and could almost visualize the cup of tea that she was often with. "These are just filthy."

"We don't have much budget for page washing." Lexi stood up and walked to the balcony in an attempt to avoid Giovanni's continued gaze.

"Bleach solution?"

"Not on that one. Those pages have too much pulp content."

"I can spot clean the worst and then we can try an air bath to remove the excess coal dust. We're going to have to open the cover anyway, but that will wait until you come back." Suzanne spoke with someone in New York before she returned to the phone. "I need to go. See you next week?"

"Yes, I'll be back over the weekend. Thanks for holding things down." After their goodbyes, Lexi hung up and felt him behind her. "Stop watching me and eavesdropping."

"Work?" he asked.

"An eighteenth-century restoration. The book is in horrible condition, but it was given to us by a Trustee so," she lifted her hands in a shrug as she turned around, "what are we going to do, except save it?"

What was Giovanni thinking as his eyes burned into her? Finally, he took a few steps forward, and she thought that understanding passed across his face. "This is your passion."

Lexi leaned against the balcony as a recollection from her past rolled out with a smile. "When I was fourteen, I visited the Smithsonian's Rare Book Collection on a school field trip. I have no idea why the librarian was feeling brave enough to let us into one of the temperature-controlled rooms, but, in the center, there was this case with one book in it." The memory played as a movie in her mind. "It was stunning. The script, the bright colors, the artwork, the binding... All done by hand, all painstakingly created. It was amazing."

She looked back at the volcano in the distance. "There is a feel to the paper, a smell... It's just- it's just different than anything else." Lexi felt the weight of the sadness life had placed on her. "If I could have chosen to be anyone, *this* is who I would have chosen to be."

She faced him, and the connection with Giovanni took her breath away. When she told him the truth, would he see that she had tried to tell him who she really was so many times before? Would that matter at all? She tried to lighten the mood. "Where to now, *Don*?"

Lexi didn't know if he liked it when she used the word or if he was adding another minute to her tally, but he curled his lips into a grin anyway. Taking her hand, he led her upstairs to where the upper floor of the suite opened onto a rooftop deck. While they had a private sitting area, the roof as a whole was a bar and restaurant.

A man she didn't recognize (who clearly traveled with his own security) was already seated at a large round table just outside their door. When he saw them exit, he stood with a smile and said, "*Don* Giovanni!" before taking her partner in an embrace. When his eyes fell on her, she could see his head-to-toe assessment, and she unconsciously drew closer to Giovanni. The man took her hand and kissed it, squeezing it within his massive palm. "A pleasure," he said in English.

Lexi decided to keep her knowledge of Italian to a minimum and smiled in return. "Good morning."

Giovanni didn't bother with introductions, instead pulling her chair out and sitting next to her once she was at the table. A waiter instantly deposited a colorful cocktail in front of her along with a plate that held a small, round *brioscia* split and overflowing with what she assumed was sorbet. The strong, sweet pomegranate taste paired with the same juice in the cocktail, which was also accented with mint. After some discussion with Giovanni that she didn't understand, the man turned to her and smiled warmly. "Are you enjoying your visit, *Signora*?"

"It's a beautiful country." Although she assumed this was the fellow *banker* that Giovanni had planned to meet, she found it odd that he would bring her along to any sort of real business dealings.

"You should take in the spa here," he said. "There are many services that you would enjoy."

Lexi tried to avoid shifting her sore ass against the seat and thought that a massage might not be a bad idea. Giovanni smirked at the discomfort she hadn't been able to hide well enough. "Thank you. I may take that advice."

"I'm taking Alessandra to Ursino. I'm sure she can make use of the many options this afternoon."

The conversation in the car came back to haunt her, and Lexi felt sick to her stomach. Each service, each shopping purchase, each meal: each was part of an organized, detailed, money laundering strategy. Sitting at the table and agreeing to a spa treatment had just made her into an unwitting participant in a much larger scheme. She had mistakenly thought she had a clue as to what the game was, but she had barely been at the real table.

The man accompanied them back to the suite and, while he and Giovanni participated in what seemed like an elaborate goodbye conversation, Lexi stood on the balcony and watched the scenery. She was conflicted. Although he had openly discussed prostitution and drugs while they were in New York, Sicily had added a significant level to her understanding of what Giovanni was a part of.

Every single thing that he had confessed left him well-protected; at the same time, Lexi couldn't help but see his words as him trying to explain that he trusted her. Just as she was trying to tell him that she was more than he would come to know, was Giovanni trying to convince her that he was more than his reputation and record? How much did Lexi really believe? How much was she willing to accept?

Giovanni's presence was a heat behind her, and she turned to face him. "Who was that?"

"A friend."

"A banker?" Frustration filtered into her words. "Another amateur doctor?"

"We should go," he said, not answering and extending his hand.

"I don't want to go. I want you to answer." Lexi crossed her arms.

"Do you remember how you left the last hotel we were in?" Giovanni asked, his hand still outstretched. "I don't mind carrying you to our next destination if you refuse to walk."

Doubtful that he wouldn't follow through, Lexi stalked passed him and he grabbed her arm. His voice vibrated against her ear. "Know when to let it go, *bambina*. Some things you don't *need* to know. Some things you may know later. Some things you may never know." When she tried to pull away, he maneuvered her hand into his and took her into the hallway, where the elevator was already open. "Enjoy this day," he whispered. "Enjoy the time with me. Don't think about anything else."

They walked into the rising heat, and Giovanni weaved through the town as though he knew it well. He pointed out things that he thought might interest her and suggested places she visit during his absence later that day. When they arrived outside a large cathedral about fifteen minutes away from the hotel, Giovanni lifted a white scarf embroidered with tiny flowers from a street vendor, passing the man payment before he draped it over Lexi's head while she laughed. "What are you doing?"

"Come on." He gently tugged her through an open gate and up small steps to where a pair of iron doors was open. "I want to show you something."

"Need a quick confession before you deal with your banking?" she quipped as they stepped inside. The massive *Cattedrale Metropolitana di Sant'Agata* was astounding both in its beauty and history, and it was impossible to see the feat of architecture without being amazed. Lexi's own religious upbringing had been minor at best and, excluding Christmas and Easter, nearly nonexistent.

As she looked upon the detail in awe, Lexi listened to the history lesson that Giovanni provided while he slowly led her through the church. "This cathedral was built in the late-eleventh century and destroyed less than a hundred years later by a fire and earthquake; only the apse survived. The bell tower was erected in 1387 before a clock was added three hundred years later, and then the entire thing was left in ruins after the earthquake of 1693." When she looked at him, surprised by his knowledge, he shrugged. "Some bankers study art history to better prepare themselves for their multifaceted work."

"Art history?" That was missing from everything she had read about him. As she thought back on the files Sam had slipped her, so much of what she now had learned about Giovanni over the course of a few days had been missing. "Of all the things to study, why that?"

"The best way to understand a people- their hopes, their fears, what it will take to win them and lose them- is to study their art." He continued to walk with her. "Art is a language of the soul; you can lie about a lot of things, but art reveals that which the tongue cannot bear to say."

Walking down an aisle toward a chapel at the end, he continued his lesson. "Agatha was born to a wealthy family in Catania but, rather than marry, chose to dedicate herself to the Church. However, when the prefect saw her, he fell madly in love and tried to force her to renounce her vows, sending her to a brothel when she refused." They stopped at the fresco that decorated the Chapel of Saint Agatha.

"Sounds like a punishment you'd find fitting for a disobedient woman."

He ignored her commentary. "After he nearly killed her himself, an earthquake threatened to destroy Catania and the prefect, who was truly a coward, fled, with Agatha dying after never accepting his advances."

"That's a horrible story."

"It's the story my father told my mother, right before he married her here," Giovanni touched the small gate that surrounded the altar area, "in this chapel."

"And I thought the story was disturbing! Seriously?" Lexi looked at him, appalled. "Who the hell threatens a woman with that story on her wedding day?"

"It wasn't a threat; it was a promise."

"I can only guess the promise he was making if he thought that prefacing it with a story about a man who murdered a woman because she didn't return his lust was a good choice." Lexi crossed her arms and leaned against the gate while Giovanni smirked at her aggravation.

"He told her to consecrate herself to Saint Agatha."

"Lapsed Presbyterian. I don't follow."

"It was his way of telling her that she had nothing to fear from him. That he would wait for her forever." He looked up at the fresco. "That he'd rather be destroyed by an earthquake than force her to love him. That he would face the volcano before he would leave her behind."

"And still, shockingly, she bit him."

Giovanni met her eyes and laughed. "Yes, she did; and, knowing my mother, he's lucky that's all she did." He put his arm around her waist and steered her toward the exit. "I promised you a library, Alessandra."

As they approached the street, Lexi pulled him to a stop. "Why did you bring me here?"

"Other than to see you in a white dress in church?"

"I'm serious. Why?" None of this made sense: not the way Lexi felt about him, not the way he treated her, none of it. Coming to a church and his makeshift history lesson made even less sense, and she felt more off balance than she had before.

He looked back at the nave of the church, as though somehow the answer was locked in the tabernacle or chiming from the bell tower. His voice was low and laced with an honest answer. "I'm not the villain you think I am, Alessandra."

"Rarely, Gio," she said, forcing herself to look away, "are we the villain in our own story."

He kissed the top of her head and let the veil fall to her shoulders, nodding slowly. "And most often, *bambina*, the best we can hope for is to be the antihero."

14

Ursino was everything Lexi had ever imagined and more. Looking at the massive stone structure, it was easy to see that the *Biblioteche Riunite Civica e A. Ursino Recupero* began its life as a Benedictine monastery. She noticed the sign that noted the library was closed for another hour. Pointing to the notation, she offered, "Grab a cup of coffee?"

"I don't know that your fellow librarians would appreciate you bringing coffee into a building that even I couldn't afford to replace."

The door in front of them opened and an older gentleman stepped into the entry. He welcomed them with a hearty *"Bongiorno."* As they walked inside, Lexi leaned against Giovanni's shoulder. "Why am I surprised that the library is closed because of you?"

"You shouldn't be."

The loud door clanged shut, and Lexi looked behind them, noticing that none of the bodyguards had come inside. "We're alone?"

"Save *Signore* Francelli who can, of course, answer any questions that I cannot." Their shoes echoed on the ornate tile floor as they stepped inside the first of several rooms. Six glass bookcases were overflowing with books and brochures; letters lay displayed alongside manuscripts. There was a beautiful writing desk near an antique arm chair and the wall was decorated with oil paintings. "In 1912, the town purchased the majority of Mario Rapisardi's personal writing space after his death," Giovanni said casually. "Much of what is in here is contained nowhere else. His correspondences and many of the fragments of his poetry were never formally published."

He followed a few feet behind her while she traveled into a larger space. "Libraries make up the north wing of the monastery. You may not know, but the original monastics here were women: nuns who made their precepts the preservation of literature."

"Is that who I would have been a few hundred years ago?" Lexi looked over at him, the memory of the church fresh in her head. "A nun locked in a library until she stumbled into a prefect with little concern for the word *no*?"

Giovanni walked passed her, as though investigating one of the cases in the center of the room. "The difference between that prefect and me is that I wouldn't have fled. Eventually, you would have said *yes* because you wanted to, not because I couldn't take *no* for an answer."

Lexi sighed and shook her head, following behind him and looking at a collection of religious pamphlets. The small tag identified the materials in the case as a Psalter and martyrology from the thirteenth century. "This is… I don't know what to say." Unconsciously, she curled her hands around his arm as he stood with his hands in his pockets. "Stop making me fall for you."

When he turned, their faces were almost touching and he leaned forward to kiss her gently. "Stop thinking you aren't caught already, and you won't have to worry about falling."

Lexi wasn't sure how to take his words and, when he stood tall again, she let go of him to walk forward. Even the floor, with its hand-painted artwork, was stunning. She was mesmerized everywhere she looked, but Lexi thought she might die from oxygen deprivation when she stepped into the main collection. She had never seen anything like it. Her eyes were drawn to the ceiling as she tried to take in all of the images amidst a library that put her fantasies to shame.

Giovanni stood a few feet behind her. "This is the only room from the monastery that remains almost intact in its original configuration. The floor is Neapolitan ceramic- majolica of Vietri; the polychrome cornice determines the vault. Those," he pointed to a series of separations, "were frescoed by Giovanni Battista Piparo: Virtues, Arts, and Sciences. Above the frame," he drew her attention back to the ceiling, "are the medallions containing portraits of the Holy Fathers of the Church. The sequence, from the Novitiate to here, is one of the few examples in Catania in which rigidity finds true expression."

The huge rectangle was penetrated by light through the side windows that were placed throughout the walls. The four corners of the room curved with wooden shelves that covered the space with wall-to-wall books. Lexi was in a dream and didn't want to wake up. She turned around and looked at him, wondering what he saw as he watched her completely laid bare.

Giovanni had been right. The world was revealed through its art and architecture, and he had found hers. He had discovered how to make her and how to break her. Lexi forced her eyes away from him, trying to reveal the majesty of the library as the source of her tears. "Thank you," she said, turning her gaze back to him. "This has been the most amazing experience of my life."

"Better than your fourteen-year-old self at the Smithsonian?" Giovanni took her hand, and she noticed that the old librarian waited for them by the door.

She didn't answer, looking one last time over her shoulder at the collection as they exited the building and the librarian removed the closed sign for a group who had already gathered. She could see Raphael and Ricardo waiting for them and, when she glanced around, identified the other bodyguards mingling in with the crowd. Giovanni led her to an outdoor café, where they were seated and coffee was brought over. "It might be easier for you to just have an IV drip set up," she smarted over her own cappuccino. "Cheaper, too."

"Are you offering another option to keep my mouth satiated, *bambina*?" Giovanni asked as he drank from his espresso. While Lexi tallied another point lost in the game and looked around the square to try and minimize her blushing, he added, "I will be occupied most of the afternoon."

"Lots of loans to issue? Debts to call in?" Lexi tried to keep the words lighthearted, but a heaviness descended whenever she remembered who Giovanni was and why she had met him in the first place.

He didn't bother with a reply. "I expect to be back to the hotel by four which means that *you* will be back to the hotel by four." Giovanni nodded his head toward the two bodyguards closest to them. "Raphael and Ricardo will be with you, but I've told them to stay back unless you ask for them or they notice trouble."

"Why do you leave Raphael with me? You told me in New York that he's your number one. No one here is looking to do anything to me; I don't need that level of protection. On top of that, I can't imagine you hire slackers so Ricardo could probably disarm a dozen guys while getting a manicure."

"I'll let him know that you think so highly of him," Giovanni said with a laugh.

"I don't need two security guards."

"Two babysitters then."

Lexi sighed his name and dropped her head back. "Can't you be serious? You're all *Sicily is not New York* and then you refuse to take your key guy with you. Why?"

"Because Raphael protects the most important person in the room," Giovanni said, never looking away from her. "He is always assigned to the person *I* deem the most important, not the person who is at the most risk."

"That's not me. Don't make that me." Lexi's lies made it difficult to cope with the rising heat. "I don't deserve it."

"I'll decide who deserves what and why." He slid his fingers up and down the hand that she gripped the mug with. "And I've decided Raphael is with you. Push me, and I'll assign you all of them or, better yet, outfit you with your own personal detail."

Lexi couldn't read him at all. His book was a language she didn't know, and she couldn't predict the end. It was chilling. Rather than tell Giovanni the truth, she wanted to run away, but the mere thought of not waking up next to him had become such an agony that she couldn't bear to contemplate any reality.

"Tell me what you are thinking."

"No."

"No?" With eyebrows raised, he chuckled. "It must be bad. *Dirme.*"

"I can't." Lexi looked into her coffee and wasn't sure she could stomach anymore.

"There is a large world between *can't* and *won't*." Giovanni beckoned over the waiter who already had a second demitasse ready and replaced the empty cup. "I think there is little you *can't* do, baby girl."

"I can't be what you want me to be. I can't be what you need."

He blew out a long, slow exhale. "Where is this coming from?"

Lexi clutched the cappuccino to avoid shaking. "Why did you come find me that first night?"

"Perhaps I wanted to finish what we'd started in the car."

"You had plenty of unfinished business at the club." She tried to swallow down the nausea. "Why didn't you leave me alone? Why didn't you just let me walk away?"

"I was worried about you." He still moved his fingers along her hand, and the movement made it harder for her to think. "I needed to find out why you mattered."

"I'm your biggest mistake," she whispered.

"It's the lies that we believe that are the most destructive and the hardest to recover from." They were silent for a few moments before Giovanni stood up to walk around the table. He knelt down in front of her. "The greatest mistake a man can ever make is to be afraid of making one. A mistake has the power to transform you into something better than you were before. And, even if you are my greatest mistake, mistakes can be redeemed." When Lexi raised her eyes to his, he used his thumb to wipe away the single tear that fell down her cheek. "Admitting when we're wrong is courage- not weakness. Only the brave can admit change and not see it as defeat."

She wasn't brave, but she couldn't do the lies anymore. Giovanni had uncovered her and he had broken her, remaking her into the person she wished she could have been all along. She had nothing left, and Lexi saw herself as the villain of the story. While she doubted she could be the heroine, she could, as Giovanni had told her at the church, shoot for the antihero. "I need to talk to you."

"Tonight." He stood and pulled her into his arms. "We will fly back to Menfi when I return. You can tell me whatever it is you wish to say, and," he stepped back in order to gaze into her eyes, "I meant everything I've said to you. You have nothing to fear from me. There is nothing you can say that will put you at my risk."

"Only in your debt." Lexi looked away, and he tipped her chin back.

"I told you before. I'll cover the chips. Let someone else play the game." Giovanni kissed her forehead and beckoned Raphael closer. "Wherever she wants to go, whatever she wants to do," he ordered. "I should be back by four."

Raphael nodded before he offered, "*Signora*? Do you wish to walk or should I call for the car?"

Lexi didn't want to do either. She wanted to hold onto Giovanni in the square and scream the truth, but she didn't. She let him go, squinting beneath the brightness when she turned to Raphael. "I'd like to get sunglasses. Is there somewhere nearby?"

It didn't take long for her to walk far enough away that Giovanni disappeared into the crowds of the plaza. After stopping at a vendor for a pair of dark glasses, Lexi took Raphael's advice to walk the main street. The architecture was beautiful; although her heart was heavy, Lexi had found a glimpse of freedom. She had made up her mind to tell Giovanni the truth, and there was an ease to her spirit that had been missing.

While she strolled the strip, Raphael and Ricardo dropped back. She couldn't always see them, but the feel of someone watching her was too ever-present for her to believe she was alone. Shortly before one o'clock, they returned to the hotel and were seated at the rooftop restaurant for lunch. As they were finishing their meal, she felt her handbag vibrate against her leg and took out her phone, laughing softly at the identification before she answered it. "Seriously? *Mio Padrone*? You made *that* your contact name?"

She heard him chuckle. "Enjoying your afternoon?"

"Just thinking." She stood up and walked away from their private seating toward the bar. "You?"

"*Ti immagino qui con me,*" he said seductively before adding, "but busy."

"Then why are you calling me? Stalking tendencies trump business dealings?"

"I wanted to hear your voice. What are you doing?"

"We just finished eating. I'm sure you'll receive a detailed report and will be pleased to know that no one had to force-feed me."

He laughed again. "I'm glad to hear that, although I quite enjoyed force-feeding you."

Lexi tried to hide herself in a hallway off the bar that led to a back staircase. She knew that she was deeply blushing and used their distance to reel in his hold on her. "I think I'll take advantage of the spa later. Not sure anything can top Ursino." She smiled at the memory. "One thing though."

"What's that?"

"I'm not Theresa. You don't need to try and make me think I'm alone; I can feel that I'm being watched. If you're going to send me with more men than you tell me, just say it. It's less creepy to know they are there."

Giovanni was quiet for a moment. "I'll keep that under advisement."

She walked back into the brightness of the rooftop deck and could see Raphael and Ricardo still seated at their table. "Can I, um, can I ask you something?" Lexi hesitated to bring up the conversation from the night before, but when the thought filtered into her mind alongside her own feelings, she knew that asking him from afar would be the only way she would ever have the guts.

"You can ask me anything."

"Did they love you?" She swallowed down the angst that the question caused, but it didn't make coming to terms with her own feelings any easier. "You said that you didn't love them, but did they fall for you?" *The way that I have,* she tacked on silently.

He was quiet for a few seconds, and Lexi wondered if the call had disconnected. "I would hope not." Giovanni took a drink of something, and Lexi heard the cubes rattle in his glass before he spoke again. "I doubt that any of them saw more than the man I showed them, and that was evidence enough to prove that they needed to be elsewhere. So no, Alessandra, I don't believe any of them felt something more than attraction."

"They never contacted you after things didn't work out? To ask to try again?"

He chuckled darkly. "Definitely not. And, on the rare occasion we saw one another, they made no attempt to approach me." Giovanni sighed again. "What we've done... What you've experienced... It's been an introduction, but it's the lower rungs of a high ladder. They knew how high they wanted to go, and, when it wasn't high enough for me, they opted to get off where they were."

Lexi looked down at the artwork that was painted on the concrete floor. She had enjoyed everything that Giovanni had put her through, but how much more would he throw at her? How much more could she endure? When she reached her limit, would that be the moment he tired of her? The thoughts strangled down any ability to tell him her feelings and she said instead, "What happens if I can't climb high enough on the ladder?"

"There's no *high enough* for you, Alessandra. Wherever you stop will be the top."

She didn't know why, but the tenor of his voice led her to believe that he was telling her the absolute truth. Was it possible that, if she felt she could go no further, he would find satisfaction in what they'd already experienced? Or would he long for more? Her brain told her that she was just a plaything until he moved on, but her heart vehemently argued that she had to take him at his word. "How do you know that will ever be enough?"

"Because *you* are enough," Giovanni promised. "I can't imagine a life without you, Alessandra. I don't want to." He sighed again, and Lexi imagined that he was struggling to tell her the words just as she struggled to accept them. "When we get back to New York, we'll walk the ladder together. At whatever point you want to stop, just say the word. I don't need more than what you are willing to give. I just…" His voice faded into a whisper. "I just need you."

Lexi wanted to tell him that she understood and that he was everything she had never wanted in her life. That somewhere between his approach at the bar and her on his lap in the car a blinding bolt of lightning had cut through her soul. That he had brought her back to life and that she loved him. Her mouth opened to pour out her heart before her brain took over. "It's really beautiful up here."

"It is," he agreed after a few seconds. Giovanni changed the subject, ready to hang up the call. "Finish your lunch and enjoy the day. I'll see you in a few hours."

"Okay," she said, weaving between tables to get back to the private patio. "*Ciao.*" By the time she returned, Raphael was standing. He lifted her purse from the chair where she had left it and, after taking it, she put the phone back. Sandwiched between the two men, she returned to the upper level suite and opted to sit on the balcony and relax. After her sudden question at the end of the phone call, she just wanted to forget the chat with Giovanni altogether. An hour of solitude worked wonders for her, and Lexi called the spa to make arrangements once she felt more herself.

"*Bongiorno*! Spa Etna." A woman's accented voice musically greeted her. "How may I help you?"

"*Bongiorno.* I'm calling to make an appointment."

"*Sì, Signora.* I see you are calling from our master suite. *Don Giovanni* has already notified us to expect you at your leisure."

Of course he did, Lexi thought, rolling her eyes. "Awesome. What, exactly, did *Don* Giovanni sign me up for?"

"I have you for our luxury beauty package, complete with a soak in the baths, followed by an exfoliation and deep tissue massage, facial, manicure/pedicure, and hair salon treatment for the styling of your preference."

"Are you sure he didn't drop off a photograph of *his* preference?" she snorted.

"I'm sorry? I don't understand."

Lexi felt awful for putting the attendant on the spot, and guilt flooded her apology. "*Perdonami*. What I meant to say is that *Don* Giovanni seems to have covered everything."

"*Sì, Signora*. Should I be prepared for your visit now then?"

"Yes, thank you. I'll be right down. *Grazie*." After hanging up the bedside phone, she grabbed her cell and wrote a quick text before leaving it on the night table. *Thanks for the spa afternoon. I'll see you in a few hours.*

Lexi walked downstairs into the main sitting area, where Raphael was working at a computer while Ricardo sat in a chair by the door. Both stood when she entered. "I'm going to the spa. I'm not sure it's bodyguard appropriate."

"The spa has already been notified of our arrival," Raphael said, walking toward the door.

"Of course it has," she muttered.

When the trio arrived at the salon that took up most of the hotel's first floor, she saw women in a variety of stages of treatments as they wandered around. While Lexi would have been annoyed by the presence of bodyguards, the patrons seemed to ignore them. When she noticed men lingering in a sitting area that was stocked with coffee and a view of the entire spa, she understood why. How many mob wives and girlfriends were here? How was it that she was now counted among their numbers?

A woman met her at the entrance. "*Bongiorno* and welcome to Spa Etna. *Donna* Masseretti?" Lexi debated correcting the assumption but instead nodded, and the hostess walked her away from her security. She followed the girl to a multi-room suite that was larger than most hotel accommodations where she was given a thick, white robe and slippers. "This is your room for your stay. Strip and dress in the robe. Your attendant, Marisa, will be in to walk you through your first treatment."

Marisa turned out to be a very kind, fit woman with a friendly smile who looked like she was in her sixties. Her silver hair held a streak of blue and was braided down her back. After explaining that Lexi was to soak in the tub in order to decompress before experiencing an exfoliating treatment followed by a deep tissue massage, the woman pointed to the chamber that surrounded the salt bath. "Then you'll float for half-an-hour. No stress will be left. You will feel like a feather."

She would be stress-free for all of five minutes before she told Giovanni that she had once been employed by the FBI. At the close of that conversation, stress would be the least of her worries. "It all sounds amazing," she lied. It sounded expensive and invasive.

Lexi wasn't altogether thrilled with knowing the tiny woman in front of her would be rubbing her down in volcanic ash and washing her off in the shower, only to massage oil into her naked body. Not to mention, while the room seemed secure, she was sure someone, somewhere was watching. She could practically feel eyes on her.

The bath was an interesting mix of heat and light. Illuminated like a hot tub, the water cycled through purples, blues, and greens, giving an almost meditative quality to the soak. Marisa returned and had Lexi lay on a teak table where she was exfoliated with a mixture of ash and clay; a wave of embarrassment hit before Lexi began to feel the stress start to dissipate. So what if she was completely naked? Clearly the woman had seen all of this before. The scrub was so relaxing that, when it was time to be hosed down with the high powered jet system, Lexi thought she might be nearing sleep. "Not yet," Marisa teased. "You can sleep on the real table."

That, however, proved to be impossible. Marisa looked frailer than she was; the woman's hands were a machine, kneading Lexi's muscles like dough. By the time the ninety minutes concluded, Lexi wasn't even sure she'd be able to walk into the salt bath.

"I will give you a few minutes to relax, and then I will explain the pod to you," Marisa said. She made herself a cup of tea with an electric kettle before pointing to a glass next to the table. "The water will help flush out any remaining toxins. Drink the water. *Only* the water," she directed as she added a hearty teaspoon of sugar to her own cup. "You need to hydrate your cells. You may have tea," she chuckled, taking a drink, "*after* your salt bath."

"Coffee with milk?" Lexi asked with a grin, expecting the coming admonishment.

"No!" Marisa shook her head. "That isn't good for anyone, ever, but especially this late." Although Marisa's accent was definitely not Italian, she had embraced the idea of no milk-saturated cappuccinos or lattes after midmorning.

When the therapist took her tea and left, Lexi slipped back into the robe and drank the water, wondering what the hell kind of minerals turned it metallic and almost acidic. She had to rub her tongue on the roof of her mouth to try and dislodge some of the flavor. She found a bottle of still water on a counter and washed down the lingering aftertaste. She felt so loose; her muscles had been worked over and made lax. In addition, she was exhausted and wondered if she could take a nap in the salt bath.

After chasing the tall glass with the remainder of the bottle of water because the metallic finish was so strong, she heard a noise in the front room, but her therapist didn't return. The massage had really done the trick. She was so tired, and Lexi needed to hold onto the wall in order to walk. "Marisa?" she called out. She could feel someone in the room, but she didn't see anyone.

"Raphael? Ricardo?" Maybe they had come to check on her. She had been gone for a while. "Gio?" Weren't they going to dinner? Had he come to get her because it was after four o'clock and she was late? Lexi stumbled against the table and overcompensated by leaning against the wall to stop from falling. How much had she drank at lunch? She didn't remember having more than one cocktail. Had the bartender made it overly strong?

Warning signs were starting to go off, but her body was too dull to respond to her raging brain. Something wasn't right. She stumbled back toward where she had left her clothes. Had she brought her phone? Could she call Raphael to come get her? Stepping into the dark room, she sobered up when she heard the noise behind her. There was nothing quite like the sound of a slider skating over the barrel of a gun as a bullet chambered to fire. "Don't move," the voice snarled.

Lexi thought she was going to pass out. She was going to be shot and could barely stand up. Her body refused to listen; she started to collapse. She recognized the voice behind her when he cursed, and Lexi wondered why Raphael was going to shoot her. The shadow in front of her tore through a hidden door into the hotel, and Raphael was forced to choose between catching Lexi and running after the ghost. "Ricardo!" he called out. "*Inseguirlo!*"

Who were they chasing? Why had someone been in her room?

"*Signora!*" Raphael was shaking her and smacking her cheeks lightly. "Alessandra! Open your eyes!" He lifted her into his arms like she was a small child and ran into the spa. The bright lights from the hallway felt like fire against her face, trying to force her to stay awake.

Was Raphael mad at her? Why was he screaming? God, she felt so sick. But first, sleep. She was so tired. "*Signora*, wake up! *Sveglia!*" He was yelling in Italian and English. Why? Couldn't Raphael just be quiet? Didn't he know she was tired?

The elevator made such a loud noise, but the door to the suite was even louder. Raphael carried her up the steps to the bed and dumped her on top of it. Her robe wasn't tied tightly and she worried he might see something that would get him shot. She tried to retie the belt, but her fingers weren't working. She didn't care. She would care after she woke up. "No, no, no! *Sveglia*! Open your eyes!"

She heard Giovanni's voice and the slamming of the door. Why were Italian men so damn loud? Not Italian- Giovanni didn't like being called Italian. Sicilian. Loud and deaf Sicilian men. Why was he still yelling? Didn't he know she was trying to sleep? "Alessandra! Where the fuck is she?" Was someone with him? He was running up the stairs and she wanted to tell him to be quiet.

Lexi tried to open her eyes, but it was just too bright and she was so tired. "Gio?" Her voice sounded slurred. He would be angry that she was drunk. It wasn't New York. Things weren't safe. But they were- they had to be. He had told her she was safe.

She heard something about a glass and then Giovanni was barking orders. He grabbed her and carried her into the bathroom. Lexi didn't want another shower. Marisa had just given her a bath. She wanted to sleep and tried to push away from him, but she was too tired to win. He held a glass of warm water that smelled awful in front of her and demanded, "Drink this."

She batted at the glass and tried to turn her head. "Alessandra," he growled. "Fucking be obedient for once in your goddamned life." He put the glass against her mouth and forced her head back. Her arms were barely able to work, and she was helpless to fight against him as he choked her with salt water, ordering another glass while she began to puke.

Giovanni turned her head over the toilet and held her hair, sighing with relief. He forced more of the disgusting mixture on her when she paused to breathe, and Lexi began vomiting again. Tears were coming and she wasn't sure what she was choking on anymore. She couldn't understand anything he said, and she fell against him, completely unconscious.

Lexi dreamed of Giovanni, but he was angry and yelling. His voice sounded so far away. Frazzled. Old. "*Lui scappa, voi lo inseguite, senza preoccuparvi se qualcuno viene ferito!*" Something about chasing people and people getting hurt. What was going on? He was drowning her, but then she was in the church and he told her that he would risk the volcano. Were they going to Mount Etna? Why was he afraid of being burned by lava?

Light-blocking curtains kept the room dark, but Lexi opened her eyes and could see the glow from downstairs at the top of the steps. She heard multiple voices; most she didn't recognize. The mix of English, Sicilian, and Italian didn't made sense. She picked out something about ketamine and being lucky.

Although she felt like her body was weighed down by exhaustion, she stood and was surprised to find that she wasn't in the robe anymore. Where were her clothes? She hadn't brought any other outfits. They weren't staying. Lexi's brain wasn't able to organize linear thought, and she felt spent. She touched her shirt and knew that, with all of the buttons, it was Giovanni's. But if she was wearing his shirt, then what was he wearing?

She carefully stepped onto the first stair. The voices died instantly, and Giovanni was quickly in front of her. "Alessandra? What's wrong, baby girl? Why are you out of bed?"

"What happened?"

He looked over his shoulder. "Go get some iced water." Turning back to her, he forced a smile. "Back to bed, *bambina*."

"We aren't staying," she said, trying to focus. "We're supposed to fly home tonight." She felt a little woozy and stumbled, but Giovanni caught her. He carried her back to the bed and tucked her beneath the blankets.

"You aren't going anywhere right now. Tomorrow, you'll go back to New York."

That didn't make any sense. They weren't leaving for several days. She didn't understand. Were they going back to Manhattan because she had drank too much at lunch? Because she was late at the spa? Raphael appeared in the doorway with the glass of water, and a memory came into focus from the haze. "Were you going to shoot me?"

After handing the water over, Raphael disappeared. Giovanni held the glass against her lips and said softly, "Drink." His gentleness scared her as she took the glass from him with trembling fingers. "You're leaving for New York in a few hours. I need you to rest so that you can handle the flight on your own."

"Why are you sending me away?" Nothing was making sense. Why did she feel so damned out of it? "What did I do?"

"You didn't do anything." Giovanni pulled her against him, and she deeply inhaled of his scent. "I promised to keep you safe. Part of that means you have to go back to New York while I take care of some things here."

"What happened to me?" Lexi nuzzled into him when the tired overwhelmed her again and wasn't surprised when he didn't answer. Her eyes closed into an empty sleep.

When Lexi woke the next time, there was a bedside lamp on; an outfit of slacks and a blouse along with underwear and a pair of flats were on the foot of the bed. The sling bag she had brought from Menfi was there as well, and she sat up, groggy but awake. There was a glass of water on the nightstand, and she took a drink of it before stopping.

The water from the spa. Lexi had finished a glass of disgusting mineral water after her massage. Part of the conversation she had overheard when she woke the first time filtered into her mind. It wasn't mineral water; it was drugged water. Someone had drugged her.

She tried to piece together the afternoon. There had been a noise that she had gone to check on, but no one had been there. Had she wanted to get dressed? To go back to her room? She couldn't remember.

Raphael had been there. Was he going to shoot her? No, he was pointing his gun at someone else. Someone had been in her room. Raphael had opted to stay with her instead of chasing the person, and Giovanni had given him hell for it. She remembered his angry voice: *If he runs, then you chase him regardless of who gets hurt.* Had Giovanni meant regardless of whether she was hurt? The salon patrons? Who was at risk of getting hurt?

"You're awake." Giovanni leaned against the open stairway into the room. "It's probably better that your body woke on its own."

"What happened to me?"

He sat down next to her on the bed. "What do you remember?"

"Nothing that makes sense. Everything seemed fine. A bunch of spa treatments. A massage. A glass of horrible mineral water." She saw him wince. "Then I don't remember much. A noise, a gun, Raphael saying to not move, passing out." She tried to focus. "You dumping salt water down my throat so I would puke."

"How do you feel now?" He stroked her cheek, and she curved her face into his palm.

"Okay, I guess. Tired but awake. What happened, Gio?"

He straightened. "Your testing came back positive for ketamine. I don't know how high of a dose based on how quickly you were throwing up, but high enough that it knocked you out quickly." Giovanni exhaled a deep breath and looked at her. Lexi could see concern etched in the lines around his eyes. "That's why you're going back to New York."

"What? No." She shook her head, but the movement tossed her brain around in her skull and made her feel nauseous. "I don't want to go back without you."

"You're on a private flight to Rome where a friend will meet you and take you back on his jet."

Lexi gripped his arm. "What the hell are you talking about? Gio, no. No, I-"

"Don't." Giovanni closed his eyes, and Lexi didn't know how to process his behavior. His voice turned colder, as though she were his property to command. When he looked at her, the compassion was gone. "For once, Alessandra, listen to me and don't question. Don't fight back. Don't make this a struggle. Get dressed and get out."

"You *want* me to leave." Why did that realization hurt so much? Someone had drugged her; Lexi should have been running for the door.

"Wait for me at the apartment, for however long it takes."

"And do what?"

"Go back to your life." He pulled her against him and kissed her lips delicately. "I need you to trust me."

"Come with me," she whispered.

"*Quando chiudo gli occhi la sera, l'ultima cosa a cui penso sei sempre tu.*" He kissed her head again and stood. "It's time to go. I'll meet you downstairs."

She dressed in the simple outfit he'd had brought for her and looked at the woman in the mirror. Her hair was limp and her eyes were vacant. She quickly pulled back a ponytail before slipping into the shoes and walking downstairs. Giovanni was speaking low to the men gathered, and he turned to her when she walked off the last step. "You'll be to Rome in two hours," he said, gently touching her face. "You'll immediately leave for New York. Try to rest."

"Please come back with me." She leaned her head against his chest. "Forty-five if you'll get on the plane with me."

"I wish that things were so easy," he whispered. Giovanni took a step away from her, and the leader replaced the lover. "When you return, Raphael will take you home. If there is anything that you need from your apartment, he will bring it for you. You'll stay in the Pinnacle. Feel free to return to work, but someone will take you every day and bring you back."

"Am I a prisoner?"

"No." He shook his head. "You are not a prisoner- you are *protected*. You can go with friends, socialize, whatever you wish- but you will never be alone."

"That's a lie," she whispered.

"When this is done," he said, ignoring her words, "I'll come back."

When this is done. Standing in front of him, Lexi knew that not only would Giovanni not stop until he had found out why an attempt on her life had been made, but that whoever had made it would pay for that choice with the highest price.

15

Even New York was heartbroken, Lexi thought when they stepped out into the afternoon. The sky was overcast. Although September wasn't known for being especially rainy, it seemed this month had done nothing but rain since she met Giovanni.

Her flights had been easy. The small jet to Rome had been only a little over an hour and she hadn't even gone into the airport. A large man who had to be suffering in the Italian heat under the suit he wore was waiting for her at the runway and ushered her with the utmost politeness to a Falcon 900 that made the trip to JFK in eight hours. With the time difference, although she'd left Catania before most tourists had been eating breakfast, she was in New York at lunchtime.

It seemed like a hazy nightmare that hadn't even gotten fully underway. She was grateful for the sunglasses that hid her soul behind their dark lenses. When Raphael opened the door to the X5, she slid into the back seat and watched life start to come back into focus. "*Signora?*"

Lexi took the phone he extended and put the mobile to her ear. "Hello?"

"You sound so far, baby girl."

At Giovanni's voice, Lexi felt her throat swell with emotion. "I am far," she whispered. It was for her own good, but the hurt was unbearable. How had she gone from alone and functional to this? This wasn't normal. This wasn't healthy. This was a return to the hell that he had pulled her from.

"This is the last time I'm going to talk to you for a while."

Giovanni offered no explanation, and Lexi didn't care that everyone in the car could overhear her conversation and pleading. "Don't do this. Whatever it is that you are going to do- *don't*. Whatever it is that you think you have to do- whatever you think you *need* to do- because of what happened in Catania, you don't."

He sighed. "I need you to trust me, Alessandra.

"Then tell me why. Come to New York and tell me why. Make me understand."

"It doesn't work that way, *bambina*," he chuckled. When she couldn't choke out a reply, Giovanni said softly, "*Non mi stancherei mai di parlare con te.*"

"Then talk to me forever. Get on the next plane, and I'll wait for you at the airport." Lexi's words were falling on deaf ears; whatever he was doing had already been put into motion. She was lucky he was calling her in the first place.

"Hand the phone back to Raphael."

She wiped away the tear that fell down her cheek. "Make me," she challenged, trying to cover up her weeping.

She could almost see him smiling. "That's my girl." His voice was low and she knew, in that moment, that he didn't know if there would be another hello. More than anything, this was what broke whatever remained of Lexi's spirit. "It's not the goodbye or the hello that matter; it's the time spent between the two." After a few moments of silence, he added, "*Che fortuna avere qualcosa che rende così difficile dire addio.*"

Lexi didn't feel fortunate; she felt numb. She couldn't answer him and gave the phone back to Raphael before returning to the window. The skyline started to crunch over them like a boogeyman against the cloudy sky, and she knew it was only a matter of time before they were in downtown Manhattan. Giovanni had told her to wait at his apartment and to go back to her life, but what did that look like? She didn't have a life without him. From the day she had arrived, Giovanni had been there. Did he realize that what he asked of her was impossible?

"Would you like something to eat, *Signora*?" Raphael asked as they pulled in front of the Woolworth Tower. "I can send out for whatever you would like."

"No, thank you." She didn't feel remotely hungry. She wanted to cry, to sleep, to run away- anything but eat. Although she knew the answer would be *no*, Lexi couldn't imagine staying at the Pinnacle by herself and said, "I want to go back to my apartment."

Raphael shook his head in reply. "Ricardo can pick up whatever it is that you need. *Don* Giovanni has requested you stay here. For your safety," he added.

Requested. Giovanni had ordered it, and Lexi didn't feel up for the fight. "For how long? How long until he comes back?"

"I don't know, *Signora*." Raphael stepped out of the car when the door opened, and Lexi sighed before mimicking him. He stopped to talk to the concierge, who made a notation on the tablet that he worked on, before Lexi followed her two-man detail into the elevator. Raphael was quiet until they reached the penthouse. "*Signora*? Your thumb, please." He held out his hand and Lexi looked at him, perplexed, while he and the elevator attendant each used a key to unlock the keypad that was next to the call button. "This will give you the ability to lock and unlock the elevator for service."

You are not a prisoner. Raphael pressed Lexi's thumb against the scanner and, in seconds, the keypad lit up before flashing three times. The two men flipped their keys in sync, and then the attendant left along with Ricardo. "We should discuss your schedule," Raphael said, walking into the foyer. "And your needs."

"I *need* to know what's going on." Lexi sat down on the sofa nearest him. "Can you tell me that?"

Raphael, like his boss, had perfected the art of not answering a question and proceeded as though she hadn't spoken. "For working, Ricardo will be with you throughout the day."

"The last thing I need is everyone I work with thinking that I have a babysitter. No."

"He will be onsite but inconspicuous."

"I said *no*. Are you fucking deaf, too?" There was no need to be mean to Raphael; he was just doing what he had been told. Lexi wasn't angry at him- she was pissed at Giovanni. As his number one, Raphael became the stand-in for her rage. "I don't need anyone to shadow me at work. I already have to deal with the shadow of Gio's identity thanks to him coming to the Gala."

"It's not a request, *Signora*." The way that Raphael looked at her, barely hiding his grin, implied that he knew he was serving as Giovanni's reflection. It just made Lexi angrier.

"Cut the *signora* bullshit. I don't like it." She crossed her arms and leaned back in the seat. "I could always tell Security that Ricardo is a stalker."

"I could always hide a multi-man team or I could send someone you don't know and don't trust." Raphael shrugged as though he couldn't be bothered. "While *Don* Giovanni is away, I have full discretion of how to manage your safety and care. Fuck with me, *Signora*," he said, emphasizing the word, "and see just how far I can go."

Damn him. Damn all of them. Lexi sighed with frustration. "Fine. Just Ricardo- and he had better be well-hidden. I don't want to see him. I don't want other people to see him."

Raphael continued detailing her days ahead. "I will escort you to and from the building; if you have any evening outings, I will also be on duty. I live on the floor below. If anything comes up, you will call me. Groceries will be delivered twice a week. If you have any preferences, let me know; otherwise, I will make sure to have balanced options brought in."

"I can go to the grocery store," she muttered. Lexi stood up, aggravated. "What if I want to go for a run or a movie? What if I just want to be alone?"

"Alone isn't an option. Manny or Ricardo can run with you if you don't want to use the treadmill in the gym here. There is a viewing screen in the library," he pointed upstairs, "but I can take you to an actual movie theater if you want to go out."

"Why can't I just go alone?" She raised her hands. "Why does Gio think that I'm in danger?" Raphael didn't answer and that made Lexi's mind swirl. "You were in my room with a gun, Raphael. You knew someone was there. How?"

"It's my job to be prepared, regardless of whether someone is there or not."

"No." She shook her head. If Giovanni thought she could read well, then he had left a full book at her disposal. She was determined to look at more than the prologue. "I call bullshit on that. You *knew*. You were in there and so was Ricardo. You were waiting for something to go down." Lexi felt her stomach knot; her words came out on a breath. "You knew someone was going to attack me."

He didn't confirm her suspicions and her fear began to beckon the numb to return. "Giovanni knew, too, didn't he? That's why he was at the hotel so quickly. He knew." She sank back to the couch.

"Something you will learn, *Signora*, is that Giovanni is always prepared for every option." Raphael's voice was both commanding and comforting. "There is little he doesn't see and even less that he is surprised by."

"He played me."

"He protected you," Raphael retaliated.

Lexi felt her brokenness dulled by anger as the words registered in her brain. "Gio used me as bait, didn't he?" When Raphael said nothing, she looked up at him and searched his face. Although she knew who she was sleeping with, the realization of who Giovanni was and what lengths he would go to made her breathless with sorrow. "He did."

"This is a conversation you would do better to have with him."

"So call him." The edge had returned to her voice. When the sides of his lips curled slightly, Lexi knew that Raphael heard it to. "Call Giovanni and let me talk to him."

"If you have any work engagements or decide to do anything with friends, let me know and I'll make sure they are scheduled." Raphael continued as though she hadn't spoken. "You will see Ricardo and I most frequently, but both Manny and Leo may fill in or drive you. You will meet them later."

Lexi was annoyed and narrowed her eyes at him. "Since you have such a plan worked out already, what should I do while I'm here? Learn to cook? Clean? Sew? What is appropriate for the *bambina* who isn't a prisoner but who isn't supposed to leave?"

Raphael tried not to laugh at her sarcasm. "The housekeeper comes three times a week, so you have no need to clean, *Signora*, and, should you not enjoy the vast array of restaurant options at your disposal, I am able to cook for you or my wife can bring you meals."

"*Wife?*" At this reveal, Lexi was shocked. "You have a wife?"

"I do." Raphael gave her an authentic smile and nodded. "And a son."

This was something that Lexi had a very hard time accepting. Her anger dissipated as all she wanted to do was uncover a way to survive. "How does she cope with your work? With you being gone?"

"She knew who I was when she married me." He looked at his watch before he pushed the call button. "I will leave you to settle, but I'll come to check on you for dinner."

Lexi didn't mean to ask the question but, as the elevator opened, choked out, "Would you have changed for her?"

"No." His eyes searched hers for a moment before he expanded his answer. "Over the years, we have changed for each other, but, in the truest sense, who we are is who we are. That cannot be changed, *Signora*."

It was the answer Lexi already knew, but hearing it made her world real and it rushed her like a thousand daggers. With Raphael gone, the apartment was quiet. There was no way she would be able to stay indefinitely in the gigantic space. She thought of going to the upstairs library, but the idea of selecting a book that Giovanni had probably read didn't give her any peace. She still felt so tired and her eyes begged her for a reprieve from any sort of work, so going into Midtown was off limits, too.

Lexi might not be able to sleep tonight if she napped, but her grief felt so heavy and she was still trying to process her last day in Sicily. How long would the sedative stay in her system? When she wandered into the bedroom, she noticed a compatible phone charger on the console table. She plugged her phone in before walking into the closet and cursing.

Pressed and hung among the clothes she had seen before was the remainder of her jeans and shirts from her apartment. These were the only things she had unpacked and now they were here. When had he had them brought? Before yesterday? While she was in the air? Lexi sank to the floor and the bracelet was cool against her face. How many tears had she cried since meeting Giovanni? What the hell was she supposed to do? How could she possibly manage what she didn't know or understand?

If she contacted Sam, her life would fall apart. Although she had planned to tell Giovanni everything, calling Sam before that happened would make her look as though she was still working for the FBI. It would be a forcible end to everything, and Lexi didn't want that. If things were going to finish going to hell, she wanted it to be because she ended the game. Giovanni would likely call everything off once she told him the truth, but she had to explain to him that she wasn't just another agent. Lexi needed him to know that it had been real- what she had done, what she had felt for him, what she had given him. That was who she really was. Involving Sam would make it even harder for Giovanni to believe her.

She knew that life would never return to the dysfunctional *normal* it had been before. Her incessant desire to destroy Giovanni and his family would simply be replaced by her own self-destruction. Lexi would have to face the fact that her father's death would be left unpunished because she had failed. She would have to tell Sam that his years of research had been in vain and that he had been wrong. She would have to live with her love for Giovanni and the knowledge that any chance for a life alongside him was as much a fantasy as the last two weeks had been.

If she didn't call Sam, then Lexi would be alone. She had no idea how long Giovanni would be gone; she would have to navigate this life by herself. Could she do that? Was that the real test of how much she cared? If this was the life he led, was it even possible for her to manage that? His brothers had wives; even Raphael had a family. People coped, but they weren't former FBI agents. They weren't a woman who didn't know who she was when she wasn't with a man she should have never connected with. If this was her struggle at two weeks, where would she be at two months? Two years?

Lexi wrestled with the idea that Giovanni had known someone was planning an attack in Sicily. Had he asked her to come with him because he was concerned New York wasn't safe? No, she reasoned. When they were still here, anyone who saw her with him would have considered her just another one of his weekly specials. Other than the Gala, they hadn't even been seen together publicly after their initial meeting and failed dinner attempt. New York couldn't have been the threat. Giovanni was just asserting his *I-rule-the-world* attitude by bringing her to Sicily.

She tried to walk through the trip in her head. Menfi had felt safe enough. He had even encouraged her to walk the property. With the security and fortifications, the *baglio* wasn't at risk. Even Giovanni had been without the SIG when she had seen him for dinner the first night.

Catania? He had told her that Catania couldn't wait. Had rumors circulated about a woman with him? A woman that mattered? The people of Menfi had assumed she was his wife or, at the very least, his girlfriend. Had word made it to someone, somewhere that there was an easier target than

Giovanni himself? Had he let her walk into a trap? Lexi felt the numb start to branch out and she clutched her body, trying to warm herself in his absence.

Knowing the truth at this point was overrated, but she sure as hell couldn't handle the lies. Lexi needed to turn her brain off. She stripped down to her underwear and took one of Giovanni's shirts off the hanger. She buttoned it as she walked back into the bedroom and picked up the remote from the mantle beneath the TV, flipping on the television and pouring herself into bed. Fuck sleeping at night; she didn't want to deal with her own thoughts anymore, and she channel surfed until she dozed off to a cooking show.

When Lexi woke up, she was shocked to see that it was the next morning; she had been asleep for seventeen hours. Sitting up in the bed, she realized she was alone and the hurt was back. She could practically smell Giovanni on the sheets. She could feel him in the spot next to her. It was excruciating.

Whatever drugs were in her system seemed to have cleared. For the first time in two days, her mind didn't feel foggy and her body was rested. She looked out the window over The City and fingered the cool stones of the bracelet as the heavy gold rolled gently on her wrist. "You can do this," she whispered to the reflection that watched the world wake up. "One day at a time, one foot in front of the other. You can do this."

After taking a shower, she stood in the closet but couldn't bring herself to wear any of the dresses that reminded her of Giovanni. Instead, she selected slacks and a thin sweater from her own clothes. After she was dressed, she searched through the different drawers for a notepad and eventually found what she was looking for, along with the bracelet's box, in Giovanni's nightstand. She scribbled *don't wash* and laid the note on top of the shirt she had worn to bed. It smelled enough like him that it had been comforting. Could she ask the cleaning woman not to wash the bed linens, too?

When she arrived upstairs, Raphael was seated at the kitchen bar next to Ricardo. "Coffee?" he asked, walking over to the built-in espresso machine and starting the press before she'd even said *yes*.

"Thank you," she answered.

Ricardo smiled at her tightly when she looked over at him. "Did you sleep well?"

Lexi nodded. "I think I'm better. Whatever I took, however high a dose, I think it's gone now." Her heart hurt, but she left that part out as she watched Raphael steam milk. He prepared the cappuccino before passing it to her, and she thanked him again while putting her briefcase bag on the side of the bar. Did she tell him that she wanted to go to the library? Demand it? "Since I'm back, I think I should go into work."

"We can leave," he looked at his wrist before opening the refrigerator, "in a half-hour. That will have you arriving shortly after Security reports for the day." Raphael placed a bowl of yogurt and fresh fruit along with a spoon in front of her before he turned back to Ricardo and their conversation. "Eat."

Lexi picked up the bowl and walked it over to the breakfast table that overlooked downtown. She ate some of the yogurt while drinking her coffee. She hadn't eaten in what felt like forever, but the sensation of hunger wasn't there. After a few bites, she just pushed the mixture around the bowl. "You should eat more."

She grinned up at him. "You sound like Gio."

"That's not exactly true," Raphael said lightheartedly. "He would order you to eat more; I simply stated a fact."

Lexi couldn't help but chuckle. "True." Damn it, she missed Giovanni. She missed his stalking and his need to control. She missed it all. "Have you spoken to him?"

Raphael picked up the bowl and placed it in the sink. "We should leave. You don't want to be late your first day back."

No one even knew she was in the country, but Lexi's question wasn't going to be answered and she dutifully followed him down the stairs, grabbing her bag from the bar when they passed by. The valet brought the sedan from the night of the Gala to the front of the building; while Raphael drove, Ricardo sat in the back seat with her. "Are you going to just hang around the library all day?" she asked incredulously to break the silence. "I doubt anyone will do anything other than try to bore me to death."

"You won't even know I'm there," Ricardo assured her.

"This can't be the job you signed up for." Lexi looked out the window. "Who wants to hide in a library while a woman Gio could replace in an hour works?"

"*Signora*." Raphael's voice was like scraping metal. The hint of his anger caused Lexi to look toward the front seat. "*Don* Giovanni would ask that I offer you the opportunity to avoid adding time to whatever arrangement it is that you've agreed to. Comments like that one will, unfortunately, require a minute." He watched her through the rearview mirror. "And I have little patience to give you leeway with self-destructive behaviors. In that way, you were correct this morning: I am much like him."

Put in her place, Lexi returned to the window, saying nothing. Everything looked different. How had the entire world managed to change in only a few days away? The sun wasn't bright; the sky had muted to gray. The people appeared more like blurs on the sidewalk. When the 550i approached the curb and Raphael opened the door, even the air she stepped into threatened to choke Lexi with its heaviness. His voice was tight with lingering annoyance. "*Buon lavoro.*"

"Yeah," she said, "you, too." Ricardo kept several paces behind her as she walked up the steps toward the main entrance. Raphael must have already called the security guard because he didn't need to be swayed to allow Ricardo in during the staff-only time. Ricardo disappeared instantly, and Lexi visited Dr. Fisher, who was shocked to see her. "Their project was less involved than they thought," Lexi lied. "I didn't want to be away longer than necessary."

She spent the day sequestered in her office. Suzanne, her page, was excited to see her back and questioned her about Ursino. How was it? Was it as beautiful as the photographs? What was her favorite part? What was it like restoring a book in such a renowned library?

Lexi tried to embellish a life she hadn't led; her lies were believed all the while her joy was faked. Luke, too, stopped in to see her and, when their paths crossed later at the café while she picked up a late-afternoon coffee to combat the fatigue from avoiding lunch, he reached out. "I need to apologize," he said when she stopped. "Do you have a second?"

"No apology is needed." She walked with him to one of the tables by the large windows that overlooked the park. "Gio is an acquired taste. Bitter most times," she chuckled darkly, "like the coffee he likes to drink."

Luke tried to laugh at her joke, but he seemed to be struggling. "It was none of my business, and I had no right to say what I said before you left."

"It was fair," she said, trying to smile. "He has a life that, unfortunately, gets regularly reported. While some of it is a lie, some of it has just enough truth to make it interesting." Lexi refused to defend Giovanni, not when he had sent her back to New York alone. "I know you didn't mean anything by it. It's okay." She looked at her watch. "I have glue drying on a piece and need to check it. Rain check?"

"Yeah," he nodded. "Do you want to do lunch next week?"

"Sure." She walked back through the café, wondering where Ricardo was. She could feel the prickly sensation of being watched. He had to be somewhere and, at his size, should have been easy to spot. Lexi couldn't find him and, as she took the stairs to the third floor, couldn't hear him trailing her either. It was disconcerting.

Lexi looked up from her desk when Ricardo stepped into the room a few minutes after her collection had technically closed. "*Signora*, it's time to go."

The afternoon had led Lexi from nervousness at the constant hidden security to annoyance at Giovanni for forcing a life she didn't want on her. Just as Raphael had been the easy target the night before, Ricardo was a stand-in for the man that she wanted to yell at. "I know what time it is," she mocked, "and I'm not done."

Ricardo didn't seem to know what to do with her attitude, and he stepped back, the door closing behind him. A wave of confidence swept over her. That had been far easier than she had expected. Maybe she could sway Ricardo to talk to her. That thought dissipated when the door was angrily pushed open by Raphael fifteen minutes later. "Done. Now."

"No." Lexi stood up and pointed. "You can go. Rare Books is closed."

Raphael's jaws were taut as he bit down on his teeth and grit out, "Alessandra: get your things. We are leaving. It's almost five-thirty. There's no reason for you to be here. It's time to go home and have dinner."

"I know how to tell time." She returned to her chair and went back to what she was doing. "I also know how to call Security."

She wondered how far Raphael would let her push him; the answer was not far. He watched her for a moment before he jeered a grunt and walked over to her. He balanced himself against the desk and positioned his body in front of her, making it impossible for her to work. "Let me explain something to you that your time with Giovanni didn't give you an opportunity to understand."

His voice oozed quiet annoyance. "If you think, for one moment, that I will let you get away with this bullshit behavior, you are sorely mistaken. I have been kind and deferent to you, *Signora*, because you haven't been my responsibility to maintain. But now? With Giovanni away? You *are* my obligation."

"Is that a threat?"

"Alessandra," he taunted. "I'm a lawyer. I don't threaten. I negotiate."

"Do you?" Lexi raised her eyes to his self-satisfied look and was overwhelmed with the need to smack him. "I'm not finished," she said slowly. "I'm not leaving. You can't make me. Negotiate that."

His lips parted into a dangerous smile. "You can get up and walk out the door, or I can throw you over my shoulder. I don't care." She was reminded of Giovanni's threats and how he was more than happy to carry them out, regardless of where they were. "There's your negotiation. You can select the option you want."

Lexi wanted to tell him to fuck off, but, like Giovanni, Raphael carried himself in a way that told her he would follow through on whatever threat or negotiation he promised. She slammed her chair into the wall behind her as she stood, closing her computer and grabbing her bag. "In the future," she growled, "I'll tell *you* when I'm done. Not the other way around."

"In the future," he replied easily, "you'll be ready to go when Ricardo comes to get you. I don't expect to have to come back in here for your bullshit." He walked to the main door and pulled an unlit cigarette from a pack in his jacket pocket. He lifted it to the smoke detector that would activate a sprinkler system throughout the library full of books. "And the next time you threaten to call Security on me, I will make sure you understand that I know how to get this room flooded with people, too." He held the door open as she tore through it angrily.

The ride to the Woolworth Tower was silent, and Lexi ignored the men in the car. When she arrived in the apartment, she stalked into the bedroom and threw her bag on the bed, exhaling a groan. She was miserable. She knew she owed Ricardo (and probably Raphael, too) an apology, but she refused to give in. They knew *something,* and she knew beyond a doubt that Raphael was talking to Giovanni. He had to be. He just wasn't telling her. Fuck apologizing to him.

She sighed and leaned back on the bed, taking her phone from her bag and opening up the internet. Typing in Giovanni's name returned pictures she had seen, and she rotated through a few. Her thumb closed the browser before it clicked on her contacts, scrolling until she found *Mio Padrone*. She couldn't help but smirk at the designation, and she hovered before dialing. After three rings, the phone clicked and she thought he might be on the other end when she heard his voice.

"You know who you've called. Now tell me why."

The smartass response of his voicemail made her chuckle. She lowered her head, exhaling sadly before she answered the order. "I miss you." The words had barely escaped before she had to fight back telling him that she loved him. "I-I'm here. I'm doing what you told me to do and, I-I," she stammered, "I don't know how long I can do this, Gio. I don't know that I'm cut out to do this. I want to wait for you, but…" Lexi forced her tears back. "You think I'm fragile like a bomb," she chuckled, remembering his words, "but I always thought I was strong. I thought life had made me that way, that I could survive anything. But I can't survive you. I can't survive this. I'm not strong and I'm not a bomb. I'm just," she exhaled again, unable to tell him that she was done.

"I hope whatever you are doing finishes soon and you can come back. I-I-I," she stammered. *I love you*, she mouthed, unable to say the words aloud. "I miss you, Gio." The application beeped, signifying her message was automatically disconnected, and she dropped the phone next to her.

Her mobile vibrated a few minutes later, and she yanked it up, hoping to see a message from Giovanni. It was Raphael. *Dinner?*

There's food in the fridge. I'm fine.

The phone vibrated again. *I can bring you chicken piccata.* He included a smile in the text, but that didn't make Lexi feel any better.

No, but thanks. Enjoy dinner with your family. She turned the phone off and stood up.

After changing into a pair of yoga pants that she found in one of her own bags, she put Giovanni's shirt back on and rolled the sleeves up while she mounted the steps to the kitchen. The refrigerator was stocked with produce, and she pulled a few things out in order to make a salad. From the wine fridge, she searched until she found a bottle of the Catarratto that Giovanni had opened the night he had cooked for her.

It took her a few attempts to find a corkscrew and she cursed when she broke the stopper. She tried to wiggle it, but the jagged cork was impossible to get out of the bottle. Lexi refused to admit defeat and pulled a paring knife from the knife block. "Fuck you," she grumbled to the wine, trying to lodge the knife inside the stopper in an attempt to remove it. She pressed her weight against it. "You are not winning."

Instead of the bottle, she should have focused on the knife. She didn't even notice that the blade had sliced into her hand until blood poured over and down the wine. "Goddammit!"

Lifting her hand, she grabbed sheets from the roll of paper towels by the sink and pressed them against the wound. The blood started to seep through, and she ran her hand under the faucet. Although the cut wasn't long, it was deep and the blood continued to flow. The tears that came weren't from pain but rather from frustration, and she wrapped her hand in the dish towel that hung by the oven. She had no choice but to go to the elevator on the first floor. After one level, she walked into a small foyer that held a single door.

She knocked and less than a minute passed before Raphael stood in front of her, his eyes vacillating between the crying woman and the hand she held wrapped in a rag. In the background of the room, Lexi saw a beautiful redhead bouncing a chubby baby on her hip while she put plates on a birch dining table. "Alessandra? What's wrong? What happened?"

"I don't know where the bandaids are," she managed before an unintended sob escaped and she collapsed into his unprepared arms. "I just want him back."

"Give me a minute," he said over his shoulder as he stepped into the hallway and closed the door. Leading her the few feet to the elevator, it instantly opened and they went to the apartment above. Raphael walked to a large closet off the foyer and removed a first aid kit. "What the hell happened?"

"I was trying to open a bottle of wine." The cut was still bleeding when he pulled the dishtowel back.

Raphael cursed. "Let's go upstairs. I want to see what did this and get it cleaned up." He pressed the rag against her hand and followed her back to the kitchen. "A corkscrew, Alessandra. You use a fucking corkscrew to open wine- not a knife."

"I tried," she explained. "The cork broke."

"You could have asked for help."

"I didn't want your fucking help!" It wasn't lost on her, as he washed her cut in the sink and looked at it, that she had to accept his help and that fueled her tears. "Why the fuck am I here? I should be gone. This is never going to work."

"You're going to need stitches." Raphael shook his head with annoyance and sighed. After drying her hand, he pressed gauze against the wound and lifted his phone. "Manny? Get up to Gio's. Bring your med bag."

"What are you doing?" Lexi looked up at him as he took the corkscrew and managed to uncork the wine with minimal work. Why had he called Giovanni's sparring partner?

"Pain relief." He pushed the glass he poured to her as the elevator below them dinged. "Up here!" he yelled down the steps. Moments later, an athletic, muscular man arrived, holding a backpack over his shoulder. "She needs stitches on her hand."

"*Signora*," the man said with a deeper voice than Lexi expected from his appearance. He tossed the bag on the bar and opened his palm in front of her with a kind smile. "May I?"

"Why did Raphael call you?" She put her hand inside his and he removed the gauze, looking over the clean slice. "Gio said you're an MMA boxer."

"That's how I put myself through medical school." He turned her hand and assessed the damage. "And it's why Giovanni doesn't mind getting his ass kicked by me. I know where to hit." He grinned at her before going back to the cut. "Raphael's right. This is going to need closing."

He pressed the woven cotton back against the gash and unzipped his bag, taking out a tube of clear gel that would serve as the skin adhesive along with a wide bandage and some antibacterial cream. After cleaning the wound, he squeezed her hand together and applied the gel. The liquid stitches quickly dried, and he covered the wound loosely before taping the bandage closed. "By tomorrow morning you'll be fine to shower, but keep it wrapped tonight." Lexi pulled her hands into her lap and thanked him before Manny looked back to Raphael. "Anything else?"

Raphael shook his head and, after Manny had taken his things and left, leaned against the cabinets. His fingers drummed along the counter. "What are you doing, Alessandra? Giovanni wouldn't want this."

"I'm glad you know that. I don't have that privilege since he isn't here to tell me." She looked up at him. "What is so important that he stayed in Sicily? Why did he take me there only to send me back? And why the fuck aren't you with him?" Lexi reached out and took his hand. "Raphael, you shouldn't be *here*. You should be where Gio is."

He pulled his hand away and walked to where she had put the produce. He put the head of red lettuce on a cutting board and used the chef's knife from the knife block to cut it into ribbons. "What do you like in your salad?"

"Truth. I like truth with a side of honesty in my salad." Lexi took a drink of her wine when Raphael chuckled. "I'm serious. How would you feel if I was your wife and Giovanni had to explain your absence?"

"Felicity knows better than to ask." He looked back over his shoulder at her. "You'll learn."

"I don't want to fucking learn!" Her hand hurt, and she curled her fingers to try and ease the stiffness that was already starting. "I don't want this."

"You want Giovanni," Raphael said quietly. "This is the cost of that. You can't have it both ways."

Lexi didn't like where the conversation had gone. She stood and walked into the breakfast room, looking out the window. "How many women have stood in this same spot and wondered when the hell he was coming back?"

"None." Raphael continued to create a salad without even looking up. "But you know that. You know that you're different, but you still push this bullshit agenda as though Giovanni doesn't care. Don't." He brought the bowl to the table behind her. "He doesn't deserve that and neither," he added, pulling a cloth napkin from a drawer along with some silverware, "do you."

"You don't know me to know what I deserve." At the moment, Lexi felt the weight of her lies stacking up on top of her. She deserved far worse than Giovanni being gone with an indefinite timeline.

Raphael exhaled slowly. "I'll be downstairs if you need me. Eat. Get some sleep. Tomorrow's a new day."

Tomorrow was a new day- a new day of a hangover from the half-bottle of wine that Lexi drank with a few bites of her colorful salad. When she woke up on Saturday, she thought she might puke and swallowed down four ibuprofen with a glass of water before she tried to figure out the espresso machine. There wasn't a regular coffee maker, and she wasn't sure how to even turn on the wall model. As she touched the different buttons and nothing happened, she grumbled. Why couldn't anything be easy?

A few seconds after the elevator signaled its arrival, Raphael appeared at the top of the steps. "Problems?"

"I just want a cup of coffee. Is that too much to ask?"

He snickered as he walked next to her and pressed the buttons. "First, second," he directed. Two thin streams of espresso began to filter into the large mug Lexi had placed beneath the spigots. Raphael took milk from the refrigerator and, looking her over, used his head to point to an upper cabinet. "Ibuprofen is next to the glasses."

"I know. Thanks." Lexi turned and walked to the windows. "I'm hung over, not blind."

"Is this how we're going to be?" Raphael offered her the cup after the steamed milk had been added. "You're going to smart off to me because you're pissed at Giovanni?"

"Why? Not sure you can take it?"

The way he laughed implied otherwise. "*Signora*, there's little I can't take." When she said nothing, he blew out an amused breath. "Let's come to an agreement. Do what you know you are supposed to do. In exchange, I will tell you whatever I can."

"Quite the lawyer, aren't you? Everything's an *agreement* or a *negotiation*."

"We can't all be librarians," he threw back at her. "*Don* Masseretti found my knack for *agreement* and *negotiation* a skill, and was generous enough to make sure I was able to put those talents to good use."

"Sounds like you've known Giovanni and his family a long time." Lexi continued to watch the traffic below.

"Since we were young boys in Palermo. My father was friends with his father and, if you go back long enough, our grandfathers were cousins." He turned and leaned against the window to face her.

"You grew up together?" She looked at him as he seemed to debate telling her a story that might offer her some sort of insight.

"We played together when our fathers would meet. My family wasn't involved in banking," he said with a smirk, knowing she would understand. "They were friends, nothing more. One afternoon, Giovanni and I were on a playground. There were children everywhere. The son of one of

Don Masseretti's *capos* didn't like that Gio and I were together. He wanted the friendship that we had started. I was," Raphael looked out the window, remembering himself with a chuckle, "tiny. A scrawny child. One moment, I was standing; the next, I was on the ground. I was choking on my own blood and didn't even know enough to cry. I stood to fight back, but Giovanni had already taken care of it."

"What do you mean?"

"The boy may have broken my nose, but Giovanni broke his arms. Both of them." Raphael heaved a heavy breath. "Then he took off his sweatshirt and used it to try and stop my bleeding. We walked back home and I knew… In that moment, I knew that I would become whatever I needed to become to have his back the way that he had mine."

"How old were you?"

"Eight." Raphael looked back at her. "By the time I was twelve, I asked *Don* Masseretti's permission to train alongside his bodyguards. I've been with Giovanni since."

She returned to the traffic as she tried to settle this story alongside everything else she had learned. "Except for law school."

"Even then," he said with a laugh. "By the time we were in college, I had already discussed my future with Giovanni. We knew where we were headed. Law school was part of our plan to get there."

Lexi leaned back against the glass and drank from her mug, watching Raphael. "You aren't just his bodyguard, are you? You're his number one. You're his *Consigliere*." The information slammed into her like a punch. "That's why you're here with me. It's why he trusts you to be here while he isn't."

"Giovanni has always been my priority," Raphael said without answering. "Don't believe for one moment that because I'm here with you I am neglectful."

"When is he coming back? What is he doing? Where the hell is he?" Lexi looked at him with desperation. When he ignored her, she returned to the window. "Fuck your agreement. No deal." After a few minutes of silence, Raphael turned to go and Lexi said, "I'm going back to work today. Figure out whatever it is that you need to do or I'll take the subway. I'm not staying in this mausoleum by myself all day, every day."

"Fine." He didn't attempt to argue. "Be ready in an hour."

Lexi continued, trying to think of things that would fill her time. "And I'm joining a gym."

"There's a gym off of Giovanni's bedroom, and there's an even larger one in the building. A swimming pool as well."

"No." Lexi turned to find Raphael watching her from the edge of the kitchen. "I want to take classes and get back to my own life. If Gio wants to tell me otherwise, tell him to pick up the fucking phone or return a message. I'm not playing the role of a mistress in a penthouse. He can suck it up or he can let me go; I don't care which."

"There's a gym down the block."

"I don't want to see *anyone*," Lexi demanded. "Not you. Not Ricardo. No one."

"As long as you cooperate." Raphael nodded. "The second you break your end of that, the negotiation is over."

"I like to run and I hate treadmills," she said, remembering the equipment in Giovanni's closet gym. "I know my clothes were moved over. I have running gear and I plan to run outside. I don't want a shadow."

"That's not negotiable. Manny runs. Ricardo, although he doesn't like it, can also more than keep up with you." Raphael leaned against the banister of the stairs. "You aren't running the streets by yourself."

We'll see about that, Lexi thought with annoyance. "I'll see you in an hour."

She let the weekend slide without incident. She went to the library on both days, working the full schedule in her closed room. By Saturday night, she had a gym membership, and she killed the afternoon on Sunday by taking back-to-back classes. Raphael was true to his word; although she looked, Lexi didn't see anyone trailing her. As she finished a protein shake on the walk back to the Pinnacle, she wondered what Maria had cooked for the weekly Masseretti lunch.

Monday morning, she packed running clothes in her work bag. It took some maneuvering, but the bag didn't look strange and she wondered if her plan would work. At five, when her room closed, she slipped into the staff bathroom and changed her clothes, leaving her dress in a locker. Was this really the pushback that she wanted? Did she think this would be enough to garner a call from Giovanni? Lexi knew that Raphael would be pissed off and, while Ricardo seemed softer spoken, she couldn't imagine he would appreciate whatever smack down her behavior would guarantee him. Taking a final deep breath, she pulled her hair into a ponytail and made her choice.

Lexi didn't bother to look around. She was being watched and quickly sprinted down the main staircase to the exit. She had barely hit the sidewalk when Ricardo called out her name. She pretended to not hear him and began weaving in between the people. She wasn't shaking her bodyguards; she was simply showing them that she could play games, too.

She had no destination in mind when she started running. Her only goal was to piss off Giovanni enough for a phone call. When she ended up on East 58th, Lexi slowed to a stop. *Disco Ballarò* looked closed; the large building was dark. She stood in front of the massive door and swallowed down the pain that being on the sidewalk inspired.

She took a few steps forward before a car screeched to a stop behind her, and the weight against her heart was heavy enough that she thought the ground might swallow her alive. Ricardo's voice sounded far harsher than she had previously heard. He spoke one word, as though anything more would cause him to lose his temper. "*Signora.*"

What were the chances that anyone in the club knew where Giovanni was? If she reached for the door, would it be locked? Getting in the car was the right decision, but, numbed, Lexi couldn't move. This was where her life had ended and where it had started again. *This isn't the place for you*, Giovanni had said. She hadn't wanted to admit how right he was, and now she was living proof of his words.

"Alessandra." Raphael's patience had long since expired as he angrily stalked to a stop next to her. He grabbed her arm and pulled her to face him as he growled, "Get in the fucking car." Ricardo was standing in front of the open door that waited for her.

"No," she said. "I'm out for a run."

"Now," he demanded through gritted teeth.

"No!" Lexi screamed, pulling at her arm. Raphael held onto her tightly. "You're not Giovanni! You can't tell me what to do!" She didn't mean to start crying, but she couldn't help it. She struggled against his grip. "Let me go!"

Rather than say anything, he pulled her body, already devoid of fight, to the car and pushed her into the back seat. He passed the keys to Ricardo before sitting next to her. Lexi scooted to the far side and cried into her fist as she cowered against the window. "This," Raphael said, repeating his words from before, "is not what Giovanni would want."

"Gio doesn't care or he'd be here." Everything hurt, and she struggled to hold back the heavy sobs that were threatening her more than the darkness that was creeping in around the edges.

"You know that isn't true." Raphael took her arm and tried to gently direct her to look at him. "Alessandra, you know that Giovanni is in love with you. Don't pretend that you don't."

"What I know is that he ordered me back to New York. He sent me here, alone, after only God knows what happened in Catania. I don't remember, Raphael. I have bits and pieces of this- this nightmare in my head, but I don't remember. I don't know what happened to me!" She yanked her arm from him. "If Giovanni cared, then he would be here, telling me, helping me to manage this. He wouldn't be out for revenge, leaving me with his best friend as a fucking babysitter."

"We all have things we have to do that defy logic." Raphael was watching her as though he knew secrets he couldn't begin to tell her.

"I need to talk to him," she pleaded. "Can you tell him that? He doesn't answer when I call. The phone doesn't even go to voicemail anymore." She had tried several times over the weekend and, after her first message, the phone refused to connect. Instead, she received a generic *the party you are trying to reach is out of range* response. "Did something happen to him?"

"Stay at home," Raphael instructed. "Wait. When he can, Giovanni will explain everything."

"How long? How long am I supposed to wait?"

"As long as it takes."

After that night, when even her bad behavior had failed to incite a response, Lexi had found her drive to push against Raphael waning. She worked full days, followed by every evening at the gym. When she ran in the morning, Ricardo was suited up and ready for her. After her Monday fiasco, she was never alone and the men didn't even try to hide themselves.

By that Friday, she thought she was going to bust at the seams. She spent as little time as she could at the apartment, but it wasn't enough. The library had been hit with a leak that necessitated closing early which meant that she had gone to the gym well before normal and was situated in the Pinnacle by early evening. Thunder foreshadowed the massive storm that was rolling in, and Lexi had already told Raphael that she was home for the night. He was probably happy to be off-duty, and she had overheard Ricardo mention that he was going on a date with his girlfriend. Lexi wasn't ruining their plans because she was sad and lonely.

After cutting herself, Raphael had taken to making sure a bottle of Catarratto was open. He must have been replacing them, too, because she was draining a bottle every two days and there always seemed to be a new one on the door of the miniature fridge that stored an assortment of whites and rosés. Lexi took the open bottle from the night before and didn't bother with a glass before she kept walking up the stairs. Reading and wine. That seemed a fitting plan for a stormy night.

Yet the library a few floors away was a painful reminder of Giovanni. Even though she saw the boxes of her own books from the apartment sitting in a corner, she couldn't bring herself to touch them. Lexi was angry that he had moved her things over without even talking to her and refused to unpack a damned thing until she could throw the books at him one-by-one. Her fingers caressing the spines of his books reminded her of the night that felt like years ago, where she had teased him about being easily replaceable. It had been flirtation then, but now the memory just hurt.

By the time she exited onto the terrace, the storm had already started, but Lexi didn't care. She walked to the eastern view and leaned over the railing, drinking wine from the bottle and letting the cold rain soak into her yoga pants and cropped shirt. In a few minutes, Lexi was drenched and freezing. Leaning her head back, she screamed as loud as she could just as a flash of lightning tore through the sky before her rage disintegrated into tears. She drank heavily from the bottle before sliding down to the concrete pavers that made up the floor and dropping her head against her knees.

Sobbing and shivering was how Raphael found her. She hadn't heard the door open, but he had materialized next to her. "Come on, *Signora*," he said kindly, scooping his hands beneath her and taking the empty wine bottle neck between two fingers.

She wrapped her hands around his neck and cried, no longer concerned that he was the enemy. She was losing it. Even he was better than nothing at all. When he brought her into the small upper room, she wiggled and tried to stand up, grateful when he put her down. "I can walk." Lexi gulped back tears. "I'm fine."

"You look fine." Raphael offered her a towel that he must have brought with him. "You smell fine, too. This," he lifted the bottle, "was brand new last night."

"I don't need a conscience," she smarted, drying her hair. She might actually need him to help her get downstairs. Lexi didn't feel stable on her feet. She was just too hardheaded to admit that she was drunk. "Giovanni does though. He's the asshole who refuses to call and expects me to stay locked in here like some sort of trophy."

Raphael scoffed. "Some sort of *drunk* trophy."

"If he doesn't like it, he can always give me a reason to stop drinking." Lexi turned around but stumbled, and Raphael caught her arm before she fell. "I'm fine," she said again, shaking him off and grabbing the banister. "I don't need a babysitter."

Sighing, Raphael was closer than he needed to be as he shadowed her down the flights. "You need a designated walker."

"Why are you on his side? You've got a fucking wife. You should know better."

Instead of answering, he replied, "Why do you act like this? You're a fucking adult. *You* should know better."

When she finally stumbled onto the main floor, Lexi thought she might be sick. The wine, the emotion, and the walk had done a number on her stomach. "I'm going to bed," she said, waving him off when he tried to walk with her. "Unless you want to get shot in the arm, you should go."

"I'm locking the elevator," he told her as the doors opened. "When you are sober, call me and I'll let you out."

Lexi offered him her middle finger in response without even turning around. By the time she got to the bedroom, she had stripped from her wet clothes and threw herself against the bed before she passed out with the towel covering her face from the light she neglected to turn off.

While the weekdays were hard, the weekends were the worst. The library had limited hours, and she was forced to fill her empty time with walks through Central Park or sparring random partners at the gym. After two weeks, she stopped her daily asking of *have you heard from him*, and eventually stopped asking anything at all. What was she supposed to say?

It's not like the men she saw regularly were her friends. She was an assignment. She was a problem for them to keep out of trouble until Giovanni returned.

Lexi heard the elevator while she pretended to push greens around a plate. A few minutes later, Raphael arrived. He dropped a steaming dish in front of her. "You've lost weight," he admonished. "You need to eat real food."

"I'm eating just fine," she said. The smell of the lasagna was far more appealing than her undressed salad.

"A container of yogurt, half a sandwich, a protein shake or two, coffee, whatever you manage to not throw away of a salad, and half a bottle of wine every day are not *eating just fine*." Raphael poured her refilled wine glass down the sink and replaced it with a large glass of water before standing across from her. "You work seven days a week. You run. You box. You're running on empty, *Signora*."

"Have you talked to him?" It had been twenty-nine days since she had heard his voice. Twenty-nine days of sleeping in a shirt that, remarkably, smelled like Giovanni in his absence. She swore he lingered around her, and she clutched his pillow as she fell into a wine-induced sleep each night.

Raphael sighed. "Please, *Signora*. You need to take care of yourself."

I take care of what's mine. Lexi felt sick and closed her eyes. "I'm going to bed. Let Ricardo know that I'm running long tomorrow before I go into the library."

"It's a Saturday, Alessandra. Enjoy a day off. I'll take you to a show and a nice meal out."

Lexi stood up from the bar and walked to the steps. "I'd like to be on the pavement by six so that I can do a few hours before the library opens." She didn't wait for a response and left the lasagna untouched before she went to the bedroom.

She dreamed of Giovanni that night, just as she had for the last month. In her dream, she was resting against him. Her fingers hovered over the curls that covered his chest while his arms held her tightly. He kissed the top of her head and murmured things that she didn't understand. But, just as every dream always ended, she woke alone and buried her head in the sheets to try to remember his warmth and smell.

Ricardo was dressed and waiting for her when she left the bedroom in gear that would keep October's early morning chill at bay. She didn't know if he thought that her pace was too fast or if she was far slower than he would have preferred. He just ran alongside her, not commenting on her silence or her mood. From Battery Park to Marble Hill was a thirteen-and-a-half-mile trip. Lexi wondered what he would think if she just kept running to the other side of Manhattan. The truth was that she couldn't run that far and back, but that might change if Giovanni didn't return soon.

As they reached Central Park, she turned around and they made the six miles back to the Pinnacle. They had only been gone two hours, but Lexi felt some of her daily angst held at bay as she rode the elevator back up. "I'll see you in an hour," she said to Ricardo when he took her to the penthouse before staying behind in the lift.

She entered the apartment and went to the shower, stripping off her sweaty running gear and tossing it in the hamper before burying herself under the spray where she completed her morning routine of sobbing where no one could hear her above the pounding of the water. She couldn't do this much longer. She had given Giovanni four weeks with no contact. This wasn't a relationship, real or otherwise. This was torture. What the hell was he doing in Sicily and why hadn't he come back? Why was no one telling her anything?

When she got out of the shower, Lexi picked up her phone and tried calling. As it had before, the automated voice told her that the recipient was unable to accept calls. She dressed in jeans and a sweater, her preference when she wasn't really working and was just killing time repairing materials outside of public view. She didn't bother to bring her work bag and grabbed the sling purse that reminded her of Menfi before she found Ricardo waiting in the foyer. He wordlessly followed her into the elevator.

It was no longer a surprise to anyone that she was at the library to start the weekend. Luke was pulling his Saturday rotation in Circulation and smiled warmly at her as she walked by. "Back again?"

"Where better to be?" she said indifferently while he followed her into the collection.

He leaned against the door that his body held open. "Are you okay?"

"Yeah, you know." She tossed her purse on her desk. "Life."

The door closed as Luke walked inside the collection. He stopped on the other side of her workspace. "You seem, I don't know, different. Are things okay?"

"Just life," she repeated. Did she look as awful as she felt? Perhaps Lexi wasn't fronting nearly as well as she had hoped.

Luke drummed his fingers against one of the few empty spots on her desk, and she looked up at him. "Would you, um, would you like to grab dinner later?"

Lexi stopped moving and her heart leapt in her throat as she tried to smile politely. "That is... I would... No, but thank you. Things are fine with Giovanni," she lied. She guessed that his invitation assumed her constant presence was due to a relationship hiatus and tried to create a legitimate excuse. "He's traveling for business, which is why I'm here so much, but thank you for the offer, Luke."

A light pink crept into his cheeks, and he took a few steps back toward the door. "Well, if you ever- I mean, just as friends. We could grab pizza and talk about books."

The pizzeria memory slammed her with nausea, and Lexi thought she might be sick. "Yeah, totally. I'll check my schedule." When he left, she sighed and dropped her head. She didn't need one more issue at this point in her life.

Lexi spent most of the morning finishing a restoration she had started earlier in the week. Her fingers were cramping and she leaned back in her chair, annoyed that she was unable to complete a tedious repair. "Damn it," she muttered when the glue refused to hold.

"*Signora*?" Ricardo walked in and offered her a compassionate half-smile. Things had only started to get better since she had ditched him for the run a month ago. If Lexi had felt like she had more to give, she would have tried harder, but the strain of Giovanni's absence made doing much more than breathing too difficult. He waved his hand at the mess on her desk. "Break time? This will still be here after you eat something- even just coffee. It's late in the day, and you've been locked in here for hours."

As much as she didn't like to admit it, Lexi had come to like Ricardo. He seemed to take his job of watching her seriously and tried to stay out of her way while letting her know that he was there. She stood up and lifted her arms over her head, reaching toward the ceiling to open up her achy limbs. "Thanks; I think I will. I need to stretch."

He kept several paces behind her, which was odd for him. Although he blended in with the other people on the ornate staircase as Lexi navigated the floors to the lowest level, she usually didn't even know he was nearby. As she walked by the Children's Department, she stopped at the sound of her name and turned to see Theresa walking toward her. Her large belly served as a table for the books she held in her hands, and Lexi awkwardly returned the hug the woman managed. "It is you! How are you? We've missed you on Sundays."

"That's sweet of you to say," Lexi said with a soft smile. She had only met the woman once.

"When did you get back?"

"It's been a few weeks." Lexi tried to think of a justification for her absence. "It wouldn't have felt right to be at your parents' house without Gio."

Theresa looked at her strangely. "I thought you were in Sicily, working at some library exchange with Ursino."

"It's a long story. When he gets back, Giovanni can tell you all about it."

Her face changed from uncertainty to understated anguish. Theresa exhaled and looked around. "You need to go see my parents."

"What?"

Theresa lowered her voice. "Go and visit my parents," she repeated quietly.

"What's going on?" Lexi panned her eyes around the space. She didn't recognize anyone as a potential security detail, but she knew they were all around. Although she didn't see Ricardo, she was sure he was somewhere close as well.

"I'll take care of *them*," Theresa said, reading her mind. "Don't go back to work. Don't go back home. Go to my parents." She touched Lexi's arm kindly. "I'm sorry, Alessandra. I didn't know."

"Know what?"

"Go to my parents." She shook her head. "I can't... Just go." She dropped the books and uttered a cry, looking toward Lexi expectantly and whispering, "Go!" before she feigned labor pains again.

Stepping back, Lexi stumbled to Security. "That woman needs help. I think she's in labor." She watched as Ricardo stepped out from behind a bookcase and looked at her. She nodded her head and lifted her hand as if to say *do something*, and, the second his gaze fell to the sister of his boss, Lexi disappeared into the café, using its side door to get outside.

The cool breeze slapped her in the face as she ran to the sidewalk and furiously waved for a taxi. "I need you to take me to Penn Station," she said. It was just a fifteen minute walk, but she didn't want to risk Ricardo- or, worse, Raphael- finding out that she had gotten away. The cabbie pulled back into Fifth Avenue traffic, and Lexi ducked her head down in the hopes that her escape had been missed for the few minutes she needed in order to be ahead of Giovanni's men.

She tossed a twenty into the front seat and ran into Penn Station, navigating the throngs of people to find the Long Island Railroad counter. She bought a ticket to the end of the line. "One-way?" the woman behind the glass asked.

Lexi didn't know what she was going to find. "No, round-trip, but I don't know when I'll need the return."

"It's good for sixty days from time of sale." The clerk chomped her gum in time with stamping the tickets and pushed them through the sleeve of the counter. "Transfer at Babylon," she added before yelling, "Next!"

Lexi had no idea how to get from the train station to the harbor or even how to get to the island, but she would deal with that once she got there. She thanked the woman and found the terminal for her train, which was leaving in ten minutes. After an hour-and-a-half of stops on her first train, she got on the actual LIRR that would take her to the tip of Long Island. As each of the thirteen stops ticked off from Babylon to Montauk, Lexi found her concern growing.

What the hell had happened to Giovanni? Had he been arrested? Injured? Her blood turned to ice. Killed? She couldn't shake the cold and pulled her knees against her chest, trying to warm herself against the thought. Wouldn't Raphael have told her if that were true? Wouldn't someone have said something? She had searched the internet for information on Giovanni in his absence, but there had been no recent articles or pictures after the library's Gala. It was as if he had fallen off the earth.

There was a taxi waiting outside of the train station, but Lexi found a map on her phone and walked the two miles to the harbor. She saw several different charters and stopped a younger-looking man. "Excuse me. Can I hire you?"

"If you want to cruise the Bay," he pointed, "I'd recommend-"

"No, I-I don't want to cruise anywhere. I need to visit my-my family, who live on an island nearby. I don't think I'll be staying long. I can pay you whatever the charge is. I just need you to take me and wait until I come back."

"What island?" He looked at her nervously. She passed her phone to him and pointed to a small blip on the screen. "There's only one family that lives there."

"I'm aware." Lexi hoped she wouldn't have to look for another boat. "Can you take me there and wait?" When he didn't immediately answer, she heard her voice choke up with emotion. "Please. I'm desperate or I wouldn't be here."

The younger man looked like he wanted to say *no*. After exhaling a shaky breath, he nodded. "It's about ten minutes each way."

Lexi sighed with relief. "Thank you."

"Thank me when we're back." He helped her board; in a few minutes, the wind ripped through the sweater that wasn't nearly warm enough for the wind chill and her feelings.

Lexi hugged her arms around her body and watched as the boat drew closer and closer to the dock where, not a month before, Giovanni had brought her. The man steered into a free port and grabbed her arm when she walked in front of him. "Are you sure you want to be here?"

"Just wait for me," she said, stepping onto the deck. "I'll be back in a few minutes."

The beach was deserted. The afternoon sun was already lower in the sky and would be setting soon. Lexi steadied her nerves as she approached the porch, not knowing what she was going to find. She gripped the bracelet around her wrist before she found the courage to smack her knuckles against the storm door a few times.

The wooden entrance opened, and Maria Masseretti pushed the glass separating them wide. "Is he dead?" Lexi didn't bother with even a hello and she couldn't bring herself to step forward. "I just need to know."

Maria's face betrayed such a sadness that Lexi felt the ground start to shake. "Why don't you come inside, Alessandra?" She took the younger woman's arm when Lexi couldn't move and pulled her into the entryway.

"Is Gio dead?" Lexi asked again. The words caught in her throat and she closed her eyes, barely feeling the woman's hand steadying her trembling body. "I just need to know what happened to him." When she risked a look at his mother, Lexi could see the woman's tears forming. Whatever had happened to Giovanni was far worse than she had initially thought. "Please, I'm not like you. I can't do this. I can't wait and not know."

"Alessandra," Maria began gently.

"No one will tell me anything. I don't need details and I promise I won't ask. Just tell me if he's alive." Lexi looked toward the end of the hallway when a figure emerged.

"I'm alive, *bambina*."

16

Lexi ran from the doorway and flung herself at Giovanni, wrapping her arms around him and burying her head against his chest. "Oh my God," she cried. "Where? How? What?" Lexi pulled back, her hands touching him as though he weren't real. She saw Giancarlo emerge from the den off the side of the hallway, and Lexi looked between the two as she backed away. "What are you doing here? When did you get back?"

"I arrived in New York the day after you did."

The day after? That was impossible. "That was four weeks ago!" She looked between the pair again. Giovanni looked like a taller, younger version of the older man whose dark eyes penetrated her. "You've been here a month?"

Giovanni nodded his head once as Lexi tried to process what she was hearing. He didn't try to explain away his absence. He didn't hold her so that she remembered he was all that mattered. He just stood there, dressed like the playboy he had always been. His hands were shoved in his pockets, and Lexi realized he had made no attempt to hug her when she had gripped him like he was her life. He merely watched her, and she could read nothing in his gaze.

Lexi exhaled when the truth hit her like a ton of bricks. Giovanni had played her the entire time. He had wanted the challenge and the sport; the moment it had gotten close to real, this time he was the one who had opted to not extend the contract. She closed her eyes and licked her lips, before biting the bottom one to avoid having the pain that was ripping through her spill out into her words. What was there left to say? Surprisingly, while her grief was choking her, she managed to hold back her tears. There was no point for them anyway.

Lexi took another step back. Giovanni didn't want her; he had sent her back to New York, only to show up the next day and avoid her. He hadn't been able to cut her loose, so he had waited, dangling her on a string like the doll he had dressed her to be, waiting for her to eventually fall. It was this thought that made her heart feel like it was going to implode. From the silence, she heard Giancarlo's deeply accented voice. "You aren't the right woman for him."

Finally, Lexi thought. At least Giancarlo had the guts to tell her that to her face. She looked at the head of the Masseretti family and slowly nodded. "You're right," she whispered. She couldn't promise herself even a shred of dignity and feared she might beg Giovanni to take her back. Fighting the urge, Lexi turned to walk away as Maria grabbed her. His mother's eyes betrayed a pain that Lexi could understand better than ever before.

Lexi touched her hand, gently removing it from her arm. "Take care of him." Not trusting herself to say anything else, she pulled away and walked onto the porch. The sea air was salt against her skin and the bitter wind made her realize she was still standing. She gulped it in and walked as fast as she could toward the boat. She could hear Maria in the background, telling Giovanni to go after her, but the door didn't open. By the time she reached the dock, Lexi didn't expect to do anything other than walk onto the deck alone.

The charter captain was pacing when she returned. He had no desire to be on this particular island; she didn't blame him. "I'm finished," she coughed out. "We can go."

"Great," he said, quickly tossing the rope once she was on board. Lexi moved to the far side of the boat and refused to look at the house behind her. The tears came as they pulled into the harbor, and she hugged herself tightly. This was never meant to be real. The mistake was that she had believed it. She couldn't judge Giovanni for knowing when to say goodbye, even if she was broken by his inability to do so.

"Are you going to be okay?" The man asked once they disembarked at Montauk. His shirt said *Joe*, but Lexi hadn't even bothered to ask his name.

"I'm fine," she lied.

"Do you have a car or anything?" The lot was dark; even though the bars were lit up and there was noise from the patrons floating around, there were no taxis visible.

"I walked. I'll just walk back to the train station."

He looked at his watch and then shook his head while he pointed to a pickup truck. "The last train leaves in fifteen minutes. You won't make it."

She didn't know what she had done in a previous life to have found this one moment of kindness, but Lexi was grateful. "Thank you." She took out her wallet, but he pushed her hand away.

"Just remember me the next time you're in the Hamptons."

Never going to happen, she thought, but she nodded anyway. He dropped her in front of the train station; within a few minutes, she was settled on an empty LIRR car. She leaned against the window and thought she might vomit from crying so hard. After a few stops, she had calmed enough that, when the time came for her transfer at Babylon, she made it onto a waiting train for the final ninety minutes of a journey that had taken her halfway around the world only to return her, broken and damaged, to Manhattan.

She pulled her cell phone from the small purse and pressed the emergency contacts tab, dialing the number she hadn't deleted two years before. When the gentle voice asked her to leave a message, "Mom," was all that she could manage before she began to sob again.

"I'm done," she finally wept. "I can't do this anymore. I was wrong. I was so wrong about everything." She cried even harder, and her entire world was carried away in her anguish. The phone beeped in her ear; she clutched it to her heart as she continued to break down. Lexi rocked against her knees and pressed them into her chest as if that could stop her soul from disintegrating any further.

Time had no meaning. The world rushed by at a staggering pace while the train ripped from water into city. The pain from Giovanni's damage gripped her soul with the numb that had never been fully ejected, and her misery began to transform into a desolation that promised her survival over sanity.

Get out, the despair ordered as her tears receded. *Run away.* Once she got out of New York, things would make sense again. The bracelet that was a heavy reminder of her suffering brought her back to reality. Everything was a lie. Things would never make sense again.

When she disembarked at Penn Station, she got on one subway line, only to transfer ten minutes later. She stepped above ground and could see the Woolworth Tower. The lights in the Pinnacle were on. As much as she didn't want to be there, she needed to be. Lexi planned what she would say to Raphael or Ricardo if they tried to stop her, but, after passing the concierge who greeted her warmly, she found herself alone with the elevator attendant.

The lift opened into the empty penthouse and she exhaled with relief. Once she had gotten the bracelet off, she would be gone and Giovanni would be a chapter of her past that she would never read again. Even as she thought it and the tears came, she didn't believe it. He had rewritten her book. There would be little chance to avoid how much her soul would ache as she relearned how to breathe.

She had left the box to the bracelet on the console after finding it in Giovanni's night table, and she turned on a small light as she ripped the box open and tried to force the thin piece of metal into the gold. Her tears made it hard to see and her hands shook. Giovanni had broken the key in the lock, but there had to be a way to disengage the piece and remove the last thing connecting them.

Lexi couldn't handle the idea of it being there, searing his ownership into her skin, day after day. She was sobbing now, trying to get the key to fit, and its refusal to work made her knees weak. The agony of the day had quickly reached its apex, and she didn't know how much more she could take. She threw the key and swiped the box onto the floor angrily.

"I'm not sure that will work either." Lexi spun around and saw Giovanni sitting comfortably in the bedside chair. The room flooded with light at the sound of his voice.

"Take it off." Pain and rage mixed together and she stepped closer to him, her arm extended as she shook her wrist. "Get it off of me."

"It doesn't come off, *bambina*."

"Don't call me that! You lost the right to call me that the second you came back to The City and didn't even bother." She stopped, forcing back the words and trying to stop her tears. "I'm not your *bambina*. I never was."

"Do you think I've lied to you?"

Lexi stepped away from him when Giovanni stood and moved toward her. Her need pushed against her pain as he stopped only a few feet away. She hated herself for still wanting him. "Was any of it real?"

He held something in his hand. When he moved to the end of the bed, she saw that it was a manila folder. Giovanni tipped it toward her before putting it down. "*Real*, I think, is relative. Ancients civilizations believed Zeus was *real*, and that thunder and lightning were his weapons."

He removed the SIG from its holster and pulled back the slider, letting a bullet chamber. He placed it to the left of the folder before removing a small box from his pocket that went to the right. "They believed that love was the result of an arrow through the heart. But *real* is not usually what is in front of us. It's rarely what we think we see or feel. It's often something we cannot understand and can do little to control."

Giovanni took a step away from her and looked at the trio on the bed. "I would start in the middle if I were you. It's probably the closest thing to the *real* you are looking for."

Lexi kept her eyes on him, but stepped forward. With trembling fingers, she lifted the file and opened the folder. A scream caught in her throat as she stared down at the front page of her FBI record. The photograph, taken at her Academy graduation, made her look much younger than she had been even then. "What is *real*?" Giovanni asked. "Is *real* the fact that a federal agent walked into my club, intent on destroying me, and told me lie after lie to convince me to trust her?"

Lexi's fingers moved through the pages as she saw a print up of an online article about the partnership between several libraries. In the photograph, she smiled alongside two other librarians. The date at the bottom of the printout screamed at her and she dropped the folder, grabbing the gun and pointing it at him as she backed up. "You played me."

"*I* played *you*?" Giovanni chuckled. "It's funny you think that, baby girl."

"Stop! Stop with that!" Lexi shook her head. "That date is from the Tuesday that I left here, right after meeting you. You knew this entire time!"

"That file was couriered to me. I didn't look for it." He stepped forward, and Lexi tried to steady her shaking hands. "Your own people want you dead, Alessandra. From the moment you began this game, someone was a step ahead of you." Nothing he said made any sense, and Lexi couldn't process what he was saying. "I've protected you. Even when I didn't know whether or not any of what you said was real, I still protected you."

What was Giovanni's game? What was his play? Lexi had no idea, and his calm demeanor as he continued to approach her was terrifying. She shook the gun at him. "Don't come any closer."

"Or you'll shoot me?" His voice remained even. There was no rage or anger. As though he had known what she would do from the start, he took another step. "There's a bullet ready. Fire. Isn't that what you want? To avenge your father?"

"You didn't do it," she whispered.

"So finally there's something I've said that you do believe." Giovanni nodded a few times. "I didn't lie to you, Alessandra. Not even after I knew."

"You played me," she repeated. "The House always wins. You knew from the start how this would end, and you played me."

"I've done nothing but give you an exit strategy." Giovanni stood in front of her. "I promised you from the start that I would take care of you. That I would settle this debt and you'd be free of it. I told you that you could be mine and leave this all behind you. *You're* the one who tried to play me, *bambina*. You shouldn't be surprised that I know the game well enough to know when to stop bluffing."

Lexi couldn't keep the gun steady and thought she would collapse when he stepped into the barrel. "I've given you a way back to your old life. You can still walk away from this, from me. Shoot me with my own gun. Pull the trigger, call it in, and walk away. Just tell them I threatened you, that it was your life or mine."

"Stop it!"

"Shoot me, Alessandra! Pull the fucking trigger!" The Giovanni that she knew appeared. His eyes were ablaze, and he pressed his chest against the gun. His rage prickled her skin and pierced what remained of her hope. "Don't pick up a loaded gun and point it at me if you don't have the guts to pull the goddamned trigger! End this!"

"*Oltre*." The word was a sob, and, as she said it, Lexi's hands trembled to the point that she feared the gun might fire accidentally.

Giovanni sighed, and they stood across from each other for what seemed like forever before he put his hand on the gun's frame. He gently spun it into his own grasp as her fingers uncurled from the handle. Returning the bullet to its magazine before flipping the safety, Giovanni holstered the SIG while Lexi, quietly weeping, clutched her hands around her waist. "So you have the courage after all," he whispered, tipping his forehead against hers.

Lexi tore from the room, slamming her hand against the elevator as she cried. She ordered its descent when the lift opened and hid in the corner. By the time she was street level, she had managed to control her breathing enough to answer Philip when he asked if she wanted him to call for a car. It was late, and she wasn't sure she was capable of walking anywhere. "Yes, thank you."

When Lexi saw Giovanni as the doors to the recently dropped elevator opened, she changed her mind. She walked quickly to the exit and heard him say her name just as she stepped onto the street. She ran toward the corner and was stopped by traffic. Lexi had to get out of New York; she would deal with the fallout once she figured out where the hell to go.

"Alessandra!" He was only a few feet behind her and, when she looked at him, she saw the man she had fallen in love with. She saw the strength and the ability to outplay mixed with panic. Beyond that and, perhaps more frightening, was the fear that overshadowed his features. Giovanni was afraid. In that moment, although she had never planned to go back to him, Lexi couldn't leave him.

The car nearly flipped over as it spun around the corner, and Lexi's eyes were drawn to the speeding sedan. The lights of downtown glinted off the barrel that extended through the tinted window, lowered barely enough for the cylinder to fit through. Giovanni must have seen her eyes behind him because he turned just as she began to run forward. She saw the muzzle flash when her body landed against his, and they both slammed into the sidewalk.

Everything hurt. Lexi had experienced pain in the past, but it had been nothing like this. Her side felt like it was on fire. She couldn't breathe, and her lungs could only manage shallow stops and starts. When Giovanni rolled her to her back and cradled her in his lap, she thought she might pass out from the agony that rushed her body. He hummed her name like a lullaby, but she couldn't read his voice. What was he thinking? Had the bullet hit them both? When a prick of pain in her wrist started to flood her with a heaviness that even Giovanni's voice couldn't save her from, she closed her eyes and the world faded to black.

The first thing she thought when she woke up was that she wasn't dead. Her ribcage scraped against her lungs causing the pressure in her chest to explode with each breath. Death had to be less painful than this.

Her brain focused before her eyes opened; she was sitting up. Lexi tried to move, but the best she could do was wiggle her fingers. When she said, "Help," her voice was weak and even the little sound she did make was excruciating. A bottle of water choked her. When she looked into the black eyes that watched her struggle, fear replaced the oxygen in the room. "What are you doing?"

"You seem to be running the game," Giancarlo said. "You tell me."

Lexi shook her head, trying to take in the space around her. It looked familiar and yet she couldn't immediately make sense of it. She had been in New York. On the street. A car. A gun. "Where's Gio?"

"Where should he be? Dead?"

She saw nothing that told her what she was desperate to know. Giancarlo's eyes were cold and angry. There was no love for her: Lexi was his enemy. She had tried to get in front of the bullet, but she hadn't been able to save his son. "I'm sorry."

"You're sorry?" Giancarlo perched on the edge of the chair that was in front of her. "You're sorry? For what? For trying to destroy my family?"

"How bad is it?"

"How bad for you? Alessandra, it is *very* bad for you."

"Is he? Did the hit? I–"

"The hit wasn't for *him*, Alessandra; the hit was meant for *you*." Giancarlo sat back in his chair, watching the words filter into Lexi's understanding. "Giovanni was *your* collateral damage."

Lexi's body slumped forward. *Your own people want you dead,* Giovanni had told her. She had assumed someone had tried to hurt her in Catania to get to him, but what if that had been an attempt on her directly? She thought she might be ill when she realized that the car hadn't been a hit meant for Giovanni. The drive-by had been meant for her. When Lexi had run to protect him, she had put him in harm's way. "No," she whispered. "No, that can't be right."

"Tell me everything." Giancarlo knelt in front of her. "Tell me everything, and you may leave here with your life." When she raised her eyes to him, he held a rectangular envelope. "You may even take with you that which you sought at the start."

"What are you talking about?"

"I did not kill your father. I cannot fault you for what brought you into this life. I can respect that you wanted an answer and to avenge his death, but," he shook his head, "I didn't order the death of your father. I didn't even know he was more than a name on a list." He waved the envelope. "However, I know who did and you can also. Just tell me what you know."

The choice was there. Giovanni or her father. Six weeks verses a lifetime. Lexi dropped her head to her imploding chest. "I don't know anything."

"I thought you would say that. I think you misunderstand." Giancarlo stood up and dropped the information on the table next to the chair. "I know what the FBI knows. I have my people there. I want to know what my son told you."

The way his eyes bore into her made Lexi shiver when she answered, "Nothing."

"I don't believe you, Alessandra." Giancarlo picked up the bottle of water and brought it back to her lips, waiting for her to drink.

There was no way she was walking away from this; if Giovanni was dead, she didn't want to. The last month had been hell. Lexi had already lost everything that mattered and she found her voice again. "I don't really care what you believe. Other than stories about saints and volcanoes," she said, watching his smirk deepen, "Gio told me nothing."

"He told me that you cannot control your mouth."

"I guess you'd be used to that. I don't bite, though, so you've lucked out on that front." At this Giancarlo laughed, and it sounded so close to Giovanni's that it took whatever shards Lexi's heart had left and crushed them to dust. "If you're going to kill me, then kill me. I'm not going to tell you anything. I don't know anything to tell you."

"Your own people want you dead, Alessandra. *Your* people seek to kill you. You know far more than you think you know and you can know more still." He called out and she saw Raphael emerge from behind her. He squatted and used a knife to cut the ropes. When she fell forward and relief washed over her agonizing muscles along with the pain of sitting too long in one place, the bodyguard caught her. It took her a few minutes, but she pushed away from him to stand on her own.

Giancarlo lifted the slender rectangle from the table to offer it to her. "Find out who killed your father. Consider your debt to this family paid."

"I don't owe you anything."

Giancarlo further extended the envelope. "You owe me your life."

"Just tell me if he's alive." Lexi pushed his hand out of her face.

"If you stay here, your life in New York is over," Giancarlo said, turning away and walking to a bar where he poured himself a drink. "Is that what you will trade for an answer that will not matter in the end?"

Lexi took a painful step forward. "It matters to me."

"Why? You sought to destroy Giovanni from the start. Why risk your life and what you wanted for an answer that will not change anything you've done?"

"Because I'd risk the volcano if it meant he knew I wouldn't leave." Every feeling, from East 58th to Sicily and back to the room in the Pinnacle where she now stood, rained over her like a storm. "I'd trade it all to tell him that it was real."

"*You* were never real, Alessandra." Giancarlo took a slow drink and said something to Raphael, who picked up the envelope from the floor. "Take it," he repeated when Raphael extended it toward her. "Uncover the truth that you seek."

"No."

"If you stay here, your life is over." Giancarlo watched her carefully. "If you make this choice, Alessandra, then you are dead."

"I'm dead already."

Read Giovanni's perspective in
<u>Faultine: Giovanni</u>

or pick up the original <u>Faultine</u> in its entirety at
www.miamichele.com
or wherever fine books are sold

Book Club Questions

1. What do you believe is the significance of the title: Faultline? Would you have chosen a different title?
2. What is your initial impression of Lexi? Of Giovanni? Which character traits do you relate to more?
3. How did your impressions of the characters change as the book progresses?
4. What is Lexi's underlying motive for seeking Giovanni out? Do you believe that she changes as the story progresses? Why or why not?
5. Were there choices Lexi made that you disagreed with? How would you have behaved differently?
6. What are Giovanni's motives as he navigates a relationship with Lexi? Do you believe he ever loves Lexi, or are his actions simply to lull her into a false sense of security?
7. Do you believe Giovanni or his family are responsible for John Master's death?

8. What event was the largest turning point in this story thus far?
9. What do you think happens to Lexi at the end of chapter 16?
10. Book Club Question: _____

   _____

   _____

11. Book Club Question: _____

    _____

    _____

12. Book Club Question: _____

    _____

    _____

13. Book Club Question: _____

    _____

    _____

14. BONUS: Find the Faultline playlist on YouTube and listen to the songs associated with chapters 1-16. What do you think of the selections? Do any songs stand out to you as especially important within the story?

NOTES:

Find your next book at www.miamichele.com

<u>Also by Mia Michele:</u>

Amnesty of the Heart (Aegean Affairs, #1)

Drunk on Passion (Aegean Affairs, #2)

Happily Ever After (Aegean Affairs, #3)

Aegean Affairs Duet #1

Martial Hearts (The Club, #1)

Hosts and Hellions: the complete trilogy

Children of Hellions (Hosts and Hellions, #1)

Sons of God (Hosts and Hellions, #2)

Daughters of Men (Hosts and Hellions, #3)

Vale

Faultline

The Gospel of Persephone

Untwisting the Author's Mind

Made in the USA
Middletown, DE
08 October 2022